AIR &
ANGELS

Dodie Hamilton

With Love

Dodie H
xx

Acknowledgements

To Julie Dexter, who I do love, and John and Josie Lewin, co-founders of Spirit Knights Paranormal Investigation; to Pat and Lee Jay in Spain, so generous with their love and advice. To the artist, Martin Bonde for the painting of the Silver Horse, and to dearest Valery Foley, so supportive, and the ladies of my writer's circle. To my buddy, Anna Ryan and her beloved horse, Cromwell, who was the study for Hazlett, and who will never be forgotten.

To my friend Ralph Goins in Texas (a great finder of facts) and to the real Margret Hankin, and to beautiful Freya-Jasmine, friends here in Rayleigh.

Last, but never least, to my good friend in Alabama, Irv Brock - thank you everyone and God bless.

Other books by Dodie Hamilton

Letters to Sophie
The Sequel to A Second Chance

The Spark
Prequel to The Lighthouse Keepers

A Second Chance

Perfidia

Silent Music

Fragile Blossoms

Fettered Wings
Part 4 of the Gabriel books

The Honeybees of Lower Langley

Dodie Hamilton, The Spiritual Midwife, is known throughout the world for her work in psychic counselling and Healing, her particular interest being the Near Death and the Out-of-Body experience. Over thirty years she's given countless private consultations and appeared at the Mind, Body & Spirit Festivals. All her books and writings, no matter how real, how flesh and blood, as in say, A Second Chance, the first in the Gabriel Books, are borne of years of study and personal exploration, the late Robert A Monroe, of the Monroe Institute, Virginia, author of Journeys Out of Body, Far Journeys, and The Ultimate Journey, her mentor.

Thank you, Robert for All That Is.

http://www.chillwithabook.com/2017/08/
perfidia-by-dodie-hamilton.html

Three of my novels have one Reader's Awards:

A Second Chance won The Chill Reader's Award.

Fragile Blossoms also won A Chill Award.

Perfidia, the sequel to A Second Chance won a Chill Award and A Diamond Award.

Reluctant Angels, the Prequel to A Second Chance, and Dodie's latest novel has received The Readers Chill Award.

Dedication

This is for Doris Taylor, Ida Hamilton, and June Bonde,
and to all beloved mothers everywhere.

Air and Angels

By John Donne

Twice or thrice had I lov'd thee,
Before I knew thy face or name;
So in a voice, so in a shapeless flame
Angels affect us oft, and worshipp'd be;
Still when, to where thou wert, I came,
Some lovely glorious nothing I did see.
But since my soul, whose child love is,
Takes limbs of flesh, and else could nothing do,
More subtle than the parent is
Love must not be, but take a body too;
And therefore what thou wert, and who,
I bid Love ask, and now
That it assume thy body, I allow,
And fix itself in thy lip, eye, and brow.

Whilst thus to ballast love I thought,
And so more steadily to have gone,
With wares which would sink admiration,
I saw I had love's pinnace overfraught;
Ev'ry thy hair for love to work upon
Is much too much, some fitter must be sought;
For, nor in nothing, nor in things
Extreme, and scatt'ring bright, can love inhere;
Then, as an angel, face, and wings
Of air, not pure as it, yet pure, doth wear,

So thy love may be my love's sphere;
Just such disparity
As is 'twixt air and angels' purity,
'Twixt women's love, and men's, will ever be.

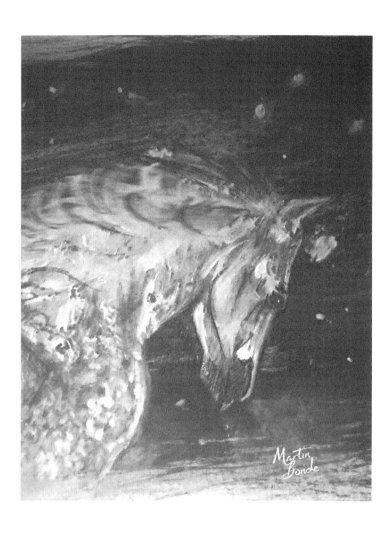

Moment of Delight

The Beeches, Comberton
Monday, 3rd April 1899

They took forever to leave: the daughter, Serena, darkly beautiful and seemingly untroubled, a perfect choice of name, and Isabella, the mother, unquiet, tiny, rustling, pursed lips and steel-corset bound.

They arrived less than a year ago throwing the house into turmoil with their non-stop Italian commentary and their yards of monogrammed luggage, and their parakeet cages and Mia, and Gia, noisy little lap-dogs (not in the least house-trained) and poor Tillie, Clarissa's Jack Russell Terrier, constantly having her toys being stolen.

Today they choose to return home, a bitterly cold day, a late snow, and a carriage waiting to take them on their way that has been in the yard since early morning, horses stamping, liveried coachmen shivering, and still the ladies linger, apparently awaiting a signal to leave.

Serena, warm in furs, turns from the window, her voice a sultry drawl.

'So Clareessa, today my mother and I bid farewell to Cambreedge.'

'Actually, you bid farewell to Comberton rather than the city.'

'*Ah certo*! The Beeches, Lark Lane, Comberton,

Cambreedgeshire, your pretty leetle home in your pretty leetle country.'

'I suppose when compared to Italy we do seem small.'

'*Si, s*o very small.' Serena took a cigarette from a silver case and lit it. 'And 'ow long do you live 'ere?'

'All of my life.'

'And 'ow long is your life?'

Absurdly, Clarissa knew herself blushing. 'I was twenty last May.'

'What day is that?'

'The 10th.'

'Ah shame! We shall miss the coming birthday as we missed the last.'

'It doesn't matter.'

'It should matter as you should've said. We might 'ave celebrated and drunk champagne. But then, with your dear papa only lately gone, to celebrate would have been wrong.'

'It would.'

Blue smoke merging with sunlight, Serena puffed on the cigarette. 'Twenty-one is an important birthday but dangerous.'

'How do you mean dangerous?'

'It comes too soon. Beauty, youth and power - we are not ready.'

'Were you ready?'

Serena slipped her furs from her shoulders and sat back in the chair, long tapering fingers caressing the cigarette. 'I do not recall.'

'You are only thirty. Why would you forget?'

'I am twenty-nine not thirty.' She shrugged. 'And I choose to forget.' She turned back to the window, tapping the pane with a polished fingernail. "Ow old were you when your mama died?"

'Seventeen.'

'She die of the consumption, I think, and you and your papa alone.'

'Not quite alone. My uncle and aunt are close by.'

'Ah yes, Professor Sarson and his wife, Mistress Phoebe. They have a house on the university campus. This I know. I have been there.'

Clarissa was surprised. 'You visited their house?'

'Si, with a friend.' Serena smiled on a memory. 'We speak of poetry and the poet, Rumi. Mistress Phoebe make tea.'

'That sounds nice. Who was your friend?'

The question is waved away. 'Oh, someone I know.'

'Uncle John is my guardian.'

'So I believe. Your papa thought you were too young to be left alone?'

'He worried, although with Margret here I am never really alone.'

'Margret? That would be Senora Hankin, your excellent cook.'

'As you say, Margret is an excellent cook and a good friend. This is her home, as it is for her granddaughter, Freya-Jasmine, when home from school. And of course we have Sally Cartwright, Margret's sister. They are my family.'

'But not your papa.'

'No.'

Grief closed in and deep wrenching pain. He is dead, dear Papa is dead!

It only seems a moment since, unwell, and more than a little sorry, he stood at the same window recalling their tour of

Italy in the spring of '97 and the people they met there, 'the charming widow, Isabella Parisi-Chase and her daughter, Serena.' And how he'd returned alone to Perugia in the spring of '98, and there: 'Knowing my dear daughter would understand how lonely Papa has been since her mama died, I begged Isabella's hand in marriage, and in a moment of delight, in Assisi where the Saint has trod, we were wed.'

That is how they arrived, Papa, ashen-faced, at the door, and the awful 'moment of delight' emerging from a carriage behind him; dogs barking, women chattering, and he with nothing to say but, 'I am so sorry.'

A generous man, given a canto from Dante's *Divine Comedy*, or the right piece of music, or even a sunny day, Charles Morgan, former Doctor of Divinities at St John's College, Cambridge, would offer his soul for a moment of delight. In the main they were usually small moments and manageable: plum cake, hot tea, and an ever open door for hungry undergraduates, as well as an ever open purse for members of the Faculty. Some moments were more irritant than delight, as was his refusal to evict a family of squirrels from the attic that earlier chewed their way through a newly laid carpet; as his continued employment of Sykes as handyman and gardener, who is a weak sort of fellow, and doesn't dig on 'account of his lumbago', and won't groom Hazlett, Clarissa's bay, 'because that 'orse don't like me and he bites.'

While there is something in that, Hazlett an ill-tempered horse, who will only do what he likes *when* he likes, Sykes should've gone years ago.

Dear Papa, he was unable to refuse a plea for help, and this, his good heart, Clarissa believes, was how he came to wed Isabella

Parisi-Chase, who, according to her daughter, was in difficulties when her husband died. 'We had no money and nowhere to live. It is why God sent us Doctor Charles.'

Now thanks to Papa's moment of delight, Serena leaves Comberton wearing Mama's furs and sapphire broach, while her mother waits in a carriage in the yard wrapped in Mama's sealskin cape.

'That is rather a splendid carriage. Is it yours?' Clarissa didn't care whose it was but having seen it call at the house before thought to ask.

'Not mine.' Serena pushed her hair from her face, a weight of glossy curls that today under a mourning veil are as black as the night. 'Not yet.'

* * *

Serena has an excellent command of English. But for intonation and the odd dropped letter one might think her raised by an English nanny. They met in Italy where, with rare candour, she ascribed her linguistic talents to her late stepfather, Samuel Chase, who taught at the University of Rome:

'Mister Samuel liked to teach as I liked to learn. A clever man, he could play piano and sing in seven different languages. He found me work teaching English in a nursery school in San Nicolo. I learn a lot that way. I was sorry when he died, and begged my mother, already twice widowed, to find a rich American husband, and young, so he might live longer. But she prefer Englishmen. She says they are '*un homo affidabile*'... reliable. My own father was Sicilian and most unreliable.'

Isabella is now three times widowed, and her husbands,

whether English or Sicilian, all reliable in one aspect, the tragedy of an early death.

Father died in the garden under the oak tree feeding last year's acorns to the pigs. Clarissa warned him to be sparing. 'They are always hungry. Put anything in front of them and they will eat.'

Serena's mother has a similar hunger. Last night, though their bags packed and waiting in the hall, she followed Clarissa about the house, breathing heavily, afraid she might've missed a bauble in the last raking.

Senora Parisi-Chase (Clarissa will never think of her as step-mother) complains of being cheated. She says Father died too soon. He ought to have altered his Will in her favour. Though she has all of Mama's things - and some of Clarissa's, even to a lacquered workbox Uncle Sarson brought back from China - she says the house should be hers.

Charles Morgan died Saturday February 25th. The Will was read March 2nd. Today, the 3rd of April, Clarissa was finally allowed to wake naturally from sleep; every other morning since the reading of the Will she was woken by Serena opening the shutters and Isabella bearing a pot of hot chocolate.

That Father left almost all of Mother's money to Isabella didn't count. They wanted the house. Every fresh assault began the same way, Serena in a silk wrapper, smiling, skin glowing, and she pouring hot chocolate into a cup and being so very Italian: '*Mia*, Clareessa, I do not ask for myself. I want nothing. *Niente!* It is for my mother - justice for one so disappointed.'

The siege, for that's how it felt, was relentless, and though wearied by it, and seemingly alone in her grief, Clarissa would not give way. Papa was not a rich man. Any money beyond a pension from the Church came with his marriage to Patricia Emily Anne Ferguson, and until the Italian affair was meant for Clarissa, as were the pearls and other precious bibelots that one-by-one found their way into a leather satchel at Serena's feet.

Now all that is left of any bauble is the gold wedding band on a chain about Clarissa's neck; all else is piled on top of the carriage ready to go to Italy, or wherever else the next *affidabile* Englishman might be found.

* * *

Another hour passes. Margret brings the coachmen into the kitchen for warmth and refreshment. Sykes takes the dogs for a walk. Sally brings coffee and biscuits to the sitting-room. Isabella sips hot chocolate in the carriage.

Clarissa asks if they are waiting for someone.

Serena stares from under heavy eyelids. 'You want us to leave?'

'I thought your mother might be warmer indoors.'

'She chooses not to return.'

'Why is that?'

'You do not know?'

'No.'

'She says she is not wanted. That as your father's wife she is entitled to the house and that you deny her.'

'Father left the house to me.'

'Maybe he did one time but that was before he wed my mother.'

'Beeches was my mother's house and before that my grandmother's. It was always going to be mine. Papa knew that. It is why he left you and your mother money. He was trying to be fair.'

There was silence. Then Serena sighed. 'I think you do not like us.'

'This is not about like or dislike. It is about keeping a promise. You are my stepsister, Serena. I have tried to see you as such.'

'You see me and my mother as family?'

'It is what my father wanted.'

'Then why not share the house?'

'It cannot be shared. You can stay should you want to but the house is mine and in trust to my uncle. My father knew that left to your mother she would sell Beeches and return to Italy, and I would be without a home.'

'Come with us. San Nicolo is a good place to live. You liked it before.'

'We were on holiday. One can be happy anywhere knowing one will eventually return. My home is here. I am in my final year at Girton. From there I hope to find work in the Fitzwilliam Museum working on the restoration of paintings. Father knew this and wanted me safe.'

'What do you want?'

'I want him back again.'

'*Si, Capisco!* He was a good man. You will miss him.'

Clarissa clenched her fist. 'Yes.'

'But not me or my mother.'

'I'm sure we shall all miss one another at times. You always have a home here should you need it. My father brought you here. It is not for me to drive you away.'

Serena picked up her gloves. 'I think you are not being true Clareessa Morgan. Your lips make nice words but your stomach sickens. You want us to go so you can resume your leetle world with your books and paintings, and your pretty college friends with their pretty leetle lives.'

'Why do you say these things?'

'It is time for such things to be said.'

'Well I have nothing more to say to you.'

'No need. Your face says all.'

'Then why are you still here?'

Clarissa is angry. This cross-examination is unfair. She tried her best to love them. They didn't want to be loved. They wanted Mama's sapphire broach, and her beaver coat and sealskin muff. They wanted china, and bed-linen, and cutlery and books from the library. They wanted things, and when things ran out, and there was only the house, they wanted that.

Pale, she stepped forward. 'If you felt so unwelcome why did you stay? You could've left the moment you heard the Will. You had no need to remain, certainly not for me. I was managing. I might've enjoyed your fondness had you thought to show it but I didn't need it.'

Serena's eyes flashed. 'We did not wait for you.'

'Then why did you?'

'It served my purpose.'

'And what is your purpose...or rather who?'

'*Non sono affari tuoi!*'

'None of my business?'

'Si! It is none of your business!"

'Then I'll leave you to it.' Clarissa offered her hand. 'I wish you and Isabella a safe journey. I'm sorry you weren't happy here.'

'*Basta!*' Serena slapped her hand away. 'I am 'appy to leave. I never wanted to come to this miserable country. My mother liked this house. She think to live here. I say *lascia perdere*! There is nothing 'ere for you. This is a cold country where people 'ave cold hearts. We are Italian! We need sunshine and laughter. We need passion and love and strong arms to hold us. We do not need resentful looks from a milk-and-water miss.'

'How cruel you are.'

'No, not cruel, a woman with a mind of my own. I need no guardian to keep me safe. In England a girl must wear black cotton stockings and her hair down and wait twenty-one years before seen a woman. In Italy a woman comes of age with the first kiss. What would you know of kisses? You will never know passion. You are too busy hiding behind your dead papa's rules.'

'Oh go away!' Clarissa held on to tears. 'You've said all you need to say. I don't care why you are waiting. It's time you left.'

'Ah look! See how the mouse turns!' Serena sneered. 'Look at the cold in her eyes. Such ice, I would freeze. Where is my dear sister now?'

'Where she has always been, here on the end of your line, desperate to catch a fish, if only a little tiddler!'

'I do not understand. What is this tiddler?'

'Forget it. It was just a thought.'

'Yes, but what does the thought mean?'

'I don't know.' Clarissa picked up the satchel and gave it to her. 'I suppose it was the word sister, and the idea that it would have been so very nice to have a sister, but then learning I had nothing.'

* * *

She had to get away. Snatching a shawl she went into the garden where to her horror she found Sykes trimming the hot-house lilac, and not carefully, wildly, attacking the tender branches with meat cutters.

'God's sake!' She ran to him. 'What are you doing?'

'I'm doin' what Master said I was to do, trimming t'lilac. He said I was to keep my eye on it and not let it run wild.'

'Yes but not this tree! He meant the old lilac running along the wash-house roof. This is a dwarf lilac and only planted a couple of years ago.'

'Well I'm sorry, Miss. I didn't know. I thought he meant this 'un.'

'Couldn't you tell the difference? One look should've told you it needed gentle handling. What are we meant to do with it now you have cut it? It's of no use in a vase. It will sag all over the place. Might as well burn it.'

'Shall I burn it then? I 'ave a bonfire goin' back of the allotment.'

'Go ahead! Throw it all on the fire. I don't care.'

She would have left him to it but suddenly couldn't bear the thought of the lilac going to the fire - so beautiful, and such a tender blue.

She gathered as much as she could and ran back to the house.

They were leaving, the carriage rumbling toward the gates, a newcomer, a man on horseback, acting as outrider.

'Wait!' She ran to the carriage. 'I have lilac.'

Desperate for them not to part as enemies but as the sisters Papa wanted, she held it out. 'Take it Serena! It's freshly cut and smells divine.'

Serena didn't move. Face averted, she sat as one carved in stone.

'Oh please!' Clarissa ran alongside.

'Say there!' The man on horseback stooped down, his face bound by a scarf against the cold and shadowed by the brim of his hat.

'Give that to me!' He gathered the lilac to his chest. 'Now step away from the carriage before you get hurt.'

Clarissa stepped back and stood watching the carriage roll away.

There was nothing else she could do.

Book One

Clarissa

Air and Angels

CHAPTER ONE

In Chancery

Fitzwilliam Museum, Cambridge
Sunday February 9ᵗʰ 1901

There are a great many stairs to the upper gallery and, as usual, the lift is out of order. John Sarson leaned against the door trying to get his breath back. In his late seventies, and with a 'dodgy ticker', he needs to rest.

Professor Sarson is here to bring his niece home to supper: Clarissa is a difficult creature to pin down these days, her work keeping her busy.

The museum is closed for the day. Beyond Clarissa and the Head Conservator all else are home for the weekend. Such institutions are often short of funds; in consequence restorative work is usually confined to out-of-the-way places within the bowels of a building or topmost attics, out of sight and mind of more popular galleries where visitors spend money.

A series of high ceiling attics with a honeycomb of smaller rooms sprouting alongside, the Conservation studios take up a whole floor. On the way through, John passed a room he took to be the main classroom where students sit at tables laden with paints and pencils and other accoutre of restorative work, and where objet d'art of all shapes and sizes is stacked about the walls.

It smelt of beeswax, pitch and turpentine and the sweat of people dedicated to the preservation of the history, whereas, a room to the left suggested a laboratory with glass cabinets, drawing boards, and walls of shelves laden with books and various optical instruments.

The room where Clary works is sparse of furniture, and so quiet one is reminded of a fashionable funeral parlour where oil of lavender masks the smell of embalming fluid, and the funeral director wears a lilac waistcoat and knee breeches, and might be taken for a bishop.

Swathed in a loose apron, hair tied back and a brush in hand, she sits on a stool before an easel. She bends to her work, floating a fine layer of gold-leaf onto the bevelled edge of an ornamental picture frame that - judging the rapt silence and mutual holding of breath - is likely to be very old, very rare, and *very* valuable. John knows nothing of her work but imagines it demanding of the eyes and the students in need of light. Today, in consideration of a costly medium in use, the many skylights and windows are shut against drafts, and he allowed in on a tacit promise of remaining silent and still.

Last year Clarissa gained the post of assistant conservator at the Museum, and is now midway through a Masters in Fine Arts under the tutelage of James van Leiden Sterne: a known authority in the field of Italian Renaissance art, particularly in the work of the *Quattrocento* painter, Fra Angelico, and the sculptor, Donatella.

'Professor van Leiden is sought after,' Clarissa explains. 'Not only a considered expert in the restoration of Renaissance Art, he is said to be an authority in the study of Twelfth Century English. What he doesn't know about Anglo-Norman poetry apparently cannot be known. I consider myself fortunate to work alongside such eminence. I just wish I could like him more.'

She sees the man arrogant and difficult to please, and though he accepts her work, often dismisses her thoughts on restoration as naive.

John Sarson suspects her frustration, and that of every other female scholar in Cambridge, aimed more at a collegiate system that allows them to study alongside male undergrads, to sit the same exams but not to be admitted as full university members and therefore unable to claim a degree.

In John's opinion she is entitled to feel unrewarded. He regards *Luna Solitaria*, her dissertation on the life of the nineteenth-century Italian mystical poet, Giacomo Leopardi, as exceptional, as is her treatise on Norse and Celtic History; both studies by any other standards worthy of a Double First.

'How is it Oxford and Cambridge are allowed to withhold female degrees when other universities throughout the world, including Radcliffe in the USA, accept our right?' she rages. 'How dare they stand aloof? It is wrong and must be seen to be so, for until it is, the unfairness of our position continues and women graduates regarded as cheap labour.'

Though sympathetic to her cause, John Sarson knows his belief that all souls, male or female, have the right to further education, is his own.

Female universities have been target for ridicule for years and women pressing for educational reform seen as harpies, and men reluctant to wed an educated girl fearing she'll one day recognise him for a fool.

* * *

James van Leiden may be arrogant, still Clarissa acknowledges his skill. Devoted to her work she is at his beck and call all hours of the day, and speaks of their latest project - a visit to Italy to look at a possible Fra Angelico painting - in whispers, as though observing the labours of a living Master.

A few years ago John helped James's older brother Kasper toward a rapid - and highly eventful - Masters in Economic Science.

Mountaineer and explorer, a man of humour and immense courage, Kasper van Leiden Sterne, or the Kestrel, as he is known after the hunting bird, believed the Earth was created for his enjoyment. While good company he was the devil to teach. Phenomenal mental recall, seeming to know any subject beforehand, he would bunk-off lectures, scaling a mountain or hacking through a jungle, causing the question to be raised: how did the fellow learn to write his name never mind gain a Masters.

If Clarissa thinks James arrogant she would be mightily thrown by his brother. A bearded giant of blue eyes and red hair, he was always on the move, always laughing and always in a scrape, rumours of drunken parties while up at Cambridge, girls secreted in the dormitory, and he at one time flying a pair of female bloomers from the roof of King's College Chapel.

James is of similar height and build yet slender and clean-shaven with fair hair and grey eyes. Graduating *summa cum laude* at Harvard, the youngest Professor of tenure at the time, he is a studious fellow, particular of dress and habits. There is no mention of him scaling mountains or hiking through jungles, a childhood accident leaving him with a limp, and so different to the momentous Kasper, it is hard to think of them as brothers.

He joined the Fitzwilliam in '99, coming to the museum

with a catalogue of written works, including the seminal, *When Walls Speak*, in which he discusses cave paintings in Northern Spain, and how research led to the discovery of a work by Jacopo Pontormo. Another of his books is entitled *Scorched Hearts (*which John found utterly fascinating), a study of letters between twelfth-century lovers Heloise and Abelard, where he posits human love and the divine as with St Francis of Assisi and the Catholic nun, Chiaro Offreduccio.

A brilliant young man, it is said that on leaving Harvard, James was courted by every leading museum, including the Louvre in Paris, the Uffizi in Florence and the Metropolitan in New York, and yet the summer of '99 found him Keeper and Conservator of Italian Art at the Fitzwilliam.

There is much discussion as to why he rejected the glamour of New York for chilly England. His was not a popular appointment. There was resentment and petty mutterings suggesting Viscount FitzWilliam didn't fund the new building for a Yankee to stroll in: it should be Britain for the British.

There is no Yankee. The current House of Leiden is Belgian born, James's father the artist, Karel van Leiden, whose family of gold merchants and jewellers can be traced back to the fourteenth-century and the merging of two Dutch families: the Van der Heyden and the Van Lyden. His mother, Alice, is the daughter of Elias Sterne, a man with no real history but of meteoric rise as a major share-holder in the De Beers Diamond Company. That connection, along with considerable academic wealth, is the reason James is here. The Fitzwilliam doing what all such institutions do - follow the money.

* * *

That John Sarson knows a little of the Van Leidens is due to a love of Persian poetry. When up at Cambridge, Kasper would visit the house on Maxwell Road discussing the poet Rumi while munching his way through buttered toast - his shoulders making a dolls-house of their home. On one such a visit he said he and his brother were made to study in different countries: Kasper to Harrow and Cambridge and James to Harvard; their maternal grandfather was keen to make connections in England and America.

Kasper said Elias Sterne was behind every family decision, even supporting the family business during the stock market crash of the 70's. 'He saw my father as weak, claiming that until his marriage to Alice, the Van Leiden goldsmiths in London, Paris and Brussels were out of fashion. "House of Leiden my ass!" He would sneer. "But for my daughter you'd be heading for the poor house along with that other washed-out Van Leiden, Mijnheer Rembrandt."'

Kasper's smile was bitter relating that memory. 'I hated the way he taunted us, whereas James, lover of anything do to with Rembrandt, would shrug: "See beyond the dirt, Kes, to the gold beneath and forget all else."'

Autumn of '94 saw Kasper leaving Cambridge for the family business in Brussels, though he was soon rumoured to be seen in South Africa, concerned with protecting the De Beers diamond mines from the Boers.

* * *

Working with gold-leaf is a costly business and time-consuming. John Sarson is weary but bides his time. He has no power here.

It doesn't matter that he was fifty years a Cambridge Don. That he is allowed in at all is a courtesy shown to his niece rather than any reputation he might have.

Clarissa is talented, beautiful and kind. Though greatly indulged by her father, she is a credit to her mother, Phoebe's sister, who left this earth too soon. Weak heart or not, Charles Morgan should've hung on to this life a little longer, if only to see his daughter's reputation grow as a skilled restorer, and, alas, to see how her fortune is lost to the Parisi women.

While this lengthy wait is for conveying Clarissa through the snow, it is also, for shame, about acquainting her with disastrous financial issues.

'All that money!' Last night Phoebe wept. 'It wasn't yours to lend. We were always going to struggle, you and I. Now it will be Clarissa who struggles.'

Phoebe fretted all night, certain they were for debtor's prison and her sister to haunt them. Knowing he had made a mess of things, and, if so inclined, his niece sending him to prison, John doubts he'll ever sleep again.

It was Kasper who brought Serena to their home. They knew who she was, the Sarson family still reeling from Charles Morgan's marriage. Until that winter evening in '98 they had not thought to see the Parisi daughter at their hearth as they had not thought to again see Kasper.

They arrived with a familiar shout: 'Halloo indoors Mistress Phoebe! Bring on the buttered toast!' Delighted, thinking they were to be reunited with a favourite scholar, John opened the door. There he was, wreathed in smiles, and standing to one side wearing a softer smile - and the late Patricia Emily Morgan's furs – Signorina Serena Parisi. There was never an explanation as to how those two knew one another and no one asked. They came again and stayed for tea, he relating his latest exploits and Serena charming. They came a third time, he talking of crossing the Sahara and she whispering of romance.

Phoebe never liked the girl seeing her a grasping creature with a ready smile and empty heart. At the time, bowled over by dark eyes, John took Phoebe to task. 'Charles should've been more circumspect. But he and Isabella seem happy enough and Miss Parisi speaks very lovingly of Clary.'

'Words.' Phoebe had frowned. 'Show me deeds rather than words. Until then I shall keep my own council.'

* * *

...and that is what John should've done when Serena Parisi paid another call. It was on a Sunday afternoon. Phoebe was out visiting her aunt. Surprised to see her, though revelling in the company of a beautiful woman, he made tea. Serena spoke of her love for Kasper and how they were secretly engaged to marry, and that she needed to settle a debt owed by her mother, but couldn't contact her lover, he trekking across the Sahara.

'It is a matter of honour,' she said. 'I can't look toward the future without settling the past.' John offered to help. She said she needed twenty-five pounds and that it would be repaid within forty-eight hours.

The Sarsons didn't have that kind of money to lend to anyone. Being retired, twenty-five pounds is a quarter of his yearly salary. He should have backed away but thinking short-term - and afraid of looking mean before beauty, he withdrew the money from Clarissa's account in West Street, and was relieved when soon afterward the debt was paid and five pounds offered as interest.

'It is so good of you, Professor John, to do this for a stranger.'

On refusing the note he was rewarded with perfume in his nostrils and soft lips on his cheek. John chose not to mention the loan or the kiss to Phoebe.

His faith in Serena and the forthcoming marriage allowed him to grant a further loan. 'It is again for my mother,' she said. 'I dare not tell my stepfather or my sister, Clary. It would break their gentle hearts. But if you could ...?'

He did, and this time for twenty pounds which was returned the following day. The transactions were always performed late evening in the Science Lab, the secrecy of the meeting adding to the delightful racing of his heart.

February '99 Charles Morgan died of a stroke and Clarissa broken-hearted. March saw the Will read and the Parisis receiving handsome settlements.

The last Sunday in March brought Serena again to Maxwell Road, and more secrets shared (a weighty diamond ring dangling from a chain about her lovely throat), and this time a loan asked of two hundred and fifty pounds.

'As you know I am in receipt of a bequest from my stepfather which will more than cover the loan. I have a reason for wanting such an amount before my Kasper returns.' She'd bent her head, soft lips to his ear. 'If I whisper the word *trousseau*, Dear Professor John, I'm sure you'll understand.'

Such a large sum of money should've sounded warning bells, but knowing she was to inherit, Dear Professor John went to his bank where the manager is a friend and a short-term loan of one hundred and fifty was agreed.

From there he went again to Clarissa's account taking another hundred, and, accordingly, late that evening, the Science Lab in St John's was again treated to the sight of a mysterious beauty muffled in furs.

This time a fortnight passed without news. What he did hear filled him with alarm: mother and daughter were said to be leaving for Italy the following Monday. Weighed down by a sense of doom he waited for a meeting but none came. The day before they were to leave he called at Beeches hoping to speak to Serena. She remained in her room, confined with 'a headache,' as did her mother, and he unable to enquire without Clarissa wondering why.

The day they left, an envelope was pushed through the letter box. Hands shaking, he opened it to find a money order for ten pounds and a note penned in elegant script. '*Do not be alarmed, Dear Professor John. The debt shall be repaid and if not by my hand then by that of a van Leiden Sterne.*'

* * *

It is a well-known saying among the faculty that a man needs to be rich to teach at Cambridge. They are not rich. He and Phoebe live on a small annuity. They have no easy way of repaying fifty pounds never mind two hundred and fifty! Plus with no property of their own, the cottage in Maxwell Road lent 'grace and favour' by St John's College, they have nothing to sell.

Some payments were made but in dribs and drabs: a five pound money order one week, then another five followed by weeks of silence; envelopes arrive post-marked Paris, but any money in francs thus incurring loss in transfer. Learning of their address in Italy he wrote asking for help. The letters returned unopened, the Parisis gone, and no forwarding address.

Interest accruing, the Sarsons were getting letters from the bank, and his friend, the manager, no longer friendly. John should've faced up to the debt, but instead panicked, transferring a further hundred from the West Street branch leaving Clarissa's account almost empty. Last night he broke the news to Phoebe, saying with no proof of payment, no paper signed or gentleman's agreement - unless a kiss counts - neither he nor Clarissa has redress.

Tomorrow, though loath to do it, Phoebe goes again to Cherry Hinton. They have had some help from Great Aunt Sheba, but as a lady of small means herself, there can't be much more to come. All now depends on Clarissa. Foolishly, he always hoped she would find out; that one day in need of money she would call at her bank. She never did. She was happy to leave all transactions in 'Uncle's Sarson's capable hands.'

* * *

Weary of it all, and dreading the coming meeting, he sighed.

'I beg your pardon, Professor.' James van Leiden looked up (John must remember *not* to add Sterne to his name, Clarissa saying he prefers not to use it). 'Forgive my bad manners. I should've offered a chair.'

'Not at all. You have important work. I ought not to have intruded.'

'No intrusion, sir.' A chair was brought. 'You are always welcome.'

Clarissa doesn't care for her boss. She maintains his appointment offends younger members of the faculty, they seeing him an arriviste, carving his way through life via the De Beers Diamonds. John finds him a decent fellow, he and his long loping walk more Texan than Belgian Walloon, and a sense of the New World striding through stuffy British corridors.

A solitary fellow, he has a house on the Granta and is not seen on campus except when, like his brother, he is drawn to early Persian poetry. Then, handsome face in shadow, he sits back of the lecture hall, and other than the hand-tooled leather boots he favours nothing to suggest arrogance.

Clarissa hates those boots. 'An elegant man used to the best tailoring and fashionable hats, what does one see at the end of those ridiculously long legs but cowboy boots. They jar and tend to confuse one.'

Born to elderly parents, and no siblings to melt the ice, Clarissa was a shy child. Now, though fiercely independent, she is wary of pursuing any really close involvement. She can be difficult at times, naive in her ways of thinking, and undeniably spoilt by her father. For all that she is a lovely girl, kind and generous. It is certain she gave everything to the Fine Arts Course, studying into the early hours, battling her way through years of male prejudice only to see the withholding of the degree.

'Theirs was a quiet house,' said Phoebe. 'Then the Parisis arrived with their thrusting bosoms and chattering tongues, Clary must've thought Vesuvius erupting again and she buried under Italian ash. Charles did wrong marrying that woman and before he died came lamenting, saying they were helping themselves to his daughter's possessions and he unable to say nay.

'Gypsies and thieves! If anything should've warned you *not* to lend money to that girl it was the sight of my dead sister's furs on her back. Trust me, as she hung onto those, Serena will hang onto every last pound of that loan. She and her mother were Charles' failing. You have made them ours.'

Means

Margret poked her head round the door. 'The florist's boy is here again.'

'Lilac in this weather?'

'Hothouse I expect.'

'And the card still unsigned?'

'Yes, the same message, "For the Lilac Lady."'

'The man must have money to burn. Leave them in water in the sink, Margret. I'll deal with them later.'

Clarissa took a sip of coffee, and then - more concerned with the mysteries of gilding than the mystery of a bouquet of lilac that, for a year or more, the second Saturday of every month, is delivered to the door - returned to her book, and the paragraph she has been reading since early morning.

'*You need a steady hand for the next sequence. Should the leaf waver, or a draught deflect your course, try blowing gently to reposition.*'

The book describes the application of gold leaf. It is usually a straight-forward process; today the words make little sense. It was the same yesterday when news of her reduced finances caused her to drop more than a casual amount of leaf on the bench and Mijnheer van Leiden's elegant eyebrows to rise. She was shaken by her uncle's confession. Anger, resentment and fear, she felt it all. There was pity too for Aunt Phoebe; seeing the brown marks on her hands as dark tides and the lines on her face gaunt ravines.

'I'm sure it is nowhere near as desperate.' While struggling to master her own fears she tried easing theirs. 'If Serena repaid the early debts she'll no doubt do the same with this.' Poor dears, they hung on her words, Uncle John, an aging English bulldog, and Aunt Phoebe his weary mate.

Clarissa did her best to soothe them, but soon left pleading a headache, the light fading and the need to be on her way home. 'Do eat something!' They'd clamoured. 'Working all day, you must be hungry.' She couldn't eat. Knowing Serena Parisi was again a cause of distress the food would've choked her.

There was an awkward parting at the door, Uncle John struggling with his galoshes and Aunt Phoebe attempting to wrap a scarf about his neck, and both so unhappy unable to function. It was then James van Leiden passed by, and seeing the open door and lamps flickering paused to doff his hat.

'A gift really,' Aunt Phoebe was to say the following day when relating the event. 'Upright fellow, one could not have wished for safer passage.'

Clarissa doesn't care for the man and would've sooner braved the weather alone, but everyone so dithery, and her own senses jangled, she conceded: 'better the devil I don't want to know than the Uncle I thought I knew.'

That John Sarson could be tricked was a shock. Clarissa had thought him a sensible man and, unlike her father, disinclined to be moved by any 'moment of delight.' Economist, a man of letters respected throughout the academic world, he had to be sensible, for if not what hope for the world.

That night she was desperate to get home, and closing the door fell into Margret's arms. Margret Hankin is Beeches right arm. Housekeeper, nurse and every way good fairy, she was here before Clarissa was born. There isn't anything she doesn't know about the Morgan family, even so, while likely to know in the end, this is one tale she can't be told. It would bring shame upon Aunt Phoebe. No one must know how, as with Father, Uncle Sarson was overthrown by the same dark eyes.

Unable to sit still, Clarissa left her book, and along with Tillie, her little Jack Russell Terrier, made for the scullery and the arranging of lilac. This is another of Serena's entanglements. The first bouquet arrived June of '99, the Parisis gone, and though sad - Papa badly missed - it was a time of calm.

Despite being stripped of priceless memories - as with the blue vase that stood on the hall table and a crystal wine decanter in the Chinese cabinet - the house had settled into old ways and Clarissa completing her Tripos.

One morning a florist's cart pulled in to the yard, the boy's arms filled with fresh lilac and the house blessed with a heavenly scent. Beyond a printed card: '*For the Lilac Lady*,' there was nothing to say who sent them. Margret said they were for Clarissa. She thought otherwise and wrote to Serena. She replied: '*The card refers to my lilac gown. Keep the flowers. All else send on.*'

So far it is only flowers that arrive every month to bloom and die. The sender may be determined to remain anonymous, but Clarissa thinks she knows who it is. Monday evening, supported on James van Leiden's arm, she was tempted to raise the subject, believing his brother, Kasper, to be the sender.

It was the winter of '99. She was on the way back from a lecture, given by James, on the life of Fra Angelico. It was a well attended class, female undergrads from Girton, Newnham *and* Lady Margaret Hall, Oxford cramming the front rows. Forced to sit at the back Clarissa complained: no one from LMH was taking Italian Art, so why were they there? A girl laughed. 'They don't care about any sort of Art. They are here for the American Magister's eyelashes.'

Clarissa sat throughout that lecture struggling to hear and left in high dudgeon. Sleet falling, and fighting to keep a lantern alight, she was almost home when peering through slushy rain she saw Serena at the gate and a stranger on horseback spurring away.

His head was down so that when Clarissa came from behind a tree he was taken unawares, and snatched at the bridle, the horse rearing and he almost thrown. 'Confound it, girl!' he'd yelled. 'If you must flit about like an ethereal mouser hang a bell about your neck so people will know you're coming!'

Then he was gone. She didn't know who he was and wouldn't have known but for a jug of cream delivered the following morning. A cat's collar with a silver bell was tied to the handle and a label: '*To the pussy cat with green eyes. The big bad dog with the loud bark sends his apologies. It was cold and he was a long way from home and hungry for a bone.*'

The note was signed KLS and she no wiser. Mildly amused, she kept the cat's collar in the Chinese lacquered box, but later found that the collar - and the box - went the way of the Parisi luggage never to be seen again.

* * *

Clarissa worked alongside the professor for more than a year without mentioning the meeting. A brief encounter with a 'bad dog,' can hardly be thought a meeting. Besides, to raise the topic would be to start a conversation and she wouldn't want to do that. It is one thing to discuss work with the man, another to talk of home and life. Bloodlessly cold is how she sees James van Leiden, a man of fine manners and clean fingernails, but not a drop of red blood in his veins, and no other passion than to restore the dead to life.

Of late she's wondered if this dislike is less to do with him and more about the encounter with his brother and the dispute that followed when Serena came to the bedroom demanding to know why he sent gifts.

Clarissa had shrugged. 'A pint of cream and a cat's collar are hardly gifts.'

'Then why he send them?'

'I imagine they are by way of an apology.'

'What apology? Why does he apologise to you? '

'Beyond almost running me down I have no idea. He did speak or rather to yell. I said nothing, though I thought a great deal, namely he was an ill-mannered oaf I'd sooner not see again.'

'You are wrong to think Kasper van Leiden Sterne an ill-mannered oaf.' At that Serena had felt able to smile. 'You do not know him. If you did, Miss Clareessa Morgan, you might choke on your words.'

'Is that so?' Clarissa had turned away. 'Then I'd better ask Margret to put the pot of cream on ice. That way your lover's gift won't be wasted and I with something cool to soothe my throat after the choking.'

After the incident of the Bad Dog, Serena didn't bother trying to be kind. Her mother might weep at Papa's funeral, but with no need for pretence she remained dry-eyed, and the sad truth revealed: the Parisis never cared for Charles Morgan; he was means to an end.

Looking back, Clarissa recalls how every day of the holiday in '97 Papa was urged to return, a packet of ribbon-tied billet-doux found after his death hidden among handkerchiefs in his dresser-drawer. Though signed Isabella the perfect English told of the daughter's hand, and '*Dearest Doctor Charles*' urged to return to his '*devoted Isabella, and to come alone so we might sit by the Arno sipping wine in the moonlight as do all lovers.*'

The Parisis are gone and no word to say if they will return. The encounter with Kasper, and the contempt afterward in Serena's eyes, has left the name van Leiden as cursed. In this she does his brother a disservice and should at least try being amenable. The problem with that is once forged a habit is hard to break, and the need to avoid the man so ingrained she avoids contact, even when he's trying to stop her injuring herself.

Monday evening the snow was deep and the roads perilous. They somehow managed to get from Uncle Sarson's without accident. The gates to Beeches loomed out of the mist. In that moment Clarissa thought on her uncle saying she may have to sell the house. It was then she began to fall.

'Say there!' Arm about her waist, and the other behind her head, he hooked her close, and she lying across his chest. 'It's okay. I got you.'

Gotcha! An American drawl against a backdrop of Flemish-Dutch, his voice is not unattractive and that evening was not so much a shout as a certainty:

'I have got you. I will not let you fall.'

Held close like that for the first time she understood what the girls from Lady Margaret Hall meant by the Magister's eyelashes. His eyes are silvery grey and his lashes thick and dark and dusted with snowflakes,

Perhaps if he'd stayed silent allowing her to retreat with dignity her opinion of him might've undergone change, but as with most men he must speak.

'Do try to stay upright, Miss Morgan. Or if not, then try to make less hasty moves. A good conservator is never hasty. No matter what is troubling her, heaven or hell, she knows to move real slow and easy.'

It wasn't offensive. He was trying to lift her spirits, and leaning against his chest isn't so terrible. It is comforting, as is his hand holding hers.

Alas, there is a time to tease and this isn't it. She has lost what money she had to his brother's mistress. The worst of it, she can never tell how the loss came about. No one must know how her father and uncle were a prey to feminine wiles. Clarissa must find a way around it and must do it alone.

Oh, but lying against him is comforting and she wanted to stay. Even so, recalling how all men - particularly this man - are a source of trouble, she broke free of his arms, and with muttered aside, slid her way through the gate.

CHAPTER THREE

Gimp

Porter's Lodge
Cambridge University
Saturday March 23rd 1901

'Off climbing, sir?' The porter nodded toward James's boots.

'Well spotted, Mr Sissons.'

The porter shrugged. 'You get to notice things in my job.'

'I imagine so, which brings us back to my question: what kind of trouble.'

'I wouldn't like to say, sir.'

'But you did say.' James wasn't going to be fobbed off. Having caught wind of a situation, and not liking the smell, he came today looking for facts, and rather than waste time going through 'normal' channels, went to the fount of all knowledge regarding university life – the Porter's Lodge.

'Having heard Thursday's lecture is cancelled,' said James, 'I enquired of Professor Sarson, wanting to know if he was indisposed. You said he was in a bit of trouble. I'm asking what kind of trouble and how big a bit.'

'The usual trouble, sir, money, the root of all evil. As to the bit - a lot.'

'Expatiate.'

'I don't know that I can say much more, sir, not my place.'

James laid a pound note on the porter's table. 'Try.'

'It's a tale that's been doing the rounds for months. A nasty bit of gossip about a young lady relative of the Profs spending more than she should, and landing him and his wife up in debt, and a house having to go up for sale.'

'Professor Sarson's house?'

'He hasn't got a house, sir. He's grace and favour through St John's. A former bursar left a couple of cottages to members of the faculty in straightened circumstances, which to my mind is the whole blooming crew.'

'So what house is going on the market, or rather whose?'

'The young lady's.'

'And the young lady's name?'

'No sir!' The porter pushed the pound note away and began sorting mail in the pigeon-holes. 'I'm not naming names.'

'Why when you've said thus far?'

'Because it wouldn't be right. So far it's whispers. No real facts, only nudges and winks. What if there's another story behind this and the young lady in question good as gold and the real Jezebel getting away with murder.'

'Has there been a murder?'

'Not so far, though with all this mucky talk going on, it ain't doing the Professor any good, or anyone else for that matter.'

'And the Jezebel?'

'That's what I said.'

'Seems to me you know more than you're telling. And that you don't believe what's being said, particularly in reference to the young lady relative.'

'Maybe I don't. Maybe I've got eyes in my head that see what other people would sooner forget, the Professor included. Then again, maybe I believe in a law that says innocent til proven guilty.'

'The best stance to take.'

'Blokes have gone to the gallows for less. A man sees a lot in my job and most of the time holds his tongue. Discretion they call it or in my case a need to be a Wise Monkey, seeing, hearing and saying nothing. There are times though when I know what's true but can't say for it ain't my truth to tell.'

'A difficult choice.'

'You're not kidding.' A Londoner - a Cockney, so James is told - pugnacious, now chasing sixty but a prize-fighter in his youth, cauliflower ear and squashed nose as tokens, the Head Porter stared from under a bowler hat.

'As for giving out names, if you're asking out of curiosity like some folks here, even them that sits at High Table and should know better, then you got enough to go on with. But if you're looking to help the Professor and his wife, which you might be, then you don't need help from me, do you, sir.'

'No, Mr Sissons, I don't.' James added a second note to the first, and taking his stick, walked on.

* * *

St Bene't's Church, Cambridge

James is not at St Bene't's for the pardoning of his sins - though if things go wrong he might be praying for that; he is here for the conquering of old enemies. The spring of 1880 found he and his brother climbing the Miriam on the Torre Grande. James was ten-years old. It was not a particularly arduous climb nor was it his first mountain. He fell, and left foot wedged between rocks broke his ankle, the pain causing him to vomit over a new climbing jacket.

Thanks to Kes's strapping he kept his leg if not his dignity. In consequence of that break he can't jump too high or walk absolutely upright, but is left with a rocking movement - in layman's terms, a gimp. Twenty years on he's learnt to affect a smoother walk but the gimp is there as is the pain in his left knee.

To say it doesn't bother him is to lie. It limits movement, and as with other cripples, he is now often mistaken to be in some way mentally retarded.

While people don't exactly lean into him wagging their hands and making exaggerated movements with their lips, the fall has changed his life.

Looking back it might be seen as the reason he graduated *summa cum laude* at Harvard: unable to succeed in physical pursuits it was down to the intellect. As Grandfather Sterne put it: 'You can let the gimp colour your world or you can use that brain of yours to show your mettle. I don't care what you do at Harvard. Just make sure you do it better than anyone else.'

Now while he will never walk pretty, he can make the gray matter dance, and combats the odd blue moment pushing what is left of the physical to the max. Today it is St Bene't's bell-tower. He aims to climb the son-of-a-bitch and while so doing brood on rumours about that good old man, John Sarson.

* * *

Rumours of the professor in debt to the bank have been doing the rounds for months - Clarissa Morgan the suggested cause. A nasty rumour, it mutters of sexual perversion and the old man lavishing gifts on his niece in return for the odd tumble. James was present yesterday in the Junior Master's john when a dollop of muck was added to the tale; the sweaty guy Steed from Classics was sniggering with a buddy in the next stall: 'If the girl is as frigid as she looks, the old man would need a blow-torch to gain entrance.'

Incensed by what he heard, a bucket used for catching drips somehow hit the toe of James's best Western boot spilling dirty water across the floor.

That he is considered outside the pack is marked by those boots. Older members of the faculty see them a leftover from a Wild West Show. Younger faculty think them unbecoming to the Head Conservator at the Fitz.

It was Kasper who found them. James soon saw them as good boots, well-made and serving a purpose in supporting his ankle. Yesterday they performed a righteous service, dousing Sweaty Steed's ankles with pissy water in the hope he'll find better to do than slander a lady's name.

Universities are run on gossip with rumours regarding illicit relationships between masters and students going on for years. In the advent of co-ed universities the dynamic is likely to change. Until then the majority of students caught kissing when they should be wishing, follow the path of 'the love that dare not speak its name.' Halls of Residence are lonely places: Freshers missing home, and sports majors needing to ease tension in their balls, Harvard was an emotional time-bomb; a Fellow had to walk real soft and look where he put his feet, for first time away from home is hard and falling in love is easy.

With the publication of *Scorched Hearts* James became the focus of more than one adolescent crush. One guy felt the need to tell the world of his passion and every Saturday stood beside the grave of John Leverett, 17th Century Governor of Massachusetts Bay Colony, reading poems dedicated to 'Magister van Leiden, the scorcher of my heart.'

If that were Kasper he'd have stood alongside quoting his beloved Rumi and everyone, including the poet, going away happy. James bore all with a resigned sigh, grateful that the guy chose John Donne and not some other daffodil as in the case of the all too current Lord Alfred Douglas.

Cambridge has its own homoerotic issues. He receives regular eye-watering fan-mail at his Granta address, and though the despair of the Faculty, he seems to have friends among the students, and is often lobbied by the Pitt Club and the Apostles regarding membership.

Rumours surrounding John Sarson continue. That there was a fraudulent bank loan is likely true; scuttlebutt regarding money usually has some foundation. That it is due to his niece is a lie – James would bet his life on that. All the same, while guys like Steed feel able to shit her good name down the sewer along with last night's prunes and custard, damage is done from which Clarissa may never recover. That being the case, James intends to pay a call on the Sarsons, settling his mind on the identity of the Jezebel.

* * *

Midway up the tower he is sweating. Why he needs to do this he does not know but do it he must. Last year it was midnight climb of Nelson's Column. In the States he would've gathered a crowd. In London a drunk and a lone British Bobby waited for him to come down. 'You're American aren't you, sir,' that and a sniff up the right nostril was all the Bobby said.

Before the Fall (how antediluvian can it get) he and Kasper were rivals, one trying to outdo the other in whatever pursuit was tried. You'd think his fall might've put a stop to that. No sir! Twenty years on rivalry still exists.

Kasper will learn of the latest escapade and follow with one of his own. With Nelson's Column he performed the same climb during the day wearing a pink bunny suit and white cotton tail. Next day he was front page news: *The Kestrel Flies Again,* his exploits seen as the stuff of schoolboy heroes.

But enough of that! James needs to focus on the bell-tower. If there is a side issue, let it be the identity of the Head Porter's Jezebel.

The first time he saw Serena Parisi she was on her knees praying. Such beauty, the mantilla covering her face could not hide the texture of her skin or the depth of her eyes. He could only stare. He wasn't the only one. Every male in Assisi's Basilica, including the marble statues, knew she was there.

His book *Scorched Hearts* was about to go to press and James was in Assisi following last thoughts on St Francis. He was due to return to Boston the following day. Then a beautiful girl dropped her prayer book.

They'd toured the Basilica together. She was in Assisi with her mother visiting an aunt. Suddenly the trip back to Boston could wait. So he stayed and for three days looked at art through her eyes. Serena is an intelligent woman knowing a little of Italian art and a little of him. 'My aunt's house overlooks the pensione where you stay. I see you. I ask who is that 'andsome man and learn of Professore James van Leiden from 'Arvard.'

How flattered he was thinking he'd been noticed. A thin-skinned guy, praise takes him by surprise, especially when falling from such lips. For three days they met every day, walking together, eating together, and he on the brink of falling in love, and she the same - or so he thought.

Then Kasper arrived on a promised break. Hands in his pockets, he strolled into a cafe where they sat sharing ice-cream. Blue eyes flashing, sunbeams on his red-gold hair creating a new Ra, he smiled and she was gone.

A light in her eyes that a moment ago said James was the only man in the world blinked out and he evicted from her heart so his brother might reign.

For a moment hatred burned until he saw Kasper wasn't taking anything she wasn't anxious to give. Then, what before had fascinated, the smile under the lashes and the red lips parting on white teeth, was so quickly, and so obviously switched to Kasper, it was laughable. And though her beauty remained, for James it never regained that first, bright shine.

Kasper was amused by the switch. 'I guess that's how it goes with a woman like that, off with the old and on with the new, and all else chewed up and spat out.' For a while it was Kasper she chewed. 'I can't say I love her. You can't love a snake that's only waiting for you to drop your pants to bite your ass.'

He'd grinned. 'Though you gotta admit bitten anywhere by that particular snake is worth the pain.'

Despite what followed - their relation ever stormy - Kasper maintained that view: 'Be glad it's not you, Gyr. She would've ruined your life.'

Around that time James was considering change, and though offered new tenure at Harvard, put out feelers to the Uffizi, the British Museum, and the New York Metropolitan. He chose not to propose the Louvre, for wonderful though it is, he saw it too close to home and Grandfather. As for that he needn't have worried - October 4th 1896 Elias Sterne died.

For a miserable old man he made a peaceful end, his face cherubic and Mama weeping at his bedside. At the reading of the Will they learned he had left the bulk of the De Beers shares to Kasper, and the rest to be shared between Anneka and James. No one was surprised. Elias had always favoured his eldest grandson, especially as - thinking toward this day and De Beers shares - Kasper chose to add the name Sterne to his title.

News of Grandfather's death hit the press. By that time James had firm offers. He favoured the Metropolitan, seeing it run by people who get things done as opposed to the British Museum whose cellars are known to be full of priceless works of art in unopened packing cases. The same laissez-faire attitude is said of the Tate Gallery; JMW Turner bequeathed his work to the Gallery on the promise they would 'take all and destroy none.'

A place like that would drive James crazy. He has to be where conservation means exactly that: paintings going among the people, not locked away in a cellar enjoyed by none but the rats chewing through the packing cases.

* * *

Having made it to the belfry, James perches on a beam gazing through binoculars over the countryside. From here he can read the dedication on the bells while hoping no one feels the sudden need to toll them.

That they are almost free of dirt suggests he's not the only one willing to risk his neck. For James, a believer in the history of art, this moment is a gift, humanity under his hand: '*Robert*

Gurney made me: Thomas Graves and Tho Fox, Church Wardens 1663.' Then another bell: *'Of all the bells in Bennet I am the best, and yet for my casting the parish paid lest: 1607.'*

The Fitzwilliam came into being in 1816 founded by Viscount Richard FitzWilliam. It has a keen fellowship, and partnered by the University should do well, though a keen fellowship is not the reason James chose to come - that choice was made when helping Kasper out of a jam.

Autumn of '98 saw the Serena and Kasper relationship on again, and the Parisis in England: Isabella wed to a Charles Morgan, retired Doctor of Divinities, and they living in Cambridge. January '99 found James in London with his sister. Grandfather's death enabled Anneka to join her fiancé, Tom Phillips, a barrister met in Antwerp now practising in Lincolns Inn.

Free to follow her heart, she pressed to have the Hatton Garden jewel shop removed to premises in Knightsbridge, an area of London more suited to the fashionable clientele she planned to bring to the House of Leiden.

'I couldn't love Grandfather while he was alive,' she said. 'But now he is dead, and I have Thomas, I can at least try to understand him.'

Anneka and Thomas were wed December '98. The ribbon on the new shop in London was cut in February '99. Time on his hands, James agreed to help the newly married couple before going to New York to accept the Metropolitan's offer. Then he received a letter from Kasper, short and to the point. *'I have a chance to join a nomadic tribe crossing the Sahara. One problem: I promised to convey that other nomadic tribe, the Parisi-Chases to London: Isabella's husband dead, and they, Veni, Vidi, Vici, moving on. They have tickets for the Paris Express London Victoria April 4th and booked overnight on the 3rd at the Dorchester. Settle any outstanding monetary debts but any other kind caused by their stay in England leave well alone - no one can fix them. Conveyance is arranged through Giovanni di Lombardi, an Explorers pal who promises a decent growler and a friendly nag for you to outride.*

Grates tibi, Kes. PS. Cavete Pulcher Viridi-Oculus Felis!'

That was it, a collection note for two people and their luggage. No way out, James wrote to that address saying he'd be there on the 3rd, but coming from London couldn't be sure what time he'd arrive. Kasper had already set plans in operation; a cable coming to Knightsbridge: '*Thank you, James, for coming to our rescue. I can't wait to see you and share memories, Serena.*'

With nothing to share but a sour taste in his mouth, he took a train from Liverpool Station that morning, stopping at an ale house in Cambridge for a meal, before hailing a cab and arriving at the house just before two.

It was cold. A hard frost had turned the beech trees to winter wraiths. Dressed in a greatcoat and hat, a scarf bound about his face, he greeted the Parisis. Serena was anxious to leave. He suggested he might pay compliments to the house but was told not to bother. 'Our goodbyes were made yesterday, and so tearful, Dear James, we would not want to repeat the same.'

Since it was of little moment to him to whom they said goodbye, he was glad to have them on their way, and making acquaintance with the horse, a good fellow, strong and with an easy stride, climbed aboard.

It was then she appeared, the subject of Kasper's clumsy Latin post-script: '*Cavete Pulcher Viridi-Oculus Felis*! Beware the beautiful green-eyed cat.'

She was beautiful with eyes the colour of fine Jade. She was also unhappy. Arms filled with lilac - blind to horse's hooves - she scrambled alongside the carriage trying to gain Serena's attention.

Though it was lilac he clasped to his chest that day, it was her, the pale mermaid, James longed to embrace. Even now he feels the touch of her hand on his, slender fingers as cold as ice and she in mourning, the black of her gown highlighting the silver white frost that was her hair.

Now he stands atop of St Bene't's bell-tower. Every muscle in his body aches but again he has conquered fear. Cupping his hands about his mouth, he called out: 'If you're wondering why I am here, Kasper, and why I gave up New York then hear this. The green-eyed cat is the reason I am at the Fitzwilliam. She is the reason I let go of other possibilities. She is the cause of my hope, and likely the cause of my pain: Clarissa Emily Morgan, the Lilac Lady.'

CHAPTER FOUR

As it Was

The Beeches, Comberton
Tuesday April 2nd 1901

She stared. 'The debt is paid?'

'It is.' John Sarson nodded. 'The money went into the bank account on West Street yesterday morning.'

'All of it!'

'Every penny.'

'And you, Uncle Sarson? Are you cleared of all debt?'

'I am, thank you, Niece, and as suggested by Mr Cairns, the manager, I have removed my name from your account. The ins and the out are now entirely under your jurisdiction and everything back as it was.'

'I see...everything back as it was.' She sighed. 'Ah well, perhaps Serena is not such a bad person after all.'

'Perhaps. There is always hope of people.'

Anxious to be on his way, and not drawn into questions regarding the nature of his salvation, John raised his hat and left, knowing the Beeches no longer feels to be a second home; there is caution where once was love.

But that is only right. He did the family harm. A man of seventy-five years, an educated man, well travelled in his youth, he should have known to look beyond the outer skin understanding that 'all that glisters is not gold.'

The question has to be asked, why so quick to give money

to a stranger. The answer is vanity. Approached by another in a similar manner he might've given a shilling in charity but never to steal. Now, but for the charity of another stranger, while the burden is lightened the debt continues.

James van Leiden paid all while wanting nothing in return: '...other than the satisfaction of being of use to you and Miss Morgan, and your promise that she will never know how it was settled and by whom.'

Clarissa won't know for he will never tell. Phoebe doesn't know. Seeing her husband closeted in discussion with the man, she suspects a great deal, but afraid to enquire remains silent. As for John, he is so broken by the affair he is left quite ill, waking in the night, heart pounding, suspecting that, along with his brother-in-law, Charles, he soon will lay under the sod.

All day yesterday he was afraid to go out, ashamed to be seen by his colleagues. The malaise in his face shows. James van Leiden was concerned. 'You are unwell, sir, rest awhile.' Said so kindly, it allowed John to say how the thought of Thursday's lecture filled him with horror. 'All those eyes staring? I don't know how I will manage, though I must, for I am paid five sessions per Semester, and while it is not a lot of money it is needed.'

That good young man offered to take his place: 'I don't have your knowledge of Persian poetry but if it would help - and me not seen a puppy parading my own work, I could talk of early English poetry.'

It was agreed that until further notice James will take forthcoming lectures. Any thanks were waved away. 'You were persuaded to believe the lady in question affianced to my brother. Whether or not the name van Leiden was offered as testament of trust and I honour bound to help. Kasper would do the same were he here, but since he is not there is no need to trouble him.

'My brother spoke of you with affection. He would be saddened to know you've been put to difficulties. So then, John,' he'd held out his hand, 'let this be our secret, yours and mine, and once agreed never mentioned again.'

Overwhelmed, John hadn't known what to say. 'I look back and wonder how I could've been so foolish. I suppose I was flattered. The young lady in question was charming and my heart moved as never before.'

James sighed. 'We all do foolish things in the name of love.'

'I am an old man. I should be beyond such things.'

'I don't know that age has anything to do with feelings. I tend to think that in terms of love the heart is ever young and ever foolish.'

Such a melancholy thought for a young and handsome man, John felt he had to ask. 'Forgive me, James, but as we are now friends, and I indebted to you for all eternity - and perhaps so I might feel less of a failure - can I ask if you've ever done ought foolish in the name of love?'

'Oh to be sure!' James grimaced. 'A foolish idea of love brought me to Cambridge. I dare say that same foolish love will send me away.'

* * *

Clarissa stood at the window watching Margret's granddaughter, Freya-Jasmine, play with the dog. Such a pretty girl, delicate skin and red-gold hair, she has the same clear, honest way as her grandmother.

In respect of the debt, Clarissa wonders if she should write to Serena acknowledging payment or simply let it go. Then, relieved to know the problem is resolved, she penned a quick note ready to post.

It is still snowing. Yesterday it was white woollen blankets, the trees bowed down under the weight; today white feathers fall. The sitting-room window looks out to the stables. This time last year it was Serena's out-post. Other than the business of lilac bouquets, there is little by the way of communication. Monday they received a note with a post box number:

'*We are between houses: be so good as to forward mail to this number.*'

Last week a letter came for Serena from a fashionable milliner in Cambridge. Clarissa visited the shop where she settled a debt of six pounds.

The milliner was grateful. 'A charming young lady - Italian, I think. She bought a rather daring lace peignoir.' The bank overdrawn and Uncle Sarson in danger of going to prison, Clarissa chose not to comment

For a brief and horrible time she thought she would have to sell Beeches. Even now with the debt paid the world shakes and she with no one to reach out to. Last night she woke in terror from a dream of the French Revolution. She knelt at the guillotine as the executioner denounced her sins to a silent crowd, 'She was a selfish woman who'd brought her family to ruin.'

Neck on the block, her last memory before the swish of the blade was of the executioner shouting: 'Try to stay upright, Miss Morgan. Heaven or hell, what 'ere the trouble, a good conservator must move slow and easy.'

* * *

Today she and the Professor visit St Bene't's. An old church with a fascinating history, executioner notwithstanding, it should prove an enjoyable visit.

Wednesday August 30th 1899, she attended an interview for the post of assistant conservator. When introduced, his name was given as James van Leiden Sterne. He politely, but firmly, corrected the speaker: 'My name is James van Leiden. The Sterne belongs to other members of the family.' Interview over he'd bowed: 'Welcome to the Fitzwilliam, Miss Morgan.'

She had the job. Until then no one had said how she'd fared at the interview; all waited on his decision, and that – boot heels clicking and the firm grip of his hand – saying who was boss.

Intent on knowing more about the man, she left the museum that day for the University Library and read of the Van Leidens, an old and venerated Belgian family of jewellers with shops in Paris, London and Brussels. The biography related James's time at Harvard, listing his publications from Italian Art to Anglo-Norman poetry and the *de Brut* manuscripts: early English poetry tracing the history of Britain through the eyes of a mythical Brutus, descendent of Aeneas. While at Harvard he took an MSci in chemistry, saying if he was to be a conservator he should understand paint, and that what he learned there brought about his book, *When Walls Speak,* an investigation into Palaeolithic wall paintings of Northern Spain and the catacombs of Florence.

There was praise too for a later book, *Scorched Hearts:* 'a work of great beauty, intensity and passion,' in which the author discusses the twelfth-century lovers, Heloise and Abelard, positing a connection between St Francis of Assisi and St Clare. That day in the library Clarissa tried, with little success, fixing the lyrical description to James van Leiden, though she did see how the words 'intensity and passion,' might be applied to his brother.

While her enquiries were about one man, Clarissa is already too aware of prejudice in Cambridge University. The idea of further education for women is held in open contempt with protest marches, the burning of female effigies, and tossing of fireworks through widows at Girton and Newnham.

New rules spring up every day: women told they mustn't be seen after certain hours in the main hall or enter the Library unaccompanied, but must wait for a male to convey her into the building. All this to battle through, plus the greater insult in the denying of a Degree, small wonder she doesn't take to one who for the next few years will tell her what to do and how to do it.

It seems she is not alone in her aversion. That day in the library a person, now known as Jeffrey Steed, Junior Master in Classics, peered over her shoulder: 'Dear me yes, our Yankee cowboy is quite the star. Prodigiously bright, good to look at, and wealthy as Croesus, one wonders how we managed before his star lit our humble English skies.' Then he'd tittered, horrid little man: 'A pity about the gimp - quite spoils the image.'

* * *

Later that day, having placed them both in an awkward position, Clarissa was brought to consider the implications of the gimp. It was foolish. She shouldn't have risen to what she saw as bait. They visited St Bene't's and were about to leave when the curate pointed out a spiral staircase secreted at the east end of the south aisle. Clarissa asked why a secret staircase.

'There are peep-holes at the top. Is this the Reformation again, priests needing to hide, or simply as you say a way of getting around?'

'I think it a mix of both,' said the curate. 'A building as old as St Bene't's has seen a lot of rearranging over the years, some of it good, and some of it cruelly unnecessary. Even now we are adapting, hence the staircase uncovered.'

'What are you rearranging this time?' said James.

'Changes are always being made. This time, among other things, we are attempting to revive the organ, a very uncertain instrument.'

Clarissa gazed about her. 'I hope you will keep things much the same. It is a beautiful church and serene. One feels safe here '

The curate nodded. 'I am glad you think so.'

'As the staircase is open, might one take a look up top?'

'You'll need to duck, Professor. It was not built with you in mind. In the main, men of the eleventh-century were considerably shorter than you.'

'It looks dusty up there,' said Clarissa.

The curate smiled. 'Is the young lady thinking to climb?'

'I don't know. Are you thinking of getting up there?'

She saw the smile and bridled. 'I don't see why not.'

'It'll be a tight fit.'

'I would like to see what's up there.'

'Are you sure?'

The curate was anxious. 'The Professor is right about tight fit. I haven't been up there in years. I don't think there is that much to see, Miss Morgan.'

'How do you know if you haven't been up there?'

'Point taken.'

* * *

The staircase was narrow and laden with dust. Elbows in and knees bent they clambered up, Clarissa bunching her skirts and ducking cobwebs. They reached the top and one after the other squeezed through a gap only to find the rest of the way closed off and they crammed together in a kind of alcove. Beyond turning their heads, there was little room to manoeuvre.

Dust rising, James coughed. 'This wasn't the greatest idea.'

She coughed with him. 'No.'

'Okay, now that we're up, I guess we'd better go down.'

'Can we hold on a minute while I get my breath?'

Clarissa was a little panicked. While getting up wasn't so hard, going down represented a whole new challenge. They will have to swap places, he to lead the way down, and that meant shuffling in a tight circle.

James wiped his eyes on his sleeve. 'As the guy said, not a lot to see.'

'I don't know why I thought there was.'

'Maybe you were thinking it might lead to the bell-tower.'

'Perhaps I was.'

They stood chest to chest, or rather, she around five-seven in height and he six-three, her breast was tucked against his gut. It was an awkward situation, and since she can't stand to be within three feet of him, this must be killing her. The situation was so absurd, and she so riled - cheeks blown out, smudge on her nose, and a curl of her hair trembling - James was close to laughing, but hung on, thinking laughter at this juncture *not* a good idea.

'I guess I'd better lead the way down.'

'Will you be all right?'

'All right?'

'Your leg?'

'Oh that's okay. Don't worry about that.'

'Might I ask how this happened? Were you in an accident?'

'I broke my ankle climbing when I was a boy. It doesn't get in my way so much. I'm used to it, and I did climb the church bell-tower Saturday and so reckon I can manage this.'

'You climbed the bell-tower?'

'Uh-huh. It's not as harsh as it sounds. There are stages to rest. '

'Is there a view?'

'Some. The bells are worth seeing. The curate was saying they've had bells in St Bene't's since 1273, and that until the middle 1600s, for a yearly fee of seven shillings, they would summon university guys to lectures.'

'My word! This is such a very old place.'

'It is. Well then, are you ready to go?'

'As I'll ever be.'

They swapped places, inching around the other so that he felt her heart beating, and he thinking maybe she's not as brave as she'd like to be.

Boot-studs chinking, he stepped down. He felt her hesitate. 'Maybe if you hold onto my shoulder you'll feel steadier.'

'I'll do that. I'm sorry I dragged you up here.'

'Actually, I think I dragged you. But that's okay. It will give us something to look back on when we're old.'

Fingers looped through his collar and her breath warm on the back of his neck, she leaned down. 'And to tell our grandchildren.'

In that moment James knew he cared for the girl and probably always would. And that whatever the outcome, the loss of the Metropolitan and the Uffizi, they rattling down an ancient staircase in a thousand-year-old church is a memory that will make his choice of the Fitzwilliam always right.

CHAPTER FIVE

The Cut

Lecture Theatre, Cambridge
Thursday May 2nd 1901

What was that? She sat, fists clenched and disbelieving. Did Bunny Carpenter and those girls from Newnham actually cut her?

She was late getting to the lecture, a problem at home, Freya-Jasmine with toothache, and Doctor Brooke called. He is a good man and kind. When Papa was ill in the winter of '86 he came every day. Margret Hankin says Papa wasn't the only reason he called, that Paul Brooke is sweet on Clarissa.

Margret is aways hinting of likely husbands and never more so than after the bank problem. 'You need to take the worry of this house off your shoulders. Beeches is too big and too old for you to manage alone.'

Clarissa used to argue the point, saying she was able to stand on her own two feet. Then she learned to let words stay unspoken, for Margret was once happily married, and lost her husband and her daughter to typhus, and can't bear to hear anyone mocking the idea of marriage.

'Arthur was a good man. He came to me young and I to him. We struggled to get started. What with the loss of our first child and the birth of our daughter, we went through heaven and hell together, and but for that filthy disease we'd still be together. My daughter, Elizabeth, and her man, Reardon, were a matched pair. Death took all three and our Freya-Jasmine the only one to escape. Love is a gift how so 'ere it comes and shouldn't be scorned, for knowing how to gild a picture won't keep you warm on winter nights.'

Clarissa likes Paul Brooke. Were she inclined to marry, he is exactly the good sort of man she would hope to find. But she is not inclined to do anything so silly but rather to seek merit within herself, whatever that might be.

Before Papa died they looked toward travelling the world. They would discuss the idea, fetching the globe from his study - so much to see in all that blue - pointing out places of interest and drawing up an itinerary.

The plan was to complete her Tripos and then do the Grand Tour of Europe, before widening their scope visiting relatives in Vermont. Italy was to be the first step, a taste of what they might find. They were to commence with Florence and then go on to Rome by way of Assisi. Fate had another path in store for Charles Morgan, which found him in San Nicolo one morning sharing a late breakfast table with a mother and daughter, and who took their morning coffee at the pensione where the Morgans were staying.

Life changed that day. The Big Plan was set aside never to be picked up again. Father didn't go to Assisi; he declared a preference for the pensione's shady garden and the company of Senora Isabella Parisi-Chase, while the daughter, a sudden Fairy Godmother, took Clarissa by the arm. 'You shall go to Assisi. We will go together and visit the Basilica admiring the frescoes.'

How she smiled that day, her dark eyes suggesting a private source of amusement. 'Everyone should visit Assisi, in particular the Basilica. I go there when I am lonely. It is a 'ver good spot for fishing.'

Clarissa thinks of that moment now and wonders if the 'fishing' that year was for an elderly English gentleman or had she a more tasty catch in mind.

Time has moved on. The Parisis are not missed, though there are times when Assisi is remembered as a hot day, sunlight blazing, the sea as sheet metal, and Clarissa with the wrong kind of hat. There was kindness that day in a back-street market. Serena bought a hat with a wide brim and a strip of scarlet chiffon which she wove it about the crown as poppies in a field of straw. 'This is you.' She'd settled the hat on Clarissa's head. 'Fire among the ice.'

* * *

The hat awaits the summer in a cupboard. It was the only good thing to come from the meeting. Serena referred to Clarissa as fire in ice. If ever there was a mix of opposing passions it is Serena, with a face for all seasons and no one knowing what made the day or how the sun would set.

Clarissa had thought the Parisis gone; their essence clings as this evening will prove. The hall was abuzz, girls from Newnham *and* LMH Oxford occupying the front rows and the rest of the hall given over to male undergrads. Then Clarissa saw Bunny Carpenter, a friend from Fine Arts studying post-grad Chinese pottery, sitting in the third row with the Crichton Twins, Pam and Paula.

What luck! There is an empty space beside them. 'Hello Bunny!' She waved her note-book. 'If that seat is going idle might I fill it?'

Good God! The way they scowled you would've thought

a snake had crawled through the door. For a count of ten - Clarissa counting the beats - nothing was said, three pairs of eyes continuing to stare, until, as though rehearsed, with one accord they turned away.

Head down and cheeks burning, she stumbled to the back of the hall, and squeezing on the end of a row opened a notebook pretending to write.

What is this? What have I done that they stare so?

From then on she heard little of what was said but stared at the dais, watching gaslight flicker about James van Leiden's head. She was here at another of his lectures when he spoke of the *Roman de Brut* by the twelfth-century poet, Robert Wace. Though well-attended it was agreed later the subject matter - a translation in Norman-Frenchverse of Geoffrey de Monmouth's History of Britain - was by-the-way. The real attraction was the speaker's cool good looks and double-knotted Harvard tie, plus, as one LMH girl put it, 'the added attraction of impeccable Latin with a spritz of Yankee drawl.' Tonight the Yankee drawl speaks of the life and loves of Peter Abelard and Heloise d'Argenteuil, with quotes taken from his book, *Scorched Hearts,* a copy of which Clarissa sees on the laps of most students. Heads down, the audience traces the current quote, male and female lips moving in time and other than the rustle of pages no voice but his.

Bunny Carpenter has a copy of his book, well-thumbed by the look of it, and though reading, pauses to glance behind her, nose wrinkled as though trying to locate an unpleasant smell. It hurt. Why do such a thing? What has been said or done to cause a former friend to be cruel. During their first year at Girton they were friends. Bunny would sleep over occasionally, her Norfolk home too far away to live out. She is a terrifically bright girl; her father is an antiquarian book seller, and her mother a well-known landscape gardener.

They got on well, or so Clarissa had thought. They were not exactly Bosom Buddies, more friends to be precise. Oh, and do let's be precise! Isn't that what James day-after-day demands of his assistant, precision and clarity, and as with nightly terrors of a guillotine, the 'need to take her time?'

What was it last week? 'This is Hogarth's work. If you take your time and look again at the right-quarter of the sitter's shoulder, you'll see shading suggestive of under painting making the work less likely to be a fake.'

That was James on Thursday. A University Fellow wanted an opinion on a painting belonging to his family; a portrait of his great-grandmother, which he suspected to be the work of Hogarth but which his father declared a fake.

'Why does his father say it is a fake if it isn't?' was Clarissa's question. James had shrugged. 'Who knows. Maybe the guy was a gambler and liked to keep the lie so his beloved painting wouldn't take a hit easing his debts.'

It was a moment of whimsy, he smiling when he said it, and he was right; she should have looked closer. Why must he always be right? Can't he be wrong for once? Perhaps she should wait behind after the lecture. He might be able to cast light on why her company is rejected by a former friend, and whether it has to do with Serena and the wretched bank loan.

'Oh, please don't let it be that.' She closed her eyes offering a prayer against what she suspects, that tonight's snub is in response to a rumour currently spreading the Halls, where it is said Uncle Sarson stole from the bank on behalf of a woman. He didn't steal anything. He took, or rather he 'borrowed' from Clarissa's account.

Steal or borrow, when it comes to slander the truth doesn't seem to matter, for now, from an embezzler, John Sarson is a thief.

* * *

The rumour has been whispered about the campus for months, eventually finding its way to the Fitzwilliam studio. Clarissa isn't surprised. Despite her efforts to keep Margret from the truth she knows of the debt, as does Sally; both are silent on the matter, a clear indication they know something.

Now with the latest news, the Sarsons said to be leaving Cambridge and not likely to return, gossip moves apace, gathering dirt along the way, hinting of sex in exchange for favours and John Sarson cast as a lecher.

Clarissa knows of the latest twist; she's heard it for herself.

Most days she doesn't use the Museum lift. After Tuesday and St Bene't's spiral staircase she felt she couldn't face another climb and so this morning took the lift. It dropped down to the basement, collected four people, hauled back up to the ground floor where two cashiers got on.

They stood up front whispering. Pushed to the rear Clarissa wasn't particularly interested in what they had to say, but hearing of a university professor, a former tutor at St John's College (an old man who should know better), who'd stolen from the High Street Bank to keep his trollop of a mistress happy, she could do nothing but listen.

The whispering, and the giggling, has been in her head ever since. Until this evening, and the cold reception at the lecture, she'd managed to keep the implications at bay simply by being unable to bear thinking of them.

Now there is no getting away from it, Bunny Carpenter's face telling all. As heard in the lift, the female at the heart of the scandal is a local girl, an assistant to 'the American Magister here at the Fitz!'

Such words drub her brain, foraging and accusing while pointing out the obvious - not once in all of the rumours and chatter, was the name of the real culprit mentioned.

But then why would Serena Parisi be mentioned? As far as the bank loan is concerned she doesn't exist. Think about it, Clarissa Morgan.

No one knows of her part in the scandal, only you and the Sarsons.

It was you who strove to keep that name away from the world.

You told no one of her involvement, not Margret, or Sally, or any member of the family; more importantly, you didn't tell anyone at the bank. When asked by the manager how the situation came about, you kept quiet, or, as you now recall, you said something silly, 'these things happen.'

It wasn't sensible but then you were distraught, and in trying to save your father's reputation, he once wed to Serena's mother, you begged John Sarson to keep quiet, thinking that way neither men would carry the blame.

It was a foolish plan and bound to fail. Uncle Sarson is a central figure in this cheap novelette; he will always suffer shame, what's more, so will you.

The obvious conclusion to the tale was there in the lift this morning, as it is here tonight in the Lecture Hall: the girl the cashiers giggled about – the one who is mocked as 'She who must be Conserved,' the mistress, the trollop - who according to gossip, lures old men into parting with their cash - is you.

CHAPTER SIX

Elf

The Beeches, Comberton
Monday May 13th 1901

'Grandma come quick!' Margret's granddaughter ran in to the kitchen. 'There's an elf in the stable.'

Margret was in the heavy stage of baking, heaving dough about the bowl, her cheeks red from effort. 'What's that?'

'An elf in the stable with Hazlett.'

'What do you mean elf?'

Freya-Jasmine reached up on her toes, and hands about her mouth whispered. 'An elf or a goblin, I'm not sure.'

'Goblin! Don't be silly, child, there's no such thing. And why are you whispering?'

'Because he's asleep and I don't want to wake him.'

'You and your fairy things!' Margret dusted her hands with flour before continuing to pound the dough. 'You're like your mama, floating away on clouds. She was always seeing goblins in the woodshed and toads under the bed. I said to her, as I'm saying to you, be careful, or one of these days your imagination will get you into bother.'

'I'm not imagining him. He's there, Grandma. He's hiding behind the water trough all curled up in a ball.' Freya-Jasmine was upset. She was wasting time, and the elf looking so thin and tired. He's probably hungry too, and those loaves already baked and standing on a tray to cool look good to eat.

'Can I have a slice of bread and jam?'

'What do you want that for? You've only just had your breakfast?'

'For the elf. He looks so thin and has bruises on his face, and his dog looks hungry too.'

'Dog? Bruises? In with Hazlett!' Realising there was more to this than imagination Margret spread a cloth over the bowl, wiped her hands, and nodded to Sally to follow. 'Where did you say he was?'

'In Hazlett's stable, but don't shout, Grandma! He looks tired, and I think he has been crying.'

* * *

'*Can Miss Morgan please pop home at lunchtime? She has an unexpected visitor.*' When the note arrived Clarissa was stretching wet canvas between clamps. She wanted to finish but thinking there must be a problem - Margret never known to send messages - she unbuttoned her smock.

'Might I leave this til later, Professor? I'm needed at home.'

James set down the brush. 'Is there a problem?'

'I think there must be.' She took her jacket. 'My housekeeper wouldn't send unless there was an issue.'

'Can I be of service?'

'Thank you no.' She was off and running. 'I rode here today on a bicycle and so shall be home in a flash. But thank you anyway…James.'

A flick of her skirts, worry again in her eyes, and she was gone, racing down the stairs. Miss Independence, she hardly ever bothers with the lift. Waiting on a lift requires patience, and patience is not her strong point.

'But gosh all hemlock, she called me James.'

This is the first time she thought to call him by his Christian name. True, she was on the run when she did it, but that's okay. He smiled, and with the students on a field trip, and no one else to see, did a little jig, catching his elbow on a large easel sent it crashing. Fortunately it holds nothing of value. He awaits news of a painting said to be damaged during the floods in Florence in '78. If all goes well, the news should see James and Clarissa meeting the art collector, Giovanni di Lombardi regarding on-site restoration.

'Though why he left restoration until now is beyond me,' said James. 'Water is the very worst. If as suspected it is a Fra Angelico, then good luck to anyone who tries restoring that.'

When Clarissa bolted she left behind the note and the sketchbook that is her soul companion. Where before she would sit in a workroom for luncheon, or eat at the museum cafe, now she walks along the Backs, or takes a cushion by the River Cam sketching flowers and the wild-life that are her fancy.

She offered a similar sketchbook when applying to the museum. While that book amply displayed her skills as an illustrator, it was her written work that appealed to James, chiefly the excellently entitled, *Luna Solitaria,* a dissertation on the life and work of the Italian poet, Giacomo Leopardi.

For some time he had been toying with the idea of following *Scorched Hearts* with a biography of that same poet. Impressed with her ideas on Giacomo's conflicted relationship with his father, the *Conte Monaldo*, he had begun to hope one day he and Clarissa might work together. Now with the breakthrough regarding Christian names, the thought takes wings.

She has forgotten her hat. He picked it up, twirling it about his hand. A pretty thing of soft straw with a red silk bandana twined about the brim, it has her scent, a flower fragrance, and, as with the girl, somewhat peppy.

For some reason the combination of scents reminds him of home. There was another letter yesterday from Mama. Anxious for Father, she writes: 'He doesn't eat or sleep but spends every moment in his studio with the door locked. He won't talk to me or any of his friends. I have sent for Doctor Goossens so many times he must be sick of us. I fear your father is going into the dark again. I wish you were home, Dear James.'

Poor Mama! She has seen it all before. Father's depressions are as deep as dark as the underground caverns in Calabria, and with so many twists he loses his way, needing a guide to bring him home.

In the past only Mama and James were able to bring him peace. Others tried but with little success. When he is this far down not even Kasper can help; indeed, a word from him seems to make matters worse, as if faced with such vitality, Karel van Leiden sees his weaknesses laid bare.

Father wasn't always a shadow-man. James remembers him telling of his life in Paris when Grandfather Gustave van Leiden allowed him to work in the shop on the *Rue de Saint Honoré*, confining his jeweller's skills to the workroom during the day, and his evening to the painters on the Left Bank.

He maintained it was the happiest time of his life: irritant and joy; his skills for the design and the mounting of jewels worked alongside his love of painting producing treasure as in the oyster and the pearl.

He experimented with colour: silver and gold were malleable

in his hands. 'My head was full with ideas: I was alive. I enjoyed the paintbrush *and* the gems, taking risks that would've made the best goldsmith tremble.'

Paris agreed with him as did his loft in the *Rue de Tivoli*. Up at five in the morning, he produced some really fine work. The Demimonde flocked to his door, particularly in the new fashion of diamond engagement rings. He would sit at a bench by the window, the scent of Jasmine rising, a hurdy-gurdy playing in the cafe beneath, and his grandfather's mantra in his head: 'hit a diamond and it will shatter into a dozen pieces. Hit a piece of quartz and it will split in two. Hit all with the right hammer and they will ring like bells.'

All life stopped in the autumn of '64 when Gustave died and Karel van Leiden was forced to return home. It was there he met Alice Sterne. They were wed in the spring 1865 and in '67 she was pregnant with Kasper.

Times were hard in the late '60s in every aspect of the trade, and while the shops in Paris and London got by Brussels struggled, needing an hefty injection of cash to compete with the more up-to-date stores that were springing up all over Europe. It was during the baptism of his first grandchild that Elias Sterne pledged to refinance the workroom on the understanding his son-in-law put away all ideas of painting. 'You've had a lengthy childhood. It is time to set aside coloured chalks and put bread on your family's table.'

* * *

With no other choice, Father let go of dreams, and while he had no real love of the jewel trade, from then on he hated it, seeing his soul shackled to a workman's bench. Mama rarely talks of that time and how Father blamed her and the children for his retreat; she warned Anneka: 'Be careful, daughter. Find a man who is willing to work and dream at the same time or all else will be your fault, and you and your womb never forgiven.'

Anneka was not afraid to try new ideas. Grandfather thought her as good as any man. He would scoff, 'she has no need of a university education to prove it.' However, needing her with him in Belgium, Elias refused to allow her to wed Tom Phillips, her English lover, but agreed with her proposal when she said: 'the day figures show the shop in Brussels is outselling both Paris *and* London – I am free to follow my heart.'

Until then she made good use of her skills, the name Anneka van Leiden celebrated from workroom to counter and beyond. She loves working with jewels. Her speciality was the crafting of the elegant Girandole earrings where she defined the use of flamboyant designs with lively coloured stones.

Gifted and beautiful, with Mama's delicate face and Father's red-gold hair, her work soon caught the attention of wealthy patrons, Alexandra, Princess of Wales among them. Anneka was only twenty-three when she designed the famous *Pearl Coronet,* a delicate confection of diamonds interwoven with pink freshwater pearls that was to be a gift to the Princess's daughter.

The coronet was the talk of St James, opening the way to another commission, the *Elena Suite*, a four-piece jewellery ensemble ordered on behalf of His Highness Tsar Nicolas, the Second, Emperor of All Russia.

Long before the skiing accident, James was banned from spending too much time in the workroom 'You are the bright one,' Elias would say. 'Your brain and what you do with it is of more use to the family than your hands.'

Kasper was told to forget the workshop. War brewing again in South Africa and the Oppenheimer Company ever hungry, he was sent to Kimberley bringing smaller independent mines into the Leiden-Sterne fold.

James inherited Alice Sterne's love of colour, and on vacation during later years at Harvard would work with Anneka on the Romanov commission, rubies the chosen gems and the Russian name Elena hinting at fire.

June 1897 brought news from St Petersburg of a Royal birth, a daughter, Olga Nikolaevna, and the name of the set changed to the *Olga Suite*. Three pieces were ready: a necklace, bracelet and earrings. The trio was sent on, and a new order set in place: a triple choker of black pearls, a single ruby as a clasp; the Czarina had admired a similar set at the Court of St James.

'Any commission from St Petersburg is a triumph; to receive another soon afterward brought success to the House of Leiden and orders from all over the world that even Grandfather could not disdain. By that time such glory meant little to Karel van Leiden, the *Olga Suite* the last to bear his name, and he taking to the shadows and a sad self-imposed task of filing paper-work.

Elias Sterne scoffed. 'I believe your father has found his true vocation.' Hearing of this, and of Grandfather's bullying, James resolved to leave Harvard. Father wouldn't hear of it. 'I don't mind being the office-boy. At least with this I can close the door at the end of the day owing nothing to no one.'

This he continued to do, working in the office during the day before retiring to his studio to sit in shadow painting endless canvasses of leafless trees.

* * *

James needs to go home. Father's health is not the only worry. Cecil Rhodes is unwell, causing the De Beers London Group to question the terms of Grandfather's Will. That the bulk of shares would go to Kasper was an issue long before the Will was written, the Board getting wind of the intended bequest. 'Power in the hands of a wild man - what is Elias Sterne thinking?'

There were meetings. A vote of no-confidence was taken, suggesting the old man be removed from the Upper Board. The vote held, but then, as in death, such was Grandfather's friendship with Cecil Rhodes and long association with the Rothschild Bank the decision was deferred.

A directive was made – a proposal - where the younger van Leiden son, James: 'the rising literary star and Head of Conservation in the Fitzwilliam Museum, Cambridge, England, might be offered a seat on the Board, where his education and knowledge of European workings can be put to good use.'

The suggestion came in a letter bearing the Oppenheimer crest of Elias Sterne's sworn enemies. The letter congratulated James on his successes in the art world and his time at Harvard 'where his tenure was seen as dazzling,' earning him 'the affection of many of the foremost families in the United States of America and they looking forward to seeing him again.'

In other words, he is to haul his elegant Flemish ass back to the USA.

It's likely he will go, if only to see what is being offered, but right now, worried about Clarissa and the cornered look in her eyes, he read the note.

Unexpected visitor could mean anything and none of it good.

He snatched up her hat and sketchbook - a reasonable excuse for calling - and sprinted down the stairs, wondering what he would find, and sensing a trace of sulphur in the air, thinking the Parisi curse had struck again.

CHAPTER SEVEN

Stowaway

The Beeches, Comberton
Monday May 13th 1901

What he found was Freya-Jasmine's elf, Jacob Chase, a teenage boy of slight frame, hunched back and club-foot, whose eyes lit up seeing him.

'Mister James! Is that you?'

'Jacob?' James stared. 'What on earth are you doing here?'

'I do not know.' The boy burst into tears, hands over his eyes and his thin body shaking.

'Never mind what he's doing here.' Margret Hankin had seen enough. 'The lad is worn out. He can answer questions later. Right now he needs kindness shown or he'll fall to pieces, poor little mite. He's had a bowl or two of soup, and so if it's all right with you, Miss Clary, me and Sally will give him a bath, and then put him to bed in the small attic. He'll be safe there.'

'That's fine, Margret,' said Clarissa. 'As you say, questions can come later.'

'No! I not go without my dog.' The boy howled. 'Amy die without me and I die without Amy.'

'Hold on there!' James crouched down. 'No one needs to die. How about if I take Amy back to my house and I look after her?'

'No! She cannot go away from me. I found her. She kept me warm at night. She is mine, and because she is mine, I must look after her.'

'Well, that is the right idea, but how about if I get a tub out in the yard and give Amy a scrub. The sun is shining. She'll soon dry. And she seems to me a kinda classy dog that won't take to being matted and dirty like that.'

The boy wept. 'I do not know, Mister James. I am afraid some man will come and take her away and I shall never see her again.'

'No one will take her. I give you my word. She will be waiting for you when you are rested. Isn't that right, Miss Clarissa?'

'Absolutely right, Mister James!' Disturbed by the boy's anxiety, she was on her feet. 'We shall lock the door and bar the gates. No one will come to take anyone away, dog or boy, while we are here.'

So it was done. Margret led the sobbing boy away. James took the dog into the yard. 'Do you have an out-door faucet?'

Puzzled by what was happening, life so uncertain these days, she led him to the stable. 'There's a tap and a hose. What about towels?'

Jacket off, straw boater hanging from a branch of a tree, and sleeves rolled, James bent to the dog. 'A couple of old rags if you have them.'

'I have some of Tillie's. I'm sure she won't mind sharing.'

'By the way your dog is wagging her tail I figure she's already made up her mind to accept the interlopers.'

Between them they washed the dog, he scrubbing and Clarissa rubbing dry. Freya, and Tillie, the Jack Russell, were running up and down, as Hazlett, the old bay horse peered over his door munching hay; questions were left for a calmer time later that day when sitting on the veranda.

* * *

'So James?' His Christian name decided now and forever, Clarissa sipped tea while waiting to hear what he had to say about Jacob.

It was Freya-Jasmine who found him and ran to get Margret, who, armed with a rolling pin, went to look. The boy was curled up behind the trough, a dog, the name Amy on a worn collar, a Rottweiler as she turned out to be, lay across him, her eyes begging them to go easy.

'It's a wonder Hazlett didn't kick him,' said Sally.

'He seems to have taken to him,' said Margret.

'Wonders will never cease, poor creature.'

'Which one,' said Margret, 'boy or the dog?'

'Both I would say,' whispered Clarissa.

Hearing voices the boy leapt to his feet, inasmuch as he could leap, a twisted spine and built up boot on his right foot weighing him down.

'Now, now!' says Margret. 'No one's going to hurt you. Stand still there's a good lad. No dashing about just tell us what you're doing here.'

At first he didn't seem to know what to say and trembled, for though it was a warm day, and the sun shining, he was afraid. Clarissa asked his name.

Great big eyes, beautiful eyes of golden brown, but battered and bruised, he peered from beneath a heavy fringe of blue-black hair.

She asked if he was hungry. He nodded. 'All right then. Why don't we go to the kitchen so that you and your dog can eat?'

Then he spoke. 'You are Clareessa Morgan.'

It wasn't a question. It was a statement to which she could only nod and agree. With that he slipped a dirty paw into hers, and sighed, a child coming home after a long day at school. 'I come with you.'

* * *

So he did, and was fed bowls of soup, as the dog was seen to relish yesterday's ham bone. As for explanations he gave none, a bowl rapidly emptying, and two haunted eyes pinned on the same woman, and he remaining unwilling to say anything that might risk losing sanctuary.

It was then the Professor arrived, and the Dam broke, tears streaming from the boy's eyes, and James, while mystified also close to tears, promising to tell what he knew when the boy was in bed.

'His name is Jacob Chase.'

'This is Isabella Parisi's son?'

'No. Not her son, a stepson...one might say.'

Such was the guarded look on his face she asked no more, but sat on her hands waiting for his story, which as he said wasn't a great deal, but what was heard implied a sad tale for the boy asleep with his dog in the attic.

'I met...or rather came across Jacob in Italy in the summer of '96. As a writer I am concerned with getting my facts right, dreading the day comments made by me are proved incorrect. I was in Assisi for one purpose, and that to verify certain data before another of my books went to press.

'I was comfortable with my findings allowing time for pleasure seeking. As with most travellers I have my favourite places. In my case,' his smile was wry, 'fitting with being seen a sober-sides, my places are churches, especially those with decent pipe organs. Now the organ in King's has a wonderful sound, deep-throated and clear, a pleasure to listen to and probably to play.'

He talked of his love of organ music and what instrument was best to be heard and where, until Clarissa brought him back asking if he played.

Red tide mantling, he blushed. 'I have a piano in the Granta house.'

'Did you play in Assisi?'

'I did not. But d'you know who did, and who played like a dream? The one upstairs asleep in your kindly attic bed.'

'That boy plays the organ?' Clarissa was astonished.

'It is how we met; music like nothing ever heard drifting down from the roof of a church in Assisi. He was playing a Chopin transition for organ. Such exquisite playing! I don't mind saying, I got down on my knees.'

'Oh James.'

'I know! His playing moved me. *He* moved me, this child with such a gift and yet struggling against disabilities. It seemed neither fair nor right.'

Gaze intent, he turned. Clarissa was again aware of the Magister eyelashes, and the depth of his eyes. A moment ago – and he usually so fastidious - he was up to his elbows in smelly dog and not bothered by water splashing his boots. Aware of this, and ashamed of former distaste, a wall crumbled and fell, and she was suddenly so very glad she worked at the Fitz.

'It is difficult for me to talk of Jacob with any kind of ease,' he said. 'I am compelled by certain promises that make my time in Assisi problematic. Yet I ask you to believe me when I say this is a good young fellow with a good heart, whose physical disabilities caused certain people to behave badly.'

'To my mind he has been treated abominably by those that should have rendered him safe. Now, finding him at your door, it would seem ill-treatment is ongoing, and his misery continuing.'

'How did all this come about?'

'I'm not entirely sure and since I know so little of his story I ought not to impress judgement on anyone. Perhaps you will allow me to tell what I do know while omitting what is not mine to tell.'

* * *

James remembers that encounter: he could hardly forget. It was his last day in Assisi, he to board ship the following morning, and Kasper now heavily involved with Serena Parisi, remaining behind. While pleased with the new book James was disappointed with his life, the lack of female company and the absence of passion. There were girls at Harvard. A pretty sophomore cared for him, but he slow to take the hint, she up and married another guy.

Kasper was scornful. 'For a bird of prey, Gyr, you are singularly slow to strike. You could have had that girl if you'd bothered to try.' When James said she was already seeing someone he'd shrugged. 'So what? Walking a straight line is all very well if in fact you're moving forward. Maybe if you were to lose your balance now and then you might hit the target.'

It was fair criticism. James is slow making decisions. Every job has a price. As with the restoration of Renaissance Art, the

---

transcribing of ancient documents requires patience. You need a steady nerve, fairy fingers, plus the ability to look below the surface as in the deciphering of old English, where four or five letters might today come down to one, as in 'yogh' for 'y' or 'thorn' for 't'.

Conservation work cannot be rushed. It is easy to make a mistake and there is always some bright fellow ready to find the error. The name Gyrfalcon came of his ability to see false from the true: the human eye having one cone per fovea, while Falcons have two and able to spot his prey from seven miles away.

The nickname was given to him by a tutor at the Boston Latin, a feeder school prior to Harvard. A lonely lad, a foreigner with a tricky leg, he lived among boys who, while inviting him to their homes, saw him as a 'strange bird', one who preferred Old English poetry to watching the Red Sox.

* * *

That last day in Assisi found him outside a church. Inside the organist was playing a transition of the Chopin prelude in e-minor. He'd stood awhile listening and then opened the door. The music switched from Chopin to Beethoven and the *Moonlight Sonata*.

A beautiful piece, beautifully played, James had closed his eyes and tried letting go of loss. Those three days with Serena had shown how lonely he had become, and how he was now eager to love and be loved. With Serena he had felt wanted, a rare sensation that, like a drug, carried hope in what was really the realm of fantasy – those three days becoming a lifetime.

Kasper arrived and the fantasy collapsed. Half-formed words

that had begun to grow in his mind, wife, family and children, crumbled to nothing. It wasn't the loss of Serena so much as knowing that while he woke every morning with a sense of anticipation she was there until something better came along.

In that church in Assisi he woke to the real world and a sense of being observed. Squinting through hazy sunbeams, he gazed up toward the organ loft. A small gnome-like figure gazed back. Ashamed, thinking he'd intruded, James touched his hand to his heart: 'Forgive the intrusion. I was lonely.'

The eyes blinked once and were gone. A thing ungainly stumbled through upper recesses of the church. A door closed softly and James left with a sense of pity and the words, '*the wounding of little things*,' in his head.

The 'little thing' - Jacob Chase, as he came to be known - followed James to the pensione that evening: 'He said he knew I was kind by the way I listened to his music and that he wanted me to help him run away.'

Clarissa was moved by his story, and by the teller, who looked as if he understood the boy, having shared similar difficulties. 'A sad story.'

'I didn't know what to do. I asked of his parents. He said he was an orphan. He'd never known his mother and his father, Samuel Chase, an Englishman, had lately died, and he, Jacob, forced to live in a hospital for the insane.'

'How did he happen to be at the church that day?'

'He was rehearsing for a concert. He has a good grasp of English. And, as you'll see, he is keen to speak his father's tongue. I felt bad about leaving him behind. It's true I was leaving for Boston the next morning, but I should've tried to understand his situation.'

Caught between what he wanted to say as opposed to what he could not, James picked his way forward. 'His father taught at the University in Rome. When Jacob's mother died he moved to Assisi placing the boy with nuns at the Santa Maria Residential School for children with physical disabilities.

'The school was Jacob's home and he was happy inasmuch as a child can be happy living that way. Jacob was schooled by a priest, an organist, who along with Samuel Chase fostered his love of music. His father loved him, working several jobs to pay boarding fees.'

'Poor boy.'

'I suppose compared to the average boy's life he was poor. He didn't seem to think so, at least not in the early years. The problem came later in the mental asylum. He did get help from the priest who I later met, who said Jacob had a musical talent the like of which he'd never heard before.'

'You went back to Assisi?'

'I went before taking up this post to check on the boy.' He shrugged. 'I don't know why I went. I guess I felt guilty.'

'What did you hear?'

'Nothing of help to him, I'm afraid, or to me for that matter, merely another idol crashing to the ground.'

As though recalling fatigue, James leaned back in the chair, his face in shadow and the leaves of the Beech trees offering shade. 'I am sure in time you will learn all from Jacob. I can say no more other than when he sought me out his circumstances were altered and not in a good way.'

'Is he here looking for you, d'you suppose?'

'I doubt it. I lived in the States at the time. Whatever his motive, it is clear he came all this way under his own effort, and with a place, or a person in mind - he seeing that place or that person as sanctuary.'

'You think he sees this house as safety?'

'I think he sees you that way, Clarissa, though for my part I would willingly take him and his dog if I thought them a problem to you.'

He looked at her. 'Are they a problem?'

'No.' She shook her head. 'It is as I said to him. We shall lock the door and bar the gates. No one will come to take anyone away, dog or boy, while we are here. Isn't that right, Mister James?'

James nodded. 'Yes, Miss Clareessa, it is.'

CHAPTER EIGHT

Promises

Beeches, Comberton
Friday May 31st 1901

Clarissa is anxious: 'So what do you think, Doctor Brooke?'

He closed his bag. 'I think, Miss Morgan, that after many visits to your young visitor, anxious at your behest, you might think of me as Paul.'

'Oh!' She smiled. 'Is that so?'

'I think it is.'

'Very well then, Paul. How is our sudden guest?'

'Once I got by that dog of his I gave him a going over, and as far as I can tell without x-rays, he is relatively free of serious lung conditions. There are crackles which suggest infections in younger years, but nothing too insidious. However, I did detect a heart flutter that I'll follow through.'

'What do you mean flutter?'

'There is some slight arrhythmia that, working on the idea of infection when younger, might indicate strain.'

'And you plan to follow this up?'

'I do. It might be nothing at all. I shall know more later.'

'What about his back?'

'I don't see any real change in that. His spine has a C-shape curve suggestive of scoliosis. We could try a back-brace in effort to stop it becoming more pronounced, but at seventeen I think it may be too late.'

'And his foot?'

'As with his spine there are exercises that will help. Other than that he needs new boots with a soft lining. He was born with this issue. Unfortunately, through a lack of medical help and understanding, the condition of the foot was left unattended, and a poor situation made worse.'

'Is there nothing we can do to change that?'

'There are ways of numbing the pain of contracted tendons, as there are massage techniques which I have suggested to Mrs Hankin. Beyond that I'm afraid the boy must learn to adapt to these issues.'

'Coming all this way with nothing and no one to help other than a mangy dog, I would say he's already fairly adapted.'

'I suppose, though I can't be happy to see you landed with this. Other than a minimal of explanation via a third party, you don't know his history or what brought him here. For all you know he is a rascal and a thief, and every day you and your household in danger.'

She frowned. 'I'm sure he is no such thing!'

'How can you tell?'

'Because he neither looks like a thief nor acts like a thief. He's simply a poor lonely boy who has been treated badly by the world.'

'Does he say so?'

'He says very little. He accepts what is given and is grateful.'

'Street urchins live by their wits. Looking grateful when about to steal your wallet is the first lesson.'

'I must say you have a very one-sided view of life...Paul.'

He grinned. 'Not at all. I am merely being sensible.'

'And I am not?'

'Of course you are! I am simply saying you don't know any-thing about this young fellow other than what you've been told.'

'...and what I was told is enough for me to think him neither a rascal nor planning to murder me in my bed. Moreover,' she was annoyed, 'what was said came via an esteemed colleague, who until I said nay was willing to take him into his household and do all needed to offer a new life, and who wouldn't leave him with *anyone* if he thought them in danger.'

Paul shrugged. 'I'm sure the professor would never willingly bring harm to your door. Nevertheless I have reservations and not only on the idea of theft but of disease. This boy comes of a country whose way of life is not as our own. Italy has a history of poor hygiene and known to be lax in medical practice. It's likely his bone condition is due to birth and ignorance on the part of a doctor rather than ill-treatment. Even so, Jacob said he came here by way of cargo-ship hiding in the hold among rats and other foul creatures. So, however you champion his cause, you must accept that along with a twisted spine and club foot, the boy may have brought other ailments.'

What he said made sense but it didn't matter. She didn't like what he said, for not only did he question Jacob's honesty, he aimed a gun at the holy-of-holies, James van Leiden, and nobody does that.

She poured what was left of her coffee down the sink, a hint for visitors to be on their way: 'I don't know about Jacob. But in terms of what one knows of anybody I could tell you of two people, adults, lately staying here, whose names I knew along with how many sugars in their tea. And while they didn't murder us in our beds they took everything they could carry from this house and smiled doing it. So, though not sure of

Jacob's background I think what is in the heart is what matters, and I see his heart as good.'

Paul Brooke left feeling ill-used for his charity, he coming to the house to tend Jacob and no bill presented. Chastened, Clarissa wrote inviting him to lunch on Saturday, and Sykes, the gardener, hand delivering.

Paul wrote back saying he'd be delighted to lunch and also that he might accompany her and Jacob to King's Chapel that afternoon, 'where the boy could get a closer look at the organ.' He said he was a chorister at King's a good many years, 'which means I can take you behind the scenes.'

Margret Hankin smiled. 'Yes, and while you are there, he'll want a kiss and a cuddle by way of payment.'

* * *

Clarissa sat in the garden gazing at the blue sky thinking of James while trying to work out who-is-who in the Parisi-Chase association. Serena said Samuel Chase was her mother's second husband. They met in Assisi. She said he was multi-lingual and would act as a guide to tourists, leading them to places of interest. 'Mister Samuel was a clever man. He was also a drinker. He left Isabella with many troubles. It is why she never speaks of him or that time. Neither her heart nor her English can manage it.'

It seems no one can speak of anything; all are constrained by promises or lies. Clarissa's doubts about the Parisis are fuelled by what happened to Uncle Sarson, and fuelled again by the way James van Leiden picked his way through any conversation about them as through crossing a field of thistles.

One always knows how James is feeling: he has a sensitive

mouth that speaks even when he is silent. If happy his mouth is a curly smile, when bored, it is downturned and morose, and when angry his mouth becomes a thin white line. In his response to Clarissa's question about Jacob, was he Isabella's stepson, there was a screeching of brakes.

* * *

Fitzwilliam Museum Cambridge
Friday 31ˢᵗ May 1901

They were talking about the damaged painting. James was saying it would be hot in Florence and that Clarissa needed to think what to take.

'When are we to go?'

'I am thinking late July.'

'As soon as that?' She set down the bottle of turpentine. 'I'm sorry, James. I don't think I will be able to go.'

'Why not?'

'Because of Jacob. He is only just beginning to sleep through the night without waking from some horrible dream. Though he's better than he was, this life is still new to him. And with Sally accompanying us to Italy as chaperone, I don't feel I can leave Margret with the worry.'

'Is he that much of a worry?'

'No. Half the time we don't know he is there. The dogs are noisier than he. Margret says he is a quiet boy, too quiet for a seventeen-year-old.'

'Is that his age?'

'It seems so. I overheard him saying Thursday was his

birthday. I hope so, for on the strength of that I invited Doctor Brooke to lunch tomorrow.'

'Doctor Brooke?'

'Margret's doctor. I am hoping you will come. Nothing too grand. A light lunch followed by a visit to King's and Jacob looking at the organ there. He should be able to manage that. Anything else would be too much.'

'You may need permission to get real close. I can help with that.'

'Thank you but Paul Brooke is a former Kings scholar. He has arranged it so Jacob can be heard by the choirmaster in the hope he might be considered a late scholar. But you will come to lunch? The weather being fine we thought to eat on the veranda.'

'It sounds something I sure would enjoy, and the idea of Jacob for late studies is first class. I applaud Doctor Brooke. E'en so I have a lot to do and the trip to Florence the least of my worries. My father is unwell which means going home. Along with that I am asked to attend meetings in the States. I can hold that off for a while but sooner or later will have to give in.'

'I'm sorry to hear about your father. Has he been ill for some time?'

'He suffers from chronic melancholia. I don't know the medical term for it. I only know when he's down, he's down, and no getting him back. As for how long, I reckon it's been there most of his life waiting to happen.'

'It must be difficult for your mother.'

'We've all felt it at some time but more than anyone Mama has been at the sore end of it. So you see I need to go if only to relieve her for a while.'

'I do see, and while not meaning to make light of this,

perhaps a meal with friends would help. I know Jacob would want you there and I surely do.'

'You do?'

'Of course! You should be there. You are the cause of Jacob's new freedom. But for you he would still be struggling against all manner of difficulties.'

'I don't know that I am the cause of his freedom yet I mean to help keep him free. Has he spoken to you of his difficulties?'

'Not to me but to Freya-Jasmine who he sees his equal. Not that she tells me much. She'll say what she thinks he *wants* me to say, which is not a great deal. When not confiding in her he talks to Margret, who he calls Miss Hanky-Panky, though how he, an Italian, arrived at that I do not know.'

James laughed, delighting in the name and the woman thereafter ever seen as Miss Hanky. 'And she doesn't mind?'

'She dotes on him, seeing him the boy she never had.'

'I get that of your Margret. She is everyone's favourite grandmamma.'

'Indeed, a case of love at first sight.' She smiled. 'Not that I believe in any such thing. I see that idea, along with everlasting love, to be the work of poets, and dangerous, leading us into a fog from which we never escape. Even so, where Margret and Jacob are concerned it is the only explanation.'

* * *

James watched her run away. She does run as fast as she can, never to loiter either at the Museum or on campus. Time moves on but the damned rumours suggesting a perverse relationship between her and her uncle continue.

Cowards that these people are they mewl and slaver in the background doing all they can to hurt. Knowing the truth it leaves him wild with anger. The priest, Father Anthony, said after Samuel Chase died, Isabella refused to pay school fees. She cashed the annuity her husband left for that purpose and had Jacob removed to a charity hospital in Spoleto, where, according to the priest, 'a musical genius was left imprisoned among halfwits and lepers.'

It is another strand of information tying James to a promise of silence and he trapped in a cage of his own making. He should've left the old Professor face the music. At least then the real wrongdoer would be known.

Campus news says the cottage lent to the Sarsons is 're-deemed and restored, and they living in digs in Brighton with not a penny to their names.' It's nonsense. They live in a cottage in Norfolk on the estate of General and Mrs Phillips, the parents of Tom Phillips, Anneka's husband.

While it's true the Sarsons are not rich, neither are they poor, both earning money, Phoebe helping on the estate and the Professor in receipt of a pension from the University while assisting the General in his memoirs.

The move was arranged in March; the Vice-Chancellor of-fered the Professor a pension if he, and his wife, would move on. Since they had nowhere to go, and James knowing of a cottage on the estate where he stayed weekends during the opening of the Knightsbridge shop, he got in touch with Anneka.

He helped them move. Clarissa was told 'not to worry. They are staying with friends and would let her know their progress in due course.'

The Professor insisted on secrecy. 'If we leave it alone for a while people will find a new source of interest. I have caused my niece enough pain. I must not cause more.' The Sarsons wrote of their new home without offering an address. Until they are settled, they would post mail via Great Aunt Sheba in Cherry Hinton – Clarissa could do the same.

James thought they were wrong to exclude her. He saw it as one more secret adding to a mounting mass that would one day fall on his head.

He said: 'Don't you think Miss Morgan will find this all rather odd?'

The old man had shaken his head. 'She's a trusting girl. Always has been. Her father was the same. It is how he ended up married to that awful woman.'

His glance was bitter. 'Trust is a family trait.'

* * *

King's College Chapel
Saturday June 1ˢᵗ 1901

The Queen dead and buried these five months, Britain is at last laying aside mourning weeds. Colour is back in fashion and Clarissa dazzling in lemon silk with a hat of the same colour, a sky blue feather drooping over her beautiful eyes, a lemon parasol in her hand, dainty blue boots on her feet, and every head turned in admiration.

Smiling, she introduced James to Paul Brooke as though presenting a cherished uncle: 'My mentor and friend, Professor James van Leiden.'

They crossed the quad, Jacob holding on to Clarissa and

James somewhat set-back, he having imagined the doctor to be old with a greying beard where in reality is a handsome chevalier in a dashing Panama hat.

They were received into the Chapel by the choirmaster, and brought to the organ, where Jacob - eyes on stalks - pounded the floor in glee, his skinny legs jumping up and down like nutcrackers. Clarissa retreated to the choir stalls to sit observing all: Paul Brooke, steady and solid, speaking with the choir-master, while James - golden in a shaft of sunlight – stood aside; he who knows more than anyone about Jacob allowing another to claim the floor.

In that moment Clarissa saw another tableau played out, and that of a Flemish boy, who at the age of ten broke his ankle, and thereafter grew reconciled to playing second-fiddle to his brother.

Though glimpsed through sleet that winter's evening Kasper van Leiden Sterne's power was unmistakable, he and his horse of one flesh, muscle moving with muscle, and the hands holding the reins that of steel. The combination was compelling, a scene from a Wagner opera, Man and Superman challenging destiny. In that moment one could appreciate Serena's passion and comprehend a brother's loyalty.

* * *

A gnome-like figure, Jacob is seated at the organ and so excited that even from this distance his ears seem to quiver. At first there were muddled notes, lots of squawks and crashes, indefinable sounds, he settling in the seat and struggling to reach the pedals.

The squawks went on for some time, the choirmaster leaning over to help adjust the stops. Clarissa is anxious. She has been on tenterhooks all week, thinking this try-out a good idea but also frightened for Jacob. It's a risky business and other than what's been said she with no real idea of his skill.

It is getting late, light changing in the chapel and the stained glass windows so many jewels. With the feeling of air being sucked through huge bellows there was a moment of silence before sound blasted forth, glorious sound, reaching for the Heavens and people turning to stare.

'Oh my Lord!' Every hair on Clarissa's head rose in salutation.

Moving fast, she left her seat, all but running through the choir door.

Outside she made for a grassy verge and bench seat, and snatching off her hat sat fighting to breathe. The music! All that extraordinary love rising from a poor misshapen body - it was beautiful and at the same time cruel.

Eyes closed, she clutched her hat, silk tearing and she struggling with tears. Later she will remember what he played, recognising those first chords as the introduction to Bach's Toccata and Fugue, but at that moment the piece did not have a name - or if it did it would be known: 'In Defiance of Pain.'

Music, glorious music, continued to swirl about the grounds, and every path leading to the chapel now teeming with people, students and Fellows, all hurrying along - some beginning to run.

Hushed and suspenseful, all were urgent to share the moment.

Clarissa sat alone at the bench, her soul wrenched.

After a while she was aware of James standing nearby and not offering assistance, simply being there, his tall figure a sentinel.

It was enough.

CHAPTER NINE

Misgivings

Beeches, Comberton
Tuesday September 17 th 1901

The letter arrived in the afternoon post. Clarissa was packing for Venice, continually changing her mind, that frock wrong with those shoes, or that skirt with that blouse. Sally ran back and forth between bedrooms in the same eager excitement. Margret watched them fuss over what to wear for the journey, a light-coloured gown or dark, and wondered why Clarissa bothered - she could wear a flour sack and still set the world alight.

'What do you think about the lemon silk, Margret?'

'It will crease something shocking.'

'Oh, pooh, will it?'

'You know it will. Haven't you got enough jammed in there?'

'You can never have enough pretty frocks. Isn't that right, Sally?'

At that Sally paused (forty-three last birthday, the youngest of the Cartwright sisters by ten years, and pretty, with blue eyes, flyaway hair and thoughts to match). 'Should I pack another, Miss Clary? I've put two in already.'

'Yes, another. We don't know where we might go.'

Margret yawned. 'Three frocks by all means but do you really need three hats. I would've thought the straw was enough. It's the same with that turquoise velvet cape and the blue chiffon gown. They are lovely, and you do look a proper picture in them, but will you wear them?'

'I hope so! The cape is gorgeous and I love the gown. Don't forget we are dining with a Marquis's nephew. We must have some nice things. Everything else is so horribly sensible and the chiffon goes to nothing in the trunk.'

'I suppose.' Margret stroked the chiffon. 'Where did you get it?'

'Rome. Papa bought it when he bought the leather pants.'

'Oh those! Gracious me, I hope you're not thinking of taking them.'

'I would if I could but I doubt we'll have time for riding.'

'Good thing too! Men's britches for riding and leather at that! I wonder where your pa got the idea, and in Rome too.'

'There's more to Rome than Papal Palaces and what's wrong with wearing pants when riding? Side-saddle is all right but not half the fun. I love Italy. It's ancient and yet ahead of time. Anything can happen there.'

'Is that so?' Margret sniffed. 'In that case, you and your professor spending so much time together you'd better keep a hand on your heart.'

'We are colleagues going to Florence to save a priceless painting. I promise you nothing like that is going to happen.' Clarissa smiled. 'Why say nay? I thought you wanted me to find a man and get married.'

'I do, but there are ways and means, and flitting about a foreign country isn't it...though I must say, if I had a choice, it would be him.'

'What about Doctor Brooke? I thought he was your ideal.'

'Maybe he still is. A professor is all very well going to places never seen and meeting all kinds of people. I should imagine you'd have an interesting life. But if you're looking for a safe bet then a doctor is as safe as you can get.

'Poor Doctor Brooke! He is a mite ponderous but not that stodgy.'

'I said nothing about stodgy. He's a lovely fellow and comes with extras. No more hanging about surgeries along with ordinary people. He can sound your chest in the comfort of your home with hands still warm from sleep.'

'Oh tush.'

'Don't you tush me! I'm saying there are advantages to marrying a doctor especially when it comes to having babbies. He that put them there can be the first to pull 'em out. Sounds like a bargain to me.'

'Margret Hankin.' Clarissa sighed, thinking the lemon silk, and her beloved house-keeper, a lost cause. 'You are a very bad woman.'

'I know.' Margret carried on along the landing. 'And look where it got me. By the way, you've a letter postmarked France.'

* * *

Brow furrowed, she read the letter again, looking beyond the words to a message within the message that may as well be written in invisible ink.

'Dear Clarissa Morgan, I write to see how you are and if you are well.

We are in Paris off the Rue Saint Sauveur. It is a comfortable apartment affording warmth and security, but still Isabella and I miss you as we miss a greatly lamented husband and father. We see Beeches a second home, and look toward to a time when we together again.

I imagine you keep the same friends and gaining new at the Fitzwilliam Museum. It is pleasant to me to know you share time with my dear Kasper's brother who I remember from Assisi in '96 as the most gallant of men.

You will not know this but before you and I met I shared three rapturous days with James. We visited the Basilica he pointing out the beauty of the paintings and I so happy to be with such a charming and handsome man.

So charming - un vero gentiluomo - I tell you, my dear Clarissa, he quite stole my heart. Though no word of love passed my lips I was mad with love for him, as I believe he felt the same for me, our hearts beating as one.

I can't tell you of the pleasure of those days and his gentle hands. I wanted the moment to last forever, and but for family situations, which I know you understand only too well, I would still be with that man.

He paid me many courtesies, unasked and unexpected, and was particularly gracious in sharing his wealth while not demeaning my poverty. In short, I lacked for nothing. Had I stooped to ask the world would have been mine.

I say this not to unfold secrets, but so you might see and understand my situation regarding any payment of outstanding debts, for which I am not to blame, my mother the debtor, and I forever forced to beg on her behalf.

Imagine my joy when I learn from your letter that, though miles apart, this good man continues to maintain care of me, as I now know which silent suitor sends me lilac. All this has left me feeling humbled and grateful, and also aware that a door I once thought closed is ever open to me and mine.

But enough of that! I shall say no more other than to rejoice in the knowledge that such a man exists, and that with you by his side as work-mate, he will always be cherished. Hoping we meet again soon and talk of such things with open hearts, and no need of tears, yours in sisterly affection,
Serena Parisi-Chase Morgan.'

* * *

Clarissa stood by the door, the sun warm and she cold as ice, a question pounding her brain: is Serena saying James settled the debt and that it was done for love of her, and he and Uncle Sarson keeping it secret?

'She is contemptuous as ever in this letter.'

Margret is ironing. 'Don't worry about that – it's in her nature. What you might worry about is her seeing this a second home.'

'Oh don't say that! It makes me afraid to leave in case they come again with all their horror while I am in Italy.'

'Don't be silly! You want to go. I know you do. So come on! Don't give way to doubts. Stay strong, for whatever brought that woman into your life, and that man, for that matter, is still to be known.'

The day passed slowly as anticipation emptied away. Clarissa stared at the trunk in the hall thinking everything is spoiled, the straw hat ugly and what to wear in Florence of no consequence. Serena is known to James. They had a romantic connection in Assisi, a fling, Margret says. He is the one sending lilac, not Kasper, and by the sound of it the debt still unresolved.

'She writes as if they were lovers.'

Margret shrugged. 'It's what she wants you to think.'

'She says they were together for three glorious days.'

'Three days or thirty, she's not with him now.'

'She says he has gentle hands.'

'As that dog out in the yard can testify and Sally when he mended her bike. He had gentle hands then and every other day. The professor is gentleman born. You should know it. He's been here often enough, bright and shining.'

'A bright and shining lover according to her.'

'I don't see a lover in that letter. They've had a bit of a fling, that much feels right. Even so, I don't recognise the chap she writes about. She makes him sound like one of them giggylos.'

'You mean gigolo.'

'I know what I mean! I am saying that is *not* our professor. She makes him out a fumbling fellow who don't come out in the daylight, only under cover of night, singing and sighing, and nothing honourable.'

'He was in Assisi in '96. We know because he met Jacob then.'

'The professor is a clever man. You'd expect to see him in Italy and other out-of-the-way places. You can't hold them meeting against him.'

'I don't. I'm putting two-and-two together. Samuel Chase died in the winter of '95, Serena said so. It makes sense she and James met in Assisi.'

'I thought you said he was there checking his book for facts.'

'That's what he said.'

'There you are then.'

'As far as I can tell I am nowhere. Whatever his reason he met Serena and in the Basilica, she saying it was a good place for catching fish…and before you ask she meant men and according to her James still in her net.'

'Pah! Mucky woman!'

Clarissa hurts with a pain in her chest and a sense of being utterly alone as never felt before, not even when Papa died. 'Mucky or not she is beautiful. I imagine she could catch a whole shoal of fish if she felt so inclined.'

'I saw nothing beautiful about either of those two. I thought them cold and hard as iron, saccharine on top and rank poison beneath.'

Margret leaned on the iron, steam rising. 'Best thing you can do is chuck that thing on the fire. One thing is sure. She sent it with a message, and that was to tell you to keep hands to yourself, he's mine.'

* * *

University Library
Tuesday August 13th 1901

Yesterday James sat in King's Chapel listening to Jacob wander his way through Bach's Goldberg Variations. The choirmaster was amazed.

'Where does it come from?'

Equally perplexed, James could only shrug. 'Born with it I'd say.'

'I'm sure that is so.' The choirmaster was curious. 'Does he talk of his beginnings, of tutors and how such skill arrived?'

'His father was his earliest tutor *and* a musical prodigy who, I've since learned, lost his way through drink and an unfortunate marriage. I am told he was a superb pianist but never finding his place.

'There was a priest who, recognising the boy's potential, did what he could to help. He was known as Father Anthony of Padua but was born Paolo Andreoli - which should give you an idea of the quality of teaching.'

'Paolo Andreoli, the organist?' The choirmaster was taken aback, as would be any lover of music, the name known throughout the world as a virtuoso of the pipe organ. Before he disappeared from his home in Milan he was thought to rival 18th century Guillame-Gabriel Nivers. 'I thought he was dead.'

'To this world he is dead and has been since the winter of '75 when, in his words, "he stopped chasing the perfect note and found peace in the Lord trying to help mend imperfect children."'

Jacob rarely mentions the priest. Although grateful for support there is caution in the boy's eyes whenever the name Father Anthony is mentioned, a sense of fearing another Judas, and that having been once locked behind asylum doors it could happen again.

While he won't talk of his life in that place he will speak of music, and in respect of 'where does it all come from?' has an answer. 'The pipe organ is not new to me. I was born playing that as I was born playing the clavichord and piano. My baby fingers flew, and my feet, ugly though they are, danced on the pedals.' He smiles, a reluctant angel with eyes of liquid gold. 'Life, death, pipe organ or piano: the difference is only in the name.'

* * *

James is in the Library trying to control anger. An hour ago he was summoned to a meeting with the Vice-Chancellor and questioned on the rightness of spending 'excessive time with a female undergrad.'

After he'd picked his jaw off the floor, he asked of the undergrad. At first no one cared to speak out. Eventually one slug crawled out of a hole long enough to offer the name Clarissa Morgan: 'of whom much is said regarding an association with a former tutor. We had hoped the sordid business was laid to rest but now learn you're provoking trouble taking the same young woman on a ridiculous treasure-trail to Italy.'

In reply James referred them to the Fitzwilliam: Miss Morgan has some association with her former college but as of last year has worked as a paid employee at the Museum and any tuition given under the auspices of the Museum and *not* the University. He spoke of Sally Cartwright acting as chaperone throughout the trip - which, by the way, is no treasure-trail, but an investigation into a possible Fra Angelico painting. For details of this they should apply to the Fitzwilliam, *and* to His Highness, the Marchese Giovanni Carlo Arello di Lombardi, at the Villa della Rosa, Fiesole, or to the Palazzo Lombardi in Como, Italy, with whom Miss Morgan and Professor van Leiden will stay at some time during their research.

With that name and those addresses he delivered a shock to the University finances, the Marchese a known patron of the Arts and particularly generous to both Oxford *and* Cambridge University.

From a sudden silence he was ushered to the door with many apologies and mutterings of regretful misunderstandings and was begged to convey the Vice-Chancellor's good wishes to the Marchese, a generous benefactor.

'Yes,' said James, determined to have the last word. 'And short on patience when dealing with fools.'

* * *

Now he sits trying to arrange his notes on the use of Black-Light. Last year he ran into a friend in Brussels. They discussed the idea of x-ray photography detecting compositional change, and how it will help reveal the history of a work, and, hopefully, put paid to forgeries.

If he sets aside the boardroom nonsense, this week can only be seen as a good week, especially with regard to his latest publication detailing his father's part in the creating of the Russian Jewel Suite. A letter arrived today from St Petersburg granting permission to publish providing he uses the original title, the *Elena Suite:* Tsar Nicholas insisting on privacy for Princess Olga.

Opening that letter was a great moment, he having been assured by both the Belgian and American Consulate that it wouldn't happen; the Russians were bound to block publication. As yet he's told no one. He is waiting for the right moment to tell Clarissa who he knows will be pleased.

With Florence in mind he needs to speak with King's choirmaster. While it is certain Jacob will be accepted as an organ scholar, he must audition. The choirmaster agreed. 'The onus is on us of the University to bring the boy under our roof, for make no mistake, other universities will want him.'

'We can't teach him anything,' he'd smiled. 'A talent like this comes complete. We can provide the odd trick or two but there is nothing about music he does not know. My one issue is the size of musical spirit compared to his body. I fear that one will eventually prove too much for the other.'

A bleak prognosis, but not unexpected, it is one of the reasons why James applied to Wards of Court. Responsibility for Jacob is now vested in the law with James as his guardian, pro tem, so that unless one comes with higher claim the boy is safe, and the attic with a view of St Bene't's tower his room.

Much of the time now is spent on caring for Jacob's body so he might catch up on health as well as educational needs. He does catch up, arms, brain and heart open to all: one day taking fencing lessons to strengthen his back, another with him perched, grinning, in a Cambridge Blue Boat as a coxswain, with a megaphone in his hand and he hoarse from shouting. In the face of these many advantages the boy sometimes quails, and fearful of losing all retires to bed until drawn out by the strong arm and leathery tongue of Margret Hankin, who, though loving the boy, keeps a firm hand:

'He's a good lad, but like any late starter can't keep up the pace. At which time me and a bit of cream custard act as a prop.'

Custody now being a matter of Law, James has stepped away from enquiring Jacob's beginnings. If there are issues regarding the Parisis they are not his to question. Even so, that Jacob came to a stranger's home through all kinds of danger shows how desperate he must've been. One has to ask, what safe harbour had he hoped to find when making that journey. James believes the answer is in the name Clarissa Morgan. At some time in the boy's hearing she was mentioned as such and he one day taking a chance to stow away.

Jacob planted that notion in James's head one morning as he was fixing the chain on Sally's bicycle. 'Oil make you dirty,

Mister James,' he squatted nearby offering advice. 'Is okay. Find Clareessa Morgan. She makes everything all right."

* * *

The bell rang for the last quarter startling James, he meant to be researching Black Light but instead fell into a reverie.

Heads down and everybody scribbling, the Library was busy. Steed from Classics shares the same table. He is here most evenings grubbing up on Japanese Erotica, supposedly gathering material for a thesis on the artist, Genji Kyasha Makura, while in reality following his own fetid way. Last year he arrived drunk one evening to the house on the Granta. When James thought to make coffee the guy followed to the kitchen and there declared undying love. That he was shown the door resulted in curt nods when passing.

For some reason now he wants to communicate. Noisily shunting a chair about the table he removes a photograph pinned to James's folder.

A keepsake, the shot was taken at the University Ball of 1900, he having plucked up courage to jump the queue asking Clarissa to dance.

That evening they circled the floor to Strauss's Blue Danube waltz, he stunned to find himself dancing, and by the look of her elevated brows she the same. It was a good moment, for while not exactly floating he made a decent job of it, head up and back straight, and she in a white gown as starlight in his arms. It went so well he dared to claim another waltz, and poor old Carter from Queens pencilled in next on her card, hating James ever since.

Really he shouldn't carry the thing around, because, quite frankly, while in this particular shot she is the Beauty of the Night, he looks like the archetypal Mad Professor, crooked white tie and hair on end.

James was pinning the photo back on the folder when the guy leaned close, the stench of unwashed linen preceding a lock of greasy hair.

'I can see why you'd want to hang on to that. It must have been quite a moment, the band playing, you looking so manly, and she, Clarissa Morgan - verging on a virgin - a picture of feminine beauty.'

It wasn't that he was over loud, it was the Library and none speaking, thus his whispering dropped into silence as a stone into a lake.

In that moment James knew what it meant to see red. Red was all he could see. All that nonsense in the Chancellor's office – old maids gossiping – he was on his feet, fist hauled back and Steed about to hit the floor, when a Fellow from Christ's reached out, holding him still.

'*Pudeat te*!' His voice rang out.

A man across the Library got to his feet: '*Pudeat te*!'

Another stood. '*Pudeat te*!'

And another: '*Pudeat te*!'

So it went, every man in the Library standing to rebuke Steed, the Latin condemnation 'for shame!' repeated until he fled. Then, as if a hand pulled a switch, silence was resumed, and the Library a library again.

CHAPTER TEN

Imp from Hell

Beeches, Comberton
Friday September 20th 1901

'Amy, come!' He crawled out of bed, and now, as every morning, stands at the window waiting for the moment when St Bene't's Church bells chime for the early morning service - sound ringing and pigeons scattering.

'Look how they wait.' He sighed. 'Every morning they dash away frightened by the bells. Why sit there?' The dog with paws on the window-ledge grunted indifferent: 'Birds, Master Jacob. They know no better.'

The bells rang. The pigeons flew. Jacob laughed and then knelt to say his prayers, first to the Lord Jesus (The Lamb of God his favourite) and then to Saint Cecilia, Patron Saint of Music, and finally a Prayer for the Dead for Papa Samuel, who every day he misses so very badly.

It is not easy getting down on his knees, overnight muscles in his legs contract and cause pain, even so he will do it.

He kneels by the bed, Amy alongside, snout resting on her paws.

Mistress Hankin once saw her do this and smiled. 'Bless it,' she said. 'The dog is pretending to pray.' Jacob stayed silent though he could've said: 'There is no pretence, Mistress. Amy prays – all creatures pray.'

She prays now, Jacob providing the words and she agreeing:

'*Agnus Dei, qui tollis peccata mundi: miserere nobis. Agnus Dei, qui tollis peccata mundi: miserere nobis. Agnus Dei, qui tollis peccata mundi: dona nobis pacem.*'

After awhile, as it goes with Jacob, words become music, sound streaming through head and heart and he oscillating like the strings of a violin until the pain in his head, back and legs is gone. He can arise then and go to the little bathroom under the stairs, his bathroom now, and wash, dress, and be ready for the day and the gift that life has become through the Lord God, Mistress Hankin, Freya-Jasmine, and the Golden one, Clareessa Morgan.

Life is so precious now he tries walking on tiptoe, afraid to rattle the world causing change, and as with air confined in a blocked organ pipe, a bursting forth, and all back to where it was and the misery of the Refugio.

Papa died December 6th 1895. January 2nd Jacob was removed from school. He shed no tears when leaving. There was no goodbye to Sister Juliana, the librarian, who saved story books with the best pictures, as there was no goodbye for Rocco, the blind boy from Napoli, a friend of many years.

It was as well they didn't say where he was going. Had he known, he would've tied himself to the altar of the Basilica and never let go.

No one said where or why, not even Father Anthony, who had guided Jacob through music since he was born. They said he was to attend a Candlemass blessing. He did attend a service but then was taken to the mental asylum in Spoleto. The Parisi ladies left him at the gate, the doors locked behind him, and if it wasn't for a conversation heard in the summer of '99 he'd still be there.

There were times when he disbelieved what he heard thinking he dreamt them. Other times he was certain of what he heard, a man's voice, angry and deep throated as a bourdon bell, sending Jacob a message, and telling of a special name. Whatever reason is true he thanks God for it, for those whispers brought him to England and safety.

Downstairs a door slams making him jump.

'Jacob!'

'Yes, Miss Hanky!'

'Are you up?'

He is up off his knees. '*Si, sono sveglio!*'

'Good, because you've breakfast down here waiting, and then early service and you playing that dratted organ again.'

'*Si*, I come.' Grinning, he snatches his clothes and whistling, makes for the bathroom. Another good day has begun!

* * *

Margret watched him scrape the empty plate. 'Do you think you can get any more off that plate?'

'I think I have enough.'

'I think so too. And therefore what do you say?'

'I say, "*grazie, Senora Margret Hankin, per una buona colazione.*"'

'Mm,' she sniffed. 'In English if you please. Then I know you're saying something proper and not being cheeky.'

He grinned, flashing his beautiful eyes, and as usual she is undone.

'I thank you, Mistress Hankin, for my very good breakfast.'

'You're welcome.' She began to clear the table. 'Now get a

move on for I've promised to see you to the church door in time for them to get sorted, though why they have to have a service on a Friday I do not know.'

'You not stay for blessing?'

'Not today. I've too much to do.'

'I am to play Chopin prelude in e-minor.'

'Are you? Well, no offence, but to my mind that's another reason not to come. I've nothing against you playing. I'm sure you're the genius everyone says you are, but that organ makes my teeth ache.'

'It is not good but still I play. Today is special blessing for the soul.'

'I'm sure it is as I am sure my soul is in need of blessing. Right now with Miss Clary and Sally away I've too much on my plate.'

'Like my breakfast.'

'Yes, you cheeky monkey, like your breakfast...though I'd rather you eat and get some flesh on them bones than dwindle away.'

'I no dwindle.' He got down from the table. 'I eat plenty. I grow every day. See?' He stood against the wall where years ago Doctor Charles drew a line measuring his daughter's height. 'I already taller.'

'Well.' Margret bent to look. 'You look promising.'

'*Si.* I look promising. Can I ride Hazlett to church?'

'I'll take you. I know you and that horse are bosom pals but he can be an evil beast when he wants, and I don't want Miss Clary coming back to bother.'

'Okay, I go.' Then he was gone, shuffling back upstairs to clean his teeth, and to comb his hair, and to stand before the mirror in a smart new jacket hoping to find another promise.

Poor Little Lump! Margret could've wept. Every day he's in better health as every day he looks in the mirror but never sees what he wants to see, a straight-limbed young man in love with life and Miss Clary.

''Cos he is you know,' Margret told her worries to Sally before she went on the trip to Italy. 'He might only be pint-size and we inclined to see him a child, but he is seventeen with the same feelings as any other lad.'

Sally agreed. She said she'd seen it in his face. 'The way he looks at her, like she's the breath in his lungs. It makes me afraid for him.'

'And for her! I worry how it's going to end, him living here stunted the way he is, and she seeing him a younger brother. If he can be satisfied with that then fine, but as I said, he's got feelings and a foreigner at that, hot-blooded. I think it can't end well. But, that might be me looking on the dark side and everything going to work out nice and cosy.'

Margret has a tendency to look on the dark side. What woman after losing her husband and daughter to sickness doesn't worry for them that are left. She used to worry for the world, but then, trying to be sensible, settled for worrying for three: her sister, her granddaughter Freya-Jasmine, and Clarissa Morgan. Time moves on and she's back to worrying for the world, in particular a stunted dwarf with the face of an angel and soul to match.

* * *

Five minutes to nine Jacob sits at the organ. At the end of the service he is to play a transition for organ of the Chopin prelude in e-minor. People sit and wait. There are more here today than Sunday. 'That is down to a nice bit of sunny weather, Jacob,' says the curate,' and your music.'

Where music is concerned he has learned to show rather than tell. People are always surprised by his playing. The congregation of St Bene't's are surprised when they come in and surprised when they go out. They think an imp from hell ought not to make good music. Friday is a busy day. Some will think to leave early. He will begin to play and they will be stuck, their hearts filled with love and their eyes full of tears - Chopin is like that.

Last Sunday he stayed after morning prayers to practice. The curate listened for a time and then hid in the vestry with a 'bad cold.' He said Jacob could play the piece but only rarely. 'People have homes to go to and lives to lead. They mustn't be made to feel too much. Life is hard enough as it is.'

Jacob loves Chopin. The prelude in e-minor was Papa's favourite. In the summer he would sit at the piano, every window open, the Sisters working in the orchard and the juice of ripening apples in the air. In the winter he played the same piece, marking the close of the year, wood smoke rising and snow falling on the East Window causing the Madonna's robe to sparkle.

One time Jacob asked what his father heard when playing that piece. He smiled. 'I hear your mother telling me it's time to come home.'

Though loved, Anna Chase has no place in Jacob's memory; she died so long ago. Sometimes, when playing the organ he thinks he sees her, and she a fairy princess riding a silver grey mare on the Caelian Hill. Papa Samuel said she was a princess. In reality she washed floors at the Rome University where he was the English Master, and then one day they ran away together.

Lawyers say the older Parisi lady was Papa's wife. Mother and daughter did sit with him during the last moments. One day a priest came and words were said over joined hands, beyond that there was no marriage, they living in San Nicolo and only visiting Assisi when needing money.

The day Jacob was taken from the school Sister Juliana spoke with the young Parisi lady. 'There was more to that marriage than a ceremony. A promise was made to a dying man and now your soul stands perjured.'

Sister Juliana's words flit about his head like anxious moths. He lets them flit, for no matter what lies people tell even as a child he understood what was being said.

* * *

Assisi is popular with tourists. Drawn to St Francis and his purity and love of animals, people come from all over the world to breathe the air he breathed and walk the ground he trod - a million voices and dialects.

Papa Samuel used to take people around the city. He knew the places to go and the people to see. Multilingual, a musician with a fine ear, he could speak whatever language required and expected his son to do the same, so that by his seventh birthday Jacob could converse with most anyone: one day Hindi with a lady from Nepal, the next a man from France.

People flocked to these tours when Jacob wore a harlequin jacket and hat with bells that Papa made. Sister Juliana threatened to burn them. 'You make your son out to be a clown.' Papa Samuel agreed. 'Yes and get paid for it. How else can I keep him at your expensive school?'

They would tour the city and finish outside the Basilica, Papa going around with the hat, bells jingling, and Jacob singing, '*Vieni tu Re Onnipotente*,' which means 'Come, Thou Almighty King.' He would sing the same verse in as many languages as they had time, leaving listeners to work out what went where, for in his rarefied world all sound is music.

Last month the tailor, Mr Peacock, came to measure a new jacket. A long thin man with long thin hands, he whistles through his nose. That night Jacob composed a song: '*L'uccello che suona melodie sul becco*.'

Next day he was in the garden pulling weeds and singing when Mister James came by. 'I wondered what tailor Miss Clary might use. I see it's the same rare bird that plays a tune on his beak when debating my cricket flannels.'

They laughed so much Jacob got sick and was sent to bed.

Poor Mister James was in trouble. Miss Hanky said he was not to encourage the boy. 'It's good to hear him laugh but knowing what we know of his heart we must be careful, for he is by no means out of the woods.'

The next day Jacob asked the gardener what she meant by 'out-of-woods.' Sykes wasn't sure, but thought it meant he must keep taking his pills. He does take pills, little white dots kept in a bottle by the bed, and when ill he puts one under his tongue. Doctor Paul says they will help ease his heartache.

Jacob's heart aches when he sees Clareessa Morgan. A different ache, a good ache, his heart reaches out to embrace all things and all people.

If this is what the pills are for he can live with that - or die if needed.

* * *

Having delivered the lad to St Bene't's, Margret is back to worrying for the world again. Unable to sit still, she takes a brush to non-existent cobwebs in the front bedrooms while continuing a one-sided conversation with Sykes, who is up the ladder clearing gutters and making a poor job of it.

Nerves strained she slapped the brush about. It's too quiet. She likes noise and hustle and bustle. Freya-Jasmine back at school, the dogs moping, and no one running up and down stairs, it doesn't feel right.

She worries about Miss Clary and the Professor. She thinks Serena's letter will change everything, and that will be an awful shame because until then they were beginning to fall in love. Now Margret is alone with no one to cosset only this useless article! Lord knows why Miss Clary kept Sykes. When the doctor died she had a chance of finding a decent gardener but soft-hearted, let him keep his place. 'And he about as useful as a bucket with holes in it!'

Sykes poked his head over the sill. 'You say somethin' Miss Margret?'

'I was just wondering what time to collect Jacob.'

'You're allus wonderin' about Jacob.'

'I dare say I am.'

'Well, when you see him tell him to keep his dog out of my potato patch. I swear it's him digging spuds up.'

'More likely it was Tillie. Jacob's dog is a well-behaved beast. It never does any harm. And she's a she, not a he.'

'I don't care what it is. It needs to behave or it'll get what's coming.'

'Pah!' Margret snorted. 'You better not do anything to that dog or you'll have the Lord God and all His angels to deal with.'

'What are you talking about?'

'I'm talking about Jacob this morning asking if dogs are buried in the churchyard. When the curate says no he says why not. St Francis said all animals have a place in heaven. That it is only humans that have to pray to get in. Poor curate! I don't know how I stopped from laughing.'

'That boy's a bit soft in the head.'

'He is not. He's a good lad, a musician and an artist. All artists are reckoned to be a bit poetic.'

'He fancies himself a gardener.'

'Yes, and a good one from what I've seen.'

'Maybe. I just wish he'd stay out of my shed. I spent all of last winter sizing them plant pots. Now they're all jumbled up.'

'That's because he's filling them with flowers instead of sizing them. It's what they are there for.'

'Aye, but what sort of flowers! He mixes 'em up all over the place.'

'Never mind mixing!' Suddenly angry, Margret poked her brush in a corner dislodging a spider. She would've trodden on it but remembered Jacob saying not to kill spiders, and so, a life saved, put it out of the window. 'He knows what he is doing. He and that priest worked in the garden in his old school between music lessons. He told Freya-Jasmine he did a bit of weeding in the asylum in a piece of ground back of the kitchen – it helped him breathe.'

'That mad house sounds a right bad place. I bet he's glad he's out.'

Margret sighed. 'Let's hope he stays out.'

* * *

Service over, Jacob sits on a tombstone waiting for Miss Hanky. It's a small graveyard, well tended, people bringing fresh flowers every day. He loves flowers, along with music they are his favourite thing. When he was a boy he had six favourite things: Jesus, music, Papa Samuel, Father Anthony, his friend Rocco and Sophocles, the school goat. The day he was sent to the Refugio every favourite thing vanished, only the Lord Jesus remained.

Now he has so many favourites he can't count them. Jesus is first. Jacob has a secret favourite second. Jesus will know what it is. But as Mister James would say, that's okay: the Son of God forgives all sin no matter how bad.

Nuns in the Refugio said most of the things Jacob likes are sins, and music at the top along with blasphemy and the sin of false pride. The first day there his clothes were taken and he dunked naked in ice cold water. Clad in cotton trousers and a shirt with the name of the Refugio on the back, he had to line up with other children against the wall to have his sins 'observed.'

Music is a sin, they said, as is singing and dancing. When he dies - which was every day promised – he will burn in Hell for wanting such things.

He talked of his teacher, Father Anthony, who was famous as an organist and played for the Pope. He told of his father, Doctor Samuel Chase, who taught English at the Sapienza University in Rome and took pupils for piano lessons.

Mother Superior said Father Anthony was not a true priest, and that Jacob's father was a drunk who lost his post for meddling with kitchen maids.

Jacob said the kitchen maid was his mother and that his

father didn't drink, wine made him ill. He soon learned to be silent. If he said too much he was made to lie face down before the altar on a stone floor begging forgiveness for being born in the shape of an Imp from Hell – a gobbo – who if he persisted was flogged, as were other children, until blood ran down his back.

Imp from hell? He didn't know what they meant. Sister Imogene, who smiled a lot but never in a kindly way, told him: '*Il tuoi deformità rispecchiano i tuoi peccati,'* which means, 'your deformities mirror your sins.'

He wept. He had always known he was ugly but not because of sin.

There was a small pipe organ in the church next door but covered up and not allowed to sing. Father Anthony said the nuns were losing a chance to praise God and that Jacob would be paid for making music. After that he was allowed to play on that organ and others. Soon he was moving from church to church, sometimes playing all day, his back hurting and he too weary to sleep.

Mother Superior would always wash her hands after counting the money, saying a demon's touch had soiled her skin. Even now he wonders what he did to be born a demon. His sin must have been bad to leave his spine twisting like a snake and his foot the cloven hoof of a goat. Goats are not so bad. He had a favourite in Sophocles, the school goat, and thinks to save his pocket-money, five silver shillings a week, to buy a goat as a present for Miss Hanky.

Jacob thinks of many things but doesn't always want an answer. These days he thinks a lot of the Refugio garden, and of his cell next to the garden, a whitewashed wall dividing night from day. One year he was ill with a fever, life ebbing and flowing through dreams. So ill, and so tired, he didn't care to live, and lay watching shadows on the walls, sometimes seeing a silver-grey horse prancing, and a lady in a white gown come to take him home.

Thinking the lady might be his mama he prayed to Jesus that day for a sign: should he stay or go. It was then the talking began in the garden.

A man and a woman argued, words passing back and forth. He couldn't hear all but thought they spoke of a boy who was ill and close to dying.

'*Goddamn-awful place*,' said the man. '*Isn't there somewhere better?*'

The woman, whose voice Jacob seemed to know said the person was too ill to be moved and would die if disturbed.

'*Dying or not*,' was the reply, '*were he in my charge I'd have him removed pretty damn quick and none would stand in my way.*'

The woman was annoyed, where, she asked, with this ugly malady could he go, and who in the world had the time and patience to care.

The man lost his temper, anger piercing an air-brick by Jacob's head: '*Where else but where you and your sainted mother sought aid for your eternal malady. And who but the green-eyed girl, Clarissa Morgan, Beeches, Lark Lane, Comberton, Cambridgeshire, England.*' Bang, bang, the man struck the wall with his fist marking every word. They moved away leaving Jacob wondering if this was a sign. He had prayed to Jesus should he stay or go. Here was the answer - a new life in a name and an address.

The Lord Jesus heard his prayer and now he plays in the King's Chapel, Cambridge. The choirmaster plans to present

Jacob to the musical world in December when he sits an audition. If accepted, he will become a scholar at the University and thereafter the whole world will know of him.

Contented, knowing he has Jesus for his friend, he waits for Miss Hanky and a warm bed in the attic. Not yet out-of-the-woods, and tired after playing, he will take a little white pill and be glad to sleep, for the more he sleeps the sooner time passes, and his secret favourite home then from Italy.

Book Two

The Falcon

False Colours

Italy: Tuesday September24th 1901

'Such beauty.' Clarissa shook her head. 'I have no words.'

'*Si! Veramente.*' Her companions nodded. 'No words.'

They came as a party to the Chapel Niccolina in the Vatican Palace: Clarissa, Sally, Giovanni di Lombardi, the art-collector, James van Leiden, and the Monsignor who gave them entry. For almost two hours they toured the chapel looking at various frescoes and discussing the life of Fra Angelico.

From there, weary and wanting to take in what they had seen, Clarissa, Sally, and James returned to the pensione in Florence.

'I never thought to see his work close up like that.' James was on a high. 'To be able to wander around and take our time was great. And so quiet! I know it was early morning. After so many visits I'd come to think of Rome as the City of Bells, not a moment passing without them tolling somewhere. Today was so quiet it felt surreal, as though Fra Angelico watched along with us.'

Clarissa nodded. 'I felt so privileged.'

'As did I! I guess the name of Giovanni di Lombardi carries weight even here within the Vatican City.'

'You think it was Signor di Lombardi that saw us gain early entry?'

'I think he must. I don't imagine the average tourist gets to see what we saw today and with time to wander around.'

'You don't think *you* might have anything to do with that, James?'

'In what way?'

'In the way of who you are. You're not exactly unknown in the world of the Italian Renaissance. Not only have you documented Fra Angelico's life, you have restored work of the *Quattrocento* period to great acclaim. I know what is said of you, James. I've read the reviews. Having been quoted by the Uffizi Museum here in Florence as the "safest hands in the Kingdom of Conservation," I imagine the Vatican was as pleased to see you today as we were pleased to be there…even at five in the morning.'

He smiled. 'I admit to finding that a bit of a pull. But then, if one wants time to wander, it's that or late in the evening, and then you have the issue of artificial light. The Vatican City is a popular tourist site. Even as we were leaving they were preparing for more visitors.'

'I did see the lines gathering.'

'It is the eternal dilemma of all such places. They need the money that today's tourists bring to help mend yesterday's damage.'

'I suppose. I was surprised by the clarity of the frescoes.' She stretched, her hands in her hair, easing the weight of curls from her neck, her breast a luscious pillow. 'Centuries of shuffling feet, dust rising and hands reaching out, and yet the colours were luminous. It is as the Monsignor said: "Fra Angelico was God's paint-brush." '

'I am glad you enjoyed it.'

'Signor di Lombardi is an interesting man. His questions were so precise. I imagine you could find space for him at the Fitzwilliam.'

'With his knowledge of art he would surely be an asset, and, of course, being of the Italian aristocracy, a man of infinite connections.'

'Aristocracy?'

'Yes. He is of the Lombardi family with connections to the Royal House of Savoy. Quite what connections I don't know. Kasper has a close bond with the man and knows more than I. I think he is referred to as His Highness, Il Marchese Giovanni Carlo Arello di Lombardi.' James smiled. 'I dare say there's a more to his name and title but I guess that'll do for now.'

'Why was he not introduced so?'

'I'm not sure. I was told his friends know him as Giovanni di Lombardi. I guess for the short-term we are included in that.'

'He is a serious sort of man. How old is he?'

'Late thirties, I think. Not much older than me, though I agree he comes over as something of a heavyweight.'

'I imagine carrying such a title is heavy.'

James shrugged. 'Italy is a world of titles. The whole of the Peninsular was once a mass of provinces, each with its own principality. The country as a whole is unsettled, if not from political unrest then plagued by disease. In '78 there an outbreak of typhus. Thousands died, Giovanni's people among them. While his lands and properties were retained, I heard he spent most of his childhood in Florence with his Uncle and cousins, the di Vallagras.'

'I see now why he is so very serious.'

'His tragedy doesn't end there. Kes said there was a difficult marriage, Giovanni's wife older than him and he vilified for loving her. Then, as if not enough, she died during pregnancy and he left distraught.'

'Poor man. Perhaps that's why he doesn't bother with titles. He finds life worry enough. I heard you preferred not to attach Sterne to your name, James. Is that right?'

'It is a different situation. Sterne is not my name. It belonged to my maternal grandfather. Van Leiden is my father's name.'

'Yet your brother carries the name.'

'That is his choice.'

'Did you not like your grandfather?'

'He could be a difficult man.'

Sensing discomfort she veered away. 'The Marchese reminds me of you.'

'You think I am heavyweight?'

'I think you are both committed to what you do.'

'I guess so.' James shrugged. 'I don't know much about him. As I said, he is Kes's friend. They play polo together and are members of the Explorers Club, climbing mountains and hacking through jungles *et al*.'

'You disapprove?'

'Not at all! If it gives pleasure it is enough. Either way my feelings would be of little account. My brother was born to raise new worlds and none gainsay him. As for the Marchese, other than a mutual love of Fra Angelico, we are new to one another. He owns a stud farm not far from you. I keep a horse there and because of the Kes connection have use of his gallops.'

'So we are neighbours?'

'Yes, for part of the year. I meant to say, but as we were caught up creeping about Rome in the early hours, I forgot to mention it.'

'Yes, as you say, "creeping," and yet so very worth it.' She got to her feet, shaking out her skirts. 'If you'll excuse me, James, I shall find my bed. Sally is next door to me. I doubt she'll sleep until I am settled.'

He got to his feet. 'I hope Miss Cartwright enjoyed the day.'

'I'm sure she did. On that subject, Sally spoke to me earlier where we both agreed that, the Marchese living in a hilly area, it might be better if she stayed here in Florence tomorrow rather than make the journey.'

'Certainly if that is her choice.'

'She would prefer more leisurely strolls about the Piazza, and has made a friend of a guest here, a Mrs Bellamy, who is older than Sally yet with similar likes. They are drawing up a plan of where to go and what to see.'

'Say!' He grinned. 'I reckon that's kinda nice.'

'I thought so. It leaves me happy knowing she is the same. Perhaps tomorrow we might message the villa saying we shall be one less.'

'I'll get onto it first thing and while I am at it talk with the proprietor here so Miss Cartwright has all she needs.'

'Thank you. Sally and Margret are dear to me, more aging aunts than anything. I'd like to preserve them for as long as I can.' She gathered her shawl. 'I bid you good night, James. It was a wonderful day, truly memorable.'

A smile on her face, but no real warmth in her eyes, she was gone, a wall again erected and they back to a nodding acquaintance.

* * *

James had to get out. Walking fast, he made for the seat of old government in the Piazza della Signoria. Then, his leg aching, and along with Clarissa's 'aging aunt' needing to rest, he stopped at a cafe, ordered a glass of wine, and lighting a cigarette sat watching the Florentine world revolve.

The Piazza is busy. Height of the season and the evening warm, people are out promenading and dining in bars and cafes, while horse-drawn buggies with flowers woven through the horse's tails trot about the square.

He has walked here so many times it feels like home. The summer after breaking his ankle he came with Father while Kasper navigated the Apennines with friends. As a recuperative holiday Florence was not the best idea. Father elected to climb to the top of the Duomo, all four hundred and sixty-nine steps. James went with him and was in such pain afterward, he was forced to use crutches for the rest of the trip. Father was annoyed. He'd come following the French painter, Fabre, and needed to get into the hills. James spent the next month hobbling about on his own and but for the pain enjoyed it.

It's possible those early weeks cemented a fondness for Florence. Confined to close quarters, he came to know the city well, and the Piazza his to explore. In this city one shares one's time with statues. They are everywhere, some ugly, others supremely beautiful. In the Loggia James is a man among super-men. Neptune, God of the sea and Perseus, slayer of Gorgons, warriors of the classical world snarl at passers-by: masculine power displayed in a clenched fist and in muscular thighs.

Kasper would love this crew, sitting at a camp fire singing bawdy songs and drinking Jim Beam whisky before joining Hannibal hauling annibal elephants across the Alps. James would prefer the company of Michelangelo's David, the statue that used to stand outside the Palazzo Vecchio. A quiet hero, David was charged with killing the giant, Goliath, enemy of Israel, which he did, armed with a sling-shot and five small stones. This is Florence. Add a harlequin hobo dancing with a little short-haired dog, and such is the view from the cafe.

Tonight one vision surpasses all and that of Clarissa reclining on a couch, a hand in her hair and the other looped through the ties that lace her gown. A long day, and they up since dawn, she is weary. The buttercup silk of her gown draping the couch is crushed from travelling yet as lovely as the wearer.

Silent, barely responding to his questions, she lay on the couch, her thoughts anywhere but Florence. James sat looking out over the city, and yet he knew her every gesture, for as she lay so he lay with her. On that humble terrace he gripped the wall, a thorn from a rose piercing his palm, but still it was his hand in her hair, and when for modesty's sake she resisted loosening the ties at her breast his need overrode propriety, his hands about her shoulders, easing the silk down, and leaning close, their breath mingling, his lips tasting the perfume of her skin.

* * *

He straightened - cigarette crushed under boot; the Substitute Man, as Kasper calls him, is in control again, and the dreamer silenced.

Given a choice Florence would be his city and a villa in the Fiesolean Hills his address. How absurd to talk of choices when a short time ago he had a first-class ticket to live and work here. The hope of gaining Clarissa's affection was why he chose the Fitzwilliam. Until lately he believed that was possible.

Last Monday he was in the Fitz basement wading through

a batch of paintings bequeathed to the Museum. While there he thought to test the new telephone extension. 'It's only me checking the line.' When she answered a smile was in her voice. 'Hello *only you*. This is *only me* saying come home, you've a deputation of ladies from the University mixed tennis group wanting to know if you're free on Friday, to quote, "knock about a bit."'

That was Monday. Overnight a fog descended, and from then on polite conversation was in place, and an empty smile blurring everything seen and felt, even to diminishing his pleasure when looking at the frescoes.

It's not that she is uncivil. She simply isn't here. He hates it! And while willing to hope a little longer, be hanged if he's fool enough to continue a dream that is already beginning to feel like a nightmare.

Wine glass empty he returned to the pensione. For the next two days they are in Fiesole and a first look at a possible master-piece. Hopefully things will be easier. If not then the Uffizi's offer to drop by for a chat will be accepted, and the door to the Fitzwilliam, and all hope in that direction, closed.

* * *

Clarissa folded the skirt into the trunk. Apart from travelling clothes, all else needed for their stay is at the Villa della Rosa. A cart arrived yesterday to collect luggage as a maid enquired of 'the English ladies appetite,' what they liked to eat and drink, and all else to make their stay comfortable.

While she enjoyed Rome yesterday a greater part of the trip was spoiled by the letter. If Serena had wanted to ruin their stay in Italy she couldn't have done better. Earlier this evening they sat on the terrace, James with a copy of John Donne's poems, and Clarissa wanting to shout: 'If it's you sending the lilac for God's sake stop!'

Sykes did the house a favour chopping down the hothouse tree. More foresight than his employer, he caught a glimpse of the future and the day a letter would drop on the mat and a handsome Prince turn into a frog.

Clarissa ought not to have come to Italy, but a coward she allowed it to follow through. Now any questions regarding the debt must wait. Florence is for being happy - not for looking under stones.

Yesterday she woke from a dream where she sat listening to Bunny Carpenter tell a packed lecture hall of the death of a once brilliant Cambridge professor, whose life was ruined when he stole money to keep his trollop of a mistress: 'you know her: she who must be conserved.'

The dream stayed, leaving her miserable, and she afraid that, on returning to Cambridge, she would hear of Uncle Sarson's demise.

'Oh Lord!' She covered her face with her hands.

Life at the Fitzwilliam has lost all joy. She used to walk everywhere. Now she rides Sally's bicycle and never stays on campus. Lunchtime sandwiches are now taken by the river. Certain former joys – small yet so very satisfying – have been abandoned. The weekly art class has gone as has an involvement with a local chamber choir, a thing she used to love and now misses so very much. Music, along with fun, is off limits - she afraid to hear another girl whisper 'slut' when passing in the corridor.

Along with home there used to be another sanctuary. James seemed to know what was happening and was so careful of her feelings she would smile thinking he should carry a placard: 'Clarissa Morgan is neither trollop nor slut.'

Serena's letter put paid to that. The winks and the knowing smiles are not here in Florence. There is a man sailing under false colours.

That night she went to bed, and restless, dreamt she danced down in the square to the 'Blue Danube' waltz, while on the terrace, his face pale as the moon, James read from his book *Scorched Hearts* to an invisible audience.

Then his words changed; they became a quote from her favourite John Donne poem, 'Air and Angels.' He read until his voice trailed away, stopping at a low point in the verse when to continue would've brought promise.

'*Thrice I have loved thee, before I knew thy face or name:*
So in a voice, so in a shapeless flame, angels affect us oft,
and worshipped be. Still when, to where thou wert, I came,
Some lovely glorious nothing I did see...'

CHAPTER TWELVE

Hobson's Choice

Villa della Rosa, Fiesole
Thursday September 26th 1901

They ate among the oranges and lemon trees of the Villa della Rosa estate in front of a fine old house of ochre paint-washed walls that every spring, according to the Marchese's Aunt, the Senora Eufemia di Vallagra, are hung with ropes of mauve-coloured wisteria, and smelling, '*come il cielo è arrivato*,' as though heaven has arrived.

The house has a superb view looking across the hills toward the Duomo cupola and the many warm-tinted rooftops of downtown Florence.

With luncheon over, and accompanied by a hustle of yipping Pekinese dogs, they toured the house room by elegant room. In a turquoise tinted drawing room they marvelled at Ming dynasty vases so fine one was afraid to touch in case they shattered, while above them hung a pair of Nicolas Hilliard miniatures, and he the artist to England's Good Queen Bess.

The library was an antiquarian's paradise. Rare books lined the shelves while illuminated manuscripts from as far back as the eleventh-century sat in glass cabinets. At the end of the room a Chinese lacquered cabinet displayed a collection of butterflies pinned to black velvet glorious even in death.

One room led to another, where from crystal chandeliers, to silk covered walls and velvet Ottoman couches, and on down to Persian rugs, the air breathed of years of hunting for the rare and the beautiful.

Eyes wide, and skirts held tight to her knees, Clarissa walked breathless throughout. Elbows in and nerves on edge, she wondered how anyone could rest in comfort among such priceless artefacts, and she was glad of dear old Beeches with its sash-windows and faded cretonne.

James was anxious for the Senora. A deaf lady of advancing years, her fragile wrists weighed down by gold bracelets that clanked when she moved, she tottered along on spindle-heeled shoes. '*Mi permetta, Senora*!' Afraid the dogs might bring her down he offered his arm and tottered along with her.

From the house they moved to the stable yard, a place the Marchese clearly adored. He stopped to pet the horses, knowing every beautiful creature by name, and talking with grooms enquiring of their health. From the stables they entered an immense aviary, where tens of multicoloured birds of every breed and colour flew overhead in a world of chattering and cheeping.

The last part of the tour led down a series of narrow steps to a grove of olive trees and the Lombardi family chapel: a building seemingly hewn out of the side of a hill. Inside there was a blue velvet-cushioned rail upon which to kneel, two hard-backed chairs and a stool. A shelf cut into the far wall served as an altar where a cross gleamed and candlelight flickered; beyond that it was empty - one might have stepped into a hermit's cave.

The Marchese had said very little throughout the tour. He'd walked alongside or stood with his hands behind his back, his dog, Shona, a sleek Doberman Pincher, at his heel. Any questions regarding the house were answered by his secretary, a man by the name of Charles Anouilh, who wore dark glasses and paced the ground as if measuring steps, which, as she was to learn, was indeed the case – the man being almost blind.

In the small chapel the silence was profound, not even a bird sang. It was a holy place where for centuries people knelt bringing their sorrows and their joys. Tears filled Clarissa's eyes. 'It is beautiful here.'

'*Si*, beautiful.' The Marchese nodded - his reply strangely ambiguous. 'If there is a heart to be found in the Villa del Rosa it is here.'

* * *

They rested in an oval sun-room sipping champagne and eating confections while the knowledgeable M'sieur Anouilh kept them amused with gossip from the Badia Fiorentina, an ancient abbey in the centre of Florence, where in the year 1436, Fra Angelico headed a team of workers for sixteen *soldi* a day.

The mystery painting was brought in. James was on his feet ready to be thrilled and tormented. Eye-glasses on his nose, he stood perusing the painting. Then he stepped away in silence.

'Perhaps you feel as I do, Professor,' said the Marchese. 'This is not so much the work of Fra Angelico, but more in the style of his old friend and mentor, Pietro di Giovanni.'

'It could be.' James was noncommittal. 'There is considerable damage.'

'*Io so*. Can anything be done to help the same?'

'I don't know. I wouldn't like to hazard a guess.'

James is puzzled. Even with this amount of damage a practised eye would know this is not Fra Angelico. Certainly that man would know. The Marchese is a known collector of the Gothic Renaissance with spies in major auction houses on the look-out for members of the nobility down on their luck.

A fist full of notes, and not a tax-man in sight, it is said he, or Charles Anouilh and his team of helpers, manages the bulk of the collection. Along with those seen today there is a strong-room of priceless antiquities. Hence, there are ice-making machines in the yard for hot weather and blue prints drawn to install electricity with the hopes of creating a temperature controlled atmosphere.

For sure Giovanni di Lombardi, or *Il Maestro*, as he is known, knows the story behind this fractured creation as he knows flood water did not cause the damage. Distortion of the support-frame suggests water involvement but not a flood. Had this come through the storms of '78, the Arno overflowing, it would be thick with mud and not a painting so much as a tragedy.

While there is a tragedy of a kind here on the table there is nothing natural about the spoiling. Howling gales didn't cause the rip along the lower shelf any more than a puncture on the left flank is the result of rats - more likely the heel of a woman's shoe. Beyond thinking the work survived the centuries lodged in an attic and now surfacing when yet another scion of the nobility is in need of cash, James has no idea how it came about.

He wonders if this connects with rebuilding work at the Badia Fiorentina. The abbey has been the scene of several finds during the last couple of years, the Uffizi currently working on a Fra Angelico found in a cellar. If this is the work of Pietro di Giovanni, known as Lorenzo Monaco - Fra Angelico's master and brother monk - then it belongs to the laity of the *Fraternita de Gerusalemme*, and not the Marchese, no matter how long his name and pedigree.

Beyond the clank of bracelets and dogs scratching, the room is quiet., Clarissa sits on a sofa with the Senora who, sleepy as a summer bee, murmurs of the past and how the Lombardi family suffered: Giovanni coming to the Vallagras as a boy after losing his mother, father, and three sisters to, what the Senora called, 'the sweating sickness.'

She said he'd known terrible tragedy, his wife dying in childbirth. There was a strange moment then in that sleepy monologue when the old lady ceased mid sentence, as though suddenly, and violently, aware of a stop-sign:

'Carina had a rare kind of beauty, scintillante, as seen again, alas, in her brother, Vincenza. The Vallagra family say Giovanni must continue the line. He say no........his wife was of a lifetime and not to be repeated.'

* * *

James knows he should say something to ease the strain but caught in the impasse of wanting to investigate the painting while suspecting double-dealing, he digs in, recalling a conversation recently where he laughed at a subject matter that now profoundly strikes home.

It was when Kasper called the Granta house. Bored and unhappy, he said he was weary of Serena. There affair had become a poisonous wound guaranteed to fester: he wanted to find real love with a real woman, not forever scratching an itch. He signed off laughing and talking of Hobson's choice: 'Since there is no such thing as real love, he would stick with what he had.'

The Tudor tale of the farmer Thomas Hobson hiring out horses without giving his customers a choice is new to James, whereas the nub of the tale - a case of that or nothing - pops up on a regular basis. It is happening today, a carrot dangled before the flesh and blood James, a man of principle, who, irrespective of wealth, works hard for his living, pays his debts (and those of his brother's mistress), and who in early years chose to stand by his father rather than suck up to Elias Sterne for the sake of De Beers shares.

The other James is more legend than reality, the Harvard whizz-kid – '*the safest hands in the kingdom of conservation*' – is infinitely more fragile due to an early loss of mobility and constantly being compared to his brother.

Egged on by his grandfather, James tried proving brain is better than brawn. If advantage might be gained in pursuing a subject - no matter how obscure - he would find it, seeking approval through academic excellence.

A passion for learning became a way of living. His awkward manner made him a stranger to society. His reserve was seen as arrogance and he without a partner at the Prom Ball or a pretty girl to kiss under the mistletoe.

The young professor found fame in other ways, leading expeditions through caves of the Calabrian Mountains, writing best-sellers, and scaling stone monuments with only a London policeman and lonely drunk for company. These were single flights of fancy, one might say, and mostly carried out at night, until one particular flight of fancy found him working in a lesser known museum in England, and his argument for being there the greatest fancy of all: to fall in love with a woman who does not love him.

Now he is offered the chance to redeem a masterpiece while uncertain of the rightness to do so. Had this been a straight-forward deal, and the name of Lorenzo Monaco suggested, he would've come to Florence. If the Italian architect and painter, Vasari, thought enough of Monaco to add his name to his *Lives* along with that of Michelangelo and Leonardo da Vinci, who is James van Leiden to say him nay.

As though hearing his thoughts, their host stepped forward. 'Am I to take from your silence, Professor, you are unwilling to consider restoration. If so I do understand. You came looking for the right thing and found wrong.'

'As you say, I came looking for the right thing.'

Giovanni di Lombardi turned to Clarissa. 'What are your thoughts on this Miss Morgan? Do you think the reviving of this forlorn item a hopeless task, or might there still be a trace of God's paint brush beneath the debris?'

Colour high, she looked at the work. 'I'm afraid I don't know enough to suggest one painter from another. It has taken a beating, and the chances of good coming from bad must be slim. Having said that...'

She gestured. 'Whatever the provenance, I do know that if anyone can give this life it is James van Leiden. So from that point of view, *Signor Marchese*, one might say you brought the right man to the wrong thing.'

She looked up. 'But then I'm sure you know that.'

* * *

They dined late that evening. James decided that, whatever the issue, the painting needed to be cleaned, and set to work in the laboratory.

It was the best thing he could've done, for with only a lovebird in a lemon tree for company, he realised he was somewhat overreacting.

The Marchese is an avid collector but also a generous man, museums and galleries throughout the world benefitting from his goodwill, and not only in minor works. He recently donated a Donatella bronze to the Louvre and a sixteenth-century bible thought to be a Tyndale to the British Museum.

If there are reasons to question provenance James should still make the piece safe, for if this is a Lorenzo Monaco it is a rare find, and being the centre panel of a triptych, points to the possibility of other finds. Tempera on panel, at first glance the painting does suggest that name, though minus the cusps he favoured, the manner of gilding and elongated figures speak of the man.

Still James feels let-down. The trip to Florence is not as hoped. Doubt regarding the painting, *and* Clarissa's reserve, have left him edgy. They are invited to a Masked Ball at the Pitti Palace on Friday. James knows it will take more than a turn around the floor to bring her into his arms.

Earlier in response to praise of his skill he had a chance to mend bridges, but, concerned for the painting, he made things worse. Giovanni said he would leave *both* conservators to discuss work needed, whereupon James said he preferred working alone: '*too many cooks will surely spoil this broth.*'

As always when anxious, a Yankee drawl got caught up in a Belgian snap, bullets ricocheting about the room and Clarissa wounded. Now she walks among the roses with a new suitor, their host knocked sideways by her beauty, his silent gaze following her about as though the door to Aladdin's cave has opened and he glimpsing the rarest of treasure.

* * *

Clarissa walks in the garden with Giovanni, banks of roses wet with dew, and gas lamps casting a golden glow through the trees.

She breathed the sweet air. 'The Villa surely lives up to its name.'

'Roses are my passion as they were my father's. When my wife was here life was about collecting art. Now that is simply a groove I follow.'

'I am sorry. You must miss her horribly.'

He was silent for a while and then: 'Carina is missed by more than a few.'

They walked on. He asked if she was cold. 'I'll have a maid bring a fur wrap. There are several dotted about the house.'

'Thank you I am not in the least cold. It is really quite warm.'

'It is, though, as I am sure you have been told, the weather here is swift to change, Miss Morgan, and where once was warm is bitter cold.'

'I am perfectly warm. This shawl belonged to my mother. I take it when travelling. I know it will not let me down...and please call me Clarissa.'

'Thank you, Clarissa.' He smiled and was suddenly alive. 'I would like to be able to say your name as I would like you to think of me as Giovanni.'

They walked on, the garden a battle-zone, ripe peaches exploding on contact with grass, the scent mingling with that of the roses and liquid on the lips.

'The name Clarissa means Light,' he said. 'My name translates to *Il Signore Aumanta* - he who gains through the Lord.'

'It is a strong name.'

He gazed down at her before gently drawing her arm through his. 'I am a quiet man but also a strong man.'

* * *

They walked on, Clarissa aware of a change, a deepening of colour in the sky and an awareness of a million sounds and scents. The Marchese is handsome, arrestingly so with olive skin, a neat beard, dark curling hair streaked with the sun and olivine eyes. It is said he rarely stays in Fiesole and that he has an apartment in Florence and a house by Lake Como. Though reserved of nature he treats all with consideration. He had a hamper delivered to the pensione so Sally and her new friend might sit on the terrace sipping champagne.

He is a charming man, even so, having become used to judging all through James's eyes she is uneasy. This afternoon, sleepy from champagne, she sat watching the two men and wondering why the tension, when an image flashed through her mind shocking her awake: she saw herself as a baby bird her beak opening to taste whatever medicine was on a spoon James offered.

Now there is this: one man's opinion so colours her view, she walks the Villa della Rosa gardens doubting a man she doesn't even know.

'You work alongside the professor all the time, Clarissa?'

'Most of the time.'

'Do you enjoy working with him?'

Hurt by the '*too many cooks*' remark, her answer was slower than it might have been. Cast down, declared a novice, she feels she can't speak on any subject and her presence here in Florence superfluous.

'James van Leiden is a brilliant man.' It was the best she could do.

'Indeed so. His expertise is known and admired throughout the world. Do you intend to stay with the Fitzwilliam?'

'I'm not sure. I shall know more when finishing my Masters.'

'You 'ave a speciality in mind? In terms of conservation the Professor leans toward the Gothic Renaissance. Is your mind as his?'

'I don't know that I have a speciality, but if I had, it would be toward the process of gilding.'

'*Ah si! Le doratura!*' He clasped her hand, his heraldic ring bruising her fingers. 'Lorenzo Monaco made his paintings shine. He said they come alive under gold. You must visit the Uffizi. There you will see gilding of the very best. Perhaps when this visit is over you might think to return to us here at the villa to see more of Firenze. You would be most welcome.'

'Thank you. You are very kind.'

'Have you thought perhaps to travel?'

'Oh yes! And not just Europe. I want to see as much of the world as I can. It was our plan, my father and I. I'd like to see it through.'

'And your place of work?' He shrugged. 'Forgive me, but I think you are not entirely happy there, and want you to know we have museums of our own, good places, not least the Uffizi of which I am patron.'

She sighed. 'I dare say I will move on one day.'

'You must go where your heart takes you. Only then are you able to explore new ideas. *Permesso!*' He took a cigar cutter from his pocket, clipped a single rose from a trellis: a tender bud of silky pink edged with gold, furled, yet on the brink of breaking free.' He offered the rose. 'Perhaps, Clarissa, when considering change, you might remember this evening; we two walking among the roses where another rose might one day think to call home.'

They parted then, she for bed and thoughts of tomorrow and a Masked Ball at the Pitti Palace and a chance to wear the blue chiffon gown, now hanging in the closet, the maid having refreshed the many skirts.

'*'E bellissimo, Signorina*,' the maid sighed. 'Tomorrow at the Palace you will be so admired. His Highness will be proud to have you on his arm. All will smile for him and adore you.'

Yes, thought Clarissa, closing her eyes, all but one.

CHAPTER THIRTEEN

Facsimile

The Pitti Palace, Florence.
Friday September 27ᵗʰ 1901

They came on a salver, a golden filigree mask to wear for the ball, and a velvet lined jewel box containing earrings and a necklace set with square-cut emeralds and diamonds. They were beautiful.

The maid fluttered. 'Signore say they belonged to Anna Maria de'Medici, and being green will compliment your eyes while praising your hair.'

Clarissa protested. 'They are lovely. You must tell the Marchese thank you, but I couldn't possibly wear them. I'd be afraid to lose them.'

The maid smiled. 'He knew you say so. I am to reply, is alright...*e qual è la parola*?' She frowned. 'Ah si! They are facsimile. '

'Facsimile? You mean they are made of paste and glass.'

'*Si*! Paste and glass. They are also..,' the maid took the necklace from the box, '*assicurato* ...insured.'

'Oh, well in that case!' Clarissa laughed. 'I should be delighted to wear them for paste or not they are simply gorgeous.'

'*Si,* gorgeous.' The maid drew the earrings from the case. 'They 'ave the wires for ears or screws. Which do you have?'

'I suppose I must use the screws.'

'You must wind very tight, Mees Clareessa.'

'I shall be sure to do that.' Surprised by the weight of the

153

earrings, she wound the screws as tight as she could. 'They are heavy.'

'Is good. I have a trick that will help.' The maid held out the necklace. 'But what about this when you already wear the chain?'

'Could I not just wear the earrings?'

The maid shrugged. 'I think they are meant to be worn together.' She leant down. 'What is this ring on the chain?'

'My mother's wedding ring.'

'Ah, *capisco.*' She nodded. 'This I understand. Your mama *e morto.*'

'And my father. I never take them off even when bathing.'

'Keep the chain and wear mama's ring on this hand.' The maid slipped the ring on Clarissa's finger before fastening the necklace about her neck. 'Now your mama and papa are comforted by the facsimile.'

So it was arranged, Sophia, the maid persuasive and talented. With hands deft and quick, she arranged Clarissa's hair in a simple yet lovely style with soft curls piled high on her head and the odd tendril lapping her cheek.

'Oh thank you!' Clarissa saw her face in the looking glass, the jewels glowing and she with them. 'You and the emeralds have made me beautiful.'

'No Signorina. You already beautiful. I merely polish the glass.'

* * *

Truth to tell, she does feel beautiful, the gown clinging as a second skin, and so exquisitely made that, while the bodice is daringly low, heavy embroidered under-stitching supports her breasts as cradled by unseen hands.

The skirts are four layers of tulle over stiff silk and hooped petticoat, caught up at the back in an elegant bustle, and attached to the back, adding a final flourish, blue satin ribbons, so when she twirls so do the ribbons.

This day has been a revelation. The gown is dazzling as is the turquoise velvet cloak and elbow-length kid gloves. The first time of wearing should be Italy. As to the colour, the soft silky flashing and flickering, here in the warm evening air it can be whatever it wants to be: the dark blue of a lake, mysterious and still, or as the Ionian Sea, sunlight shimmering on the waves.

Mama would've disapproved thinking the colour too strong for Clarissa's pale skin. Papa knew better. He had seen his daughter grow, a willowy girl arriving through a boneless child with the winter's hair of silver and the green of spring in her eyes. It was Papa who noticed the gown that day when they strolled through the *Via dei Codotti*, where beautiful models paraded beautiful gowns. He saw the blue chiffon. 'The girl is lovely but the colour is wrong for her. Her hair is dark when it should be light. Come! I'll show you.'

Thinking of that day her heart swelled. Her father, a sweet cherub of a man, bowed his way across the marble floor, mingling ancient Latin with modern Italian; and the Mesdames and Signoras beguiled.

In terms of money they were never rich. He bought the gown that day without enquiring the price, carrying the box back to their hotel as if transporting jewels from the Nile and she Cleopatra for the day.

As a child she was told blue and green should never be seen. This day proves they work well together, the dark juniper of the emeralds enhancing the chiffon. And they are emeralds!

However slick a jeweller's trick, glass and paste never looked like this. Only a true gem would share the warmth of her body. The long earrings brushed her shoulders, while the last pendant stone of the necklace nestled between her breasts, breathing as she breathed.

She will wear the jewels with pride and with some confidence. Sophia has cared for the Marchese's guests for years. She has tricks of her own, silk thread wound about the upper earring to be tied behind the wearer's ear.

Clarissa left for the Pitti Palace feeling like a princess. Tomorrow before they return to the pensione (and England, she thinking James will shorten their stay), she will speak with Sophia, offering her thanks; such skill is hard won and worthy of recompense.

* * *

The evening warm, and the White Hall crowded, Giovanni stood watching the lovely English Miss charm her way through a glittering throng, her ravishing smile laying waste to attending Italian males.

Charming though it is, her gown is less than she deserves. If it is anything she makes it so, she with the radiance of a Fra Angelico Madonna, and while the mask seeks to hide her identity it highlights the perfection of her face.

The emeralds were a mistake. Bright eyes and innocent mouth, she needs nothing but herself. A tiara and bracelet complete the Medici emeralds. Carina wouldn't wear the tiara. She said it gave her a headache while the earrings stretched her ear-lobes. Four pieces would swamp this girl.

She has set the Pitti Palace on its ear, though that is not why he brought her. No man would think to put her on view, a thought shared by the Royal party; the Count asked '*Il Marchese intende aggiungere un Angelo vivente alla sua collezione.* Is the Marquis planning to add a living angel to his collection?'

The noise of chatter rising, he left through one of the small salons out on to the Piazza. Once in the evening air, the business of the painting on his mind, he lit a cigar, and then made his way toward the fountain.

That he was expected sooner or later at this Station of the Cross for Unrequited Lovers was reflected in the professor's elegant eyebrows.

He shrugged. 'So many mirrors. To see oneself replicated a thousand and one times is fine for handsome Harvard gentlemen and for your beautiful English Miss but not so good for me.'

Acknowledging an attempt at ice-breaking, James smiled. 'And how is *my* beautiful English Miss?'

'I cannot tell. We walked in and she was swept away. The Royal party has an eye for beauty. *Zia* Eufemia said it would be so.'

'Your aunt seems to be having a pretty good time.'

'Senora Eufemia di Vallagra was once very beautiful and though no longer young remembers those times.'

'So I saw, though I admit to earlier having doubts about your dogs.'

'You mean to fall? No. I was as you thinking her fragile. I do not think that now. The lady was born an Aldobrandini and wed a Vallagra - a fierce combination. She has more energy than me and I forty years her junior.'

* * *

They stood awhile in silence watching the splendour. Beyond what Kasper has said, and the world of art in general, Giovanni knows nothing about James. He is not easy to know. An intellectual, a lover of art and of music, he'll have his gentleman's club in Boston where he can sit and smoke with other devotees of Balzac and Voltaire. Judging the immaculate cut of his cloth, he likes good tailoring; the champagne tussore suit worn yesterday at the gallery was of Savile Row, as was the soft cream-coloured Homburg hat. Female heads swivelled and he seemingly unaware.

The word from Cambridgeshire is that he likes to ride, and that he keeps a decent mount at the Lightfoot stables. Unlike his brother nothing is known of his intimate life, no costly mistress settled in a love-nest in Paris. In that respect all is silent. James van Leiden stands alone, an enigma, and yet such a man that irrespective of infirmity, he commands respect.

Tonight the addition of a black velvet mask to white tie and tails lends his tall figure a *louche* appearance, one seeing a dashing Highwayman, who would take your money and yet with such grace, the loss would seem worth it.

Though not as obvious as his brother one suspects he is his superior in every way. Giovanni has known Kasper for years. A terrific fellow, strong as an ox and brave as a lion, he was always a hazard, especially to himself. A man who cannot resist a dare, no matter the odds - twice over Niagara Falls in a barrel - will one day do harm to himself and those that love him.

In view of that, knowing how the brothers rub off one another, Giovanni must remember to say Kasper is expected in

Florence sometime over the weekend. 'James, might I speak of the painting?'

'I wish you would.'

'First let me say you were right to suspect a problem. There is deception but not of my choosing. News of the find came via a family member whose name I cannot tell having given my word I would not. Originally the painting was passed down through a family in rightful manner. However, at some point it was removed from the family in a less than honourable manner. It is my intention to try making this right.

'The Rosary, as it is provisionally named, is the centre panel of a triptych. Though I don't have them as yet I know that right and left panels are at large, and of such beauty beneath the grime, they are worth saving.'

'I would hardly call a four-inch gash grime.'

'No more would I, which is why I must proceed with caution, so that tomorrow, or the next day - or maybe never - I may acquire the rest.'

James frowned. 'What is this, Giovanni? Why the caution? Are you in some way held in ransom?'

Giovanni's reply was bitter. 'Since the issue involves a member of my family I am assuredly held to ransom. It is a complex situation made more by a disturbed mind. I must negotiate with care, *Il Maestro* at his best, so that in time the world gains all three panels.'

'But why do you need me? The Uffizi has excellent people who have worked on a Lorenzo Monaco.'

'I would like to be able to do that. It would put a stop to this painful conversation, but, along with family involvement, a vested interest within the museum makes that idea impossible.'

He sighed. 'I know you suspect fraud, and I am sorry - for while there is wrongness, it is not mine.'

'Why couldn't you tell me this from the start instead of wasting time?' James was angry. 'I'm not asking anyone to break their vows. God knows I'm up to my neck in my own promises and know them for the curse they are. But you should've said, trusting I would've helped whomsoever the artist *or* the problem. Instead you left me thinking ill of you when I needn't.'

'I would wish it that simple.' Giovanni ground the cigar butt under his heel. 'I have been troubled by this particular work for a good many years and only in the last month seen light at the end of a very long tunnel. If I did cheat it was in fearing you would not come to my aid. In that I ask your forgiveness.'

Both men stood a while in silence surveying the glittering throng about the Palazzo. Then Giovanni spread his hands. 'In point of wasting time did you manage to secure a moment of Signorina Clarissa's dance card?'

'Not a chance. By the time I got back from handing in her cloak there was nothing left. So many fanciful signatures, I figured most of the House of Savoy here this evening wanting to dance with my junior conservator.'

'The lady is much admired. With respect to that I would say the word junior when applied to talent and beauty of this calibre is a mistake. Too many times said and the Fitzwilliam Museum will lose a valuable skill. I do not think you would want to be left alone in your artistic endeavours.'

'Perish the thought.' James held out his hand. '*Grazie, Marchese, per avermi onorato con la tua lotta. Farò tutto il possibile per aiutarti.*'

'*Va bene.*' They shook hands. 'Thank you, James.'

* * *

Clarissa hasn't stopped dancing. Her feet hurt, if not from the tread of heavy patent boots then from sparks ignited on the marble floor.

The ballroom is a fairy-tale place of white stucco, glass and sparkle where crystal chandeliers hang suspended from the ceilings and huge mirrors on every wall. When they first came in, along with other guests, they climbed the longest flight of stairs, going up and up, silk gowns whispering on marble. They then waited in line to be presented to the Royal party. Giovanni said not to be anxious; she would be welcome wherever she went. Eventually, aware of rows of gold braid and of glittering jewels, and of eyes smiling through fantastical masks, she made a good curtsey. Someone asked how long she planned to stay, and had she visited the Boboli Gardens, if not they were picnicking on Sunday and would love to see her.

More introductions followed and more masks and smiling eyes, names offered as from a children's fairy tale: the Principessa this and Count and Contessa that, and Clarissa a ballerina turning on a bejewelled trinket box without a hope of remembering names.

The orchestra struck a chord, a ripple passing through the crowd, men donning white gloves and ladies bending to scoop their gowns. This evening the Marchese does not dance: Clarissa will partner another gentleman with scratchy medals on his chest and a neat moustache under his nose.

They joined the opening parade, the ladies in glorious gowns, osprey feathers nodding, and men resplendent in white tie and tails. The orchestra played and they danced the Grand March, weaving patterns about the ballroom floor. Happily she did not falter, her partner a strong leader, and she recalling such a dance from the Cambridge May Ball.

A waltz, a Mazurka and a Polonaise, the evening sped on with more smiling eyes, and she attempting conversation while trying to catch her breath.

If she had an anxious moment it was with the first glimpse of the other gowns. Ladies of the Savoy Court follow *haute couture* in swallow-line gowns with embossed satin trains. The blue chiffon is beautiful, though compared to those worn tonight it is simple in style - countrified as Serena once said.

Apart from the Grand Dames and chaperones seated on sofas about the edge of the ballroom, Clarissa wore the only dark coloured gown; all the other ladies in pale tints. This gave her a fright, and made her feel self-conscious, until she looked at her dance card. Then seeing but for one space it was full, she forgot her fears and danced on.

Now having saved the space she looks for James. It was he who caused this to happen. She wants to thank him and remember this night forever.

There he is! Head above the rest, bright hair shining, he is with the Marchese at the entrance of the ballroom. They are talking. Whatever the painting issue it seems it has been settled and both happier.

The dance is winding down. She is anxious to gain James's attention before being claimed by another. In this moment is it not a stranger's arm she wants about her waist, it is his arm, and though it won't be the Blue Danube as in the May Ball of 1900, she won't care as long as they are together.

James van Leiden, he of 'the gentle hands,' is a difficult man to know, forcing her to acknowledge her shortcomings while questioning her thoughts to a point where she is uncertain of everything. Dedicated to art in a way never imagined, he is in search of perfection and harsh on those with a lesser reach. Even so, while he is difficult - and secretive regarding his association with Serena - they must share this last waltz or the evening will be spoiled.

Good! He has seen her and is coming, making his way through the crowd, polite as always conscious of doing things the right way. Lips turning upward and eyes soft, he is smiling, seemingly glad to be here as she is glad.

'Oh come on!' Heart beating, she stood on tiptoe wanting him to hurry, and not to be too polite - not right now – for if he does take his time he risks losing her as a partner perhaps in everything.

'Oh James! Darling, please hurry!'

Head up, his gaze holding hers, as if sensing danger, he moves faster, cutting in and out of the people, silent, no longer apologising.

Too late! He is here, the Other One, cutting across the ball-room floor - dancers giving way before him as if it is the right thing to do.

A giant of a man, he eats up the ground with every stride, not on horseback this time or wearing a mask. Face bare, he comes as he would have the world know him. 'Hello green-eyed mouser.' Amber eyes glowing, Kasper van Leiden Sterne leaned over her. 'It is time to get your cloak. The big bad dog has come to take you home.'

CHAPTER FOURTEEN

Leaf on a Tree

Beeches, Comberton
Saturday September 28ᵗʰ 1901

'But are they well, Mistress Hanky?' said Jacob, hands behind his back, knowing she wouldn't be pleased to see how red and sore they are from scrubbing a kennel he found on the local rubbish dump.

'I'm sure they're fine,' said Margret. 'Why do you ask?'

'I miss them, and Miss Sally, who makes everything pretty.'

'Yes, Miss Sally is a bit on the artistic side. She wanted to go to university but it never happened. Women didn't bother in those days. Mother said she should've worked in a flower-shop. She'd have pretty things to arrange all year round. But never mind that, why are you bothering about Italy? This is the third time today of asking when they're coming home.'

'I worry.'

'Worry about what?'

He shrugged. 'I do not know.'

'Is it because you think they might miss your audition?'

'*Si*, my audition - that and other things.'

'Such as?'

'I do not know.' He spread his hands. 'I just want them here.'

'As do we all, lad. The old house hates 'em away. The walls are groaning. But don't fret. Miss Clary will be home and my sister if she can bother to write and say when. I've heard nothing so far. If they do the whole three weeks Freya-Jasmine will be here and everything back to normal. Talking of normal?' She beckoned him forward. 'What have you done to your hands?'

'Nothing.'

'Don't tell fibs. They are rubbed raw and I know why. You've fetched a bit of rubbish home from the tip and thought to take it out back trying to make it serviceable and me not knowing.'

'It is a kennel for dogs big enough for Amy and Tillie.'

'And that's all right, but you shouldn't have made your hands sore. You need them nice for playing.'

'The kennel was dirty. I make clean.'

'Yes and get me into trouble with the choirmaster when he sees them. It's the same when you groom that miserable horse. You have to look after your hands. Now go inside and we'll put some cream on them.'

Jacob sighed. 'This organ business is a bit of a do.'

'A bit of a do?' Margret hid her face in her apron trying not to laugh. Bless him - he's picked up her saying. 'Come on then, let's have a look at those hands.' She bathed and lathered them with cream wondering why he is so anxious, his face screwed up. 'You do know they'll be home in time for your audition, don't you? Miss Clary *and* the professor said so.'

'I know.'

'They're not the people to break their word. And it's not for weeks.'

'I know.'

'Then what's the fuss about?'

The boy sighed. 'I think they do not like one another.'

'Go on!' She gave him a little shove. 'Why would you think that?'

'They are not happy as before. Mister James weeps.'

'Weeps? What are you talking about? The professor is a grown man. Grown men don't weep. And what's he got to weep about? He's on holiday in Italy with his favourite girl.'

'I do not think she is his favourite.'

'Oh, but she is, Jacob! Believe me. She's top of the tree with him.'

Jacob shook his head. 'He not top of tree with her.'

'Possibly not, but that's none of our business. Right then! That's you sorted.' Having had enough of the boy's far-seeing eye, Margret changed the subject. 'Now go and get your coat. I'm going to the professor's house to sort out the new curtains. Since you're so worried about him, you can come and hold pins, and while you're at it, keep his chap, Johnson, from bothering me.'

* * *

Croft House, as it is called, is very big and very empty. Margret wondered why a single fellow like him needed a house this size. Beyond books and wardrobes full of fancy suits and jackets, everything lined up in neat rows, boots in another wardrobe and hats on a shelf (his man Archie Johnson showing a pernickety mind), many of the rooms are empty.

Sally said she wasn't surprised: he's come of money and used to houses this size. Margret said yes but why bought and not rented. 'It's not as if he's going to stay. Sooner or later he'll go back to America or home to Belgium.'

That was said a couple of weeks back when talking of new curtains for the front windows. He was in conversation with

Miss Clary, saying they would be delivered when they were in Italy, so he would ask his man to fit them.

It was then Margret butted in. 'Pardon me, but you'll not want a man fitting anything. He won't know what to do as he won't know your ways. Give me your address. I'll see to it.'

'Are you saying you know my ways, Miss Margret?'

She'd nodded. 'In this I think I do. You'll want them particular, and as I am a particular sort of person I reckon I could do them justice.'

He'd smiled his beautiful smile. 'I reckon you can.' The following day a set of keys was delivered, two pound notes, and a message: *I told Archie you were coming, even so, you may have to negotiate space, he being far more particular than I. I suggest, Dear Miss Hanky, that like the Greeks, you come bearing gifts: your rhubarb crumble will do it if not your flapjacks.*

At first she thought, beggar Archie and his particularness, but then, anticipating trouble, the professor usually right, she baked a crumble *and* flapjacks, nipping them and a pot of fresh cream into her basket.

It's as well she did, Archie Johnson is a bachelor of long-standing and awkward with women. She found him in the basement complaining of the daily help, he having come in for sake of the curtains to find she'd not been in.

It took several pieces of flapjack to soften the edges but now they get on. Margret sent Jacob for Sykes and a carpet beater. 'Mind you come straight back. Me and Mr Johnson have our work cut-out to make this right.'

* * *

167

Jacob took the dogs for a walk and then thought to groom old Hazlett. He likes the horse and the horse likes him, they share conversation, the dogs sitting listening. He told Hazlett he is to play at St Bene't's on Monday for a wedding. 'The bride asked for you,' said the curate. 'The organ being a bit of a blighter we didn't have requests for music before you came.'

The organ is a bit of a blighter. If this was the gilded pipework of King's Chapel he would've played Wagner's *Bridal Chorus* but knowing it wouldn't suit St Bene't's he plays a lighter piece as in Mozart's *Ave Verum*.

The curate is kind as are people of the congregation. They stop to talk with him. He answers their questions and is glad to be accepted but all the time he worries for Miss Clareessa. As with the congregation, people at King's are getting used to seeing him. At first they would stare. Now they walk on, he as familiar to them as a leaf on a tree. It is then, being familiar, he hears things, and they gossiping knowing a leaf wouldn't tell.

Yesterday they talked of St John's College and an old tutor who became involved with a female undergrad causing 'a bit of a stink.' They said the old man is ill and if he dies, the 'stink' will start up again and names will be named, among them, 'that young beauty of a conservator.'

Jacob prayed to the Lord Jesus last night hoping the young beauty is not Miss Clareessa. Now he is tired and can't play as he should, and so prays some more, knowing a leaf on a tree has one spring and one summer, after that comes the autumn and a fading and falling.

* * *

'Take the weight will you?' Margret stands on a stepladder fastening hooks, while Archie Johnson takes the weight. It sounds easy, but the material is embossed brocade and makes her arms ache. By the time she's done she will have earned the two pounds. She did offer to split it but, a gentleman's gentleman, Archie said he wouldn't dream of it.

Sykes is in the drawing room and too quiet for comfort. Margret sent Jacob. 'Go and see what the fellow's up to.' Jacob went and found the gardener hanging over a Grand Piano looking at a row of photographs.

'That professor fancies our Miss Clary,' says Sykes. 'See? That's them dancing together at a ball. Look at his face - he's moonstruck. He'll be lucky. He don't stand a chance with that doctor bloke hanging about.'

Jacob stayed silent. He understands moonstruck. He sees it now in Mister James's house - Miss Hanky blushing, and the man, Archie, who is not that way inclined, left nervous. He has seen it in the cow-shed in Assisi. When a calf is newly born, the Sisters, angels in white coifs, sing hymns at the birth, and the calf so bedazzled by the beauty of the world unable to stand upright.

It is better not to think of such passion. Jacob knows Miss Hanky likes Archie and he knows Archie likes men. He knows Doctor Brooke loves Miss Clareessa as he understands she looks toward Mister James. He is younger than them all yet feels the same passion; moreover, his love is tinged with a gratitude no one would understand. He does not speak of it, but keeps it in his heart, especially when with Sykes, who, sad inside, makes fun of finer feelings.

Papa Samuel used to have a piece of wood with a mask on one end and a metal box at the other; it was called a stereoscope.

If you put the mask to your eyes you see a picture of snow falling on naked ladies. Another time it showed the same ladies playing with a beach ball. After Papa died, Jacob took it with him to the Refugio where the Mother Superior threw it on the fire.

Now Jacob has an imaginary stereoscope. When he looks through the mask he sees a lady riding a silver horse. The silver horse is a younger Hazlett, with a smart red bridle, and bells plaited in his mane. The lady has golden hair about her shoulders. She smiles and, holding out her hand says: 'Don't be lonely, Jacob Chase. Climb aboard, and you and I will ride into the sunset.'

* * *

Four o'clock he woke from a dream where he was entangled in curtain material and couldn't breathe. Miss Hanky was saying not to be silly: 'Mister James is particular about curtains and wants them hanging straight.'

He slept to wake again from a nightmare where he had lost his imaginary stereoscope and was like one mad, weeping and throwing things around, desperate to find it. He finally found it under a cushion in the organ loft at King's. But when he looked through the mask, a man looked back.

The man smiled. 'Dying or not,' he said, 'were he in my charge I'd have him removed pretty damn quick, and none would stand in my way.'

Jacob woke remembering the photograph on the piano in Croft House and the man standing beside Mister James. What's more he knows the words heard in his dream. He heard them in the Refugio when close to dying.

This morning he asked Miss Hanky, 'Who is that man?'

'That's the professor's brother,' she said. 'He used to come to see Serena Parisi when the other two were here. Their affair was supposed to be a secret but I knew about it. Miss Clary's poor father not long dead, it was my business to know. He never came in doors. He only ever waited at the gate or sent a carriage. His name is Kasper van Leiden Sterne. Cain to the professor's Abel or Shadow to his Light, I don't know which.'

CHAPTER FIFTEEN

Right Thing

Pensione, Florence, Italy
Tuesday October 1ˢᵗ 1901

The painting leaves for Cambridge today. It should be at the Fitzwilliam by the time he is home. After a layer of dirt was removed, James saw how Giovanni had arrived at the name. A rosary looped about the Recording Angel's wrist is an unusual appendage for a work of the period, making the painting ever more rare.

James had thought to use the next few days to further restoration, but with Kasper's arrival - and a letter from Mother begging help – his stay in Florence will be cut short. Seeing this as something of a mixed blessing, he spoke with Clarissa, saying while he had to return home, she and Miss Cartwright could stay, the Marchese offering the Villa for as long as they wanted.

Things then took another turn. Sally's new friend, Dora Bellamy, a wealthy widow in Florence in pursuit of Michelangelo, suggested she might like to visit the Bellamy house by Lake Como: 'My son, the Reverend Charles Bellamy, arrives tomorrow. We're hoping to visit friends en route to the Lake.'

One look at Sally's eager face and the comfortable way the women had with one another, Clarissa agreed she should go. Mrs Bellamy offered addresses: 'There is the odd American but we are mostly English domiciles who, while lovers of *la bella*

Italia, like to keep a foothold in the old Country.'

Sally leaves with the Bellamys on an early train. Clarissa, who'd promised to attend a picnic at the Pitti Palace, leaves on Thursday with James seeing her as far as the coast. Kasper offered to see her back to England:

'You came with an escort. You should return with the same.'

She refused: 'I believe I can cross the English Channel without mishap.'

Kasper arrived to take part in a Polo match in Rome. The Royal Court of Savoy plays the Italian Olympic Team and Kes wearing the Marchese's colours. When not practising polo he walks in the garden, sits in the sun room, or is anywhere Clarissa might be. He was surprised to see her. 'You never said this wondrous beauty is your assistant. If I'd known I'd have visited months ago.'

'I didn't think you'd be interested.'

'In the usual way you would be right but she is beyond the usual. How did she come to be with you?'

'We are colleagues. We came to see the painting.'

'Oh brother, do you even know your good fortune!' He closed his eyes. 'I would have a colleague who looks like moonlight on snow and whose lips are as warm raspberries in the first sweet melting.'

This is the way of it: Kasper means to have Clarissa and not as with his other affaires but from now until forever. An image revolves behind James's eyes. He sees emeralds flash. Clarissa is in his brother's arms. The Royal party smile thinking the god Eros provides the best in floor-shows.

* * *

The Polo match is not until next Saturday. Monday saw Kasper prowling the villa hunting his prey. He had missed Clarissa; she was at the Uffizi Museum with the Marchese observing the restoration of a true Fra Angelico.

Restless, he'd continued to prowl until suddenly was gone, seeking new romance while blissfully ignorant of the trouble his former romance had brought to Cambridge. Kasper doesn't know of Serena's part in this, or of the money borrowed by John Sarson and the heartache left in her wake.

He should be brought up to date, and not because James settled the loan, but for the rightness of it. The Sarsons regularly send two or three pounds to James. Their struggle to pay is enough to hold someone to account.

Tuesday evening there was a knock on James's room. 'Why the sudden sensitivity?' he said. 'You never knocked on a door in your life.'

'Then it's time I learnt.' Kasper sat out on the terrace, and then, lighting a cigar, began asking questions. 'Why didn't I know of the girl?'

'You do know of her. She lives at Beeches in Comberton.'

'I spotted her once coming through the snow. She looked sad. I did think to turn and sweep her up but I was in the usual tangle and not the best company. I knew a little of her history. In fact, a *lot* of her history - a constant stream of information. Seeing her now, I think misinformation a better word.'

'Who speaks of her in a wrong way? But then don't tell me, I know.'

'Who else. But why didn't you tell me about Clarissa Morgan? You've been with the Fitzwilliam nigh on two years. There's been a lot of conversation between us in that time but never anything of her.'

'As I said, I didn't think you were interested in hearing of my colleagues.'

'You are my brother. I am interested in everything you do from writing books to shinning up St Bene't's bell-tower.'

'You know about the bell-tower then?'

'Of course! Isn't that what this is about - anything you can do I can do better - including the wooing of the fair sex?'

'I wouldn't know.' James went to the bathroom, and then, former issues niggling, he returned to the terrace. 'Was it worth it?'

'What?'

'Taking the name Sterne?'

'Oh not that again!' Kasper sighed. 'If you are referring to finances it was definitely worth it. The rest didn't count.'

'It counted with Father.'

'Everything counts with Father. Even rain on the window pane counts with Father. You should know that, Gyr, you've tried lifting him enough.'

Knowing that to be only too true James pulled up a couch and sat, recalling another evening when he did the same, his arm over the wall and a thorn piercing his palm. Now his brother pierces his heart.

'I wrote of her in a note to you,' said Kasper. ''Ware the green-eyed cat.'

'I know but at the time it didn't mean anything.'

'Does it mean anything now?'

'Can't say it does.'

'Come now, Professor. Don't go all foggy on me. You're the educated van der Leiden. The Harvard crush as opposed to the brute. Aren't you always saying tell the truth and you won't have to worry about covering your tracks?'

'Hah!' James snorted. 'Never in a million years. That was your way of keeping vengeful husbands off your back. And forget the van *der* Leiden. Unlike you, I am in no need of embroidery.'

'I like the embroidery. It makes the other fellows jump about a bit. As for vengeful husbands, that does sound like the old me.'

'A new you! Hallelujah! The world can breathe again.'

'All right then, lay off. I know I've skeletons in need of burying but I am not alone.' Eyes sharp, he looked at James. 'You're not entirely blameless. There was the sophomore who doted on you. And there was Assisi! You never did come clean on that.'

'I had nothing to come clean about. You made sure of that. The sophomore is a happy memory. The other thing, three days in Assisi, can be summed up as a momentary lapse of concentration.'

'And as I said at the time be glad it wasn't you. She would've driven you mad as she's more than once driven me. But it's wrong to talk of her so. That was another time and another me. I can't step back now.'

They sat in silence, digesting what was said and what it meant for the future. Then James nodded. 'It meant something the first time I saw her.'

'Ah! That's when you understood my postscript.'

'Yes, the green eyes. But what is this really about? We've always kept secrets from one another, trivia as with St Bene't's tower and Nelson's Column.'

'We're not talking trivia. We're talking life and death.'

'Are we by God!' James was stunned. Until this moment he'd hoped Kasper was just curious. Now he sees he is in deadly earnest. 'You are a man with varied needs, Kes. I can't see you changing.'

'I can change.'

'And a Kestrel? Can a bird of prey stop hunting?'

'It's a matter of wanting to.'

'It is not a matter of wanting to.' He clenched his fist. 'It is a matter of genetics. The Kestrel is conditioned to hunt. He doesn't know any other. If the weather is rough he can bide awhile on an empty gut. But sooner or later he is hungry and then all good promises thrown to the wind.'

Kasper sighed. 'I guess you really don't know me.'

'I guess not, anymore than you know me.'

There was silence and a sense of levelling. 'Okay, so we don't know one another. Just let me know the syllogy of things, like what this girl means to you, when did you meet and where and why.'

'I met Clarissa the day I hauled Serena and her mother to London. You might say we met because of you. No force of nature as you would have it, merely a sequence of events caused by the note you sent. But in terms of that hauling, are you and Serena at odds again?'

'We're always at odds. It's how she works, lovers on a short leash and any pleasure entirely her own. I was the same, but not anymore.'

'Are you sure?'

'As sure as I know you are in love with Clarissa Morgan.'

'Who says so?'

'I do,' Kasper flicked ash from his knee, 'as does your face, your hands, and every other part of your heated body.'

'Careful!' James snarled. 'Don't try making sport of this.

My thoughts on Clarissa Morgan are not yours to play with.'

'I'm not playing.' Kasper tossed his cigar. 'I am trying to be a good brother, enquiring your feelings, not wanting to step on your toes. In face of that, I reckon the best you can do is to be civil and answer.'

'I don't know that I have any feelings to tell. I have thoughts on all sorts of things. Feelings are another matter.'

'I don't want to know about *things*, James. I want to know about people, indeed one person, and that person only.'

'Then you are out of luck. I am the Substitute Man remember. I don't deal with people. They are too much trouble. I stick with things. It's the same with love. As someone once said, "Love is an idea perpetuated by poets, a sleep-inducing drug meant to keep humanity from seeing the real world."'

'Oh confound it, do shut up! You're talking drivel and you know it.'

'If I am it's because I'm tired and in need of sleep.'

They gazed at one another, a door closing on childhood. Kasper took up his coat. 'I'll be on my way.' He paused at the door, hand on James shoulder. 'Are you certain of what you say, Gyr, and why you are saying it? Be truthful, you of the fine brain and ultra sensitivity, the brother I love. Can you say, hand on heart, you really don't have any feelings on the matter?'

There was a pause. The night was warm. What sounded like bees thronged the lemon trees. It is surely an unusual event at this late hour, and though thrifty, seems somewhat sad, they coming in the dead of night to rob the last sweetness of a dying flower.

In that moment, quite honestly - though he kept his hand far away from his heart -James van Leiden had no feelings about anything.

CHAPTER SIXTEEN

White Waistcoat

En Route to Milan, Italy
Thursday October 3rd 1901

Until Kasper suddenly arrived, the plan was for James and Clarissa to stop overnight in Milan before visiting Henry van Leiden, an elderly relative of James, in Montceau-les-Mines, France. Following an overnight stop, they would proceed to Boulogne: Clarissa for the ferry, and James for Belgium and his home in Leuven.

Clarissa suggested she could go on alone from Montceau-les-Mines; James didn't need to go all the way to Boulogne. He wouldn't hear of it.

'I don't doubt you can find your way. You are a woman of infinite resources as our short spell in Italy showed. Even so, I must do what I feel to be right and good manners nothing to do with it.'

His term, 'infinite resources,' grated, as did his smile, however, having been bruised more than once she is learning not to rub against a stone.

Rain, mist, and sudden cold, it was an uncomfortable train ride, made more by Kasper's last minute decision to join them. The two brothers sat side-by-side when they might as well be on opposite sides of the Poles. Clarissa had a window seat and for part of the way was entertained by a young lady of Freya-Jasmine's age petting a little Scotch terrier while advising her

179

maman on the latest fashion in bonnets.

The young lady left at Palma. Clarissa was sorry to see her go but soothed her mind with passing views and memories of the Riverboat on Sunday and the tour of the Uffizi on Monday with the Marchese.

They were met at the museum by a guide who said that construction work on the building was started in the six-teenth-century by Cosimo Medici, and that the museum came about 'through the machinations of a man with a passion for magic, Francesco de' Medici, Grand Duke of Tuscany.'

The tour was a history lesson with tales of intrigue, and of wife against husband, and brother against brother; it left her wondering how in all the scheming they had the time, or the desire, to consider art.

They spent time behind the scenes looking at the world of conservation, men and women working with the latest in technical equipment, and where a senior conservator worked on an actual Fra Angelico. He explained some of the procedures. It was a special moment, for not only did he include Clarissa in his observations, he asked her opinion and listened when it was offered.

At the end of the visit she thanked him, saying she hoped to come again. He smiled. 'Take care, Signorina Morgan, or you may catch the Uffizi bug, where the word is, as it is everywhere in the world of art, forget the condition. If it is old and beautiful bring it to me...but under cover of night.'

It was then (a quixotic character delighting in sudden moves) Kasper van Leiden Sterne hove into view, his tall frame replicated in the glass-fronted cabinets, and he with no apology for gate-crashing beyond, 'Oh, so there you are. I did wonder.'

While Clarissa didn't care to see him, familiar with the man and his ways, the Marchese accepted his presence with quiet patience.

Midday the public arrived and everywhere soon crowded. In the bustle, Clarissa was separated from the rest, borne up a staircase to the Gallery where a subject of division was on display: Titian's *Venus of Urbino*.

In his book, *A Tramp Abroad*, Mark Twain calls the painting, '*the vilest, most obscene picture the world possesses.*' Papa thought it beautiful. 'If one looks with the right eyes one sees what is there - a woman in love.'

Both the Titian and the Botticelli Venus are depicted as naked. The Botticelli maintains modesty covering her body with her hair. Titian's Venus doesn't try. Purring sexuality, she gazes out at the world replete and powerful.

While the nudity is startling, Clarissa thought the work daringly beautiful rather than obscene. On her way out of the gallery she dropped her programme. A man picked it up, tipped his hat and moved on. It was Kasper. He had been looking at the painting and with sensitivity, unlike the arrogance of the Pitti ballroom he chose to leave her to her own thoughts.

On the night of the Masked Ball he behaved like a brute. He'd pushed through the dancers. 'Hello green-eyed mouser. The big bad dog has come to take you home.' Furious, she'd whispered, 'I promised James.'

'Too bad!' He'd grabbed her hand. Sure of his power, every woman easy prey, he led her onto the ballroom floor. 'He should've got here sooner.'

Though livid (what was she a doll to be handed about) she'd suffered him, people applauding thinking the episode a romantic gesture. When the music stopped he would have spoken but in no mood to listen she went looking for James. Sadly, he was angry and with a curt bow left her stranded.

Clarissa felt their quarrel is long-term, and they vying with one another since birth, and while no quarter is given, there is no real enmity. That night, after the waltz, a change came about where their rivalry took a bitter turn.

In the Pitti Ballroom, a room full of mirrors, everything seen and seen again, she'd stood alone, cold air on her bare shoulders and a once beautiful blue gown in tatters. Still people applauded. The Marchese did not. He observed all with a frown and then, offering Clarissa his arm, brought her and Senora Eufemia to the Royal Party to make their goodbyes, signalling servitors to escort them to the Villa - the old lady chuckling: 'I look forward to seeing more of you, my dear. *Si rende la vita interessante.*'

Such was the Masked Ball, an evening of mixed blessings. Now she is on her way home sadder, and no wiser of James's part in the state of affairs.

As for 'making life interesting,' as the Senora suggested, she feels lost and alone, steam rushing by the window and a precious friend now a stranger.

* * *

Cold, she sank deeper into her furs, retreating to thoughts of the Marchese, who throughout the last few days conveyed concern with his hand at her elbow. A man in command of his life and feelings, he guided her through the following days. They were together on Sunday, the Royal picnic having moved aboard a steamboat on the River Arno. They talked. Clarissa seems to think she told the story of her life, Mama dying and how she and Papa planned to travel.

He seemed interested in everything, especially Jacob, saying the boy and his music were folklore in Assisi, Father Anthony known to him and news of Jacob's talent spreading. 'If there is anything I can do to further his career please let me know. I am in Cambridge soon. Perhaps we might meet. If, as you said, he is to audition in December, I should very much like to be there.'

He spoke of his life, or not so much of *his* life but of those around him, in particular his secretary, Charles Anouilh, a French mercenary who had served Giovanni's father. 'I have an image of my mother as like the shining sun, but nothing of my father. I saw Charles as I see him now, razor-thin with the keen eyes. Wherever I was he was also. If I fell from Strong-bow, my first pony, he picked me up. *Altrettanto*, if I was bad, as with the time I threw stones at a stray dog, he was there with an 'eavy hand. He taught me so much, mostly how to tell right from wrong. His sight began to fail here in Firenzi when thieves raided my uncle's house. A swordsman, the best in Italy, he killed every one, but was cut about the eyes. He has some sight, and what is not there is seen in other ways. Charles, or *Lucciole*, glow-worm, as he is known, taught me how to ride, how to fence, and how to live.' Giovanni touched his hand to his heart. *'Il mio più grande amico*! I trust him with my life and my soul.'

* * *

He came to the station. 'You do not have to go, Clarissa.'

'I think it best.'

'Then let me get you a decent brougham and four of my good

horses. They will take you wherever you want to go in comfort.' When she protested he'd draped a fur cape about her shoulders. 'At least take this along with a fur bonnet and a book to read. You have a long journey ahead. You may find the atmosphere colder than before and in need of diversion.'

How right he was. While the original plan was for Clarissa and James to travel alone, eleven o' clock this morning Kasper arrived in one of the new motoring cars. Such a racket, everyone gaping, he drove the contraption to the station, left it there with a valet, and joined them on the platform.

'It suits me to go to Milan. I have business there.'

A whistle blew and Clarissa was lifted aboard: 'Look to your boots, Kasper,' said James. 'The horses have been busy.'

The train moved out, Giovanni doffing his hat. Before saying goodbye she thanked him for the Uffizi. She said every moment there had opened new ways of thinking, and that in the idea of art she now sees there are no barriers, and words like 'yesterday' and 'today' are meaningless. The lifeblood of artists such as Fra Angelico is kept alive in the dedication of conservators.

Passionate and humbled, she'd stumbled over words.

His grasp urgent, he took her hand. 'I must tell you, Clarissa, knowing you were coming I read your work on the poet, Leopardi. I wanted to know about you, who you were and how you felt about life. I was greatly moved by what you had to say, particularly about Giacomo's sense of isolation.'

'Yes, at night.' She nodded. 'The only one alive in the world.'

'Si! *Solo con la notte e la luna!* I read your work and thought then, as I think now, a woman who writes this way knows Italy, the passion and the pain. And that for her, coming here will be like coming home.'

With that, he brought her hand to his lips, and suddenly, green eyes gazing over her fingertips, while he was still *Il Marchese,* there was the man.

* * *

En route to Montceau-les-Mines
Friday October 4th 1901

Kasper left early Friday morning. He was gone before she came down, a note left with the concierge. Aware of James at the desk writing a cable, she slipped the note into her pocket and in the business of moving on forgot it.

She had a restless night, needing coffee and the croissant that was offered in the salon before going into the gardens. A pretty place, they had stopped here on the way down to Florence. Clarissa remembers how happy they were then, she buying earrings for Freya-Jasmine, Sally consulting a phrase book and James saying, 'Worry not, Miss Cartwright, Florence has a common language.' Then seeing Clarissa wondering, he'd grinned. '*Si chiama amore,* Miss Clary, the language of love.'

If she thought the first leg of the journey home was awkward, it was nothing compared to the next. But for an elderly man asleep with a scarf over his face the train compartment was empty. Clarissa and James were two frozen corpses and the air so cold one knew winter had already arrived.

Giovanni's gift was a copy of Giacomo Leopardi's poems. It is not inscribed; an art collector, he preferred to enclose a card rather than mark a page. There is a message on the card. She will read it when she is home.

In that moment, thinking of home, tears filled her eyes, she knowing it would take the extraordinary to remove her from the place and the people.

As though catching the thought, James looked up. 'Your people will be surprised to see you back early.' She nodded. 'I did think to cable but held back knowing Margret would see the post-boy and fear the worst - we buried under an avalanche or something like it.' For a time he held her gaze before returning to his newspaper. 'And she wouldn't be so far wrong.'

It was a foolish thing to say, he in a deep enough jam without adding to it. Frustrated, he returned to the art review. He had to do something or go mad. Hour upon hour, wheels scorching metal, she barely a touch away, and he with a million things to say and all of them wrong.

A headline caught his eye: Cecil Rhodes forced to resign his seat in the South African Government, and now his heart a cause of concern. Knowing this will create issues for the De Beers Group, James wondered if the recent invitation offering a seat on the Oppenheimer Board will remain open, and if so, wouldn't it be better to terminate his contract with the Fitzwilliam as soon as possible; after all, what is to be gained by staying.

The day before they left for Milan Giovanni called the pensione. Though their conversation was of the painting, he was clearly unhappy with events at the Masked Ball. Knowing his behaviour toward Clarissa had also been less than chivalrous, James was more than a little ashamed. Since the Ball, beyond an odd glance at the breakfast table, he'd seen little of his junior conservator. A carriage would arrive early in the morning to bring her to the Villa del Rosa, and out to dine with the elderly senora. The two brothers were left to stare at the moon, Kasper saying he wished he'd never come to Florence. When asked why, he wouldn't say. He didn't need to, he has eyes and sees what all Florence is seeing - a coloured waistcoat.

* * *

Sunday on the Piazza, Giovanni wore a yellow waistcoat and sand-coloured silk jacket. Seeing Clarissa on her way at the station, his waistcoat was dark olive, and he sporting the latest single-breasted frock-coat. Before coming to Italy James ordered similar, though not as dashing; he opted for fawn cashmere where the Marchese favoured peacock blue velvet.

At the railway station the man was every inch the Italian *Signore*, hair trimmed, clean-shaven, and the beard gone the way of a cutthroat razor. All marvelled but the one that was meant to, for she doesn't know Florentine history, therefore misses the significance of a coloured waistcoat.

Seven years ago *il Marchese's* waistcoat was a statement of sorrow and intent. Today it foretells a new era: *Sono libero di osare amare di nuovo* - 'I am free to dare to love again.'

Giovanni di Lombardi is the nucleus of a particularly influential group of people in Florence, patrons of various charities, followers of the arts, and all in some way connected in with the Palace. A man of charm and considerable wealth, he is considered one of the most eligible men in Italy.

According to Kasper, he is likely to stay so - he once wed to the art historian, Carina di Vallagra, the Senora's niece, a woman of beauty and intellect, ten years his senior, who he is said to have adored.

Their union lasted three years, but then as with so many

great love stories tragedy befell, Carina dying during pregnancy. She died in the winter of '94, the coldest winter on record, and mourned throughout the artistic world. Flowers were piled on her coffin. Nobility followed the bier, and none more grief-stricken than her husband. It is said his wife died in his arms, blood from her mouth staining his breast and from that day, no matter the occasion, he wears a white silk waistcoat in remembrance.

He is known to have lovers. One lady in particular is a constant companion, the American opera singer, Sadie Ambrose Pennington, who keeps a villa in Como sharing the Marchese's love of Appaloosa horses. With all thoughts of marriage set aside he is the despair of those with daughters, every mother in Florence hoping a change of vest will herald a change of mind.

* * *

The carriage is empty, the old man alighting some miles back. It is coming up for midnight. The train is pulling into Montceau-Les-Mines station, where, hopefully the valet, Percival Stamp, and the van Leiden ancient growler is waiting. It is a pity really. Uncle Henry's house is old and not in the least comfortable. They could've chosen to stay in a modern hotel but, Henry being Father's only living relative, James felt obliged to stop.

When it comes to health the van Leiden womenfolk seem to flourish, where the men don't do so well: Pa's father dying of heart disease and Henry not so strong. A poor history doesn't bode well for the brothers, which may account for Kasper borrowing the name Sterne, he hoping to change his luck.

They are here, lights coming into view and the station sign swinging.

Cramped, and in need of stretching, James got to his feet. Clarissa sleeps on, her book on the floor and her cheek on her arm. So pale! In this absence of light one might think she has gone the way of the lovely Carina, quietly dying and James now the one in need of white weskits.

Disturbed by the thought he leaned down to wake her. Drawn by chains, he couldn't stop leaning, until, hands braced either side of the seat he hovered. Angel or Devil, in that moment he didn't know what he was, but hung above, recalling the first time he saw her, and she running alongside the carriage offering lilac to the woman that continues to hurt her.

He yearned to kiss her then as he yearns to kiss her now.

Gently, not meaning to wake, he touched his lips to a curl of her hair then hauled away, retrieving her book as he went.

It took a door slamming to wake her. Fudged with sleep she stared, a puzzled child. 'I'm sorry,' she whispered. 'I don't seem to be quite awake.'

A porter appeared, more doors slammed, and soon the moment - the kiss - was under his feet along with cigarette ash and yesterday's news.

On the platform he looked for the valet. His uncle wouldn't come, he is too old and the hour is too late. Then he saw him: Percival Stamp from Bradford, a little man, stubby and round, who has been with Henry van Leiden for years.

As always he is in black, a bowler hat balanced in the crook of his arm.

'Is that your uncle's man?' She is beside him, cold and trembling.

'That's him. Take my arm. Leave the luggage, the porter will get it.'

Two cripples together, they walked on, he with a stick and she stumbling.

The station was almost empty. They walked on. Fatigue or stress, call it what you may, James developed tunnel-vision, Percival seeming a great distance away and they taking an age to approach him.

'James.' She saw it first and gripped his arm. 'Something is wrong.'

He nodded. 'I reckon so.'

Offering support, she tucked in real close, fitting neat and tidy into his body as if she'd always been there. The valet was wearing a black armband. His eyes were red from weeping.

'What's wrong Percival?'

The words came from a long way, James seeing them coming, every letter of every word emblazoned in red.

'It is your father, sir.'

'What about my father?'

'He has passed on.'

'You mean he is dead?'

'Yes, sir.'

'How?'

There was a pause and then: 'I'm afraid he shot himself.'

CHAPTER SEVENTEEN

No Place

Beeches, Comberton,
Monday October 7th 1901

'She's on her way?'

'Yes, m'm. The 12-45 train just pulling in.'

'About time too!' Margret slammed the telephone down and regretted doing so: Mother always said be polite to those that serve since we also serve. She picked it up again, apologising to a dead line. 'Beg your pardon, I'm sure.'

She trudged into the kitchen complaining to the cat: 'I don't know what the world's coming to: the professor's father dead, Miss Clary in Belgium, Jacob thinking she'll miss his audition and my sister, Sally, late coming home, and if that's not enough, the study window is letting in rain.'

It has not been a good week. Sally's letter didn't help, she making a new friend and now on her way home via Lake Como with a mysterious postscript: '*Guess who I saw in Assisi? I'll tell you when I'm home!*'

Apparently this new friend, a Mrs Bellamy, was staying at the same hotel in Florence. She and Sally really got on. '*It was as if we'd always known one another, just waiting for the day to resume an old friendship.*'

Margret had felt like chucking the letter on the fire. This is typical of Sally making friends with strangers. She has been hurt more times than enough doing that, if not by men, then by so-called friends. Mother used to say, why can't you be like other girls? Why do you always want to paint pictures and other nonsense? You need to settle down and get married.'

Sally would stare with those big blue eyes. She was always pretty. Even in her forties she is pretty with Cupid bow lips and long lashes. Afraid for her, Mother would nag. Sally would say she's not worried about settling down; she just wants to be happy. Now she is attended by Mrs Bellamy's son, the Reverend Charles, vicar at St John the Divine in Diss, Norfolk. '*You mustn't mind me being late, Dear Maggie,'* was the PS. *'I am having such fun.'*

That was before the bomb fell and Beeches getting that other cable: '*Sad news. James's father has died. Staying for the funeral.'* The poor professor! It's hard losing a parent. Margret sighed, and picking up a tea-tray went to see what the men were doing in the study. Jacob is in there with Doctor Brooke and Mr Johnson. They stand about the leaky window discussing what needs to be done. Jacob is on edge all the time: he keeps asking when Mister James will be home. 'She said she didn't know, and would he stop biting his fingernails; he'll make his fingers sore.'

Margret's not sure James van Leiden will stay in Cambridge. She likes him and wouldn't want to see him leave. But as she said to Sally, he'll get bored with the small town rules and the gossip that even now is going on: Miss Clary's uncle ill and blame being apportioned.

* * *

Sally arrived home at the same time as the carpenter, and what with it still raining and things needing unpacking they didn't have time to talk until the evening when it was all about Charles Bellamy.

'So you call him Charles, do you?'

Sally blushed. 'It's difficult not being on first-name terms when you're travelling together. We had to stop-over twice. I couldn't keep calling him the Reverend Bellamy, could I?'

'I don't know if you could or not. From what I saw you seemed very cosy together. Was his mother not with you then?'

'Dora gets tired easily. She slept most of the way back and so it was up to me and Charles to keep conversation going.'

'And did you?'

'Oh yes!' She laughed. 'We talked about everything from Sunday sermons, to keeping a congregation awake, and the baby-sitting of owls.'

'Baby-sitting owls?'

'His housekeeper found a nest of chicks. The mother owl had died, poisoned, he thinks, and Charles has been hand-rearing.'

'That's a bit out of the way, isn't it? Not exactly the sort of thing you expect to read about in a Parish Weekly.'

'Charles is an out of the way sort of person.'

'So it seems. He has a housekeeper. Not married then?'

'No, not married. His housekeeper comes in from the village every day, and a charwoman to clean and other things.'

'You seem to know a lot about the Reverend Charles.'

'I know what he has told me, and, of course, Dora, being his mother, talked of him all the time before we met.'

'Like him do you?'

'Very much.' Sally yawned and rising, gathered her bits and pieces together, a sure sign she wasn't about to say more.

'And does he like you?' Margret had to ask, for seeing the

pink in Sally's cheek, and sensing change ahead, she was both glad and sorry.

'I believe he does. He did say he'd like to visit soon, and if you could spare the time, to speak to you and Miss Clary.'

'That's all right then.' Margret took the tray to the kitchen. 'It's a bit sudden to speak about anything but at least he goes about things the right way.'

'He wouldn't know the wrong way. Oh, I forgot to tell you!' It was then climbing the stairs, her step weary but heart and soul as light as air, she remembered Assisi. 'Guess who I saw on my travels?'

Margret rolled her eyes. 'How would I know who you saw?'

'Try!' A girl again, eyes sparkling, Sally hung over the banister. 'Who do you most *not* love in the world? And I don't mean poor old Sykes. Who gets your dander up quicker than anyone and her mother a close second?'

'No!' Margret came to the bottom of the stairs. 'Not those two?'

'One of them.' Eager to talk now the topic of Charles is broached and a seed sewn, Sally sat on the top step. 'There she was, Serena Parisi, sitting on a bench outside the Basilica smiling at the world.'

'Did she see you?'

'Not only did she see me, she made a point of making herself known. I saw her earlier and rather than run into her - she always looking like the Queen of Sheba - I steered Charles in another direction.'

'Ha!' Margret laughed. 'Not too sure of him then were you?'

'No, nor thinking to be. You know the effect she has on men, Miss Clary's Uncle John a case in point, I couldn't manage it.'

'So what then?'

'Dora was inside. I went to join her thinking Serena was leaving, and I think she was until she saw me. Next I know she's in front of us, all smiles and lilac lace peering under a parasol. I introduced her to Charles. She asked questions: how long was I here? And how is our dear family at home.'

'"Dear family?" The cheeky madam!'

'That's what she said. I didn't say much. I didn't want to. I felt the way I always felt when she is near - a grey mouse wanting to hide.'

'And what was the reverend doing?'

'Not a lot.' Sally frowned. 'Though I do remember him taking my hand, a thing he hadn't done before. She talked of Cambridge, how she misses us all. I asked of her mother. I felt it only polite. She said - honestly, I nearly choked – that Isabella was in America with her new husband.'

'Never!'

'Yes! Straight out, her eyebrows lifted as if it was something wonderful. And do you know what, Maggie, I felt sorry for her.'

'What, Serena? You felt sorry for her?'

'I did. I don't know why but I got a terribly sad feeling in my chest looking at her, thinking of the people who wander the world like lost souls and never settle. It seemed wrong. So I said to her, "I wish your mother well and I wish you the same." It was then Charles took my hand.'

'Well I never! Married and in America and Serena not with her. You'd have thought she'd want to go. All those millionaires, she'd do well there. But then,' Margret sniffed, 'she's already got one in the professor's brother.'

'Or the professor.'

'Yes...or him.'

Though they smiled about the connection they didn't laugh. Sally was so happy the roof could've fallen and she none the wiser. On subject of that, thought Margret, the reverend coming courting is a bit sudden. But then, when love strikes like that, hot and fast, they've no time to duck.

Aged fifty going grey, and on the skinny side, he seems a decent enough fellow, and utterly gone on our Sally, his moustache twitching wanting to kiss her. Margret wonders how Mrs Bellamy feels about this. She is probably glad: a widow, on her own and not entirely well, she'll see Sally as company and a reliable daughter-in-law, and overall the best news for an aging son.

* * *

The leak is fixed and one less worry. It's only nine o' clock but Margret is ready for bed. It's no good going up at the moment; Jacob is in Sally's room, they talking together, and he asking the inevitable question - when will Clarissa be home. In point of fact she needs to come home. It's a shame about the professor's father, but Beeches is not right without her, and while talking about Parisis is mostly in jest, Margret is uneasy, wondering why Serena was alone in Italy and where was the professor's brother.

Miss Clary once mentioned Assisi and that the church there, the Basilica, was Serena's self-confessed hunting ground, she and Isabella going there when out of funds and looking for help. The question is - if Serena was there seeking a new benefactor, and not interested in going to America, where does she live now and what happened to their place in Paris?

Those words, 'our dear family,' gave Margret a fright, tapping into a thought that is always in the back of her mind that the Parisis are not done with Beeches. Those two did a lot of damage when they were here, and though they are gone, the damage remains.

Margret locked the back door, sliding the bolt, fulfilling nightly duties while continuing a conversation with the cat. 'I mean, look what Serena did to Miss Clary's uncle. It seems as if lying in wait like a bejewelled spider is her way of paying the bills. It makes you wonder, where did it start and why. Is Serena like this because of her mother or just naturally evil?'

When questioning her dislike of the pair, is she being fair, Margret only needs to watch Jacob when their names are mentioned. It's hard to put into words other than, seeing a cat a mouse will freeze, its little body quivering; as a bird, seeing a sparrow-hawk will hide until the danger is passed. That's Jacob whenever their names come up, and that is why Margret and Sally have learned to speak of them as 'those two,' rather than upset the lad.

* * *

There are letters on the mantle: one bearing the university emblem, the other from the museum. They arrived lunchtime. Margret can't stop looking at them. She sees official looking documents the way she sees a cablegram - the bearer of bad news. They might be about the museum roof, water coming in after all this rain, and builders brought in to deal with the problem.

She hopes it is not connected with a rumour brought to her attention by one of Miss Clary's friends. The young woman, a Miss Carpenter, was in tears. She said she hadn't been the friend she might've been, that the latest gossip was started by a member of the faculty, a man called Steed, who sent a letter to the Fitzwilliam demanding the removal of '*a female of low moral fibre whose presence brings shame to the Museum and all associated with it.*'

That was Friday. Then they were told there was no such letter; the rumour was a lie from start to finish. The Fitzwilliam is said to be amused: '*if they were to take notice of letters telling them to sack someone, then the museum would have a staff of one and he the sacker.*' They can laugh but Margret can't, no more can Jacob who heard about it. He knew that once planted an idea gives the 'no smoke without fire mentality' a cause to make trouble.

Miss Clary didn't know what was waiting in Belgium but went to keep the professor company. She doesn't know what's waiting here when she gets home, but as Miss Carpenter said, they will get through it as a family.

Weary and heart-sore, Margret switched off the light. On her way to bed she passed Sally's latest painting hanging at the top of the stairs, a picture of Beeches with roses round the door and the motto: 'No place like home.'

Yes, she thought. Let's hope Serena Parisi never feels the same.

CHAPTER EIGHTEEN

Notes

Hallerbos Forest, Belgium
Wednesday October 9th 1901

'Might I carry the basket for you, Mevrouw van Leiden?'

'Thank you, my dear. It is rather heavy.' Alice passed the basket. She smiled at her sons ahead, James carrying the funeral urn, and Kasper a sheaf of flowers. 'And you see we are reduced in numbers and battle-worn.'

Beyond the odd group of walkers, they were the only people in the forest, the van Leiden family having chosen today to travel to Halle scattering the ashes of the deceased among the trees.

'I understood your daughter has left for England.'

'Yes, this morning. As you are no doubt aware, Anneka, and her husband, Tom, are awaiting a happy event, and this their first child, they are naturally anxious.' Alice sighed. 'I wish I were closer to Colonel Phillips's estate so I might be more involved with my soon-to-be grandchild's life but, as with many grand-mothers in these modern times, I must love from the sidelines.'

'I'm sure Anneka misses you as you miss her.'

'We are very close. I know she dislikes the distance, but the shop in Knightsbridge does well with her at the helm.'

'Does she plan to continue with the shop after the baby is born?'

'She does. Tom has hired a nanny for Norfolk. There is also a lady called Phoebe who lives on the estate who Anneka very much likes. She has agreed to help mind the baby when needed.'

'They sound so very organised.'

'That is the lawyer in Tom. A good man, he is always ahead of the game, as Kasper would say, and meticulous in the care of his wife.'

'How nice.'

'*Ja*, nice, that good English word which though small can say so much.'

They walked on, Clarissa feeling reproved though not sure why, unless it is a tone in Alice's voice when speaking of the Phillips, they with greater share of territorial rights than she would like.

Poor lady, she is going through a stressful time. Karel van Leiden's body was discovered Tuesday, October 1st in a disused farmhouse close by the house, his dog, Pepper, alongside, both dead from gunshot wounds. Knowing there would be doubt regarding the manner of his death, Alice had help in Oleg Anders, the lawyer and prominent member of the De Beers Group.

Oleg suggested they bury the dog and nothing said; 'For unless there is proof of suicide, the coroner cannot rule out accident or murder.'

There was a note but that disappeared along with the dog. Most of the time the family converse in their own tongue, still Clarissa understands that Anneka, heavily pregnant and in floods of tears, begged her mother to have her father cremated rather than interred, 'so we all need suffer no more.'

When news came of the death, Anneka was in Leuven spending time with her mother before confinement. An 'open' verdict declared at the inquest, she suggested Hallerbos forest as resting place; 'It was father's favourite haunt, especially when the bluebells are in full bloom.'

The family withheld cremation until Kasper arrived. If there is an overriding emotion within the house it was of grief laced with anger, Clarissa woken one night by Anneka's husband condemning Karel van Leiden: 'While I am sorry for your mother and brothers I feel only disgust for your father.'

Tom Phillips was furious. 'His was a cowardly deed. He knew you were coming here. You'd think he might've waited until his first grandchild was brought to being before pulling any damned trigger.'

He was not alone in his anger. Kasper would not attend the crematorium. He saw it a dishonest way of doings things; either his father was given a decent ceremony or 'they should burn him like Guy Fawkes on top a bonfire wearing a foolish hat.'

* * *

Having dined that evening, Clarissa took a stroll in the garden, thinking of the day and that strangely distracted ceremony. No one wept, at least none she saw. There was a sense of needing to exhale, the family having held their breath for years. It was noticeable in Alice, her face slack and her hands hanging loose as if she had nothing to hold. Kasper was more at one with the trees than what took place on the ground; James was on his knees digging his dead father into the soil, squashed bluebells marking his pants.

She was on her second tour of the rose arbour when Kasper arrived. Elegant in a tuxedo, as with the rest of the family dressed for dinner, he loped down the path toward her. 'Might I join you?'

'Please do.'

Hands behind his back, he walked alongside, his long tread adjusting to a shorter stride. For a while he was silent and then he bent his head.

'Thank you for being with us. It can't be easy for you and no way to end your trip to Italy. So, *bedankt*, Clarissa, my mother is helped by you being here.'

'I am so very sorry about your father.'

'As are we all. We should've known it was a possibility and been on our guard. My father was a broken man, his talent as goldsmith and painter deserting him. I admit to finding his choice of leaving hard. Whatever my grief I hope I never have to end my life doing harm to those left behind.'

Unable to respond, she resumed the walk about the grounds. Bergen, their house in Leuven, has fine gardens. While close to the town it still maintains the air of the country. Three times they paced the garden, nothing said until by the lattice gate when Kasper's long fingers pursued a rose.

'I meant what I said.'

Not sure of his meaning she waited.

'I was wrong to do that, crash about the ballroom floor like some kind of fool. I apologise, and as I said in the note, will try to make up for it.'

Oh, the note! She hadn't read it. That night on the railway station news of the tragedy pushed other issues aside, she with her arms about James. The Harvard scholar fled, and a birthright remembered, he begged forgiveness for not being with his father when he died: '*Mijn arme vader! Vergeef me!*'

Since Kasper's note was still in the pocket of her travelling gown she thought best to say nothing. 'How is your shoulder?'

'I beg your pardon?'

'Your shoulder? I heard you say you were hurt during the Polo match.'

'Hurt?' He made a wry gesture with his mouth and stood seemingly debating the word. When he did speak it was to himself rather than her. 'Since I was challenged on a point of ungentlemanly conduct, I'd do better claiming my hurt as gained on the Field of Honour rather than a Polo game.'

'Gracious!' She frowned. 'That sounds positively barbaric. I thought Polo was an elegant sport. You have quite changed my point of view.'

His smile was grim. 'I wouldn't want to change your mind on anything yet having played Polo for years I must say that, while looking good through a camera lens, there is little elegance on the field, especially in Rome. Italian sportsmen play to win and Saturday a bloodbath.'

'I thought your team won.'

'We did and we won well, the Marchese on top form.'

'Oh, Giovanni played?'

'He wasn't meant to. He had a back injury and was supposed to rest. He changed his mind, and by far the best player was welcomed back.'

'He played well?'

'Ferocious, nothing stood between him and the target. Unfortunately toward the second half I was the target.'

'And your shoulder?'

'Nothing rest won't cure. It's the man that is maimed, and, not to put a fine point on it, will never be the same.' When he switched topics Clarissa was glad. There were words within his words she wasn't sure she liked.

'So you are to leave us tomorrow, Clarissa?'

'It would seem so. The plan is to catch an early train to Calais, and then the ferry to Dover, and on to Cambridge. Your brother did mention calling on his sister in Norfolk but I preferred to go home. My family will be anxious.'

'I hope it won't be as demanding as your journey from Florence.'

Florence? For a moment she was lost, the idea of being there, and all that she saw and heard, was overshadowed by events here in Belgium.

Kasper was watching her face. 'For me, events here in Leuven have removed what happened in Florence to such a distance as to feel unreal.'

'Yes, and me too! A veil dropped between then and now.'

'I'm sorry. One's tragedies should remain one's own. They ought not to impinge upon the life of another, especially one so dear to my brother.'

Impulsive, she turned. 'Mijnheer van Leiden Sterne...Kasper, I understand your concern but there is no need. This is your family's tragedy. No one can imagine your pain, as none can imagine the extent of your father's troubled mind to put you to such pain. We are friends you and I. Friends should be able to share pain. If not there is no friendship. Wouldn't you agree?'

Kasper gazed down at the lovely face and was silent, replacing what he might've said with Giovanni's anger: '*This is a gentle woman with a gentle mind. Do not treat her as others of your harem. Self-respect along with good manners, and she might see beyond the brash exterior to good intent, and not your customary need to haul another woman to your bed.*'

'It is what friendship should mean.' He sighed. 'I talk too

much. I suppose I wanted you to know, heathen or not, I would not have you harmed in anyway. I would have you adored, Clarissa Morgan, and in that make you a promise: if you should need me I am here.'

Later she looked at the note. '*In the joy of seeing you I behaved like a fool and for that I apologise. I would not hurt or offend you, and hope, in future, to prove my words.*' In respect of notes Clarissa has her own and is waiting for an opportunity to slip it into James's pocket. She won't re-read it, for if she did she might lose her nerve and throw it on the fire. A short note, three sentences to be precise, it says all that is in her heart; he may answer it as he may.

* * *

Alice van Leiden sat by the window. 'Thank you for bringing James home. While I love all my children he is the one to soothe my heart. We miss him here in Leuven and always have.' She looked up. 'Is he happy in England?'

Clarissa was careful in choice of words. 'The professor is respected by all at the museum as he is admired by the university students and faculty.'

A thin sort of recommendation, Alice had continued to stare, searching for reassurance. 'I want him to be happy. If unappreciated he will not stay. James is as his father. He needs to be loved and know he is.'

Such sadness in her gaze, Clarissa hugged her and was surprised by the sudden weight on her breast, as if in the moment - comforted by a stranger – Alice could rest. It has to be said the crematorium was a cheerless place; Alice standing by the coffin, rosary in her hand and a look of wanting an answer without knowing the question. A bell rang and the coffin disappeared behind a screen. Then, head up and shoulders back, she had an answer: she is Alice van Leiden Sterne, daughter, woman and mother - she will survive.

That morning, before they left, she pressed a jewel box into Clarissa's hand. 'This bracelet is of my husband's making. I saw it this morning and knew he would want you to have it. It is delicately fashioned and unique, as was all of his work. Take it in remembrance of a good man who simply lost his way.'

* * *

Kasper watched them leave from an upper window. Seen through a square of glass they are a married couple leaving a hotel, luggage loaded and smiles exchanged. She is lovely in a grey travelling gown. The red fox-fur bonnet sits well on her pale hair. He has seen the bonnet before and the cape. Both are gifts from Giovanni, the maid at the villa busy last week removing price tags.

Mouth sad and yet strong, Clarissa stands aside, a stranger and yet not.

He has known of her for some time. Serena Parisi would regularly hold a mirror to her soul, and this girl one day remembered as a sister, and the next reviled as 'Missish' and out-of-touch with the modern world.

This sort of commentary happened on a regular basis and if Clarissa was not under the magnifying glass then it was James. Serena was ever curious about him, as though time spent with him in Assisi made her greedy for more.

'Where is your brother?' she would ask. 'Can't you invite him to Paris for the weekend so we might get to know one another again?'

From another woman such curiosity would incite jealousy. But knowing how *this* woman's mind works - the need to possess and to possess entirely - Kasper would smile and shake away, preserving James's sanity with his own.

As for Clarissa Morgan, God knows who Kasper thought to meet that night in the Pitti Palace. He probably wasn't thinking at all, but following a pattern so known he only needed to a push a button in his head and the game is on.

She was a game, or the possibility, when seen through the snow a while back. She wasn't a person then, neither did she have an identity or a name. There was a face, and a thought maintained until chance might turn the thought into a deed, a kiss of those perfect lips, and the glistening possibility of being the first to conquer virgin territory.

It was all of that and at the same time nothing, for in those days Kasper had another game to play, and that of keeping a slippery fish from escaping his net.

In the first few weeks of meeting, Serena Parisi ruled as a queen over a part of his anatomy that was always hungry. She would smile: '*Well, here I am. What are you going to do to keep me?*' In the beginning, as with other women, he'd paid his dues: the De Beers' shares taking a hammering. There was also a diamond ring, a huge thing with an ugly stone that, if offered as a gift, most women would be insulted - not Serena. She wore it about her neck as a passport to other riches.

For a while there was mutual trade until, fearing old age, she upped her price. It didn't matter that he said he is not for marrying. She was deaf to that as she was deaf to the fact he did not love her, some coldness within her - or him - made the thought of life with her intolerable. They are parted now. She has the Paris apartment and several thousand guilders. He has a huge sense of relief. There is darkness in Serena that is felt rather than seen. The male member recognizes it and leaps up panting until one day it cowers recognizing the image of a spider feeding on her mate.

Now, standing at the window watching love retreat, he knows to look on one woman while defining the faults of another is wrong. James wouldn't do it. He might recognise the wrong but wouldn't use it to justify his feelings for another. But then justifying feelings is not what this is about; this is Kasper mourning the loss of his father, and of Giovanni, his friend.

Giovanni was angry the morning after the Masked Ball, and so mindful of his roots, he lapsed into the old Umbrian dialect leaving Kasper struggling to understand - not that he could mistake the intention. *'If you were not invited to my home I would ask you to leave. As, if you were not a friend of long-standing, I would challenge you to reclaim your honour – and mine - in a way suiting us both.'*

The man excels with a rapier. Unlike his Italian contemporaries, he was trained in the fast French manner of swordsmanship by Charles Anouilh, who before he was blinded, was said to be the finest *schermidore*.

In another life Kasper would've accepted the challenge, but this is the friend of his heart, and the woman is Clarissa. So he bowed his head admitting fault and a degree of reparation was made, but only a degree as the Polo game proved. It was a good game, fierce and fair, until the final whistle. A bell called foul and the fight was on again. Giovanni's pony, *Il Vento Selvaggio* - Wild Wind as he is named - made a sudden sharp turn, and then - two pairs of elegant nostrils flaring – it skidded to a halt a pin-prick away from Kasper's face.

That day he was left with a wrenched shoulder from pulling the reins, a puzzled glance from the rest of the team, and satisfaction in Giovanni's eyes, and the knowledge a friendship is over, and not for any clumsy wooing on his part, but because *il Marchese* had marked the woman for his bride.

It was in his face on the Polo field as it was on the Riverboat that Sunday, people seeing what others saw, the old-world assertion of *droit de seigneur*, and the need of a queen to rule by his side. How the House of Savoy, the Vallagra family, and the Church of Rome, will see this is another matter.

There is also the occasional lover, *and* the glamorous Mrs Ambrose Pennington and her Appaloosas: they will all have a say in this story.

* * *

Along with a bruised ego and a lifetime of guilt, Kasper brought another souvenir home from Florence - a straw hat found in a trash can at the Villa del Rosa, and Sophia, the lady's-maid, resentful.

'Miss Clareessa said I could keep it.'

Fifty lira changing hands, and the hat was his. A pretty thing, a red silk bandanna tied about the crown, it is in his room. That last night in the Villa, his heart aching for the loss of too beloved souls, he packed the hat along with his Polo kit, thinking it's all he'll ever own of the woman and so worth saving.

Rumi says lovers pitch their tents in non-existence and that even without wings they fly about the world. Kasper must find a place to pitch his tent, and wingless, offer love without hope of gain, for he is his father's son, and but for a change of heart he too might be found one day nursing a shotgun.

CHAPTER NINETEEN

Missing Piece

Greys Farm, Norfolk
Friday October 11ᵗʰ 1901

Gladys Phillips smiled. 'So nice seeing James again. Kind and well-mannered, if a little sad, he is one of my favourite people. I thought him sad last time he was here. Now he seems even more reserved. Dutch roots, I imagine, and Anneka sharing a similar vein. But those boots! Can you not have a word with him? Perhaps say he's tall enough without wearing those.'

Exasperated, Tom Phillips sighed. 'They are not worn to increase his height. As you say he's tall enough. The boots are necessity rather than an indulgence. They support an injured ankle.' Tom is anxious as well as annoyed, his mother in a forgetful way that started a year ago and is getting worse. 'If he is sad it is because his father has died and in a particularly difficult way to accept.'

'Oh, I am so sorry. I had forgotten.' Shocked, her smile collapsed and he left regretting his harsh tone.

'I thought best to remind you.'

'I am glad you did. I mustn't say anything like that again. I don't know how I could forget. It is so hard on the family, particularly Alice. But then, it is always the wife who picks up the pieces. Look at me and your father when he fell. It took months to get him right. Now poor Phoebe Sarson has similar grief.'

'I hardly think Father tripping over the dog compares to Professor Sarson's difficulties. They are a world apart. ' He took her arm. 'But anyway. Time's getting on, why don't you get a good night's rest?'

'It's only nine.' She looked at the clock. 'Isn't that a little early? '

'Not if you're tired. You were up early today. All the excitement, Anneka and I back home, you must be worn out.'

'I suppose. Very well, if you think it best. As you say, I was up early.' She collected her knitting bag and kissing his cheek made for the stairs.

'Would you like me to send Martha to you?'

'No, not, Martha. She was baking all day. You could call Phoebe. I'm always happy with Phoebe, and I'd like to know what the doctor said this morning, and whether we should rethink nursery arrangements.'

'No need. As said before we left, when we're here we'll have a professional nurse. Phoebe will only be involved if she wants to be and for that we shall have to see how her husband progresses. Anyway, go and get settled. I'll pop down to the cottage. James is there now catching up on things.'

'Oh that's good! A kind man, a gentleman, even with those boots, he will help, and the Professor needs kindness.' Mrs Phillips climbed the stairs. 'I fear the world has done him harm.'

'One could say that.' Tom went to the cabinet, poured a generous shot of whisky and drank it down. 'Then again one might say he brought it upon himself there being no fool like an old fool.'

* * *

'Oh Rumi! And an illuminated copy!' Pleased with the book, John Sarson tried sitting up but couldn't manage it. 'That is so kind.'

'I'm glad you like it. I saw it in Florence and thought of you. Now please, take it easy.' James eased him back on the pillows. 'When you're on your feet again we'll have time to rustle through this and others beside.'

'Yes, we shall rustle, won't we?'

'You betcha!' Glad of a reason to turn away, James put the book on one side. It is three, maybe four months, since they last talked. He wasn't well then, suffering a chill, his wife said. This is no chill. This is a very sick man.

'You say you've seen a doctor. What did he recommend?'

Peevish, John shrugged. 'What do they ever say these fellows, but a lot of quibbling and quoting of herbals but no real facts to go on.'

'What herbals?'

'Blood strengtheners and the like. Beyond that he suggested rest.'

'Did he perhaps refer a consultant?'

'He didn't refer anyone and didn't need to, for I know what ails me as does Phoebe.' John Sarson looked up, his face suddenly serene. 'As do you, dear James, and have done since you walked through that door. I am to meet my Maker and none but a priest needs consulting on that.'

James didn't argue. If this is where the man finds himself, a dire prognosis offered, and he coming to terms with it, then none must interfere.

Though forewarned, Phoebe saying her husband was long since diagnosed with angina but that his condition is worse, seeing him is a shock; where once was a roundish fellow with a merry smile, there is a pyjama-clad skeleton.

Dear Miss Phoebe, she was thin of face yet steadfast. 'He's always had a problem. He takes pills, sometimes they work, sometimes not. The physician talks of weak anterior walls that sooner or later will rupture. While that is medical science, and there's room for it in the world, I prefer my late sister's diagnosis. She said Charles and John were brothers under the skin, with eager souls, willing hands, and hearts too big for their bodies.

'Our doctor, who knows John well, came to see us. He said I should be prepared. I said I was prepared the day we met. The doctor has a sad marriage and so didn't understand. I explained. I said, when you love as John and I love, every day is a gift as every day is a loss, life moving toward the moment when the door will open and someone other than John is there with notice of death in his hand. It was always a case of borrowed time. Knowing that, we made much of what we had, no matter the issue. Though unable to have the children we wanted, and struggling to make ends meet, every day was good.'

Tears hung in her eyes, then a memory entered her mind - a harsh memory - and her tears were glaciers. 'That loan put his heart under stress. I could close my eyes and wish it away – he could not. No matter where he goes the debt follows and our niece constantly slighted. He knows, as do I, this has ruined her life, and that it will take a miracle to give her back a future. It is Clarissa's burden that is killing him, and if I'm not careful it will kill me.'

When James helped her to a chair she clung to him. 'He needs your help. Not money this time! I know you settled the loan and I bless you for it. This is different but will still place you in a difficult position.' She spoke of a letter wanting dictating. 'I don't know what's in it. I only know every day since he fell ill he has prayed for you to come and, in his words, save him.'

For a while she spoke of other issues. She said the Phillips were kind, particularly the Colonel, who has concerns of his own regarding his wife. Mrs Phillips suffers memory lapses and though only in her early sixties is generally vague. Phoebe said how things alter. A few short months ago they came to Norfolk seeking refuge, now she divides her time between sick rooms.

'In the morning I help John to sit by the window. Then I help Gladys be ready for the day. The Colonel wanted to hire a nurse but was afraid of alarming his wife. Nurse and friend, he said I am the best of both worlds.'

She smiled. 'Please don't think we made a mistake coming here. I love the cottage as does John. Thanks to you we're safe no matter what happens. And I do believe there are sweeter times around the corner along with sad. Mrs Tom Phillips, your sister, is expecting. In the last month or so she has looked to me for comfort. I was happy to give. We are told one door closes so another opens. I'm hoping that with the closing of this door I shall continue helping Gladys while enjoying the friendship of a young mother and her child.

* * *

It is late. James is packed ready to leave. He did think to stay with Anneka another night but with so much hanging in the air - another book about to be published and a meeting tomorrow at the museum - he resolved to catch the 10-40 train, which should bring him into Cambridge just after midnight.

The meeting at the Fitzwilliam is not his idea; he learned of it when telephoning the house. Archie said he was glad the professor was coming home, and not to worry the drapes are up and everything shipshape. He said he would make sure the boiler is hot and leave a covered supper-tray with smoked salmon, a light salad, and buttered shortbread to follow.

'By the way, sir, the museum roof has problems with leaks, and the top floor closed down while they deal with it. So I'll stay over tonight, if you don't mind. Then I can get you straight in the morning.' James didn't argue, though a bit of an old maid, Archie beats coming home to an empty house.

He carries the letters back to Cambridge, two in his left breast-pocket and one in his right. The two in the left are addressed to different people but carry the same message. They aren't long, the content, and what it means to convey, is as honest as the man who wept while dictating.

James had sat throughout with his head down wanting to shout: 'My dear fellow! I shall deliver these if that is what you want, but is there no other way? For no matter how they are received, and by whom, these letters will put you and Clarissa to more shame.'

Even now, and time passing, he mentally rewrites every line, changing this word, erasing that, trying to stick with the intention while lessening the impact that this blood and bones confession will have on the dusty minds of Cambridge University and the Fitzwilliam. No good can come of this, for in seeking to demonstrate innocence, John Sarson creates a thicker stew. He wants to set matters right, but being a gentleman he can't bring himself to name the woman at the heart of the scandal. This so muddles the issue that anyone reading the letter will come away convinced Clarissa is to blame for the whole shebang, and John Sarson the good uncle covering for her.

At one point James was so disturbed by what he was hearing he sprang to his feet. 'You should talk this over with your niece. Miss Morgan ought to know what you plan to do and say.'

The old man had wept. 'I can't involve her further, and in that I have another letter and ask you to give it to her when the time is right.'

'Surely you want to give this.' James had protested. 'I would bring her here to the cottage. Then you can say all you want in rightful manner.'

'No!' Apoplectic, John Sarson had started up in bed. 'She must not come here! You must not bring her. It would harm you as much as her, we seen as some vile *ménage e trois*. She must be kept as far away as possible.'

He'd pressed the envelope on James. 'I am asking much of you, but dearest boy, it is because I trust you above all men, and as such, ask this last thing - keep her away until I am gone, for I am ashamed to look on her. '

* * *

The letters are to be given on John Sarson's death. Such a task fills James with horror. If he had his way he'd roll down the window and cast the lot to the four winds. Instead, he waits, hoping a better way can be found.

The day might be remembered as one of passing on macabre messages. At Norfolk he said farewell to the Phillips and then drew Anneka aside, delivering a message neither is likely to forget. 'Don't speak now or afterward,' he'd said. 'Let me say what I must and leave it at that.'

He'd taken a deep breath, and then: 'Father came to me in my sleep last night. He wanted to tell Tom he was sorry. It wasn't planned, the need overcame him. He sends love and a special kiss for Poppy.'

She'd gaped, eyes wide and lips forming the words: 'A kiss for Poppy?'

'He said you'd know what that means.'

'I do.' A single tear had tracked down her cheek. 'It's what we planned to call the baby should we have a little girl.'

Now sitting on the train he wonders if he did right, that perhaps he should've waited, or just kept quiet. But then he thought, 'it happened. I saw him as clear as day. He was happy and wanted his daughter to be the same.'

Time getting on, he looked out of the window trying to gauge where they were, but it being night, his face gazed back, the window a blackened mirror, and he reprising a dream that came this morning on the stroke of four.

One, two, three... the clock on the mantle had chimed, and for a moment he had thought it was St Bene't's bells calling the faithful to Sunday service.

Bells did ring but it was those of the Left Bank he heard, and he aware of his father as a young man and how he must have looked when living in Paris.

In his twenties, yet instantly known, he sat at a bench, a leather apron about his waist and a jeweller's hammer in his hand. A beautiful day, hot sun poured through the window liquefying a line of rubies that lay on a strip of black velvet cloth - thirteen rubies of the finest quality.

One, two, three... James counted them. Then, seeming to

know they were meant to signify the Lord Jesus Christ and His Twelve Disciples, he asked if his father had received a new commission from the Russian Court.

His father had shaken his head. 'I fulfill an old commission. If you remember the Tsar was short-changed on the *Elena Suite*. He asked for four pieces. We sent three. This will be the missing fourth and my work completed.'

In this Father was referring to the spring of '96, when Tsar Nicholas the Second, the Emperor of all Russia, ordered a set of jewels for his wife to celebrate the coming of a new century. There were to be four elements, rubies the chosen jewel, and the ensemble to be known as the *Elena Suite* - Elena a Russian name for fire. Three pieces were ready: a necklace, bracelet, and earrings. Then they received a message: the Tsarina having been delivered of a girl, the three pieces were to be sent under the new name of Olga.

In the dream James asked what the fourth piece would it be. His father had shrugged. 'I haven't decided.' He'd pointed to a painting on an easel. 'What would you take from this work as your inspiration?'

Thinking it was the Lorenzo Monaco painting, James bent to look, but as is often the case with dreams, the image was blurred. Unwilling to make a choice, he left the bench and went to the window, gazing down at the street where a hurdy-gurdy played among brightly coloured awnings.

'*Sommes-nous à Paris, mon père?*'

'*Bien sur, mon fils!*' His father smiled, his face now reflected in the train window. 'Where else would I come but to where I was most happy.'

'Are you happy?'

'I was until you asked.' His father had paused. 'Now I'm not sure.'

'Do you have anything to say to Mother?'

'I don't think so.' The dream was changing, the sun behind a cloud, and yesterday's ghost merging with early morning rain. 'Anything meaningful was said years ago. You could say I am sorry - but then she knows that. '

'Do you want me to carry your love to her?'

'You can give her my love. I doubt she'd believe your dream. Your mother was raised a strict Catholic. Dead men visiting late at night won't go down well. It might make her even more anxious for my soul.'

'But didn't you come bringing messages of love? Isn't that what such meetings is about - love remembered and old hurts healed?'

'I didn't come to you, James. You came to me. But do give my love to Anneka and a kiss for Poppy, her little baby eager to be born. '

'What about Kes?'

'Other than to remember he is your brother, I wouldn't bother him. He has enough on his mind.'

'Is there nothing for me?' James remembers feeling so very unhappy that any word would've done. At that his father had reached out, ruffling James's hair as if he was a boy again. 'You have my love, *liefge*, and always will. '

CHAPTER TWENTY

Silence

Pine Cottage, Cherry Hinton, Cambridgeshire
Saturday October 12ᵗʰ 1901

'What do you mean they don't live in Brighton?'

Clarissa is taking coffee with Great Aunt Sheba. It is weeks since she visited. Bathsheba Falloway-Sarson is not a comfortable person to visit for along with being profoundly deaf she is argumentative, particularly on the subject of deafness, which she says she is not - people nowadays mumble.

Before her parents lost their money in the panic of 1825, Sheba, along with five sisters, lived in London, in Mayfair, a grand house with a sweeping staircase that, as she liked to point out, every evening was lit *'by the best quality beeswax candles so that it shimmered like a Fairy Castle.'*

Summer of '85, the Fairy Castle went the way of many others and Mayfair swapped for Wandsworth. Year-after-year more money was lost and with every change the rent harder to find. The five sisters, all beautiful, fled through marriage: two to the North and carpet manufacturers, two across the Atlantic to the New World, and the fifth to India by way of a tea-planter.

There was only Bathsheba -the youngest and most beautiful, as paintings on the walls do testify – but so hard to please she remains unmarried, living in a tiny cottage in Cherry Hinton close by St Andrew's Churchyard.

Today she is especially argumentative, holding forth on the

'weakness of modern education.' She says her Great Niece has no right to ask probing questions when the answers aren't hers to give. 'I can only tell what I know. They do *not* live in Brighton and never did. Your uncle is unwell but they are with friends, and in the care of a sponsor, and therefore safe.'

'I was told they had gone for the sea air.'

'Not by me you weren't.'

'Well someone said Brighton, and when asked, you didn't disagree.'

'It was not my part to disagree. I am simply the mediator. You write your letters. I pass them on but not to an address in Brighton.'

'Where then?'

'I can't say.'

'Why can't you?'

'I promised I wouldn't.'

Clarissa clenched her fist. 'Who did you promise?'

'I promised your uncle and by that, I suppose, their sponsor.'

'What is this sponsor? Who is he?'

'I understand he is a person of great good faith, who has more than once come to their aid.'

'Do l know him?'

'I don't know if you do. I only know you are required *not* to know your uncle's current whereabouts. He doesn't want you going there.'

'And Aunt Phoebe? What does she want?'

'At the time they moved, early March as I recall, they were told their presence was causing gossip, and the sooner they left Maxwell Road the better. I imagine the one thing then on Phoebe's mind was concern for her husband's heart, whether it could stand another beating.'

For a moment Clarissa couldn't speak, her mind fixed on the statement and the implications. 'And I visiting them would be the beating?'

'Not at all! They were anxious for you, child, and still are. It's why they want you to stay away. Your uncle will be in touch when he's better. '

'Why not now? They are my family. I am concerned for them. I brought gifts from Florence, poetry for Uncle John, and a lace collar for Aunt Phoebe.'

'And very nice too, as is my gift, the lace mittens, though perhaps I might've preferred a collar, mittens suited to an older person. But never mind. Leave them with me, I shall send them on along with your latest billet doux.'

'I beg your pardon, but I don't want to leave them anywhere but where my aunt and uncle are. Perhaps you'll give me the real address.'

'I can't do that. I gave my word, and a Falloway-Sarson's word is his bond.' She shook her head. 'You must abide by your uncle's wants, you being his reason for leaving, though I would've told him to stand your ground, and if necessary call a constable bringing that wretched woman to justice.'

'They would never do that. Lawyers and public name-calling, would surely damage my uncle's heart and not just his. Isabella Parisi was married to my father. It would be his name along with hers dragged through the dirt.'

'Sometimes a battle is necessary, and please do stop mumbling! I'm finding it hard to understand you. Young people are so inconsiderate, always sure of whom they are and everyone else old and foolish. Now where was I?'

'Proposing battle.'

'Yes and the more public the better. I tell you, if I'd had my way, and not learned of the change of address until *after* the event, I would've locked the door so they couldn't leave. For make no mistake, no matter where they go the lie remains, and unless something extraordinary occurs - a voice with the power to damn the lie - the word thief follows them to the grave.'

Clarissa was on her feet. 'Then I'm glad you didn't know, for that would have been a terrible thing to say and a terrible thing for them to hear. Fighting is not in their nature. They do not think fisticuffs and neither do I.'

She collected the post, the poetry book and lace mittens: the lace collar she left behind. 'There will be no waving of fists. People will get hurt.'

Great Aunt Sheba was offended. 'You may think remaining quiet saves the family honour but you are mistaken. That he should never borrow money is a fact, as you should've been in touch with your financial affairs.

'Mark my words,' she was scornful. 'The days are gone when a woman can rely on the men of her family to act with discretion. You need to be in control of your life and your purse, and none other. As I said earlier, a university education is only of use when joined with good common sense. Wake up, Clarissa Morgan, and secure your future, for while you linger defending your father's name, the damage continues, and another kind of name called, and yours top of the list.'

* * *

Needing to breathe, Clarissa took Hazlett out of the stable. He was as eager as she to get out and took to the saddle, trotting into the yard with high step and a light in his eyes. No side-saddle today, Clarissa wears the leather pants Papa bought with the blue gown in Rome. 'Two worlds in two garments, the old and the new,' he'd said. 'Wear both with pride.'

Old and worn yet soft as silk, today the pants strike the perfect note.

Hands cupped, Sykes hiked her aboard, and she led out.

Margret stood at the gate. 'Are you sure you know what you're doing?'

'No and I'm not sure I care.'

For a time all went well. They went to the Common, a familiar stamping ground. Then, all that green stretched before, Hazlett took off, nose forward, hooves flying and she flat to his neck screaming for the joy of it.

Good though it was they couldn't keep it up, Hazlett too old and she too aware of trees shedding their leaves and of a sudden turn toward winter.

This was Papa's favourite time. Mama loved the spring. Buds sprouting and daffodils pushing up through the ground, she saw it a beginning, whereas Papa saw autumn as preparation for sleep, and the weaving of blankets so the Earth might sleep through the winter. Life is hard now he is gone, and not because of current problems, it would be hard howsoever he left. It is the way he had of looking at misfortune through peaceful eyes, and while not ingenuous, he knowing the harsh side of life, his way of finding a way through.

He knew how to make a sad person glad as he knew how to address injustice. Mama was the place of earthly comforts, the binding of a wounded knee. Papa offered comfort that at times seemed as the froth on a summer dandelion yet was real and enduring. Margret and Sally Hankin more than fill a hole, but that one special person is gone and life left mourning.

The horse meandered along, stopping occasionally to crop grass. Clarissa mused on the letters at home that suggest a change of plans. She had hoped time spent in Italy would bring respite from the bank loan saga but listening to Great Aunt this morning all hope of that was dashed. Why does it linger - how boring life must be for those who feed on so small a tragedy. Is there nothing new to occupy their minds, some poor impoverished undergrad drowning in a debt, or another foolish old man caught with his fingers in the till.

No, the tale lingers, and she will never be free of it.

* * *

Turning toward home she became aware of a rider on the far side of the Common, a man on a grey horse coming out of a wooded area that backs onto the Newmarket Road. Now he pauses, seeing her as she saw him.

Directly she knew him; the van Leiden men have a way of being that sets them apart be they fifty or five thousand yards away. It came to her then that land on the far side of the Common may well belong to the Marchese, he saying he had stables close by.

Hazlett is quivering. He has seen the rider and horse, and curious, lifts his head sniffing the air. Aware of this she turned him away to a track on the right. As she turned so did the rider, his move copying hers, so that they walked alongside keeping the width of the Common between then.

As though amused Hazlett snickered, and delicately, but firmly, picked up pace, as did the pair across the way. So they proceeded until he accelerated again and both riders trotting. It was when they broke into a canter that Clarissa laughed, knowing across the way James was laughing.

So darn comical, the horses dictating the pace, and they, human puppets, obeying, she laughed, but sensing Hazlett wasn't done kept a firm grip.

It's as well she did, for with a sudden dog-like yelp he took off, and away again went all four, horses, woman and man.

Again it didn't last, how could it, they running out of flat ground and the grey more powerful. Indeed, though Hazlett was flat out, it's certain James drew on the reins, his horse able to outstrip the other.

* * *

The church soiree lulled her into a calm place. It was a small concert. Jacob played Chopin and then sang the chorus: '*God so loved the World*,' from John Stainer's *Crucifixion*, a new work that he and the curate study with Easter in mind. His audition is fixed for the afternoon of Wednesday 11th of December. It promises to be quite an occasion, since, having heard of his skill, people are contacting the university asking for tickets. It's not just local people; former scholars are making enquiries and Cambridge hotels under siege.

Jacob knows none of this, his tutor taking care not to bring such news to him. Margret was approached last week by the choirmaster: 'Make sure the boy gets plenty of rest. That way he will fulfil his potential.' According to her, the choirmaster 'will be the one with a breakdown if he's not careful.'

Unable to put it off any longer, Clarissa opened the letters to find a definite anti-climax, the Fitzwilliam Museum reporting a leaky roof and rainwater seeping through. '*In order to resolve the issue, the Board hereby suspends the workings of the Conservation area until further notice, instructing staff of that department to stay away until such time as they may resume work.*

While regretting this hiatus, the Museum assures every employee of their best interest; in proof of that please find documents enclosed showing payment of salary for this month, and the coming month of November. It is hoped that a new year will see the department up again and running.'

The letter from the university said much the same; that the Conservation Department was closed as from Monday 14th of October, and the Chancellor sending out a similar warning; 'any student seeking access to that department should contact the college tutor and not those of the museum.'

Clarissa felt the letters are about a leaky roof but also James. She doesn't know how he is involved but ties her anxiety to his mother: 'If unappreciated he will not stay. He needs to be loved and to know he is.'

Afraid to go to bed she lay on the sofa lest she dreams as she dreamt in Florence that Uncle Sarson will die and she publicly reviled as the cause.

A sweeter memory took over, that of the morning and Hazlett's mad dash. She recalled how she and James had stood, panting, surveying one another across the Common. And how, heart bursting, knowing she loved him, she'd stood up in the stirrups, fist balled and right arm pushed up into the air.

What she tried to convey in that moment can never be

known, she blinded by tears, and he across the way high in the saddle, his fist mirroring hers.

It was that way at the railway station in Montceau- les-Mines, he bowed with grief learning of his father's death, and she filled with love and admiration for who he is. That day she'd wanted to kiss his pain away but couldn't get beyond the wall of silence that is come between them. Such a high wall holding back a river of secrets is near impossible to climb, and yet, were he to lift an eyelash in need, she would tear it down with her own bare hands.

Intentions

Boardroom, Fitzwilliam Museum
Monday October 14ᵗʰ 1901

James stood gazing out on a rainy day, water streaming down the window, and his attention taken by a gargoyle on a roof opposite.

Old and timeworn, the building has stood for centuries. The gargoyle, in the shape of a toad's head soot-stained and covered with moss, has observed the building's growth and decay. The beast too has worn away; all the while fulfilling his purpose of disgorging rainwater in a particularly fulsome manner that, in James's opinion, mirrors his feelings about this meeting.

Arriving at eleven, he was met by a deputation of governors, most of whom he'd never seen before. He was conducted to the boardroom for coffee and brought up to date regarding the roof, the heavy rains of the last month revealing shortcomings in the construction, leaks appearing, and the upper floor needing to be closed down until the problem is resolved.

Conversation was of cricket and a game in Philadelphia where a US team took on England, and though losing by two games to one, earned plaudits for a 'jolly good effort.' Being an ardent fan, he joined in the discussion. The subject then turned to Italy and the tour of the Vatican Palace, and James's party having to catch an early train so they might have the Chapel to themselves.

There was laughter, and jokes about the need of strong

coffee and matchsticks to prop open eyelids at such an early hour - all very jolly.

It occurred to James that the agenda for today's meeting was prearranged and every member of the board given pointers: '*Smile and be polite for right now we need to keep the fellow happy.*' That's how it felt in that room and continued to feel until the focus turned toward the true purpose of the meeting - the mystery painting. It was then the room was transformed into a judge's chambers and the men about the table a jury.

The thought brought a smile to James's lips and a childhood game to mind in the concocting of collective nouns. Anneka was good at that as was Kasper. All three had their affiliations. An avid reader of Gothic novels, Anneka's choice had a darkly romantic turn, as in a Melancholia of Mills or a Beggary of Broken Hearts; Kasper took from his usual cock-eyed way of looking at things, returning from China once with a list which included an Idyll of Ibis, a Mystery of Mandarins and a Riot of Rickshaws (the latter from the way Coolies risked life and limb in pursuit of passengers).

As good as their offerings were James would dismiss all as simple alliteration, and when challenged to do better drew on early Saxon, and they never knowing if the words were true. Now observing these 'twelve men and true' sipping tepid coffee and munching stale biscuits, he pondered a collective noun for executioners.

He couldn't call them a 'murder' or a 'horde - crows having the former and rats the latter. If this was the Ottoman Empire they could be summed up as a Damnation of Executioners. So it was, his nerves raw from the trip to Florence and the death of his beloved father, James sought distraction while stoking an inner fire, frustrated seeing his life no longer his own.

The Lorenzo Monaco is why he was brought here today, the meeting aimed at securing information. While for security's sake only a few know the painting's whereabouts, sad to say most art collectors would care less, there being no great demand for art of the fourteenth century. In this the Marchese is a rare bird, and in James's opinion, one with longer sight and truer vision.

They spoke about this at the Uffizi; Giovanni saying the day will come when work of this period will fetch hundreds of thousands of dollars: 'Though that was the last thing on my mind when sending for you, James. My love of Lorenzo Monaco's work is instinctive as it is for roses. They live within me, keeping me alive in the way my heart keeps me alive.'

* * *

The feeling in the Fitzwilliam boardroom has little to do with Art and all to do with who gets to keep the painting. They want to know where his loyalties lie: are they with his current employer or will doubts expressed at the time of his appointment - a Yank in the Court of King Arthur – prove to be right.

As the rain eased, James was considering leaving when part of a whispered conversation caught his ear: 'the Professor and the Marchese are said to have been seen together at the Uffizi. Most likely he has already crossed over.'

He turned. 'Crossed over?'

Amid a sudden drop in conversation every man at the table swivelled and a fellow toting the coffee-pot the target.

'You, sir, with the coffee-pot? May I ask your name?'

'Gibbons, sir, Maurice Gibbons.'

'And what is your position here at the museum, Mr Gibbons.'

'I am an accountant. It is my job to verify the accuracy of any and all financial transactions appertaining to the Fitzwilliam Museum.'

'Not an easy job, I imagine.'

'No, sir, not by any means.'

'Well then, Mr Gibbons, would you mind expanding your comment as to what I might've crossed over and to where.'

'My dear Professor van Leiden Sterne.' The Vice-Chancellor was on his feet. 'I don't think there's any need for that.'

'Need for what?'

'Well...that! It seems to me you've caught one of those unfortunate off-the-cuff comments that don't mean anything other than they are lightly thought and thoughtlessly said. Isn't that right, Mr Gibbons? You were thinking out loud, offering a point of view that is yours and none else.'

'I suppose I was thinking out loud.' The accountant dug a deeper hole, but then, realising he was already cut adrift, he told it as it was. 'Although I was not offering a personal point of view so much as one overheard.'

While the Vice Chancellor chose to resume his seat, the accountant remained standing, his arm unsteady, and coffee in danger of spilling.

'Pardon me, sir.' He turned to James. 'No offence intended.'

'None took, Mr Gibbons. As you said, you were passing on an opinion. One question though - where do you think you might have heard this?'

'I heard it here this morning.' In for a penny as in for as pound, Maurice Gibbons put down the coffee-pot. '...and said more than once.'

'As I thought. ' James took his coat from the stand. 'I'll be on my way then, gentleman. Thanks for the coffee and cricket chat. I admit to being glad the Philadelphian boys put up a good show.'

'Oh but I say!' The Vice-Chancellor was up again. 'You're not thinking of leaving are you? There are things we need to discuss, anxieties we share as to the painting and who you might be leaning toward in housing the work. Not wishing to jump the gun, you know, merely anxious for the Museum.'

'I imagine you are anxious. Yours is a heavy responsibility since if I agree to attempt restoration it will be under the auspices of the Fitzwilliam. And, if my early judgement is right, then the work is a possible investment in the future of hundreds of thousands of dollars.'

'You think so?'

'Art is a fluctuating market but a good painting maintains value. As you say, not to jump ahead, for whoever worked the brush it is in need of attention. With that in mind I'll take my leave. I need to go to Boston. I was going to wait until the New Year, but a leaky roof providing an opportunity, I'll catch a night train to Ireland and be there and back soon as able.'

So it would've been left and not too much damage done, but as often happens, someone was keen to have the last word.

'Well really!' A thick-set fellow stood up, familiar as an off-spin bowler for museum. 'Surely you're not leaving like that. I mean, good Lord, taking offence over a couple of casual words hardly seems the thing.'

James paused. 'I don't know that I am taking offence over anything, but if I am, it won't be words that do it but the suggestion behind them.'

'Which is?'

'I don't know. Apparently they were said here this morning. In which case, if you were here you'd know more about the intention than I.'

The Vice-Chancellor sniffed. 'This does seem a fuss over nothing. You above all, Professor, should know how it is. Words can mean anything, for in the end it is down to the listening ear to make a judgement.'

'Absolutely! The listener hears what he is able to hear. Following that thought I am tempted to consider an abstraction of the French maxim, *honi soit qui mal y pense,* along the lines of *mal a celui qui l'entend* si: evil unto him who hears it so. Wouldn't you agree?'

The man was not amused. 'Whatever feels right for you, Professor van Leiden Sterne.'

James shrugged into his raincoat. 'I'll tell you what does *not* feel right when seeking the intention behind words. That is, that while I have been in Cambridge close on two years, and in that time, Vice-Chancellor, have come to regard you as colleague and friend, you have yet to know my right name.'

* * *

Thinking Maurice Gibbons likely to come under fire for this morning's activity, James left a card at the Porter's Lodge, suggesting the accountant give him a call at Croft House for 'when it comes to pecuniary matters, sound advice is always welcome.' It occurred to him that, while not seeking help - the family using the same Belgian firm of accountants for years - with a new book coming out, he could benefit from the advice of an honest man.

He was late getting back. Johnson had thought ahead, leaving a supper recognised as Mrs Hankins's excellent fish and broccoli pie which, warmed in the oven, and with a glass of chilled Muscadet, will taste delicious.

Hungry, he demolished most of the pie leaving the rest for a stray cat that comes to the door at night. Then a glass of wine at his elbow, he immersed his body in as much hot water as the boiler would allow.

He'd spent the afternoon investigating the roof. Staff in the Conservation wing had removed 'soft' items to better ground, which allowed him time to read the many messages of condolence on his desk. So many, he was moved, especially by the hand-painted cards, and once bathed, will add the cards to the latest scrap-book, plus Father's suicide note, and the letter Clarissa slipped into his pocket.

James wants to believe the suicide a sudden act, that Father took a shotgun to kill crows currently bothering the quail, an annual event, but then, at some indefinable moment, a switch was flipped and the gun a sudden friend. Mama had a difficult time in Leuven, churchmen and secular busybodies muttering over funeral rites. As ever money talks and nothing so loud as De Beers Shares, and suddenly a church and a bishop available in Antwerp which Mother rejected, settling for a pot of cinders in a bluebell wood.

If James were to close his eyes he would see rain falling and Clarissa holding a bright yellow umbrella over his mother's head. The last day in Leuven Mother said James could have the suicide note if he wanted.

He asked, 'have you read it?'

She said no.

He asked, 'what will you do if I give it back?'

She said she would destroy it.

As yet he hasn't read it. He may never read it, and until a choice is made it will go in the scrapbook along with other snatches of life.

* * *

There are many such scrapbooks in his apartment in the USA. He began the first on his twelfth birthday, swapping a home for a dormitory in the Boston-Latin school, and he wanting to take memories of home with him.

Kasper had laughed. 'Why look behind when you can look forward.'

In terms of looking forward, after his visit to China, Kasper was a changed man. His need to explore, the taking of dares, the treks to Alaska and other places, are the main thread of Kasper's life. Earth, Nature and her creatures are another, and infinitely more important to him than people.

The pets he's had over time, the horses and the dogs, and he unable to chastise, even when Burgundy, the Ridgeback, murdered his good boots.

After China, and the cruelty shown to animals he couldn't bear to think of meat never mind eat it. The first day home he rampaged through the house, the cook protesting, and he emptying the larder, including a haunch of venison thrown in the river, and grandfather's old valet, Tibo, fishing it out.

Eventually he calmed down, accepting that other people have a right to their choices, and that if he didn't give a little he'd lose a lot of friends.

Anneka was the first to take his part, and then Mama, they finding it easier giving way to growling looks than to argue. Father didn't mind at all; he stopped eating meat the day his mother served up their pet goat.

All but Grandfather surrendered, and he reduced to chewing alone in his room and hiding the bones. During the last visit home, though none felt like eating, fish was a choice. Clarissa hardly ate anything, but then, a stranger in a difficult position, a lack of appetite was hardly surprising.

That night at Montceau-les-Mine station, Uncle Henry's man standing by, James begged her to stay. 'Please don't go.' It was more of a knee-jerk reaction than anything. Given time he would've pulled himself together seeing her to be safely home. As it was he was saved the struggle, she holding him close, supporting him and his family through a bad time.

One other item will go into the scrapbook tonight. Johnson found a gentleman's calling card this morning while unpacking James's clothes.

He'd poked his head round the door. 'Did you want this, sir?'

James was about to say, 'that belongs to Miss Morgan. Perhaps you could pass it on,' but instead he nodded. 'Leave it on the side there.'

Elegant cream vellum, the insignia etched in gold, it is a stylish card as befits the man. It had fallen out of a book given to Clarissa. Tonight, along with the student's messages of condolence, James will affix three new items in the scrapbook: the letter Clarissa slipped into his pocket at Dover, which he hasn't read; Father's suicide note, again unread, and Giovanni's card.

If asked why Clarissa's letter remains unread he would say that while it remained unopened, past and future are in balance and open to change. The same can't be said of Father's last words, and yet they are his last words, and while they remain unknown, the twelve-year-old boy, the *liefge*, can have them say whatever he wants. The message on Giovanni's card is a Latin salutation: '*Cordis Mei Principessa:* Princess of my Heart.' A simple message, though for anyone with an understanding of the Classics, it can be seen for what it is - the opening address of a proposal of marriage.

To withhold the card is a mistake that may one day cost James dear. He seemed to know that but offered an excuse: if she didn't miss it before, she won't miss it now.

* * *

Midnight he woke from a nightmare where he was being crushed by a giant foot. Heart pounding, he felt ill and afraid, and hopes this is not how his father went through life, for if so, a shot-gun makes sense.

Grabbing a robe he went downstairs and following Miss Hanky's recipe for sleep, warmed some milk. Poor little beast, the cat was curled up by the back door. James scribbled a note asking Archie to feed it while he is away.

He was on his way back upstairs when he did a very foolish thing. Grabbing a towel, he went back down, and opening the door wrapped the cat in the towel, taking it back to bed where it lay purring.

It crossed his mind then to do the right thing, and give Giovanni's card to Clarissa. Then he thought to Hell with it! We can all play the Latin game, and - *desperatis temporibus vocant, pro desperatis mensuras* - desperate times require desperate measures. He hung on to the cat and slept.

Air and Angels

Book Three

Jacob

Air and Angels

Big Man

Beeches, Comberton
Monday October 28ᵗʰ 1901

Jacob was sick in the night, twice. The second time it was all water, and is what Miss Hanky calls 'nerves.' Now he sits up in bed gazing out of the window waiting for the morning. The clock on his table says *quarto e quattro*. He must be quiet now and wait for the rest of the house to stir.

All is silent but for the grandfather clock down in the hall; boom, boom, like the bells of the Assisi Basilica it tolls the hour. Jacob loves the clock. He gives it a hug every morning. If he misses anything of his old life it is the sound of Assisi's bells. There were so many: some heavy and stern warning of hellfire and damnation. Others, as with St Bene't's, were light and joyful, reminding the world of the presence of the Lord Jesus and the hope of Salvation.

After many months living here he knows every creaky floorboard and can usually get about without waking anyone, though Miss Hanky has the ears of a bat. The other night she caught him coming back from the stable after checking on Hazlett - the old horse being off his food.

'He's old,' says she. 'His bones ache. It's what makes him miserable.'

Miss Clareessa disagreed. 'He was born mizzy, like some other people I know.' She said that looking at Miss Hanky. They had been arguing over Miss Sally who wants to be married but her sister saying she must wait.

'They are in love,' says Miss Clareessa. 'Why should they wait?'

Miss Hanky said, 'because they don't know anything about one another.'

'They make each other happy. What else is there to know?'

'Everything! They need time or it'll be marry in haste repent at leisure.'

'Oh pooh! Be honest, Margret, you just don't want her to go.'

'Of course I don't want her to go!' Miss Hanky had cried. 'She is my sister. If she goes I won't know what to do with myself.'

'You'll be all right.' Clareessa hugged her. 'You'll have me. Think of all the wonderful trouble I'll bring. You'll be busy from now until Eternity.'

Jacob was in the laundry room when that was said. Shocked seeing Miss Hanky in tears, he was in tears. 'You will have Freya-Jasmine,' he says.

'Yes, I'll have Freya-Jasmine.'

'And me! You'll have me.'

'Oh yes.' She'd kissed him. 'I shall have you and be glad of it.'

So they stood, all three weeping and hugging. It was a sad moment and yet happy, sheets steaming on a rail and he with the people he loves most in the world. It only needed Freya-Jasmine to join the hug, and Mister James, and the dogs and Hazlett and Muffin, the cat, and life would've been complete.

Mister James is in America and may not be able to get back in time for the audition. Jacob is sad, for of all the people who should be there that day it should be his special father. Mister James stood surety for Jacob in Wards of Court. He doesn't know the details, only that when asked who would 'stand for the boy in a question of parental rights,' he got to his feet: 'I will.'

So although the choirmaster says he is a guardian and not a father, in Jacob's opinion he is exactly that and sent by the Kingdom of Heaven.

The other night when Jacob couldn't sleep for worrying about the audition, he crept downstairs. Miss Hanky was watering the plants. He told her Mister James was his new father. He said it was a secret. At first she was cross. She didn't like being told secrets; 'It means I have to be careful what I say.'

She said she had heard a whisper to the effect. 'Like the Kingdom of Heaven the professor knows a suffering child when he sees it.' Then she'd blown her nose, in tears again, saying she had probably misquoted the bible but that 'God wouldn't mind; it being true of the professor whether or not.'

Miss Hanky is funny. She makes Jacob laugh even when he shouldn't. The tailor came last week to measure for a new jacket for the audition, brown velvet and the latest cut. Mister Peacock measured Jacob and then suggested a 'silk foulard necktie in a similar brown colour shot with gold.'

He showed Miss Hanky the cloth. She said Mister Peacock ought not to be so silly -- Jacob didn't need shooting with anything: 'He is to play the pipe-organ in King's College Chapel, not a harp perched on a cloud like a fairy.'

Oh, Jacob did laugh, and so did she, and then both were sorry for Mister Peacock who went off in a huff. 'That's all right,' she says, 'he'll come round when I need a new bonnet for our Sally's wedding.'

Miss Sally is to marry the Reverend Charles Bellamy from Diss, in Norfolk. The wedding can't be until after Christmas.

The reverend said left to him, they would run away tomorrow to Gretna Green, but that he was up to his eyes in carol concerts and Nativity plays, and couldn't see a day free.

Reverend Bellamy is kind. He talks to Jacob - he does not stare. The only time he stares is at Miss Sally. Last time he was here he spoke of Italy and his mother's house in Como. Jacob has never been there and so could not say but was pleased to be spoken to so kindly. On leaving, the reverend said Jacob would like the organ in his church. 'It has a pretty sound. When Miss Sally and I are wed you shall stay with us and play to your heart's content.'

Such happiness! Jacob dare not dwell on the joy that is his life. It is too precious to carry and as the past has proved, easily broken. When Papa Samuel was alive there were lots of breakages. They took all manner of shapes: thieves in the night stealing what little they had, illness, where to sleep and what to eat: things got broken every day and every night, particularly when the wine was plentiful.

Papa Samuel used to say wine made him ill. Nuns at the Refugio called him a drunkard. At the time Jacob didn't believe them. Now, looking back, he sees wine did make his father ill and that because he drank too much.

He was a puzzle but then people puzzle Jacob - things promised as opposed to the things done. He sees now that his father made a lot of promises and while he kept as many as he could others fell by the wayside.

In Beeches Jacob has found the home he always wanted, smiles wrapped about him like a suit of armour, and everything promised is everything done, so that the fears of yesterday stay on the other side of the door.

A few days ago yesterday's fear knocked on a door again but not Beeches, at King's College, Cambridge via the Porter's Lodge.

* * *

Jacob used to share his bed with Amy and Tillie. A while back Hazlett got sick. Miss Clareessa called a vet, thereafter the dogs would sleep in the stable, a night-lamp shining and they curled up alongside Hazlett. Now Jacob has a new bed-mate, Muffin, the cat, who came with Mister James one morning: could she stay until he was back from Boston. 'I had thought to leave her with Archie Johnson but his mother is not well; he can't be there all the time.'

When Jacob enquired of the cat's name Mister James shrugged. 'I don't know that she has one. She is just a ragamuffin stray I foolishly let in.'

So the cat is Muffin, and though Jacob has not said (Amy and Tillie easily offended), it is better now at night, the cat is not so heavy nor does she pass so much gas. The following day the vet came. 'Muffin is being attended to,' said Miss Hanky. 'While we don't mind one cat we don't want an army.'

At first Jacob worried thinking the dogs would be unhappy. There was a brief spat one morning in the kitchen, Tillie eating from Muffin's dish. Now they ignore one another, they 'live and let live,' as Miss Sally says.

It was that 'live and let live' comment that, when said by another, brought yesterday's fears knocking on the door.

The other evening Jacob was late from organ practice. Thinking Christmas he had stayed behind looking at carols and would've gone straight home but had a message to collect some

247

music he wanted from the Porter's Lodge.

Jacob likes the porters. They make him laugh. The Head Porter, Mister Sissons - the Big Man - never laughs, nor does he crack jokes. He has black eyes and a big nose and bushy eyebrows and wears a bowler hat. When he was on duty Jacob would run by the Lodge, feeling guilty, as if he'd done a bad thing, like talk in the Library when he should whisper or kneel in the Chapel when he should stand. There is also the fact that if they do speak, the Big Man refers to Jacob as 'Mister,' and if not that then 'sir.'

At the first 'Mister' Jacob was so overwhelmed he begged to be called Jacob. The Big Man had shaken his head. 'I can't do that. I have heard you play. As far as I am concerned Mister Jacob is the least I can do.'

That day, though he didn't understand what was meant, Jacob stopped being afraid. He thinks of the Big Man as a friend. He trusts him, so that when he speaks Jacob listens. The other evening he wanted to know when the professor was coming back; Jacob said he had promised to be home for the audition. The Big Man had nodded. 'A man of his word, he'll be there.'

He then asked where the professor stayed in America. Jacob was thrilled, thinking this was the day when he might be of use. Excited, he'd pulled out the wallet Freya-Jasmine bought for his birthday, which has a card inside showing his address and a picture of the dogs, saying, '*Happy Birthday Jacob.*'

'This is where he is.' He'd offered the card. 'Mister James wrote it down before he left. He said I was not to lose it, that if I needed him I was to cable this or the one for Harvard where I was sure to find him.'

Then he had to try not to laugh for the Big Man wears *pince-nez* eye-glasses, tiny circles of glass with a velvet ribbon on the end of his nose. They were so small, and his face so big, they looked like an ink blot on the Moon. He wrote the address in a notebook saying, he was sending the professor a warning; how a 'certain person had been seen hanging about campus asking questions.'

Jacob was reminded of Sergeant Clarke who tours the campus at night. He asked if Mister Sissons had been a policeman. He'd sniffed, 'Not in this life, though we have had the odd entanglement.'

Card back in his wallet, Jacob was about to move on when the Big Man became another Miss Hanky. 'Now while it's not for me to pass advice onto anyone - a porter not an Agony Aunt - I want you to think about what I'm saying in terms of self-preservation. Apart from the odd silly-arse undergrad mucking about on Rag Day this is a safe place. While that's down to people like Sergeant Clarke, it is also down to the voice inside a person begging them to think twice before doing anythin' foolish.'

It was quite a speech that day and frightened Jacob, the Big Man leaning forward, his eyes darkly menacing. 'All right, live and let live, people have been known to change for the better. But from what I've heard you've been burned once and don't wanna be burned again. It's like being offered a lollipop that tasted bitter last time. You wouldn't care to lick it again no matter how sweet it looked or how pretty the hand offering it. You'd be on your guard. It would be foolish to accept anything from a hand that already wronged you, and you're not a foolish young gentleman, are you, Mister Jacob. So next time someone smiles and says nice things, make sure they are nice. And if uncertain, wait for the professor.'

* * *

That was three weeks ago. Now rather than pass the Porter's Lodge, he goes another way, for while the Big Man meant to be kind it made Jacob afraid, so that now when he's out walking he thinks he's being followed, even though he doesn't know who or what would follow him.

A while ago he was sick. Now he's cold and hugs Muffin, who yawns and sighs as if to say, 'you humans are such restless bedfellows.'

He thinks about the Big Man and what he meant but that's not why he is sick - it is the audition. He's desperate to do his best and make everybody proud. Miss Hanky says, 'not to worry. Once you're sitting at that organ you're nerves will vanish and you'll knock our socks off.'

If he knew for sure Mister James would be here he'd feel better. James makes Jacob feel safe. He is not alone in that feeling. When the man happens to visit Beeches, everyone runs out to meet him: dogs, people - the lot - as if God switched the sun on.

'Jacob!' A candle flickers.

'*Si*!' Eyes wide, he sits up in bed.

'Are you all right?'

'*Si*!'

'Not ill or anything?'

'No.'

'Only I thought I heard you on the landing.'

'I went to the bathroom but I am okay, truly I am.'

'*Okay?*' She smiled. He saw her smile through the door, her lips lifting, as he could smell her, the gentle scent of waking from sleep. 'I think we've all been spending too much time with Mister James. Next thing we'll be talking of sidewalks instead of paths and trash cans instead of dustbins.'

He sighed. '*Si.*'

'You are missing him?'

'*Si*, Miss Clareessa, I miss him.'

'*Si.*' She moved on, candle light easing away and he left alone with the morning. 'Me too.'

CHAPTER TWENTY-THREE

Saving Bacon

Beeches, Comberton
Friday November 1ˢᵗ 1901

'I would say so, Clarissa, a touch of colic.' Paul Brooke straightened. 'I take it you've sent for the vet.'

'Sykes took a message.'

'How long has Hazlett been like this?'

'All night and much of the evening before. He's not been right for a couple of weeks, but this last sickness is excessive.'

'You've been in here all night?'

'On and off.' She knelt in the straw, a felt glove on her hand massaging Hazlett's belly. 'He was in such pain I was afraid to leave him.'

'Is he any better now, do you think?'

'I don't know. He drank a little water and passed hideous amounts of gas, as you are no doubt aware.'

'Yes, the air does hang heavy.' Paul knelt down beside her. 'You look tired. Let me take over on that.'

'I'd love you to take over but I'm afraid he'll bite your hand.'

'Surely not! Come on, old fellow!' Paul touched him. With that Hazlett lurched sideway, teeth almost connecting with the good doctor's arm. 'Good Lord!' He started back. 'I see what you mean.'

'That was a warning! Trust me, if he really meant it his teeth would be hanging on your arm. He's a miserable old codger

252

who doesn't read the Good Book and therefore has no interest in letting the meek inherit the earth. He plans to be fractious from now until the Last Trumpet call.'

'And you are to be alone with the beast until the vet comes?'

'He won't bite me. I am the hand that feeds. As to help, I have Jacob who is as good as any veterinarian. The problem is that the Hazlett has been in the clover, which with all this rain is inclined to be mouldy. I did tell Sykes to keep an eye on that but might as well have talked to the air.'

'I would stay with you but am needed by my own sick and wounded.'

'I know and thank you for coming. I didn't know who else to call. It was a relief knowing you are not too far away.'

'I would be a lot closer, as you know.'

'I do know and I am grateful.'

He took up his hat. 'While your gratitude is neither my aim nor my desire, I am here for you. I would shoulder the world for you if you let me.'

He left and Clarissa was alone with a horse she should hate for being such a damned misery but who is *her* misery and has been these fifteen years and as with any precious possession, she wants to keep him a while longer.

There have been many changes in the last years and but for the rare exception, all unwelcome. Papa's death brought the greatest change. While grief will always be here she'd looked toward a time when any upheaval would be settled, but like a crack in the pavement, the ruinous bank loan continues underfoot, and she never knowing where it will lead.

Last Friday she went to the Fitzwilliam to retrieve certain belongings overlooked in the confusion of leaky roofs. She had thought to find the Conservation Department empty. What she found was undergrads in coveralls decorating the top floor. A girl recognised as of LMH, Oxford, said it was a protest meeting, a notice in the common-room saying anyone who wanted to save the American Magister's bacon should be here today.

Clarissa asked what she meant by 'saving his bacon.'

The girl had grimaced. 'It's more about saving ours, for if we lose him we lose a brilliant lecturer.' She said, it's rumoured the professor is either leaving the Fitzwilliam or has already left, 'poached' by the Uffizi. She said the students feel cheated, seeing him 'hot mustard and as well-versed within his subject as was Isaac Newton, and the faculty inept.'

There was much more of that, banners hanging out of the top windows, and the message, 'SOSH : Save Our Scorched Hearts,' declaring genuine admiration for James van Leiden as a teacher and lecturer combined with the usual student need to kick over the traces.

Stunned by the idea of him leaving Clarissa was ready to shed her coat to join the protest when Pamela Crichton, sister of Paula Crichton, seized the opportunity to make a point. Heads turning, she called across the room:

'Why are you asking questions Clarissa Morgan? When it comes to inside information regarding this man I thought you'd be the first line of communication. Travelling Italy together, hunting priceless paintings, sharing hopes and dreams, you must be friends by now as well as colleagues. But then in describing your association with the Divine James a woman of your experience deserves a more appropriate epithet: bosom buddies or pillow talk, I don't know and would hate to get it wrong.'

Naturally a whole host of witty replies to that nasty bit of work were on the tip of Clarissa's tongue, every one more cutting than the last; sadly they came after she left the museum and kept on coming til she wanted to scream.

That was last Friday. She hasn't been near the Museum since, or anywhere else for that matter, preferring to stay within the boundaries of home and safety. Yesterday, thinking she couldn't bear much more of it, she asked Margret's thoughts on moving.

Margret had frowned. 'Do you mean where our Sally's going?'

'Perhaps there …but anywhere really.'

'But would she want us there, Sally, I mean? She newlywed and relatives popping up all over the place, it doesn't seem fair.'

'We wouldn't live next door just in the area.'

'I don't know.' Margret was wary. 'If it were me I wouldn't like it. I'd feel spied upon. Anyway, what about your work at the museum? You wouldn't want to leave that, would you, not after all you did to get there?'

It was in that moment Clarissa recalled another conversation on where to work and why, and she walking in a garden where a man took a rose from a trellis – a tender bud, silky pink edged with gold. 'You must go where your heart takes you. Only then will you be able to explore new ideas.'

* * *

Clarissa suffered a headache all morning and went to lie down. She slept and woke to hooves clattering. There was a carriage in front of the house, grooms attending the horses, a lady's maid hovering, a fur wrap over her arm, and down in the yard a woman, presumably the owner of the fur wrap, leading Hazlett out of the stable.

Clarissa ran down into the yard. 'Take care! He bites.'

'Never you fear, honey,' the woman smiled, 'he won't bite me. I would larrup his ass if he did and he knows it.'

Whoever she was she continued to lead Hazlett about and he tossing his head and making a fearful din. As usual he was trying his favourite trick, lunging sideways threatening to bite, and she in costly furs wading through horse-muck as if it was the most natural thing to do.

Eventually he succumbed, standing still under the woman's hand.

'Bravo!' Clarissa clapped her hands. 'I've never seen him so undone.'

The woman smiled. 'Like so many guys I know he's a lot of sham in need of tough lovin'. Ain't that right, Gianni?'

Giovanni was by the stable door. He bowed. 'Good day, Clarissa. Allow me to present a good friend of mine, Senora Ambrose Pennington of Baton Rouge, Louisiana - Como's answer to Annie Oakley. The lady over there biting 'er finger-ends is Miss Molly Tate, Miss Pennington's ever-anxious maid.'

They didn't stay that first visit, Mrs Pennington wanting to change after her tussle with Hazlett. The Marchese apologised for not letting Clarissa know of their visit: 'It was a spur of the moment. Mrs Pennington and I were coming this way, and thought to drop by. We heard your horse was unwell, and Sadie being a mender of ills, thought to help.'

They brought such warmth Clarissa was sorry when they left. As for Sadie Ambrose Pennington - the opera singer known throughout the world for her glorious voice - she fell in love with the woman there and then, and though time would bring many changes that first love would remain.

A lady in her mid-forties, plumply curvaceous and beautiful, she exuded kindness as radiant as the pearls about her throat. She said she loved England. 'I have a little *peid de terre* 'down the road from Gianni where he allows me to play with his horses. I'd like to come more often but need the warmth of Italy for my old bones.'

Head bowed, recognising majesty, Jacob was wary of the Marchese. Sadie had him at her feet, they having already met and he remembering as she remembered him. 'I don't need an introduction to you, honey-child. I heard you play and saw then as I see now an angel reborn.'

That night before retiring, eyes like stars, he knocked on Clarissa's door. 'Miss Sadie is the great lady. Please may she come to my audition? Then I can play for her again as I played in Spoleto.'

It appears Sadie visited a church some years ago where Jacob was playing. 'She asked if I would play *Santa Lucia*, a Neapolitan folk song. She said it was for someone she loved. We were in a church. Such music not allowed. We sang together. I did not think the Lord Jesus would mind such a voice. She gave me a kiss and Sister Imogene a handful of lira. I was happy with my kiss.'

* * *

It was a day for visitors. As the Lombardi carriage pulled away so another traveller arrived - Kasper van Leiden Sterne. Clarissa was in the yard in shirt and leather breeches mucking out the stables; Jacob was at King's and Margret and Sally were at the market selling the last of the summer preserves.

Kasper set his horse loose in the paddock, and shucking his

jacket began shovelling stinking straw. 'Heaven's sake!' Clarissa was mortified. 'That will be the third pair of handmade boots I've seen ruined today.'

Golden eyes alight, he smiled. 'I wouldn't worry about that. What are boots for but for shovelling muck.' They worked side-by-side in silence. She wanted to ask if it was true about James leaving for the Uffizi, but recalling Italy, and tension between the brothers, remained silent.

Other that a brief chat with Margret when dropping off the cat, James left Cambridge without saying when he'd return. Jacob says he is in America on business and will be back for the audition. Since he seems to know more than anyone what's going on in that man's head she must trust it to be so.

Later, both smelling worse for wear, they sat in the yard drinking tea where Clarissa realised any romantic inclination she might have felt toward the man was gone. She smiled at the shift, thinking not so long ago she took a reviewer's glowing description of James's *Scorched Hearts,* 'a work of great beauty and intensity of passion,' and hung it as a laurel wreath about Kasper's neck.

So much for constancy! Three male visitors in one day, all personable men, a prize for any woman, and yet she's left staring at the wall.

Margret Hankin swears by the safety in a marriage. She says that until you have a ring on your finger a single woman is sport for all. Clarissa doesn't believe that, nonetheless, the loneliness felt this morning was harsh.

She has no yearning for Kasper and while she likes Paul Brooke she doesn't love him. He knows this and too modest to presume never pushes his suit.

Beyond respect and admiration she has no thought of Giovanni and yet earlier, aware of calm strength, she'd wanted to leap into his arms shouting: 'Whatever it is I agree to it as long as it is anywhere but here!'

The thought makes her smile, for what woman would dare to run at a man like that weeping on his jewelled waistcoat. Shocked by her audacity, his coat collar ruffled, he would surely retreat into his magnificence and his Villa with its roses and its treasure and the gilded butterflies – dead butterflies.

Scandal or not, she must stand her ground and not give way to gossip, for in the end that is all it is. If she has to sell the house and move then she will. And if in the end the situation becomes too much, and she still keeping her suitors, she can always toss a coin.

'Fickle brute!'

'I beg your pardon!'

'I'm sorry, Kasper. I was wool-gathering.'

'I say draw it mild, Miss Morgan!' Kasper stretched out his legs. 'Have you any idea how painful it is to be the recipient of that remark.'

She smiled. 'What? Fickle brute?'

'No, not that so much. That at least has intimations of excitement. The other comment, wool-gathering; there is no way that can be proposed without cutting a red-blooded man to the quick.'

'It wasn't meant to. It was just a phrase that came to mind.'

'There you go again! Just a phrase suggests more wool-gathering, and I, by all accounts, an increasingly humdrum companion.'

'Humdrum?' She threw back her beautiful head and laughed.

Kasper saw the long white line of her throat so tempting he had to smile, thinking if he'd vampiric tendencies, by now his teeth would be gainfully employed.

'How do you arrive at that word when thinking of yourself? I can't imagine you humdrum even as a child. I am fairly sure you were born dramatic.'

'Ha, dramatic!' He laughed and felt a little better, because until then, a compliment from those lips - if that is what it was - he might have been another wheelbarrow and, paradoxically, equally filled with shit.

While admitting a blow to his pride he must accept the woman just doesn't see him, whereas he sees her everywhere, though after today, the image will be decidedly rearranged. Over time he has found that the first sight of a person leaves an image that rarely changes. Until today and the mucking out of stables Clarissa Morgan was a girl in a blue ball-gown seen across the ballroom in the flash of white-gold hair, a sprite, lovely and as ephemeral as a summer day.

Today's image explodes the myth of sprite, causing his heart to pound and his loins to burn in the revelation of tight leather britches, a trickle of sweat between her breasts, and dung covered boots. Even now as she sits with one hand on her knee, the other by her throat, all he can see is a smear of dirt on her upper lip, and all he wants to do is lick the smear away.

Instead, knowing what he came to do, he took the hat from his satchel.

'I believe this is yours.'

'Ah yes.' Clearly not overjoyed to see it she frowned. But then, a well bred young lady she recovered her manners. 'Serena bought me that.'

'Serena bought you this hat?'

'It was a hot day and I was ill-equipped for the sun. It was kind of her.'

'Kind?' He was bitter. 'Serena is never kind. She doesn't understand the word.' Knowing how that sounded he held up his hand. 'Forgive me. I am wrong to speak so. What's done is done and no need for rancour. As to the hat, if it bothers you I'll take it with me when I go.'

'No need.' She took the hat. 'Freya-Jasmine will find a home for it. As for excuses you need none, Kasper. You are always welcome here.'

'The hat was an excuse.' He shrugged, tongue cumbersome, he stuck in the stiff Dutch manner and the English language a burden. 'I wanted to thank you for your support of my mother in Leuven and say how much we care for you and that we'd like to become better acquainted.'

'Thank you, Kasper.'

'Also, I would like a chance to meet with the boy organist.'

'You want to speak with Jacob?'

'*Jah*! I need to talk with him, to explain.'

'Explain what?'

He spread his hands. 'I know something of him and from the onset must declare my part in his history as less than honourable. I know he is Samuel Chase's son and that for a time he was in the care of the Parisis. I know too he was a sickly lad, suffering from heart disease and somewhat lacking in wits.

She frowned. 'Lacking in wits?'

'Excuse me.' He was tying himself in knots. 'I do not mean to offend. If I say the wrong thing it is because much of what I know I was told and did not seek to question. I was told he was an imbecile with heart complaint and confined to a sanatorium in Spoleto. Again, I did not choose to question. Later I saw for myself it was no sanatorium but a madhouse with bars at the window.

'I have no excuse! There is none. I was due to go on an expedition at the time and couldn't be bothered with anything else, certainly not another's child.' He said a lot more, words slam-bang, shoved together, more and more so he might get them out of his head and into the open. Eventually, when there was nothing left to say, he ground to a halt, strangely exhausted.

'To cut a long and feeble story short, I did what I always do, I put it in the back of my mind as not my problem, and that's where Jacob stayed, buzzing like a confounded wasp, until the day I heard he'd found his way here.'

All was silence; even the day was silent, the odd leaf fluttering to the ground. She kept silence throughout, never once seeking to halt the flood of words. It came to Kasper with a greater blow to pride that she wasn't surprised by what she heard. She had a source of information in the boy himself, plus there was firsthand knowledge of the Parisi women and how they lived.

Then he was doubly ashamed seeing his affair with Serena through her eyes - the grubby manoeuvring and clandestine meetings at Giovanni's farm.

Every aspect of that association reeks of sex in a soiled bed.

Of course she knew of the affair as the housekeeper knew, people seen by him as faces at the window and mocked by Serena as nobodies. They all knew, and while the affair sullied their doorstep, beyond a man on a horse they knew nothing of the one at the heart of it: KLS - the bad dog.

For the first time he understood why a good friend was

moved to challenge him to a duel; Giovanni knew of the Parisi affair; his Lightfoot Farm a home-from-home when Kasper was in Cambridge.

All this and more is known to the woman who sits so silent, and was known when he made his grand entrance in the Pitti Palace, arrogant hand thrust out and nonsense on his lips. What did he hope she would see that evening in Florence, the gallant voyager, intrepid explorer of deserts and other wild places? More likely she saw a buffoon and a cad.

'I'm sorry.' He picked up his satchel. 'I don't know what I was thinking coming here today. I suppose I wanted there to be no secrets between us so I might come again known and clean.'

Eyes soft, she was on her feet.

'I'd like to come back, if I may, to talk with Jacob and to apologise. I let him, and myself, down.' He took her hand, pressing his lips to her knuckles, horse-dung and all. 'God keep you Clarissa.'

CHAPTER TWENTY-FOUR

Lightfoot

Lightfoot Farm, Bressingham
Tuesday November 5th 1901

Somewhat embarrassed by the disarray, Giovanni whacked a cushion in place so Clarissa might sit. 'As you see, there is work to be done here.'

'Oh no, you mustn't! There is nothing to be done. I love this place! It is so...so...' She spread her arms searching for the right word.

He offered an idea. '*Il mucchio di rifuti*?'

'What does that mean?'

Jacob sniggered.

'What?' She had to smile because they were smiling. 'Come on, tell me.'

'Is tip, Clareessa,' said Jacob, stuffing his fingers in his mouth.

'Tip?'

'Si! Where we throw rubbish. My bedroom...Miss Hanky say.'

She laughed. 'No, not a bit of it. This is comfortable and easy and warm. I could be happy here among the horses and the roses as I could be happy in Sadie's house. These are blissful places! Good heavens! If you see this as untidy, I hate to think how you see Beeches.'

'*Va bene*! I am glad you like it,' said Giovanni.

Though a trifle untidy, people from the Bressingham Theatre

Club dining here last night, he doesn't really think of the farm as a muck heap. If he could leave all else behind and rest here for a few weeks of the year, the in-fighting, and the general madness of his life - plus the loneliness - he would be a happier man, not to say a man with a better shot at a longer life.

'Come!' He leaned down, pulling her to her feet so she might see the rest of his cherished *vita inglese* and in this perhaps see more of the man.

Even as late as this in the year, the bitter cold and sudden snow, life here is a relief. Very few of his business associates appreciate the allure of a ramshackle house on the Cambridgeshire Border. They see such vacations as an extension of his friendship with Sadie and an escape route from his life as *Il Maestro*.

Giovanni couldn't live here in any permanent way: while Como has his heart, Firenzi has his soul and always will. Lightfoot Farm is not a commercial enterprise, it is a getaway where he and close friends can relax - a 'rich man's bauble,' as Charles Anouilh says. Still, the place is important, especially now with his hope of Clarissa, and it is only a hope, fragile and delicate as the Venetian goblets spun every day in his factory on Murano Island.

What can there be but hope, for even accounting for the difference in faith and in age - she twenty-three and he two years from forty - there is the greater barrier to cross - her heart lies elsewhere.

He doesn't know the nature of their difficulties but sees how Clarissa and James trip over one another like blind children only able to move at the invitation of the other. Immense passion baffled by a rare innocence, they are a bewildering combination, and self-defeating, in that such a heat can grow suddenly cold, binding muscle to bone.

Giovanni once knew a love like that, though even now he couldn't say who owned the innocence and who the passion. It was a hedonistic love; savage with sudden high and low points, he lived always on the edge of a precipice, constantly shifting to maintain his footing.

Allora, non più di questo! No more of that! Over time he has schooled his mind to look forward rather than back, for to slip into memory is to see a woman in Purdah, and a man with two faces: one for the world and another for himself. At such times the only hope is for silence and a precarious tread about the Villa del Rosa, an empty mausoleum filled with living noise.

Sadie knows about that noise, but then, Sadie knows everything.

He turned to Clarissa. 'You like Mrs Ambrose Pennington?'

'Oh yes. She is so warm and friendly. Freya-Jasmine adores her, as does Jacob, but then I doubt anyone could dislike her.'

'Some would differ.'

'I thought her perfectly charming. But then everyone has a point of view, and often as far from the truth as it can be, as I have found to my shame.'

'*Cos'è quello* shame? What is this I am hearing?'

'I don't know.' Her face was suddenly pale. 'What is it you hear?'

They were in the long breakfast room. Facing south, it is warm even in the middle of winter and furnished *a la* Sadie, filled with rich colours, heavy drapery, and long sofas with fat cushions and soft-shaded lamps.

A good room offering comfort, he has sat here many a time listening to the early morning bird-life, the Dawn Chorus, so romantically named, and he waiting for the sun to rise so he might be free of the night.

Jacob is in the garden with Charles and the little girl Freya-Jasmine. They are erecting a huge rococo establishment from this first pristine fall of snow. Sadie and Miss Sally lend a hand. There is time to talk

It is a good place to talk, even to one's ghosts.

* * *

He sat beside her. 'Why speak of shame?'

With no other choice Clarissa told of the bank loan, describing events of that day in February in the cottage on Maxwell Road: Aunt Phoebe hovering, face stricken, and Uncle John's hands shaking. 'I have brought you here, my dear niece,' he'd said, 'for I have some rather bad news to tell.'

At the time, knowing her uncle wasn't a well man, she had steeled her nerve. But never in a million years did she imagine what he would say.

Puzzled, she'd waited, until, he hesitating, Aunt Phoebe spoke for him.

'I'm afraid your uncle gave away a great deal of your money from the West Street account. He says two-hundred-and-fifty but when I spoke to the bank I learned with bank charges it was close to three hundred.'

'Three hundred pounds, Giovanni. Every penny I possessed.'

'Why did your uncle do such a thing?'

'I'm not sure I can say. I know who you are and that you'd never disclose a secret, but still I feel bad telling you, as if I am letting my uncle down.'

'*Ehi allora*! Tell me what you can. Leave the rest behind. Trust me.' He shrugged. 'I am a grown man able to fill in the spaces.'

'Oh, very well then.' Words spilled out – the faster the better to be rid of them. 'My uncle was deceived into loaning money to a woman who earlier approached him for smaller loans which she repaid the following day. This time when she came she asked for two-hundred-and-fifty pounds, saying she was getting married and needed money for a trousseau.'

Giovanni nodded. 'Such a gambit is known to thieves. They feed the fish tasty bait before hooking the line. Did he not wonder at the amount?'

'He is a gentle creature as is my aunt. They wouldn't know the ways of a thief. Being a truthful man, my uncle believed what he was told, especially when the teller was beautiful and knew the way of men and dreamers.'

'Beauty dulls the senses.'

'It would seem so, though she said what my uncle knew to be true: she'd benefitted from a Will that more than covered the amount. Oh, that two-hundred-and-fifty!' She clapped her hands over her ears. 'I hear that number even in my prayers. I shall never be free of it and the pain it caused.'

'What pain?' He took her hand. 'I cannot think the want of money hurt you. You 'ave friends. The loan would've been redeemed by a friend and speedily. Something else came - something unkind.'

'Yes unkind. It involved one bank but two accounts, my uncle's account and mine with money left to me by my mother. Uncle Sarson was trustee to that account. Not only did he draw from it, he took out a loan of a hundred-and-fifty pounds from his own account. The day after he told me I went to the bank begging for time. Even knowing I'd be refused the manager let me beg. He said my uncle was tricked by a woman claiming marriage to a wealthy man. He asked if *I* was the woman. I said no but he didn't believe me.'

'It would seem the woman in question saw your unfortunate uncle not so much an old fool as a romantic dreamer.'

'I was the fool. In that moment, the bank manager frowning, and my uncle in danger of going to prison, I felt I needed to defend him. I can't recall exactly what I did say but I surely didn't help myself. I was the romantic dreamer trying to protect the family. I soon learned I'd protected everyone but me.'

'What happened then?'

'What would happen but gossip was at work and I the chosen subject. Hah!' She tried to laugh. 'I had the pleasure of hearing about it firsthand and the story so twisted I thought they were talking of some other poor soul. But it was me they laughed at, no one else, and me they slandered, saying I brought shame to the university and should be sacked from the Museum.'

'Overnight my life was in tatters. I was someone to avoid, or to spit at when passing in the corridor, or to send obscene notes through the Fitzwilliam mail. It's my own fault.' She sighed. 'I should've let things take their course. The innocent don't need shielding. They are already known.'

Giovanni stood gazing out of the window. She joined him, slipping her arm through his. 'I should've named names. Instead, I went to ground like a rabbit. I stayed away from art classes. I sang no more songs. I took no walks along the river. I rode a bicycle to the museum, quickly there and quicker back. I hid, and this I do regret for it changed nothing. The horror continues.

Everything I have worked for is falling away, and I am unable to do anything about it.'

'Oh look!' Dashing a tear away, she rubbed a space in the misted window: Jacob and Freya- Jasmine lying in the snow, waving their arms up and down, creating wings. 'They are making angel wings.'

'Si, angel wings.' Giovanni took her hands in his: 'We shall leave this now. Later, when you feel able to talk to me as one who loves you with all his heart, and who would die rather than see you unhappy, we shall peer further into the darkness. 'For now.' He brushed a curl back from her forehead. 'One question I must ask if only to save you more pain. Is the debt repaid and by whom.'

* * *

The light fading, they left soon after in the old barouche with the covers drawn and India rubber hot water bottles to hug and to warm the feet.

He watched them go, thinking tomorrow she'll regret her moment of candour, and he losing ground rather than gaining. He would have her stay but she is uncomfortable thinking he knows more about her than she cared anyone to know. Some of her story, though new from her lips, is known to him from a tale told to Sadie; how a client took items from a milliner's shop in Cambridge without paying, and that a Miss Clarissa Morgan honoured the debt.

Being Sadie, and the creditor said to be Italian, further information was extracted. A familiar name was given, that of Serena Parisi.

Kasper says their relationship is over. 'I promise you, she and I are done.'

Giovanni neither wants nor needs such promises. Though hot-headed, Kasper van Leiden Sterne is a man worth knowing. It was he who saved the life of the Earl of Dedham's youngest son. In the spring of '94 they attempted the southeast ridge of the Matterhorn. Having achieved their goal they were on their way down when they heard young Richard Fosbury was in trouble.

A guide returned to the peak but needed help from supporting climbers. Kasper volunteered as did one other. They located Dick Fosbury and got him down. Kes was hailed a hero as was Giovanni, the second climber.

While he loves Kasper as a brother he fears for his impulsive ways. There is no obvious sophistry in the man. It is as Charles Anouilh says, 'with Kasper, what you see is what you get, and what you get is authentic.'

His behaviour at the Masked Ball is an example; he was overcome by feelings for Clarissa, and unlike his brother unable to hide it. It is that kind of brute honesty that saw an end to his relationship with Serena Parisi.

Now there is the business of the old man's folly. Though Clarissa wouldn't give a name, it appears the debt is redeemed. First immediate thought was of James van Leiden, for given the same situation - and he honour bound – it is exactly what Giovanni would've done.

* * *

The carriage rolled on. Warmed by hot water bottles, and made sleepy by the plod of hooves, they slept part of the way home,

Sally dreaming of the Reverend Charles, and the rectory in Diss soon to be her home, and Freya-Jasmine smiling in her sleep - her arm about Jacob; she being five years his junior, yet in terms of worldly wisdom light-years older.

Clarissa begins to see that while he is a calming force, Giovanni di Lombardi is challenging. Two minutes in his company and doors fly open to her soul. Before today she had no particular feeling for the man. Now seeing him in different surroundings - the ease of Lightfoot Farm - she is aware of him as a man, his handsome face and physical prowess, the strength of his body in the breadth of his shoulders, and how they taper down into narrow hips – an athlete's hips – 'A fencer,' says Sadie, 'and a truly beautiful man.'

After lunch Jacob spent time alone with Giovanni. Clarissa hopes he was able to talk of the past. While he does talk to Freya-Jasmine, he is loath to speak of his time in the lunatic asylum. Any communication comes via nightmares, and he discovered kneeling up in bed, his eyes wide, and staring at some terrible image. His one friend in those years was his music; whatever happens in the future that friendship must be allowed to continue.

Today Jacob was happy grooming a young foal. At first he was afraid of their host. Then he began to relax and to giggle and to flirt with the maid, seeming to know that nothing, however bad, can get by *il Marchese*.

Now he sleeps safe in dreams, his young face as beautiful and as pure as in El Greco's painting of the martyred Saint Sebastian: glory shining through pain, and only the blood-tipped arrows missing.

CHAPTER TWENTY-FIVE

Blue Mood

Connaught Hotel, Dublin, Ireland
Sunday December 8th 1901

'It's okay! You go on ahead.'

The busboy tried sheltering James from the rain, but the lad, five-foot nothing, and the umbrella bigger than him, it was a lost cause; not that it mattered, after seven days of raging winds and mountainous seas - plus a brief but withering case of *mal-de-Mer* - what are a few hailstones.

Once inside the revolving doors the wind ceased and James drawn into a familiar oasis of faded Axminster carpet and beeswax polish.

'Hello there, Professor.' The desk clerk smiled. 'I imagine you're glad to have the ground under your feet again.'

'Darn right.' He shed his mackinaw. 'They were pretty violent seas.'

'So I heard.' The clerk passed the keys. 'Your usual suite is ready, and the rest of your luggage under lock and key for collection tomorrow.'

'Good. Were you able to get me a ride on a ferry in the morning?'

'Well, we did get something, but the weather being the way it is, ferries grounded and all, a mail boat was the best we could do.'

'As bad as that?'

''Fraid so. If you could wait a day or two it's said to be easing off.'

'I need to be in Cambridge at least by Tuesday.' James bent to pick up his satchel. 'So I guess a mail boat is as good a way as any.'

'Very well, sir. Anything else you'll be needing?'

'Maybe a meal in my room later, fish if you have it, and if Tom Mullins is not too busy, you could give him a buzz for me.'

* * *

While hardly home-from-home, Dublin is a good place to land. Needing to move on early in the morning he'd stuck with the bare overnight essentials and this being a sixth visit was easily settled. Kasper finds James's choice of the Connaught Hotel inexplicable. 'You're usually so confounded finicky about everything, why stay here when there's better in the city.'

There might be better but there won't be anything as comfortable. An old manor house with lofty ceilings, there is space to move about, the beds a decent length and the tub the same. While the trimmings are faded the rooms are clean, bed linen fresh and lavender scented. James knows the hotel and the hotel knows James. The chair by the bed is known as is the casement windows leading onto a veranda where early morning sea-breezes flow; the whole place is as warm and easy at the end of the day as an old jersey.

If ever a man needed warm and easy it is in the wake of that crossing. It was a rough passage and while no one seriously considered crossing his fingers, James suspects this last week saw more than one passenger aboard RMS Campania renew old acquaintance with his Maker.

It wasn't only the gigantic seas of the day, it was the shrouding fog that every night held the ship in silence as if they were removed back to a time when a man at the wheel relied on the stars to get him through.

Every day felt like a lesson in survival where, between trips to the john - his body under siege - ideas for another book glimmered: a mythology of Sea Monsters as in Charybdis, the snake-headed gorgon that ruled the turbulent waters of the Straits of Messina bringing many a sailor to his doom.

While that book is still a hazy thought the good news during the trip to Boston was the launching of *The Fire Within:* his account of the Elena Suite. It had been well-received, and, according to the publisher, sales through the roof helped by an article in the New York Times: '...*a once in a lifetime opportunity to see inside the Winter Palace to the sumptuous beauty that is the Romanov Jewel Collection.*' The headline had James wondering how St Petersburg would react. The publicity fellow at Harpers said everything is good: 'If it makes Ivan look more terrible than the next man it's okay with the Russians.'

Aware of the blues that comes with the conclusion of any long-term project, James left them to it. He has a new project in mind, and while in Belgium, visited a jewel merchant where he bought fourteen of the finest natural rubies. The idea of fashioning a rosary came to him in Florence in the first glimpse of blood red beads looped about the Recording Angel's wrist. It being years since he visited the family workroom, it might've stayed an idea; instead, nurtured by a dream, and a dead man's need to complete what was left unfinished, the idea took root.

As yet there is no flowering. A dark mass hangs over James sapping strength and mental clarity. It arrived the day of the board-meeting at the Fitz, and apart from the odd glimmer of yellow, a blue-mood holds him in thrall.

The success of *Fire Within* brought joy, as did the sight of land this morning. A cable delivered on the evening of the 25th November brought a vivid flash of orange. Colours dominate his thoughts: blood red jewels, grey fog covering the sea, a blue mood gripping his brain - any happy moments is seen as yellow.

Monday evening brought anger in a searingly hot orange. James was dining with the Proctor at the Harvard Club. They were talking baseball with the odd bit of university business tossed in. They were settling to coffee and brandy when a waiter asked if James would accept a cable. The cable was signed JA Sissons and read like a line from a spy novel: *Jezebel asking questions of boy organist. Wise Monkey senses challenge to birthright.* At first James could figure neither the message nor the sender. Then he got it: Sissons is Head Porter at Cambridge - Jezebel is Serena Parisi.

* * *

The cable put an end to the dinner party and Boston, he knowing what was meant by challenging birthright. Joseph Arthur Sissons has past dealings with the law. He said he was born in the East End of London, a tough area for any kid, especially one whose father spent more time in prison than out.

He said his father and uncle were petty thieves, taking whatever wasn't nailed down. 'In the early days they'd take me with them as look-out or squeezing into places they couldn't. It was like that for years, one or the other serving time. The night of my seventeenth birthday they stole from a bloke in

Whitechapel, a Yiddisher boss-man with nasty ways and means.

'They were small fish, my dad and his brother. It didn't matter; my uncle's left hand was lopped off, as my father, supposedly the master-mind, lost his right leg from the kneecap down. I was in the local pub with my mates the night of that job or I'd have gone down with them.

'I don't know what they took. Sixpence or sixty pounds, it didn't matter. They'd encroached on bad boy's manor. He sought vengeance. It was my mother who got me right. She sent me to live with her sister in Cambridge whose husband was in the army. He said it would right me or kill me. I chose to do right and for close on fifty years that's what I've done. Being a porter ain't much of a job but it's honest and it's clean. As I said, I see a lot of things that ain't right as I saw with Professor Sarson and the Jezebel. Discretion and all that, I couldn't do much about it. One day, though I'm getting on and don't have much time, I might be able to do something good.'

The Wise Monkey message was Joe doing something good.

The following morning saw James at the booking office trying for an earlier berth and settling for a lower deck aboard the Campania leaving New York on the 1ˢᵗ of December. As it turned out he gained nothing, rough weather adding days to the journey. The only good thing about the high seas was that the sharing passenger had cried off, leaving James - lucky fellow - able to relieve both ends of his body in privacy.

* * *

The masseur smiled. 'How're you doin', Professor?'

Stripped to buff, teeth clenched and ready to be put through the mill, James was stretched face down on the bed. 'Not so bad, Tom. How are you?'

'I'm doing fine thanks to your good self.'

'I did nothing. It was down to you.'

'Ah, I am good at what I do, but you stepped up when most folk wouldn't give a one-handed masseur a go, thinkin' you need two hands '

It was in James's head to say he used to be such a person, but Tom was a-straddle, the bed sagging, and with a fist and a left elbow the size of a hammer pounding the small of his back, there was no time for words.

It was the desk clerk at the Connaught who introduced the 'best masseur in all Ireland.' Having found Tom Mullins to be exactly that, and in need of cash to set up a massage centre in the city, James invested. Tom was an engineer aboard a cargo-ship covering the Mediterranean coast. Losing his left hand in an accident he learned massage techniques while in a Turkish hospital, supplanting the loss of a hand with forearm and elbow.

He used to work in the hotel kitchens making money on the side as a masseur; now he owns a Turkish Baths in the centre of Dublin with a huge clientele. He gives the best massage and right now, though painful about his ankle, James's body is singing, blood coursing through every vein, so that any doubt in these lean times regarding masculinity is flown to the four winds.

'Regarding your current heavy situation down there, sir?' Tom grinned. 'Did you want me doin' anythin' about it?'

James laughed and, blushing, grabbed a towel. 'Trust me, Tom, if I was inclined in that direction I'd be more than happy to lie back and think of Ireland. But since I am a monastic individual I shall continue to grin and bear it until all good feelings subside.'

Tom left promising to get to Cambridge one day, 'and set up another place so you and your brother won't have so far to come seeking relief.'

Ah yes, there is that. While denigrating the Connaught Kes is more than happy to mine the Mullin's gold. When coming to England he will pay ahead for Tom to visit, and though in the matter of sexual predilection his choices are clearly defined, he is comfortable with any service on offer.

'You need to expand your mind,' is his thought on the matter. 'This is nothing to do with a side street in the *Rue d'Aerschot* anymore than it's about a sly fumble in the men's shower room. This is about the freedom to feel what you need to feel without a sense of wrongness. The man is a magician. He can do more with one hand and an elbow than any woman I know.'

Then he'd laughed. 'God help me, I wouldn't want a woman to know what Tom knows. I'd become a tyrant overnight, locking her away in a tower, food on trays shoved under the door, and me eventually dying of exhaustion.'

* * *

When talking of love Kasper has a dour point of view. 'As far as I am concerned love is sex with ribbons in its hair, and until the bows are undone damnably boring.' He said that on the eve of James's eighteenth birthday. He was home in Leuven prior to Harvard. He'd finished with the Boston-Latin, and, *Sumus Primi*, in terms of academia, was ready to climb a higher ladder.

It was a small get-together that night, Kasper brought his

Cambridge friends, easy going twenty-year-old undergrads; any friends of James were still in the USA. The difference between Belgium and the USA is in the word *still*. New England was James's life. After living so many years in the States it couldn't be any other way; home vacations were endured rather than enjoyed.

Kasper was schooled in Cambridge, England, the distance of the Channel and a few hundred miles as compared to an Ocean taking a week or more to cross. It's easy to see how Grandfather learned to love one grandson more than the other - while one was a next door neighbour, the other was a stranger.

That year the birthday gift was a trip to the *Rue d'Aerschot*, an area of Brussels known for the relaxation of the body and the mind - in other words a whore-house and James first in line to enjoy a lovely lady.

And she was lovely. Her name was Portia. She was slender with long hair the colour of a blackbird's wings. Her skin was as burnished copper and her eyes a wondrous silver grey. In truth she was every man's ideal, a face seen on an obelisk and worshipped as Bastet, Lioness and protector.

Mind-numbingly lovely with a gentle touch and warm arms; she was everything she could have been and thus rendered James impotent.

It didn't matter what she did or how she did it. Mouth or hands, and with those long hennaed fingernails, all that he might have been lay curled up asleep in his lap and he mortified. It was too much. She was too much! She was the words of a song, a book and a poem, the enchanting face briefly glimpsed through a carriage window. She was the woman who every day of his teenage years - and doubtless those of every other guy – waited, naked, in the back of his mind; the wet dream of all wet dreams, and because she was all of that, he could not do what was expected and so did what he could.

* * *

To say he made love to Portia - which is surely not her name, she a Niobe or an Estella - would not be true. His act of turning the tables was as instinctive as shielding one's face from a blow; the eighteen-year-old boy ran for cover, and the Substitute Man took over. Among a blur of soft flesh and new tastes, what hands and lips went where, he couldn't say. His senses led him plus a smattering of locker-room hints. One memory sends up a flag, that of her eyes widening, and a purring noise back of her throat that, heard from a real woman as opposed to a siren, would likely cause him to faint.

Thank God a stubborn kind of humour allows him to smile as well as to grit his teeth when recalling the event. He never told Kes about it, and she, Niobe, didn't give him away. On the contrary, an understanding lady - older when standing in the light - she put on a show, and in what he took to be Arabic, told of a gentle lover and the pleasure of his elegant company.

'Elegant company,' he liked the phrase holding it to his heart in the hope of soothing a humiliated soul. In terms of his performance as a lover he has nothing to say. If there was pleasure that night it didn't belong to him, and he can't say of the lady, since she is paid to give pleasure or at least pretend.

James wonders if he saw something of Portia in Serena Parisi that day in the Basilica, they sharing the same darkly luscious looks and swaying walk. An unworthy comparison, he'd like to lose the idea but it returns.

Maybe Kasper is right when he says love is sex with pretty ribbons. A few weeks back he called at the house saying he wanted to find real love with a real woman. Then he'd laughed: 'since there is no such thing, I'd better stick with what I have had.' He was with Serena then, she who steals from old men, and who, by the sound of things has set her sights on Jacob and any newfound fame he might bring. Hand on heart, Kasper swears he and Serena are done, and that he is looking toward a new horizon. James remembers a day in the Villa del Rosa, and how, spellbound, Kasper had stood watching Clarissa pet a dog, her skirts trailing and her hand in the dog's fur.

Alien words accompany that memory from world-weary lips. 'Oh brother, do you even know your good fortune! I would have a colleague that looks as moonlight on snow and whose lips are warm raspberries in the first melting. And who, if I tried my every best, might stay a colleague for life.'

CHAPTER TWENTY-SIX

Writing on the Wall

Beeches, Comberton
Sunday December 8th 1901

'Hello, Jacob.' Kasper drew the chair closer. 'Do you know who I am?'

Jacob nodded. 'Si.'

'Who am I?'

'You are Mister James's brother.'

'*Sì, io sono il fratello di Mister James.*'

'No!' Jacob scowled and looked away out of the window. 'We no speak Italian in Beeches. We speak my father's language.'

'All right then. We'll speak in English, though it is not my father's language as it is not my brother's. We were born in Belgium.'

'Mister James speak American. He is in Boston America, but will soon be on his way back home to be with Miss Clareessa and me. He like Miss Clareessa and he like me. He is my new father.'

Kasper frowned. 'New father?'

'*Si.* He take me to Norfolk to meet Mister Thomas Phillips who is *avvocato.* I like Mister Thomas. He play cricket with men from Bressingham: Mister James batsman, Mister Thomas wicket-keeper, and I fielding - we won.'

There was so much love and pride in the lad Kasper smiled. 'My sister Anneka lives in Bressingham. She is married to Mister Thomas.'

'This I know. Miss Anneka is Mister James's sister.'

'Yes, and soon to have a baby.'

Jacob nodded. 'Ah *si*, *bambino*!'

While there was still caution, the boy leaning away, the chat about Bressingham went down well. It's clear he has a bad case of hero-worship for James. But then, who can blame him? For when you get down to the nuts and bolts of this, James seeking guardianship of an orphan - a hunch-back with a clubfoot at that - you see a fine deed, and as always a quiet deed.

'I did hear from my mother that James is talking with Belgian lawyers. He wrote of his hopes for you in the future.'

'Hopes for me?' With that word hostility melted away, warmed by the glow in the boy's heart. 'He speak of me with his mother?'

'Yes, his mother, Alice, who is, of course, my mother, and who in due time, when you officially belong to us, will be your grandmother.'

'Grandmother?'

'*Si! Tua nonna. Nonna* Alice van Leiden.'

'*Mia nonna*?' It was too much for the boy. He burst into tears, knuckling his eyes. 'I never had a grandmother. I would like a grandmother.'

'Poor boy!' Kasper pulled Jacob into his arms. 'I should never have left you in that place. I don't know why I did. I can only say I was another man then and not a good man.' Then confound it, if *he* wasn't also weeping, thinking of Father alone in the old farmhouse and the dog, Pepper – apart from James, the only creature Father really loved.

'*Ah no piangere*!' Roles were reversed. Now the boy was holding him. 'It will be all right. I promise.'

'You think so?'

'I know so. Miss Clareessa told me. She said Jesus loves everybody, including little children and drunks.'

'Hah!' Kasper sat up, and between laughing and weeping felt more than a little foolish. 'Clarissa says Jesus loves children and drunks?'

'*Si*!' Thinking he'd made a friend Jacob is happy. 'Mother Superior at the Refugio said my father go to hell for drinking. Miss Clareessa say no, Jesus loves everybody. I asked if He like animals. She say St Francis followed the way of Jesus loving all things pure at heart. Then she hug me like I hug you.'

The whole thing is out of Kasper's control. This pilgrimage was to set things straight making peace with himself as well as the boy. He didn't think to end up weeping; his heart has bruises enough without making more. 'I came today to say I let you down. I should've got you out of that place.'

'You did get me out! I was ill. You and the Parisi Lady were in the garden talking. I know what you said. It is here in my heart forever. "*He should've gone where you and your saintly mother went, seeking sanctuary with the green-eyed girl, Clareessa Morgan, Beeches, Lark lane, Comberton.*"'

Kasper was shocked; not only did the boy remember every word that was said, he imitated the voice - the deep timbre and the braying of an Ass.

'Is that not what you said?'

'It is.'

'That is what brought me here. You saved me.'

Enough! The Bad Dog is on the run again. This is the second time he's come seeking forgiveness, and the second time of going away mortified. He must either stay away or learn to polish up his life.

'I must be on my way. I wanted to meet you face-to-face.'

'We meet now, face-to-face, Mister Kasper.'

'We are okay then, Jacob?'

Jacob smiled. 'You sound American like your brother.'

'I could do worse.' They parted on the assurance that as Kasper is in England he will come to the audition. 'I will play well knowing you are there.'

* * *

Kasper is in England at the Knightsbridge shop. Anneka is due to give birth any day and under nursing care at home. They have a solid staff at the London shop but this being their busiest season a little help never goes amiss.

While he did come to Cambridge to see Jacob another reason brought him, and that is an old and bothersome relationship. Kasper used to think his Beagle pup, Lizzie, had the best nose for locating treasure, but when it comes to his money and his pride - Serena Parisi will sniff him out.

Last week she called Knightsbridge saying she needed to see him. He asked why she couldn't come to London. She said she'd business in Cambridge and while keen to return to Paris all ferries are grounded due to rough seas.

A siren wailing in his head causing the hackles on his head to rise, Kasper agreed to meet at James's house this evening at seven, which in Serena's terms could be midnight or not at all. Now he sits at the piano trying to remember how to play. They had lessons as children. Anneka was good. James was very good; Mama thought music might be his future. Grandfather had other ideas. He said the boy played well because he memorised note sequences; why waste time on a piano when he could challenge the world.

Kasper sits at the piano but his heart isn't in it. Serena is coming. therefore sex is imminent. It is useless to pretend it won't happen (it always did), a dark flame setting fire to a candle.

There weren't many good things about their association, but, practised and quirky, she was good at sex, creating the right effect without needing pretty words to go with it. If that was all they needed they'd still be together. But Kasper has come to understand he needs to love and be loved.

A family is now top of his list and a loving wife to come home to. Until Father's death such things belonged to other men. Now he needs them in the same way he needs air in his lungs. Serena is never in one place long enough to make a home. Like her mother, she is always running ahead of unpaid bills, the apartment in San Nicola their only bolthole. Other than owing money he doesn't know why they run. He once asked of her childhood thinking to know more. She laughed: '*Allora, Kasper.* You think to save me from myself? Trust me, I do not need saving. I am in control of my life and my destiny.'

Kasper's biggest regret in this mess is the loss of Giovanni. They have climbed mountains and trekked deserts together. They have explored the Great Pyramid and sat all night under African skies. He is cherished as a beloved friend and Kasper now left with a hole in his gut where once was love.

The incident at the Masked Ball might seem a cause of parting but the friendship had been strained for some time. Believing self-respect to be the first duty of a man, Giovanni saw Kasper's way of life as shoddy. Though only thirty seven, the Italian seems older in so many ways. A traditionalist, born of noble blood; the heraldic family motto speaks for the man: '*facta non verba* - deeds not words.'

* * *

Snow thick on the ground and a heavy frost in the air, it was gone eleven when a carriage drew up. Kasper was asleep before the fire when James's manservant showed her into the sitting-room.

'May I take your coat, madam?'

'No need.' She shrugged away. 'I do not intend to stay.'

'Very well.' Archie Johnson looked to Kasper. 'Will that be all, sir? Only I need to be on my way, my mother is expecting me home.'

'Thank you yes.'

'Goodnight, sir. Goodnight, madam.'

'Goodnight Archie.' Kasper nodded. 'I'm sorry you were delayed.'

Johnson bowed his way out. Serena grimaced. 'I do not like that man. He has the face of a mournful bullfrog.'

'He has family business and was anxious to leave.'

'Then why didn't he? He does not live here, and with his master away has no reason to remain.'

'On the contrary, his master, as you call him, is due home. And, as I shall be staying overnight, Archie had every reason to be here. He is a good man and reliable. James would not like him ill-used.'

'James does not like anyone ill-used.'

'No more do I.'

'*Va bene*!' She threw her purse on the chaise. 'I dare say the bullfrog will be compensated for his trouble.'

'Money doesn't buy everything.'

'Oh, I think it does.'

'It doesn't buy loyalty. That is either there or not. And if it is, then one works to honour it.'

'*Allora,* it is nothing.' Osprey feathers in her hair and an evening gown under her furs, she spread her hands to the fire. 'As I said, I am not staying. A carriage will return for me in an hour. '

Kasper should have been angry at this late showing but didn't seem to care; whatever this is he wants it over. 'Have you had a good evening?'

'Very good, *grazie.*'

'What was it, the theatre?'

'I dined at a friend's house.'

'Do I know this friend?'

'I do not think so. It is someone I met when I was here before, a lawyer friend of mine, a lover of the arts.'

'A lover of the arts?' For some reason her comment amused him. Of late, thinking to invest in the motor industry, he has spent time in certain factories observing assembly lines. Now, while trying to decide what particular *art* she had in mind, words like connecting rod and piston keep getting in the way.

'What is so amusing?'

'I don't know. Am I smiling?'

'You are.'

'That is a mistake. Let us talk about why you wanted to meet. I dare say that will remove humour from the rest of my life never mind the evening.'

'I needed to speak with you.'

'What about?'

She glanced about her. 'Might I sit?'

'Of course! *Vergeef me*! I forget my manners.' He pulled the chaise closer to the fire, patting the cushions. 'Can I get you a glass of wine?'

'I do not drink wine.'

'Since when?'

'Since I think for my health.'

'Have you been unwell?'

'I am very well.'

'But you don't drink wine.'

Her eyes turned on him. 'I would have a glass of milk if you have it.'

'I'm not sure there is milk. I'll look.' He found milk, brought her a glass, and then, knowing he'd need it, helped himself to a tumbler of whisky. He offered her a cigarette – she declined.

'I do not smoke now. I think they too are bad for my health.'

'I'm sure you are right. So what do we need to talk about?'

'When is James home?'

'Tomorrow I believe.'

'I hear he is to leave Cambridge. There is talk in the university. They say he is stolen by the Uffizi and moving to Florence.'

'I don't know.' Nerves jangled, he poured another whisky. 'He always had the option and Father's death created a need for change in us all.'

'In you too?'

'Especially me.' He sipped his drink, as did she, and he fizzing inside –waiting, waiting. 'I've spent my life seeking new ideas and new people. I feel the need to get to know who I am rather than what might be over the horizon. What about you, Serena? Do you look for change in your life?'

Shoulders whitely gleaming, she loosened her furs. 'I think that change is here whether I wanted it or not.'

Kasper stood against the mantle. Her words unsettle him as does her mood, thoughtful and heavy, not at all as expected. She began to talk of her mother's marriage to a Florida businessman and, as always, refers to Isabella by her Christian name as though speaking of a friend. Apparently the husband exaggerated his situation, his life not nearly as prosperous as promised and Isabella thinking to return to Paris.

Suddenly weary he yawned. 'And how do you feel about that?'

'Isabella must do what is best for her, though if things continue with me as they are I would be pleased to see her.'

Firelight flickering on the silk of her gown, she stretched out on the chaise as voluptuous as ever. Kasper was reminded of Florence and the Uffizi and Titian's infamous nude. That Serena is clothed means nothing, for whatever she wears a man is only ever conscious of the flesh beneath.

That day in the Gallery stays in his mind. Along with tourists, he queued to see the *Venus of Urbino*. As always in any art gallery where nudes are displayed the crowd shuffles along, offers a quick glance, and then - not wanting to be thought ogling flesh - moves rapidly on.

Clarissa Morgan was among the crowd. On her way out she dropped her programme. He picked it up and in that moment, as with Belshazzar's ghostly warning hand - *Mene, Mene Tekel Upharsin* - he could have written her thoughts on the wall. She was questioning Venus's hand as it lay across her belly: 'You are naked? What is it you seek to protect?'

It was a strange moment, impossible, and yet if asked he'd

swear he heard her thoughts and that they mirrored his own. That was the Uffizi. Now he waits in James's elegant house, everything in place and a place for everything, and as with the tall candles and ivory keys of the piano, all is quietly beautiful.

Desperate to have this woman gone from his life he turned to ask why she is here, and then, as with the Uffizi, her mind was open, and he knew.

'Serena?' His heart raced. 'What is it you want of me?'

She held his gaze. 'Don't you know?'

He could barely speak. 'Are you with child?'

'*Si.*' She smiled. '*Sono incinta.*'

Gatherers

Croft House, Cambridge
Sunday December 8ᵗʰ 1901

'Is it mine?'

The question rose up from his gut on a wave of nausea. She watched his struggle with a smile on her lips. He did not know what to say. He, the Kestrel, fearful of nothing, Climber of Mountains and Divider of Seas, was bereft of words, the future - his future - no longer his to decide.

Eventually the pity of it all sank in. 'How long have you known?'

'From the beginning.'

'What does that mean?'

'It means I knew the moment it happened.'

'And when was that?'

'That last day in Paris. If you recall we did what we always do. We shouted. We slammed doors. And then, the clock ticking, and you leaving to discover a New World, or whatever you do, we made time for a little diversion.'

'A significant diversion I would say.'

'*Io so.*' She took a powder compact from her purse, and with a steady hand, powdered her face and shoulders, repairing non-existent damage.

He stood gazing into the fire, the world – his world – continuing to turn but on heavy wheels uncertain as to the destination.

She extended her arm. 'Do you think this is a beautiful house?'

'What!'

'This, your brother's house? Is it how you would imagine him to live?

'I do not know how my brother lives.'

'I think you do not know your brother.'

'No, probably not.'

For a while she continued to debate her beauty, peering in to the mirror, adjusting this and that, and then satisfied, closed the compact.

'Why so disturbed? There is no need to be.'

'You are pregnant, Serena, and with, I am supposing, my child.'

'You doubt it is your child?'

'No.' Any immediate hesitancy was dismissed. 'You would not be here if it was another's. You'd be seeking fresh pasture and what to do for best.'

'And I being here means you are the best?'

'Yes, because you know I will honour the commitment.'

'It is my hope.'

'What other choices are there?'

'I have choices. I could have done this alone, and other than you being the father, you not involved.'

'I have to be involved. Raising a child alone is hard.'

'What do you know of raising a child? Are you already a father?'

'Not that I know of. I've likely had a few near misses in the past but in this I am fairly convinced you are the first.'

'The things you say!' She curled her lip. 'You should be ashamed.'

'I didn't mean it that way. Your news has come as a shock.'

'I knew it would which was why I waited to tell you. I know children are not in your way of thinking.'

'Of late they might have been.'

'What, a child of our making?'

'No.'

She dismissed the idea. 'Then you are fortunate to have avoided the issue thus far, since, by your own admission you 'ave not been the wisest of men.'

'Not the wisest nor the...' He choked on what he would've said since to speak of fortune is foolish. My God, he thought. Is this who I am, a brute juggling the news with heavy paws to see what stays and what falls?

The idea of her being pregnant is a shock. In all the time they were together he never considered the issue, and since in that time she never declared maternal leanings, he can only assume the news is a shock to her.

'How did this happen?'

'The same way all babies happen.'

'I thought you were careful. I know I was...or hoped I was.'

'Such things happen no matter how careful.'

'Then would this be what women think of as an accident?'

'I do not know what other women think. I know that a child is growing within my body and that I need to plan ahead.'

'Isn't that what you always do, plan ahead?'

'You would have me deal another way? I should perhaps run amuck, weeping and wailing, and tearing my hair? My life now blighted by a fate worse than death? Would that be more fitting?'

The words she chose reminded him of her sharp mind and command of English. While Serena might be thought of as a cold and unfeeling woman, one could never see her as dim-witted. It is the intellect behind her gaze that jars when coming up against her insane need to acquire things.

In the beginning of their relationship they - or rather he, as he sees it now, were so wrapped up in passion, the desire for gifts, for jewels and gowns and cash, seemed natural. Isn't that what lovers do, remove an item of clothing with the left hand while decorating the body with the right?

Once in Paris he made a joke of it, sliding a five franc coin under the apartment door. She pocketed the coin. '*Grazie, un deposito.*' She'd smiled when she said it but the next day had removed notes from his wallet, their association was a contract based on sex - payment on demand.

* * *

That notion was furthered in the spring of '98 seeing their apartment in San Nicolo. He was to visit Giovanni and while in Italy call on Serena. He found the Parisis in process of packing, bag and baggage in the hall and dogs yapping.

They were again on the move, Isabella to marry an Englishman and to live in Cambridgeshire. That they did not want him inside their apartment was apparent. It was gloomy inside. Any natural light was absorbed by the contents of what might have been a warehouse. Such a mass of things: wardrobes filled with clothes, furniture, sofas, tables and chairs, and in between and around - wherever there was space - boxes piled upon boxes. A layer of dust over all suggested it had been this way for years.

One image stays in his mind. There was a box half filled with household items, crockery and frying pans, and lying half way in and halfway out, an item of fancy-dress: a pair of angel wings, the feathers tattered and torn.

When Kasper asked, 'what is all of this?' Isabella, who rarely speaks, all interaction left to her daughter, shrugged. '*Del necessario per vivre.*'

The necessaries of life! In that moment he was shaken, realising he knew nothing about Serena and her mother. Gypsies on the move, and twice-married Isabella in line for a third husband, he'd asked. 'What happened to make you live like this?' At first Serena had frowned not liking the question. Then she'd shrugged. 'Nothing happened. We are who we are, Isabella and I, gatherers for the morning.'

Later he described what he saw to Giovanni: the women having to eat out, no room for a stove, every inch given over to a storehouse. Giovanni spoke of the eighteenth-century art critic, Denis Diderot, and what is known as the 'Diderot Complex'. The need to hoard is seen as a psychological issue, where the obtaining of one item leads to a hunger for the next, eventually becoming a spiralling need and the sufferer never fulfilled.

Giovanni said the condition is rife in the art-world. It is a disease where the collector will stop at nothing to get what he or she believes is already theirs. Though he wouldn't name names, he mentioned a female collector who, he said, would lay claim to an item to the point of blackmail and theft.

With Serena the need to acquire doesn't stop with things; she seeks idolatry and the gathering of men's souls. Kasper never really saw her as his mistress but more a courtesan, or in truer words, a well-paid whore, thus their relationship wore itself out. It is how the apartment in Paris came about, the money in her bank, and the diamond ring.

The winter of '99 was about fulfilling an ambition. Kasper, Giovanni, and men from the Explorer's Club crossed the Sahara Desert as guests of the Annizah tribe. After this fearsome, and often dangerous trek, Kasper realised he needed to straighten his affairs. It was about that time that Charles Morgan died. The old man's death shook the Parisis. Suddenly, Serena was talking of marriage, joking, saying she had a husband in mind, a lawyer - the one she speaks of now, the art lover - but that Kasper was always top of her list: 'De Beers shares outranking a lawyer's writ.' She wanted a settlement. If marriage was not his intention, he should make her safe with a place of her own where she and Isabella might live out their lives 'irrespective of old men dying.'

In answer he gave the Rue Saint Sauveur apartment and a fistful of shares. So their relationship ended, but before they parted, they enjoyed, alas, a final, fateful, customary 'diversion.'

* * *

In Florence Kasper said a man can change. James argued: it's not about wanting to change, it is a matter of genetics; a Kestrel is born to hunt.

Rumi said lovers don't live by the rules. He woke this morning thinking love might make the difference; that with Clarissa he needn't revert to old ways. The idea made him happy, thoughts of home and children unfolding in his mind's eye. Now, in the blink of that same eye the hope of love is gone.

'So what is it you want?' He turned toward Serena. 'Is this, us meeting here and you telling me of the child, your way of proposing marriage? Or have you come up with a more realistic way of resolving the dilemma?'

She stood before a looking glass adjusting her furs. She took so long to answer he wanted to slap her. Then, when he thought he could take no more, she looked up. 'I do not want to marry you. I never did. You will always be second choice to me as I was always nothing to you.'

He frowned. 'So what is this about then? Why are we here?'

'Because of the child! While I would sooner marry the devil than be chained to a man I do not love, the matter is not of me to decide. From now on it is what is best for the child.'

He opened his mouth to speak but she put up her hand.

'I know what is best for me and it isn't you. Believe me, I am not begging. I do not have to marry you. I have a way out. It is there outside in a carriage waiting for me to say yes. I can marry the lawyer, who, *che mi adora,* would not care if I gave birth to an elephant so long as I stayed with him.'

Again Kasper tried to speak but she closed him down.

'It is as I ask you here and now. Do you want to see your son live and grow beside you? Or do you want him to be known as another's man's child? Similarly...' Eyes flashing – a sudden stranger - she stood before him, a mother defining the terms of the birth *and* the life of her child, and he, Kasper, allowed one chance and one chance only.

'...do you want to see your daughter - who will be as beautiful as her mother is beautiful - walking beside you with her hand in yours, or do you want to give her to another, who will worship her as he worships her mama.

She held up her hand, his diamond ring flashing. 'Choose now, Kasper van Leiden Sterne! Take me for what I am, or let me and mine go now and forever.'

Lost Time

Beeches, Comberton
Tuesday December 10th 1901

Early morning Mister James came by on his big grey horse and stood under the Beech Tree, snow falling all about him like bridal petals. Muffin, the cat, knew and woke Jacob, patting his cheek so he might look out of the window.

'Mister James!' Heart thrilled, he dashed down the stairs not stopping for his slippers though the snow lay thick on the ground. '*Sei qui! Sei qui*!'

'Yes, I'm here.' Mister James hauled him onto the horse. So happy, Jacob clung to him. He was home! His adored special father had kept his promise and would be there in the audience at Kings. Safe at last, Jacob was able to tell of his nightmare. He told how he dreamt of the audition. He was there in the organ loft. Everyone was waiting for him to play. But he couldn't read the music. The score for his choice of music - the Chopin Etude opus 10 organ transition - was tattered and torn. He couldn't make sense of it.

The dream left him afraid, thinking he had made a bad choice, the Etude a fiendishly difficult piece with skipping semi-quavers. 'I shall play badly.'

Mister James smiled. 'You will play well, and I, along with the spirit of your father, shall be proud.' They turned the horse, named Argent, through the gate into the yard and on toward the warmth of Miss Hanky's kitchen so that the day might begin.

* * *

James removed his hat. 'I thought I'd better come by to say I'm back.'

'I'm glad you did.' Miss Hankin stoked the boiler. 'We've not had a day's peace since you've been gone. Every five minutes, will you be back in time or should we go and get you. I said to him, how the heck are we supposed to get to the professor? It's an ocean we'd have to cross not a road.'

'I did think he might be anxious.'

'Anxious isn't the word. He's driven himself and everyone else in this house crazy. When did you get back?'

'I got into Cambridge late yesterday evening. I was lucky to get here at all. Most of the sea-going vessels had been grounded due to the storm. I would've come later today but felt I needed to catch up on family issues.'

'Is there anything else but family issues these days?'

'It sure doesn't seem that way.'

'At least you're here now. So come and sit and don't be a stranger. You're welcome here whatever the hour.'

He sat. 'I was concerned it was rather early.'

'No need. What with one thing and another I've been up and down most of the week never mind the night. If it wasn't the lad being unwell it was the wretched horse, and if not that then Miss Clary.'

'Clarissa is unwell?'

'Perhaps not unwell. She is upright, if that's anything to go by, head up and back straight. But what with the trouble about the old uncle, he sick, and that awful tittle-tattle, I know she is feeling it.'

'Confound it all! Not that bank loan nonsense again!' He was up and on his feet. 'I beg your pardon. Cursing helps no one. It's just that this is the very last thing I had hoped to hear.'

'It's not what any of us want to hear, but it's the same with all skeletons left unburied - they will rattle. Still never mind.' A cup of coffee before him, she pushed him down. 'Sit and rest. We've a long day tomorrow to look forward to and a run on all of our nerves. So best we need to pull together.'

'Thank you for the *we* Miss Hankin.'

'Well we are in this together. You are part of us, Professor, and probably always will be.' She shook her head. 'I tell you, there's something nasty at work in Cambridge, people with too much time on their hands and not enough good will. We must watch out for such and if we can, stop them in their tracks.' She tied an apron about her waist. 'Now can I get you a bit of breakfast?'

'Thank you I have eaten.'

'And what have you eaten?'

'Johnson left a couple of things.'

'He's a good man is Archie, and if I may say devoted to you. I've seen the way he cares for your things. You could do a lot worse than Mr Johnson.'

'And I am grateful for it.'

'Good. So, you've eaten, but what about a juicy herring fried in butter.'

'I like herring.'

'There you are then.'

So James sat down again to eat in probably his most favourite place these days, Beeches kitchen, bright and warm, and filled to the brim with loving charity. He sat, glad to be back in Comberton feeling the warmth and saving questions for the right moment. Then the inevitable need arose, and moved by a delicious smell, he asked: 'Does Clarissa like herring?'

'If they're not too bony. These have been filleted so she'll have a nibble and when my back is turned offload the rest to Muffin here.'

'Ah yes, Muffin.' He stroked the cat. 'Thanks for looking after her.'

'She's a nice little cat. We didn't mind having her. I hope you're not looking to get her back. Jacob's fallen for her and she for him.'

'I guess that is okay. Acquiring her was more a need on my part than act of kindness. If she's happy here and you do not mind then fine.'

He waited a little longer but then with no obvious sound of movement other than that of Jacob singing he had to ask. 'Is Clarissa an early riser?'

'Usually she is. Not quite up before me but close. It's how I know when she's unwell, bedroom door shut and curtains pulled. Here you are!' She slapped a plate in front of him and his mouth watered. 'Eat that and then maybe a slice of toast. You're a busy man. You need to keep your strength up.'

James didn't need prompting, and shedding his jacket, set to, every mouthful better than the last, until the plate was empty and another question on his giveaway lips. 'So is she not well at the moment? You did say she had been under stress and it is coming up for quarter after seven.'

'Ah dear.' Miss Hankin sat down with him, a softening gaze suggesting she knows that while he is here for Jacob, it will always be Clarissa. 'As I said, her uncle is ill, and she's barred from seeing him. It wears on her. Until of late she stopped going out, clinging to the house like a waif and stray. I was bothered for her health, especially as she couldn't get to her work.'

'I believe they have located the problem with the roof.'

'So I heard. The weather held everybody up. I don't know what it's been like where you were but it's been shocking here. Rain and gales and snow, it's put a stop to all manner of things. Even so,' she looked up, her mouth tight, 'as we have found - life goes on and times change.'

'Good changes?'

'Depends on how you see them. The bible says the Lord God created the world in seven days. You've been away close on two months. It being Cambridge, and a university city, a lot can happen in two months.'

The last bite of herring sudden dust in his mouth, he took up a napkin and wiping his mouth waited. There were preliminaries, he sensing a choosing of words, and Margret Hankin offering softer options first. 'My sister Sally is newly affianced. She and her intended, the Reverend Bellamy, who you met in Florence, are due to wed in January. It's to be on the 28th. It was his father's birthday. His mother - a nice lady, if a trifle strong of opinion - asked if it might be that date. So they are to wed and live in a pretty rectory in Diss, and my Sally a vicar's wife, and I to lose the best sister a woman ever had.'

James understood times really had changed. This is not the Beeches of yesterday. Uncertainty shifts the tiles on the floor as it rattles slates on the roof. Miss Hankin is afraid, contemplating a future she knows any minute may change. 'It will all work out well in the end.' He took her hand. 'I met the reverend and thought him a good man. I'm sure they will be happy.'

'I don't doubt it. If there is such a thing as a perfect match it's them. They look through one another's eyes and breathe through one another's lungs, joined in less time than it takes to break another's heart. They will be happy and do good things together. I shall rally. It depends what else comes to pass.'

'What else has come?'

'As I said, times are changing.' She drew her hand away and was up scraping plates, washing dishes and preparing lunch, minding her chores so she didn't have to think of the loss of a sister and other impossibly dear people.

'We've made a new acquaintance, a gentleman caller, which has occasioned dinner parties here at Beeches and me looking to cook fancy food and drink fancier wines, and run off my feet, and while all for good and pleasant reasons, none of it bodes well for me. '

His first thought was that Kasper had called. He has been in Cambridge, staying over last night and by his note on the piano plans to return, he taking the express to London for changes of clothes and discussions with his lawyers. While ignorant to the nature of his legal concerns James assumes Kasper used his time in Cambridge well, whereas he wasted time contemplating a seat on the Oppenheimer Board, before rejecting the same knowing Grandfather would've risen from the grave seeing such a partnership as treason.

'Has my brother called?'

'Yes, Mister van Leiden Sterne did drop by. He didn't stay.

He was busy arranging an expedition into a jungle in South America or some such place.'

'Did he come just the once?'

'He came twice. The second time was for Jacob. I asked Miss Clary what was going on. She said it was old business. I dare say the lad will tell you as he will tell of another gentleman who came recently and keeps coming.'

Keeps coming? Here it is - the real news behind the offering of herrings and toast. James didn't need to ask. He knew who it was that came and keeps coming - even so, his mouth ever a traitor, it got ahead of him.

'Would that be an Italian gentleman?'

'That's him! Signor Giovanni di Lombardi.'

Now the name was out she could relax a little, filling in the details. James listened. There was a lot to be said, as in, 'the signor ever-such a nice gentleman. Sally was pleased to meet him as was the Reverend Charles, he sending them a bottle of champagne and a hamper of biscuits in Florence.'

Arms braced, she leant on the sink: 'It turns out he's not just a signor. He is a titled gentleman with a villa in Italy and a place in Norfolk.'

There was a list of visiting days and descriptions of trips to the gentleman's stables: 'They all went, Miss Clary, Sally, Freya-Jasmine and Jacob. I could've gone but didn't bother. I stayed home counting my bruises. Freya came back fizzing like a glass of lemonade about a pony by name of Soubrette. A dear little thing, she says, it dances rather than trots. Anyway, the pony is hers whenever she visits the stables.'

* * *

It was at that point - she wringing the same dish cloth - James's knew he was not alone in his despair that, while Miss Hankin can contemplate the loss of a sister with a degree of hope, this new visitor with his houses and ponies is a greater threat. Norfolk is across the way but Italy is a whole new world, and as said of America - 'an ocean she'd have to cross.'

James searched for words not only for Margret Hankin but to comfort himself. 'I have met the Marchese and have no reason to doubt he is anything other than a gentleman.'

'I'm sure he is. He was nothing but polite. Sally thinks the world of him, especially as he knows the reverend's mother, Mrs Bellamy who has a villa close by his lady-friend and they belonging to the same artistic set.'

'I see.'

'Yes and so do I. It's all so cosy, everybody knowing everybody, and they all wrapped up in a nice warm bundle and me on the outside looking in.'

'You've been together as a family a long time,' said James. 'I can't imagine Clarissa leaving you or your granddaughter out of any equation.'

'She wouldn't! Not in a million years. Every decision made is dependent on us Hankins - me, Sally, and Freya-Jasmine. This is Clarissa's home. I have no money neither has Sally. We live on her generosity and that of her father and always have. We depend upon them. It's why I keep a little respect referring to her as Miss Clary. She knows that and appreciates me. It's why she fought so hard against those other two when they tried taking the house.'

'Other two?'

'The Parisi women! It was when the doctor died. He left the

house to Miss Clary, it being her mother's and before that her grandmother's. Those two didn't care. They'd been left money but wanted more, Serena saying Beeches belonged to Isabella and Miss Clary had no right keeping it.'

'She said that?'

'She made a right song and dance about it, threatening lawyers. Poor girl, they made Miss Clary's life a misery. She stuck it out. She knew given to them two thieves the house would've been sold and me and mine out on our ear.'

'That must have been difficult for Clarissa.'

'They never let her alone, and even now I doubt it is over. When it comes to taking what she thinks she's entitled to there's no one like Serena.'

'I didn't know about the house.'

'No, but you knew about the debt, didn't you. The money she stole from Miss Clary's uncle.'

Suddenly it was James in the hot seat and contempt in Miss Hankin's eyes and he unsure of the target. 'To some degree I know about it.'

'Of course you do! It was you paid it off. To my mind, taking that money was her way of paying Miss Clary back for not getting the house.'

'I don't understand you.'

'Don't you? Well think about it. I don't know how much this is worth. It's a nice house and so probably worth a few hundred if put up for sale. It's why she took from Professor Sarson, he being a trustee. So he got a few pounds back - he was never going to get the rest, Serena seeing Beeches as owed to her.'

'I'm not sure Serena is that Machiavellian.'

'Maybe not, but she got the money didn't she? And she

doesn't have to worry about giving it back. You took care of that. We know all about it, as we *all* know you and Serena had a romantic dalliance in the past.'

'Dalliance?' James frowned.

'Yes, in Italy. Mind, that's your business and nothing to do with anything. The only way I know is the same way Miss Clary knew. Serena told her.'

'Serena told Clarissa about that?'

'She sent a letter laying it all out. And while she didn't go into details, she did say you'd paid the debt for love of her and that she was grateful.'

'Grateful?' He was on his feet. 'Good God!'

'I don't know about calling on God. It's a bit late for that, my dear. We got the letter a few days before you went to Italy. I don't mind saying it did you no good in our girl's eyes, which is a shame, because until then you were the only one. But that's that. I mustn't be unkind. I've made mistakes of my own without polishing yours, for I'm sure it was a mistake as it would be for any decent man caught up in that woman's wiles.'

Lost for words, James could only stare.

'Anyway that's old history. We've a new dawn to face and, while I'm sure he is a better sort of person, we've another Italian to worry about and all else is gone by the board, Doctor Brooke included. It's where they are now in Norfolk. Jacob stayed home, worried about the audition as did Sally to give me a hand. Miss Clary and Freya-Jasmine are guests of the Marquis's lady friend, a Mrs Ambrose Pennington - another of your lot.'

'My lot?'

'I'm sorry. I didn't mean to say that but I am cross with you, Professor. You never really put your heart into winning the girl.

You were too nice about everything. Instead of fighting for her in the old-fashioned way, you tiptoed about as though afraid to tread on her feelings, and she all the while desperate for a sign you cared. Then along comes this Italian fellow, who knows what he wants and how to get it, and where are you - traipsing about America, and she stolen from under your nose. As for the other lady, Mrs Pennington, I just meant to say she is an American. Miss Clary really likes her. She seems a nice person; an actress with big hats and furs, and a smile. I was quite overcome.'

'Is that so?' Head reeling, James made for the door. 'Forgive me, Miss Hankin, but I can't imagine you overcome by anyone.'

'Can you not?' She shook her head, eyes empty. 'Well, let me tell you, Dear Professor, the day I hear they're moving to Italy – which trust me is not so unlikely - I shall be so overcome I'll close my eyes and hope not to wake.'

Division

Beeches, Comberton
Wednesday December 11ᵗʰ 1901

'What about my tie?' Jacob is panicking. Mister Peacock dropped the foulard neck-tie off yesterday: 'A gift to the young impresario.' Brown silk, it is very pretty but tricky to tie. This is his third attempt and still it wriggles.

'Give it to me!' Freya-Jasmine took it, and turning him round, fitted it quickly and neatly about his neck. 'I know these things. My college scarf is an absolute bounder. I have to be firm and keep it in check.'

'What is bounder, Freya?'

'I'm not sure. My tutor says it a lot, particularly when the boy's rugger team are out. I think it means like a ball bouncing all over the place.'

'Ah *si*! My foulard tie bounces. I need to be firm and keep in check.'

'Yes, and your silly nerves. Please don't be afraid, Jacob. You will be wonderful and everyone will say so. We shall be there, your family, listening and smiling and being so terribly proud.' She gave him a kiss and danced away in a new taffeta gown and a bonnet, a blur of beautiful colours.

It is decided that, as legal guardian, James is to accompany Jacob to the Chapel and the family arriving later. The audition is set for three-thirty. James arrived at the house at two. Miss

Hankin gowned in sober black let him in.

'Bit early aren't you, Professor.'

'Good day Miss Hankin. There is method in my madness. Is he ready?'

'He's been ready since dawn. If you wait here, I'll go and get him.'

James didn't have to wait. A picture of misery, limping and hoarse of voice, Jacob clumped his way down. ''ello Mister James. We go now?'

'Yes, we go now.'

'Is early for audition?'

'A little.' James helped him into his coat and, cold and snowing outside, tied a muffler about his neck, the boy lethargic under his hands, turning this way and that and the family collecting on the stairs. Then he was ready and stood with hands hanging at his sides. 'Have you got everything you need?'

'*Si.*'

'Your music is already there waiting for you.'

'*Si.*'

'Yes, and everything is arranged as you would want it.'

'*Si.*'

There was a flurry of hugs and kisses, Jacob accepting all but with the tragic demeanour of one going to the scaffold rather than an audition.

James took his hand and nodding to the rest drew the boy out of the door.

'Mister James!' Jacob saw the Wolsey parked on the road and let out a yelp of delight. 'It is a new motoring car!'

'You betcha! The driver and I thought you might care for a tootle about the town on your way to King's and maybe stop for a malt at the drugstore.'

Limp forgotten, Jacob was off and running. He got to the car and seeing the driver screamed with delight. 'It is the Big Man!'

'Yes, it is Mr Sissons. Since he will be attending your audition today, he has kindly agreed to act as chauffeur pro tem.'

James was adjusting goggles about Jacob's eyes when Clarissa caught up with them. 'James van Leiden.' She grasped his hand before turning away. 'You are the kindest of men.'

* * *

Clarissa woke cross with herself this morning thinking they ought not to have stayed in Norfolk overnight on Monday, that it created unnecessary travelling while giving Margret too much time to think.

It was the pony, of course, and the doll's house in the attic, and all the costumes that as an opera singer Sadie Pennington had collected over the years. Freya-Jasmine is besotted with the woman. The feeling is mutual, Sadie with no family of her own delighting in the child, and they whispering and giggling together, sharing a similarly scatty humour.

Love of Jacob brought Freya-Jasmine home yesterday, wanting to be with him on his audition; beyond that she had no desire to leave Sadie, happy there in a way not seen before and already planning the next visit.

Her grandmother is aware of this and fearing a change makes her feelings known. 'I don't think you should let the child visit too often. Mrs Pennington is a nice lady but very loud. I worry that too much time with her and my grand-daughter will be chewing gum and singing "*Home on the Range.* "'

This was said this morning following a month of similar comments, thus catching Clarissa on the hop and causing a snappy response. 'Better that, don't you think, than forever looking on the dark side of things.'

Margret Hankin was born intuiting problems. Nine times out of ten she is right but of late, Sally to be married and talk of moving, plus the appearance of Giovanni di Lombardi, she naturally views the future with doubtful eye.

'About time!' This was the greeting yesterday morning arriving home. 'I hope you know you've had me worrying all night when you'd be back.'

'As you see we are back in plenty of time.'

'I should think so.' She'd stomped into the kitchen. 'So much for consideration! Since when did you stop caring about people's feelings?'

There followed a long tedious rant about the inconsideration of youth, and how 'the older you get the less say you have in your life.' While used to this complaint from Great Aunt Sheba, Clarissa didn't want it in Beeches.

'Oh for heaven's sake! Can we at least get inside the door?'

'On the subject of consideration and those that do and those that don't,' Margret was determined to be heard, 'the professor came yesterday asking about Jacob. Six o' clock he came, more or less stepping off the boat from Ireland. Now that is consideration.'

'James is back?' Clarissa's heart had lurched.

'Yes he's back. I made him breakfast.'

'Jacob will be relieved. Did he leave a message? I mean, did he have anything in particular to say?'

'I'll say he did.' In a rare moment of malice Margret Hankin's worries tipped over into spite. 'He said it was him that repaid the bank loan. What's more, he did it for love of Serena.'

'I see.' With that Clarissa had picked up her bag and made for the stairs, Margret following, and though seeming to regret her remarks continuing in the same vein. 'He didn't actually say he loved her. But he must've done, why else would he pay. He didn't know your uncle at the time or you. It had to be for Serena. In all fairness I can't recall what he said. My mind was on other things, the Italian signor for one and where that's leading. I told the professor about him, I said the next thing you'll hear is Miss Clary moving to Italy.'

Yesterday at quarter to eleven Clarissa went into her bedroom, closed the door, and pleading a headache stayed there for most of the day.

A part of her had wondered if it was James. Even before Serena's letter she'd thought he might be involved. Uncle Sarson's refusal to discuss payment gave her the idea: 'he abiding by a promise to a certain person *not* to tell.'

So the truth is out and the debt again on Clarissa's shoulders. Alone in the bedroom, head in her hands, she thought to ask a favour of Giovanni. It was a small idea at first, but the more she thought the more the idea sickened. How can anyone ask a favour of a man who'd just declared his love!

Thinking on that she'd ran to the window and regardless of snow threw it open to lean out over the washhouse roof gasping for air.

For the last two years a monthly bouquet of hothouse lilac has arrived at the door with the message: '*For the Lilac Lady.*' The washhouse lilac is old. It was planted the day she was born and has struggled through twenty-three winters to produce the odd blossom, and every year was reviled as a nuisance 'for getting under tiles.' It blooms, it withers, and then along with the despised hothouse lilac, is tossed on a bonfire to die unloved and unappreciated.

Yesterday a younger Clarissa closed the window: Papa's girl, the one who believes in eternal love and the kiss that wakes a sleeping princess.

'Hush!' Finger on her lips she asked patience of the older Clarissa: 'Wait before you ask a favour of anyone. If a lilac tree can keep hoping so can you.'

* * *

James knelt in the church praying for Jacob and the triumph he rightly deserves. He also prayed for himself and a letter he plans to deliver to Beeches where he writes of coming to Professor Sarson's aid: that he admired the man and felt obliged to honour the van Leiden name. It was a difficult letter to write for however brief he cannot deny the 'dalliance.'

Sighing, he sat back in his seat. Joe Sissons was on his right next to the aisle and Archie Johnson on his left. 'Who's in the seat next to you, Archie?'

'I don't know. It was reserved along with ours when I got here.'

'Okay then.'

Joe Sissons grinned. 'And we three anxious uncles chewing our fingers.'

'I'm nervous enough for any uncle,' said Archie. 'What about you, sir?'

'I want him to do well.'

James cast an eye about the Chapel. As they are seated left of the central aisle so the Beeches party is the row to the right. Clarissa, Miss Hankin and her sister, Freya-Jasmine, and a woman James takes to be the exotic Sadie Ambrose Pennington, are flanked by Giovanni at the aisle. The good Doctor Brooke and the Reverend Bellamy sit at the far side.

With a growing sense of division - us and them - James was greeted earlier by a cool smile, the Marchese elegant in a sable coat and dark homburg walking toward the West Door with Clarissa on his arm.

'Good day to you, Professor van Leiden.'

'Good day to you, *Signore Marchese*.'

'This promises to be an exciting day for your young charge. Is he ready, do you think?'

'Entirely so.'

'You have faith in the boy?'

'As do we all.'

'*Allora, può solo fare bene!*' Giovanni nodded and moved on with a rustle of silk, the world parting before him and his beautiful companion.

James is grateful for Joe and Archie; but for their loyal support he could not have borne this day with any kind of ease. Monday he learned of another kind of supporter. Word of him 'crossing over' to the Uffizi has reached epic proportion and he greeted by banners bearing the letters SOSH, Save Our Scorched Hearts, hanging from the many flying buttresses. Students are protesting his loss, which has caused yet another message from the Vice-Chancellor: '*Would the professor drop by. We have matters to discuss.*'

James is in no rush. While the protest movement is the work

of students his gut tells him bigger forces are at work.

It was Joe Sissons who came up with the idea of the car. A part-time cabbie, he works the rank with his horse, Neptune, while taking on the odd private business. The Wolseley parked out front is the latest private business, Joe hired by Vickers, the manufacturers, to attend functions promoting the car.

'I'm to be at a party in Cambridge tomorrow which is why I have the car. If you're willing to give it a go, Professor, we could give Mister Jacob a bit of thrill before his big moment. It might help calm his nerves.'

The idea was put to James late Tuesday evening, they meeting in a local bar to talk about the cable. Joe said he'd seen the lady in question, Serena, the Jezebel, once in the tea-rooms across the way and twice on campus.

'She was up to her eyes in furs but I knew her from when she would meet the old Professor in the Science Lab. I heard she was asking about the lad. It bothered me.' He'd shrugged. 'It could be something and nothing. People can change. I cabled you in case she hadn't.'

Now they sit together, three nervous uncles. In terms of nerves they are more anxious than Jacob. A shivering wreck entered the chapel. He sat at the organ and an angel pulled a switch, ghosts of former musicians coming to his aid, so that along with them the boy might have his moment of glory.

* * *

Giovanni leaned close. 'Do not worry, Clarissa. He will be fine.'

'I know. It's just that he is so precious to me, like the young brother I never had. I don't want anything or anyone hurting him.'

'I am assured by Sadie he is a musician with a great future ahead of him. With that in mind the thing to consider is not so much what happens here today but what should happen tomorrow.'

'Yes I know, but I can't think of that!' She protested. 'Not today! I understand what you are saying. I know we have to think ahead, but let's please get him through this before worrying about tomorrow.'

'*Certo!* I meant only to say that with regard to his future, and to yours, my life, my way, and my heart, are entirely at your disposal.'

Clarissa heard what he said but couldn't respond. This building has known centuries of music, piety and prayer surging up toward the woven wings that is King's Chapel ceiling. She understands what Giovanni is saying and the weight of it, but feels today she'd best stay with love of Jacob and none other.

Before he left she sought him out. She didn't bother with the attic, if you want to find the elf look to the animals. Such is his love of creatures he knows when they are ill and, as in the case of Hazlett, must be prevented from doing himself harm sitting up overnight in the stables.

This morning he was in the woodshed hiding a dish of porridge under a piece of sacking. He gave a guilty grin. 'I leave dinner for fox.'

'And your breakfast porridge by the looks of it.'

'I no like porridge.'

'And the fox does?'

'*Si!*' He'd shrugged. 'Better'n me.'

'I have a gift for you.' She'd fastened a St Christopher medal about his neck. 'We've all had a hand in it, even Sykes. It has your name and address engraved on the back so that if you ever get lost you know where to find us.'

As she said to Giovanni, he is the brother she always wanted. She loves him and knows beyond a shadow of a doubt that Papa loves him too.

Giovanni frowned. 'Is it true James van Leiden is Jacob's legal guardian and that he has applied for continued care?'

'There is court order in place to that effect. Why do you ask?'

'In terms of the boy's future with you and the family it is an important point. That Jacob was born outside of this country will complicate issues. Do you think James means to carry the guardianship through?'

'I'm sure of it. James van Leiden would never put his name to anything that he didn't mean to carry through.'

'You think a great deal of the man?'

'In terms of this, his promise to take care of Jacob, yes I do.'

'And in other things, in matters of the human heart, *your* heart in particular, where do your feelings lie?'

It was then Jacob entered the chancel, his diminutive figure seen against the golden backdrop. A ripple passed through the congregation, people whispering. In that moment Clarissa was as certain of her answer to Giovanni's question as she was of her name. Later, looking back over the day, she sees her eventual reply as contradictory to the first as nay is to yay.

* * *

Midway through the second piece James breathed out. Jacob is playing well, the people in the Chapel mesmerised, and this audition going down in history as the most exciting and the most heartbreakingly sad.

The first choice, the Chopin etude, opus 10 number 4, is difficult. James sat on tacks throughout. However, once Jacob began to play the idea of a teenage boy sitting an audition was a joke. Age has nothing to do with his skill. This is genius at work. One must look beyond this day to a place known as Timeless where genius in names such as Mozart and Beethoven reside.

Jacob's second choice is the Etude, opus 10, number 3. It is not a favourite of James, since, subtitled *Tristesse*, one is tempted to make much of the idea of melancholy with lots of hand-waving and lugubrious expressions, over-egging it, as Anneka said, when as a teenager James hung over the piano like a dying swan. With Jacob there is none of that. He lets the melody speak for itself. Usually applause has no place at this kind of gathering but this is not the usual, and so as he brings the piece to a close there is applause, gentle applause, and he bowing and smiling, the pixie's ears seen in Assisi pointed and rosy-red.

James fought the need to stand up and shout: 'Remember this day! You will never know the courage of the boy and what it took to get him here.'

Across the aisle Clarissa sits motionless, tears on her lashes. Miss Hankin and the rest of the family are the same, a wave of love reaching out.

Jacob takes another bow and sits in preparation to play a final piece that, according to the program, 'is a special choice - an Italian folk song.'

People settled eager to hear more. Then the day went horribly wrong.

'Sir?' Archie Johnson got to his feet. Pink-cheeked, he leaned toward James indicating the aisle. 'I believe this lady is looking to sit next to you.'

James turned. Serena stood in the aisle, Kasper beside her.

* * *

Joe Sissons gave up his seat so they might move across.

Kasper apologised: 'We were held up in the snow.'

James didn't give a damn for his apologies. They could not have chosen a worst time to arrive. Until this moment Jacob was happy. Now, face ashen, he stares in their direction as though paralysed.

A glance across the way shows the family closing ranks; even the young girl, Freya-Jasmine, leans toward her grandmother seeking comfort. James saw then that, while he knows a little of the boy's history, these people know the boy. They see him every day, when he is happy and sad. He is family, and irrespective of being Ward of Court, their fear for him remains.

Then Sadie Ambrose Pennington rose to her feet, and the matter of what to do in a family crisis was resolved by more experienced hands.

'*Grazie! Mi scusi per favore! Grazie*!' Smiling, she made her way to the end of the row, and then the consummate Diva - furs sweeping the floor - she flowed down the central nave like a radiant many-sailed ship.

The Chapel was agog, the congregation fluttering. Sadie Ambrose Pennington is known throughout the world as the *American Song Bird*, her face seen on sheets of music in piano stools from here to Botany Bay.

Afterward Jacob would describe his feelings, how very

frightened he was seeing Serena, and how in that moment his faith deserted him:

'I wasn't Mister Jacob, a scholar at Cambridge University. I was what I am, a hunch-back dwarf who happens to play the organ. And across the horizon, only a boat ride away, is Italy, and Spoleto, and a white-washed cell with bars at the window where I was ever afraid.'

At the Chancel Sadie paused, and facing the congregation, spoke of the song that she and Jacob 'had thought to surprise you all on this winter's day.'

She said they had 'chosen to offer that which describes the beauty of the earth, and while over the centuries the Chapel has heard all manner of music, a simple Neapolitan song like *Santa Lucia* is always a joy to the ear.'

One hand on her bosom and the other gesturing to the audience, she nodded to Jacob, lifted her bright face and sang. If in this display Jacob was taken by surprise the audience never knew, for not only did he play with great aplomb, he adopted a showbiz manner lifting his arms and sighing.

It came to James then that, along with Samuel Chase, the boy had spent his early years on the streets of Assisi surviving the cruelties of life by playing and singing, and that this showy manner was a knee-jerk reaction to danger.

They, the two them, sang three verses. Then Jacob's supporters, young choristers squashed in the pews, who'd sat in silence throughout the Chopin, added their voices, and the rafters in this great old building ringing.

It was a far cry from Chopin and yet it was marvellous.

CHAPTER THIRTY

Miracle

King's College Chapel, Cambridge
Wednesday December 11ᵗʰ 1901

It might have been the look that made up her mind. It wasn't much, a turn of the head, a glance, and yet so filled with loathing it shook Clarissa.

While Serena never claimed to like her stepsister, she had never outwardly declared enmity. If there was any obvious feeling it was indifference bordering on scorn. She sought to preserve her energy for more worthwhile pursuits as in the hunting of hidden treasure, and once found, stowing away the same, a smile on her lips and a paw raised in warning - claws lightly visible.

There was the odd flash of temper as with the cat's collar and the jug of cream but swiftly dispelled. The one time she did display anger was the last day in Beeches waiting for a carriage to take her and her mother away. At the time Clarissa didn't know the carriage, now recognising the coat-of-arms, she sees it as a Lombardi on loan to Kasper when in Cambridge.

That last day saw anger, Serena believing Isabella had been cheated of the house. They took so much and always overnight. One day a Chinese cabinet was missing, the next day the blue vase, and sadness lingering where once were memories.

Margret would shrug. 'Think of it like this - a well fed beast sleeps; a hungry animal will chew on anything. If losing stuff means keeping your fingers then that's all right.' She knew the

Parisis wanted the house and in those days would sit into the early hours watching the stairs: 'She was frightened for you, Miss Clary,' said Sally. 'I used to say don't be silly; they are human beings not murderers. She would look at me - "So? It wouldn't take much, a ruck on the stair carpet, a little shove, and this house and everything in it is theirs." '

That anger is here in King's Chapel and while not afraid for herself, Clarissa thinks of hungry animals and the need to keep people safe.

Margret is happy for her sister but afraid of being left old and alone. Papa always said that whatever happens she has a home as does Freya-Jasmine. While that remains true Clarissa needs the support of a man she trusts. She had hoped that might be James, but now, knowing of the loan, and he here in the Chapel with Serena, she let go of hope and, closing her eyes, prayed that, right or wrong, dearest Papa will help her through.

'Giovanni?' She turned to him. 'I was wondering whether we might invite the van Leidens and their guests to Beeches for a small celebration tea. An informal meeting perhaps, bringing a few of Jacob's friends together while offering a united front. What do you think?'

In those few words she made a choice, putting her trust in strong hands, and in seeking his advice, and while not actually acceding to his earlier statement offering hand and heart, she did acknowledge the same.

A tall man he stood with his dark head bent and face absorbed, listening to words that while unspoken could be heard if he had the will to hear.

'I think it an excellent idea, Clarissa.' He nodded. 'It beards the lion in his den while clarifying a situation.'

'*Sì! Io pensavo anch'io.*' Thinking she might've made a mistake in the Italian, she repeated the phrase, stammering. 'Th...that is what I thought.'

'No, *amore mio!*' Gaze brilliant, he took her hand. 'You didn't get it wrong. You got it all entirely right. Come! We do this thing together.'

They made their way across the aisle: James, Kasper and Serena, turning toward them. Clarissa didn't offer her hand to Serena. She couldn't manage that, but with teeth set she could smile.

There was a brief hiatus, a ruffling of feathers at this frontal assault, anger flashing before being tidied away under lustrous lashes. Then, too sure of her own beauty to be bested by another, her composure was restored.

'Dearest sister!' She kissed the air. 'It is so good to see you.'

Clarissa was unable to meet James's eyes; not that it mattered, he was in that closed-down stance he adopts when under fire.

Heart aching, she remained silent, for having made a choice she can only follow where it leads, Giovanni's hand covering hers, his gold ring, the House of Lombardy, vivid against the whiteness of her skin.

* * *

Once inside the house, Margret and Sally looked to the arranging of tea. Sadie uncovered the piano and began to play, while Freya-Jasmine, skipping about, acted as maid. Unaware of the ground shifting beneath them, everyone seemed relaxed and happy - everyone but Jacob, who hid in his room taking the dogs with him. Clarissa left him alone, thinking he must find his way through this without undue fuss. Eventually, drawn by the music, he crept down to stand alongside Sadie, and there he stayed, she a temporary lighthouse, and he afeared of being shipwrecked.

Clarissa wandered about with a sense of being two people, the child that lived and grew inside these walls and the woman that will leave. She hated the idea of Serena being there but knew it needed to happen if only to show the love felt for Jacob. That she is here is no coincidence. Other reasons may have brought her again to Cambridge: Kasper or James, yet the boy by the piano - musical genius as he is hailed with talk of concerts and private soirees - is why she was at the audition. A snippet of conversation heard this afternoon from the row behind pointed the fact: '*Yes, very beautiful! I heard that, as his sister, she contacted the bursar reserving a seat in the van Leiden row.*'

Knowing what sister meant when Papa was alive, and what it might mean in a Court of Law, the word filled Clarissa with horror. Suddenly afraid for Jacob she looked to where Giovanni stood. He, feeling her gaze, glanced up, nodded, and fear subsided. One way or another, the people here in this house are to some degree sealed within Clarissa's fate, and yet, beyond a nod of the head, nothing is declared, only that the man is here and she glad of it.

* * *

Quarter to six the doorbell rang: Serena and Kasper. While they were in the hall being relieved of coats and boots, Jacob grabbed Clarissa's hand, dragging her into the yard and to his hidey-hole, Hazlett's stable.

'Why is she here?' He was shaking. 'What does the Parisi lady want?'

'I don't know, but whatever she wants she can't have it.'

It wasn't enough. With first-hand knowledge of the woman and what she can do, he needed stronger assurance. 'Where is Mister James? He is my special father, the judge said so.'

'Yes, as you say, he is a special father and won't let you down.'

'They will take me away.' He paced the floor. 'I know they will.'

'They will not!' She paced with him. 'I won't let them.'

'*Oh mio*! I knew they would come.' Still he paced the floor, his foot dragging and he looking ill. 'They will never let me go.'

'*Ora* Jacob?' Giovanni stood at the door. '*Cos'è questo trambusto?*'

'*Signore?*'

'I ask why you make a fuss.' He stood stroking Hazlett's nose. 'You played well today. You should be happy proving your worth to all who listened.'

Jacob bowed. '*Chiedo scusa, Altezza. Avevo paura.*'

'In English, if you please. We are not alone.'

'Your pardon, sir. I was afraid.'

'You have no need. You are safe here in this stable and, with time, and Miss Morgan and the Lord's good grace, you will be always safe.'

'Highness?' Puzzled, Jacob stared.

'*Allora.*' Giovanni took Clarissa's hand pressing it to his lips. 'As I say, time and Miss Morgan's good grace, you will always be safe.'

'Oh! This I see!' Jacob's eyes widened. 'Then Miss Morgan is also safe.'

'*Si! Io sono Il Marchese di Lombardi!* ' Giovanni shrugged and was suddenly so Italian and so very handsome. '*Mi prenderò cura di tutti voi!*

'I am the Marchese di Lombardi.' Clarissa understood the smile as she understood the words: 'I will take care of you all.'

* * *

The sun is setting and the sky heavy with snow. James gazed into angry clouds, accepting the reality of the day that, somewhere between a Chopin etude and a Neapolitan folk song, he lost the love of his life to another man.

Proof of loss was in their clasped hands; Clarissa's hand eclipsed by Giovanni's. He met them earlier on the way to the audition. They were together then yet apart in that taking a man's arm is a matter of etiquette. Now she is enfolded into his life, and while a promise is not yet given it is assured.

James didn't used to be an angry man. As with other excesses he saw it a destructive force and wasteful emotion. Today he is beyond anger.

Some weeks ago he knew a feeling akin to this. It was in the University Library and Sweaty Steed playing foul with Clarissa's name. He was angry then but in a hot way. There is nothing hot about this; it is an ice cold hand clamped to his chest where his heart used to be. It arrived with such force it unscrambled the mechanism that is James van Leiden, so that for a moment he stood outside of life looking in at a younger Serena.

Hair pulled back, sharp collar bones and the body of a teenage girl, she stood before a looking-glass. She was practising her smile, titling her head from side-to-side, offering expressions, frowning and laughing, and standing beside her - a conductor with a silver tea-spoon - her mother, Isabella.

Anger drew him to his feet this afternoon. Joe Sissons left his seat for one across the aisle. She could have had that but chose to be on the other side of James. Her beauty a source of attention, she let the moment work for her and squeezed by to sit with her arm through his: ''Ow are you James?'

It left him sick, knowing the whole performance was not about him but about Clarissa. 'Look!' Serena was saying. 'See what I can do, dearest sister. I can lie and cheat and steal and this man will still adore me.'

He'd wanted to strike her. He is not alone in his torment. Kasper is unhappy as seen by a note left on the piano. A rambling screed, he wrote of a bible story and how Belshazzar, King of Babylon, met his end. The story says the king mocked God's Holy name by allowing his servants to drink from sacred vessels, thus a ghostly hand was seen to inscribe a death sentence on the wall:

'*Mene, Mene, Tekel Upharsin:* Thou art weighed in the balance and found wanting.' Kasper added his own thought: 'I too have been weighed in the balance. Please God I will not be found wanting.'

Weighed in the balance is how James feels. He always feared he would lose Clarissa and now understands he has none but himself to blame.

Joe Sissons touched his arm. 'Are you all right, Professor?'

'I am all right, Joe. Just give me a minute.'

James needs to make his way to the wretched tea-party, Jacob will be looking for him, but he can't seem to move. He thinks of Phoebe, the old professor's wife, who said Serena's debt had ruined Clarissa's life, and that it would take a miracle to give her back a future.

The miracle has happened; it is there in the hand holding hers.

That hand foretells the future. In the coming weeks word will go out that His Highness, the Marchese Giovanni Carlo Arello di Lombardi, esteemed patron of the Fitzwilliam Museum and the University of Cambridge, is to wed a local girl. At first it will be a whisper, and then, when not denied and good wishes passing back and forth, it will become a roar, a transition will be made, and a slate wiped clean, and soon Clarissa seen as a sacred icon.

Everything said before of debts and misbehaviour will be dismissed as too ridiculous to be true, and she raised among her female peers worthy of calling cards and in every possible way people seeking an introduction.

James should be glad for her and her family. Marriage to such a man means a good name restored, the bank loan a distant nightmare, and that good old man, John Sarson, relieved of obligation to his niece, and the letters in James's pocket - death bed confessions - never written.

'I must visit the old man to let him know how things are.' He reached out to Joe. 'What do you think? Could you and Archie come along with me? It's only Norfolk...not like Italy.'

'No need to ask. Norfolk or Italy, when it comes to standing by a pal there ain't no difference.' Concerned, Joe Sissons took James's arm. 'But we should get going. I need this car in the garage and you need to be at the tea-party. Your boy is there. You don't want him bothered by undue influence.'

They made their way to the car: James feeling his way like a blind man.

She is gone. The safest pair of hands in the world of conservation has dropped the most precious treasure, and all because he waited thinking tomorrow... and tomorrow and tomorrow.

CHAPTER THIRTY-ONE

Safe not Sorry

Beeches, Comberton
Wednesday December 11th 1901

The door opened and Jacob flew at him. 'You came!'

'Of course I came. How are you?'

'I am better now.'

'That's good.' James hugged him. 'You played wondrously well.'

They hung together, Jacob with his head on James's chest. Then Jacob sighed. 'I was good but I could've played so much better.'

'We could all play so much better but somehow that never seems to happen. It is the nature of the beast.'

Jacob pulled away. 'Beast?'

'Never mind. It's only a saying.'

'I know about the beast. I have seen him. He has big red eyes and big teeth. I saw him today in the Chapel and I was afraid.'

'I know.'

'I see him here but then *Il Marchese* make it go away.'

'Did he? I'm glad.'

'Mister James?' Uncomfortable about what he had seen, the boy shifted from one foot to the other. 'Shall I say how His Highness make it better?'

James smiled, poor wretch. 'Will it hurt me to say so?'

'*Sì!*' Jacob nodded. 'I think it will.'

'Then leave it, dear boy. Let me learn for myself.'

* * *

He soon learned why it would hurt. Though in different parts of the house, Giovanni in the sitting-room listening to the Reverend Bellamy, and Clarissa helping serve food, a connecting cord bound them together, visible in a light blush on her cheek and his ardent gaze.

In Florence one was struck by the upright bearing and solemnity, though only in his thirties he seemed so much older. Now, while the upright bearing remains, all else is changed. He radiates goodwill and certain suppressed feelings known by him alone. The saga of the white waistcoat and a wife mourned for seven years is done, and he clad in a suit of bullet-proof armour that only Clarissa's glance might pierce.

On the way to the house James passed Paul Brooke, another loser in this game of love, who had paused to commiserate. 'I suppose we should be pleased. At least now the wagging tongues are silenced.'

James approached them both. Giovanni's grip was firm and his glance untroubled, whereas Clarissa was subdued, her face a pale cameo and she standing slightly behind her lover shielded from the world.

Looking for a hiding place, James would've spoken with Kasper but he is another unhappy soul, and other than to say he'd call before leaving, didn't want to talk, wouldn't talk, but went out to the yard clearing snow.

Avoiding the study where Serena held court, James circled

the house. For a while Jacob dogged his footsteps, nervous, talking of the audition and of his duet with Mrs Ambrose Pennington, until suddenly swerving away to help outside with the snow. It was a good time to leave but James stayed pursuing pain stuck with an idea he might never see her again, until Miss Hankin drew him into the kitchen. 'So here we are. The king is dead, long live the king.'

It was pointless pretending he didn't know what she meant, and so he shrugged. 'Or to the victor the spoils.'

'You make it sound like gaining her for wife was a battle.'

'It might've been seen so.'

'I don't seem to remember you putting up much of a fight.'

'You can be cruel when you want, Miss Hankin.'

'Really?' She grimaced. 'Am I being cruel when I say she would've done better with you? And the family, for that matter, who, knowing who you are, and liking you for it, would've been glad to have you in his place.'

'If that's a compliment it feels distinctly back to front.'

'It is how I feel about it.'

'Has Miss Morgan said anything about promises exchanged?'

'No and she won't yet. But then who needs to be told. One look at the fellow's face and we all knew what was going on.'

James frowned. 'You know, Miss Hankin, You might try being a little respectful of Clarissa's choice. The Marchese is a member of the Royal House of Savoy, which may mean little to you but means a great deal to Italy. A wealthy man, educated, speaking several languages, his patronage would be a gift to a young person like Freya-Jasmine. She would benefit from his help as would you if you let him. I have been to his home and know he treats those of his household with consideration.

So, while understanding your position, and your regret at the thought of leaving Beeches, you'd do well to remember who he is and what he represents.'

'I am sure he is a very nice chap and that he will take care of Miss Clary. I am just saying I would rather it have been you.'

'Or Doctor Brooke or anyone else not living half-way across the world.'

'Well, maybe Doctor Brooke. He is a good man. But he wasn't the man Miss Clary wanted. It was you she cared for, and but for that woman, Serena, over shining like polished brass, I'd be seeing out my old age with you.'

Determined never to think that way again James let the remark go. 'So will you try seeing the good in this and live in Italy?'

'Oh no! I'm not doing that. Italy wouldn't suit me and I wouldn't suit it. I'll go with our Sally.'

'And Freya-Jasmine?'

'Well that's another thing.' She sniffed. 'Just because I'm a miserable old woman doesn't mean I should get in the way of her life. She loves Miss Clary. If she wants to go to Italy and be schooled there all well and good. From what Mrs Pennington says there are some very good schools in Florence.'

'You are talking about not seeing your granddaughter for months on end. Can you bear to do that?'

'I can bear anything but the child thinking she missed out. She'll have the best with Clarissa and if Italy is what she wants so be it. I don't hold my breath. Going with Sally is no bed of roses. I'll be the old maid sister, the hanger-on nobody wants, not even Sally, a new wife in need of privacy. They won't know what to do with me. I'll be a nuisance and the older I get the bigger the nuisance. But I don't have a lot of choice. It's that or Italy.'

'I do understand and I sympathise.'

'I know you do. I don't suppose you need a housekeeper, do you? I know you've got good old Archie but there's always room for a little 'un.'

'And I would have that little one and welcome if only for her salmon and broccoli pie, but it would seem I too am on the move.'

'Where will you go?'

'I don't know.'

'I did hear rumours but thought that was all they were.'

'That *was* all they were, but now with this...I might as well make the rumours fact.'

She patted his arm. 'We are a sorry pair. But nothing is decided yet. Things can still change.' She would've said more but seeing Serena heading their way found she needed to check the hens. ''Cos you never know, Professor. This time of the year there are all kinds of wild animals running loose seeing what they can maim and kill. Better to be safe than sorry.'

* * *

Serena smiled. 'Dear James. 'Ow are you?

'Thank you, I am well.'

Today, though bitterly cold, and she swaddled in luxurious furs, she carries a fan on a chain about her wrist, and opening the same cools her face.

'My brother Jacob was very good today.'

'Your brother?'

'Yes, my brother. My mother was wed to his father. We can

claim kinship and plan to do so. You too have plans for him, I think.'

'I am awarded guardianship, if that is what you mean.'

'Ah yes guardian! It is a good word.' She tapped her cheek, the black lace fan flattering her eyes. 'And the law approved of this, he being sickly of health and in need of good care, and you *not* of his family?'

'My circumstances were considered by the Court and found sufficient.'

'Of course! One expects nothing more. This is a nice house.' Eyes covetous she glanced about and James recalling talk of her desire for this house. 'Yes, a good house, and as we know with time and patience, and new information presented, things can change with houses as well as people.'

'I dare say.' He bowed. 'You must excuse me. I have things to do.'

'What kind of things?' She put out her hand, the fan resting on his sleeve. 'I did hear you are to leave Cambridge.'

'I have made no decision.'

'Your students protest your absence.'

'They are students. They would protest the sun shining in the sky if they thought it jolly to do so.'

'Ah yes. They are children. I understand this. Children are not sophisticated. They cannot hide their feelings. They run with hearts wide open. They make banners with the title of your book and fly them from the rooftops.'

He was silent.

'Scorched Hearts is the name of your book, no? A wonderful name! *Così sensuale!* It says much of you, James van Leiden. That you are a man of great passion and that as with any fire all you need is the flame.'

He remained silent - her words dust under his feet.

'Your students say that their hearts are scorched by the thought of you leaving. I understand 'ow they feel.' Lashes long on her cheeks she pressed the fan to her bosom as though protecting her heart. 'I felt pain when you left me in Assisi. Three days of love and I scorched never to love again.'

* * *

Clarissa was on the landing. She saw James pause to speak with Giovanni and then he left. She wanted to run after him: 'Don't go! I love you and will always love you,' instead she continued to the bathroom.

She washed her face and tidied her hair, and opened the door to Serena who pushed by to be violently sick over the lavatory.

'Do you need a doctor?' Clarissa stayed with her.

'No doctor. We both know what this is.'

'How can I help?'

'You could get milk and allow me to lie down a moment.'

Clarissa lit a lamp in the blue bedroom and drew the curtains. Then she ran down into the kitchen and taking a jug from the larder poured a glass of milk.

'Is there a problem?' Giovanni was behind her.

'Serena is unwell.'

'Do we need a doctor?'

'I don't think it is that kind of unwell.'

'*Cos'è*?' He frowned and then nodded, understanding. 'Perhaps it is Kasper she needs.'

'Better to let her rest.'

Serena sat on the side of the bed. She took the milk and then sighed: 'I remember this room. I was comfortable here.'

'It is a nice room.'

'Nice? Oh *la*!' She grimaced. 'Was there ever a country and people for stifling feelings. And you, the perfect English rose, uprooted and bruised, are past master at hiding yours. Look at us now. You bathe my face and bring me milk. Why so meekly accepting when really you want to shout and rail.'

'I have guests and prefer not to make a fuss.'

'Why not make the fuss? Why not shout and scream for once in your life letting the world know how you feel? After all that has happened here in this house, do you not think you deserve to be heard?'

'Depends what you mean by deserve.'

'I mean so many things. Why not speak of them here and now, Clareessa Morgan, and I again under your roof and vulnerable.'

'Vulnerable?'

'*Si*, vulnerable.' She shrugged. 'I am unmarried and with child. What better time to unloose your chagrin.'

'I won't do that. As I said, I have guests, and while there is much I could say I'll not be a bully. I'll leave that to you.'

'Ah, so you can use words sharply.' Serena stood before the cheval mirror inspecting her face. 'I don't know why you won't admit your loathing of me and my mother. You never wanted us here. From the start you felt your papa had made a mistake. You hid your feelings but I saw them.'

'If you knew I felt that way why did you stay?'

'I suited me to do so.'

'Then you can hardly complain about my thoughts on the

matter.' Clarissa shook her head. 'I don't understand you. I never shall. Who are you, Serena, that you dare question my feelings. Have you forgotten what you did and the way you hurt people?'

'I have a good memory. I remember every day and your loathing of us.'

'Do you remember stealing from my uncle?'

'I took nothing that wasn't mine.'

'How was that money yours? And please stop speaking of what happened as if talking of strangers in another town. The people you hurt are not strangers. They are my family. They live close by, or used to. They are dear good people who never did you a moment's harm. They didn't deserve this.'

Serena started forward. 'I took from them what you took from me. See this house!' She slapped the wall, gas-light flickering. 'It belongs to my mother. Isabella was wife to your father. What belonged to him belonged to her.'

'My father gave you money that was meant for me. You took that and everything else you could carry. You didn't need to take more, especially that way. It was cruel and ugly, and the pain you caused is still happening.'

'If there is pain you are to blame not me. Ah!' Drained of colour Serena sat back on the bed. 'Now you cause me and my baby pain.'

'I'm sorry. I didn't intend this to happen. I don't want to argue with you. I want to get away from all of this and start a life where you are not.'

'And that is why you agree to marry this man. You do not love him yet he is rich and a way out.' She nodded. 'I understand, though 'ow you manage I do not know, he mourning the most beautiful woman in all Italy.'

Clarissa was done with it. 'Do you need the bathroom again?'

'No. It will pass.'

'Then should I call Kasper?'

Serena was silent. Then she smiled. 'Why Kasper?'

'You are unwell and need to leave. And if he is the...' Unsure of how to continue Clarissa was silent.

Serena filled in the gap. 'If he is what...the father of my child?'

Clarissa remained silent.

'Yes, say nothing, for in this you know nothing, particularly about my feelings for James van Leiden. You live so long with your good Papa you've no idea of the world. You think love is one man and one woman. That a woman can have two lovers and enjoy both doesn't occur to you.'

'You're wrong.' Clarissa gazed at her. 'I am not blind to the world. That you have more than one lover doesn't surprise me. I just wonder if it is love, or if it is exactly as you say - you enjoying them.'

'Are you saying I cannot love?'

'I don't know. I simply wonder if in all of this you have ever loved. If not, and you carrying a child, then it is a shame and I am sorry.'

'I have loved.' Serena leaned forward, her gaze dark. 'I still love. That I don't have him within my grasp is an error I seek to rectify. And I will rectify it, though it takes me a lifetime. As for shame, where love is concerned I do not accept the word. There is only love and that is enough.'

'I would agree with you if I thought you understood the idea of love.'

'I understand better than one who spends her life dreaming.

You dream you are the Marchese's adored one. Impossible! I promise you that will never happen. Have you been to his villa in Fiesole?'

'I have stayed there.'

'And what did you see?'

'I saw a rather striking house. Was I supposed to see other than that?'

'It is a rather striking house. People go there to gaze at it and the treasure inside. It is a store house of rather striking things, every item handpicked, nothing like them in the world, and all signifying the same.'

'And what is that?'

'The Villa del Rosa is not a house. It is a shrine and a living testimony to the man's love of his wife. Carina di Vallagra was said to be the most beautiful woman in all Italy with moonlight in her hair and eyes of topaz. You will never be happy there, for you will share your life with a ghost that has haunted the villa for seven long years.'

Clarissa covered her ears. 'Please stop!'

'I will stop as one day you will stop dreaming and know what all Florence knows. You did not give your life to a living man - you gave your life and your youth to *un vedovo,* a widower, a shadow of a man who married for love and who will die loving the same.'

CHAPTER THIRTY-TWO

Pals

Lightfoot Farm, Norfolk
Thursday 12ᵗʰ December 1901

Packed and ready to go, Sadie sat watching sparrows fight over a crust of bread. Then bored, she went to find Gianni. He was out and not likely to return until the evening. She hitched a ride back on the cart, the housekeeper left stripping beds and Charles at the kitchen table polishing Gianni's boots and frowning, as if to say, 'go find a man more your age, fool of a woman.'

Charles Anouilh: secretary, bodyguard or hired butcher, no one knows the true history of the man. It is said he began life as the bastard child of a local priest, and that his mother, a nun, took her life when Charles was but a boy. From the age of seven, so the story goes, he was raised by Benedictine monks before leaving in his teens to become a soldier. Gianni's name for him is *Lucciole* - glow-worm. He said that as a child he was never afraid at night, for no matter where he was or when, Charles was always there – his eyes shining through the darkness.

It is certain he loves his charge, watching over him like a dragon safeguarding an egg. This last summer he saved the egg from breaking. There was an anti-monarchy protest outside of the Duomo. A fanatic threatened Gianni with a pistol. Half-blind or not, Charles Anouilh was ahead of it. A knife flashed and the would-be assassin was dead - his throat opened up like sliced ham.

So many strange and exotic tales are said of the man - Sadie tends to believe them all. Today he was right to arch his brows: she shouldn't have come.

On this day seven years ago Carina di Lombardi died, all of that glowing beauty and raging storm returned to the earth. Gianni will have gone to Mass this morning. While not wishing to come between him and duty, Sadie thought to drop by to see if he remains steady in his decision to return to Florence.

She and her maid, Molly, leave today on the 3-15 train to London. Hoping to do a little Christmas shopping they are booked in for two nights at the Grosvenor. Gianni and Charles leave some time tomorrow and all four to meet at St Pancras Saturday ready for the noon-day express London to Milan.

Gianni has found love and is loath to leave that love unwatched. Sadie understands and would have stayed if only to be there at Beeches on Christmas Eve when a knock at the door brings St Nicholas to Beeches in the shape of Gianni's groom, and Soubrette, the pony, a Florentine blessing in a red satin bow tied to the saddle.

A child like Freya-Jasmine is Christmas and the birth of Our Lord shared with the living as well as the ghosts of yesteryear. It is a shame to leave but it was the right thing to do. As she said on the way back from Cambridge yesterday. 'If you want to marry Clarissa Morgan you must continue as before. You won't have a problem with the House of Savoy. They don't doubt you, and won't doubt your choice. It is to the lesser houses you must look.'

Anxious for him, she'd pursued the issue. 'You will be observed as never before and must remain the *Signore* they think they know and love. Greater issues as with the matter of Christian faith can be resolved by greater minds. The little things will condemn you, a broken dinner date or an empty chair at an evening soiree. Before they were the mishaps of a busy man and not worth a cent, but once wed to an outsider any mishap will be seen as the fault of the English girl and she suffering because of it.'

Knowing what she said to be true he'd remained silent throughout the journey, gazing into the darkness, hand on his knee, the Lombardi ring, the joy and the bane of his life, reflecting the lantern glow.

Sadie pursued her intent with caution. They are friends yet to presume too much in this is to cause offence, a certain look in his eyes, and an end to friendship. It is a look she has come to respect; a thing of lightning it will come out of nowhere, on the Polo field, in the managing of home issues, anywhere. When it does arrive mind your manners, for it suggests His Highness senses discourtesy, and while not yet offended, the wrongdoer - commoner or king - better back-off before a door closes on him for once and all.

It is said his father was the same: a goodly Signore, a just man, fair with those who played fairly but merciless when wronged. Seven years ago Giovanni Carlo Arello di Lombardi was wronged in such a way it was thought by those that knew he might never reclaim his honour.

Sadie met Gianni in the summer of '91. A leading coloratura, at the peak of her profession with a voice like a bell, she was on tour with the New Orleans Opera Company, playing to packed houses in all major European cities.

Travel weary from so many weeks on the road, and after the fiasco that was Verona's *Aida,* she needed to rest.

The plan was to present the opera in Verona's Roman

Amphitheatre with the Maestro, Giuseppe Verdi, as a guest. It turned out to be a disaster.

Head filled with visions of ancient Egypt, the stage director had carpenters erect a monstrous pyramid centre stage that on the night of the performance no one could get into or around. He imported chariots along with male and female bare-chested slaves leading wild animals up and down the ramparts: a lion actually breaking free during rehearsal, and the poor half-crazed creature, wounding several members of an already depleted orchestra.

Thinking bigger and better, the director brought in local choirs to add to the chorus, none with stage craft, so that on the night, dodging camels and heavy scenery, people were falling off the stage. Then a flaming torch carried by one the slaves set fire to a banner, and men with buckets trying to douse the flames. In the midst of this chaos, Sadie Ambrose-Pennington, the *American Song Bird,* sang *Retorno Vincitor* to an hysterical audience while treading through donkey shit in her bare feet.

Florence was to be a rest and the Pitti Palace an intimate soiree with Italian music from Monteverdi to Puccini. It is to the heartbreakingly sad V*issi d'Arte* from *Tosca* that Sadie remembers meeting Gianni. That evening in Florence she sang of the love of Life and Beauty to a man with darkness in his eyes.

Later that evening at a reception she was introduced to *Il Marchese* and his beautiful wife, and though he smiled, the darkness was still there.

A friendship formed that day that kept Sadie in Italy long enough for her to never want to leave. It saw the end of her marriage to William T Pennington, he skipping to Reno divorcing Sadie to wed Betty Redway, his long-time secretary and lover. Bill said he'd had twenty years of running from one bed to another, he didn't want another twenty, and 'would Sadie be a pal and not take him to the cleaners. Last seen, his boys - twins born eighteen years ago - six-foot and growing, are gonna need every dollar.'

Bill is a good guy. It wasn't his fault Sadie couldn't conceive. He was kind and patient and adored children and but for the Tour would've hung on.

Sadie was a pal. She took what was hers to take: fifty-per-cent of the shares in Idaho Copper Canyon Mines and the Appaloosas. Bill did wobble over the horses but she hung on. God's sake, every day away she'd wept not seeing her babies, she wasn't gonna give them up so Bill could sell them at auction. There would no more tours and no more husbands; the horses were hers, bought with the proceeds of her first sell-out concert, and named the Ambrose Appaloosas after her daddy.

That was ten years ago. She keeps in touch with the Penningtons, Bill not doing so well, the Wall Street panic of May taking its toll. She sent a message: 'If you and Betty are looking for a bolt-hole there's always one in Italy.'

Carina once asked why Sadie didn't fight for her marriage. In Italy a broken marriage is the wife's fault, a woman suffering anything rather than be shamed in divorce. Sadie had a villa by Lake Como when Carina said that. She was singing at *La Scala* and having the best time of her life with the best sex from the love of her life. If so inclined, she might've offered Orlovsky's aria from *Die Fledermaus*: *Chacun a son gout* - each to his own.

As it was she said nothing and with good reason, for that summer day Carina was sporting a black velvet eye-patch, and under the patch a blacker than black eye. All was not well at the Villa Rosa. That their idyllic marriage was in trouble was the Big Secret; that it stayed so was nothing short of a miracle.

In those days Giovanni was as guarded about his thoughts and feelings as he is now. Carina might occasionally lament *il suo bel ragazzo indifferente* - her beautiful indifferent boy - but quietly mocking and always smiling, so that when the bomb did explode only the few knew and they were family.

Sadie knows a little of what happened on this day seven years ago, and can say - hand on heart - she wouldn't want to know more. While opinions regarding the mystery surrounding Carina's death are whispered abroad, no one really knows what happened, perhaps not even Gianni.

One man will know more than anyone, and that is the sculptor, Vincenza di Vallagra, Gianni's brother-in-law. Vincenza was Carina's twin, born one minute before her. A cruel man, spiteful and vindictive, throughout his sister's life, and on until her death, he used that minute to dominate and control her.

Disowned by his own family, a gambler and a spendthrift, and loyal to no one, he is the cross the House of Lombardy suffers to carry, and the one person able – and willing - to spoil Gianni's newfound happiness.

Sadie loathes the man, thinking him rotten to the core. Now, alone in the cottage contemplating shuttered windows and gathering dust, she is suddenly afraid. She knelt and closing her eyes sought a blessing against evil. She loved Gianni the first time she saw him. Her heart belongs to him and always will no matter who stands with him or who stands against. It is as she said to Bill:

'I hold no grudge against you. You can't choose who to love. It happens or it doesn't, and if it does, you have to hold on and stay true forever.'

* * *

Greys Farm, Norfolk
Thursday 12th December 1901

Before leaving Beeches yesterday James van Leiden asked Giovanni if he might have a word. He mentioned the Fitzwilliam
and a possible sharing of the Lorenzo Monaco painting. He then
spoke of his concern regarding the troublesome bank loan and
in his customary manner was direct.

'Might I enquire if you are in any way informed of an issue
regarding Clarissa's uncle and a bank loan?' When Giovanni
said he was aware of a problem of that nature, James nodded.
'I thought so, which is why - while hoping you won't see me
treading on sacred ground - I would speak on the old man's
behalf. Too many foolish promises forbid me to discuss the loan
yet I can say the wretched thing is paid and none need worry
how. My concern is not about payment or problems caused
because of it. It is about being able to live with oneself *after* the
problems. Professor Sarson is ill and not long for this world,
and while there are reasons to stay away (his reasons I hasten
to add and none of mine), I fear that in the event of his death
Clarissa will be left reproaching herself for a fault that was never
hers. Moreover...'

He'd paused, eyes closed, momentarily stifled: 'I feel any
news regarding her future with you, *Marchese*, can only cheer the
professor's heart, he seeing a problem resolved and his beloved
niece with no lasting harm.'

With that he'd stepped back. 'That was my thought on the
matter before bringing it to you, who I know want only the best

for her, for despite words to the contrary, I believe John and Phoebe Sarson long to see her.'

He wrote down the needed address, and with a grasp of the hand was gone: a rare individual able to put the needs of another beyond his own.

That evening, before leaving for Norfolk, Giovanni told Clarissa of the conversation. Her reply was immediate. 'He is my uncle and precious to me as is my aunt. I would want to see them no matter what.'

She read James's note: *The Sarsons live in a cottage at Greys Farm on the estate of Colonel and Mrs Clive Phillips, whose son, Tom, is my brother-in-law. I took them there in March. They had nowhere else to go.'*

Lips trembling, she said, 'Of course he helped them. It's who he is.'

Doubtless other thoughts passed through her head but that was all she said. Now they are here at the farm greeted by a Colonel Phillips, a gentleman of some substance. Giovanni would've stood apart but could not, for along with an amiable invitation from the Colonel to 'to come up and have a word,' Clarissa's eyes begged him to remain.

A shell of a man, chest sucking in and out as he struggled to breathe, John Sarson lay propped upon the pillows with the worn and transparent look of one who fights to wake every morning and who'd sooner not wake at all.

A glance and Clarissa was down on her knees by the bed with her arms about him. 'Oh my poor dear uncle! I am so sorry to see you ill.'

So many emotions passed through the invalid's face; shock, bemusement, even anger, he held away from her embrace as though fearing contamination. But then he submitted, his arms about her and they weeping together.

Giovanni stood by the window brooding on the brevity of life and how we confuse all with foolish wanting. That he should be here on this particular day observing the approach of death chills his blood while stirring memories he'd sooner remain quiet. Carina di Vallagra died the night of December 12th 1894. The difference between the death-bed scenes could not be more apparent.

This room sits within the cottage roof. It holds a bed, a *cassettiera* in the corner, and a chair. It has a low ceiling, he having to bend. It is cramped and crowded with the muddle of the sickroom. The smell of rank disease hangs in the air and but for present body-heat it would be cold, ice patterning the inside of the window as well as out.

Carina died on a sable rug before an open fire, love birds singing in the aviary, roses scenting the air, a glass of good wine by her hand, and Tansy, her little Pomeranian dog, on a cushion beside her. Two different scenes, two differing lives: one of opulence, the other poverty. Yet if one were to weigh emotion felt during both events, while all are hurting, the love and pity felt here in this hovel would be seen as incalculable.

* * *

Giovanni found sleep hard last night. Everything is arranged for the return home, the housekeeper and staff at the farm taking last instructions. All heavyweight baggage is sent ahead; the paintings bought last week from a local dealer on route as is the Sevres dinner service.

Sadie and her maid leave today for London. He and Charles will follow later. All will take the London to Milan Express train on Saturday. It is all arranged, still Giovanni could not settle. These days *Il Marchese* has many reasons for wakefulness, his time stretched by the needs of the Lake Como *and* the Fiesole Estates. There are problems at his Valtellina vineyards in Lombardy and in his glass factories on Murano: workers calling for a Union while threatening the withdrawal of labour. Florence has known a huge increase in tourism, which has brought both good and bad. The whole of Italy is in a state of political turmoil. Lives are at risk, not least *his* life. Last year, a radical demanding the overthrow of Italian aristocracy held a pistol to Giovanni's head, and but for Charles's dextrous blade, an end to any kind of unrest.

Amid the many, there are now two main sources of disquiet: love for a woman in her grave these seven years, and love for one just learning to live.

Clarissa is always on his mind. He wants her for wife in the way of one waking from a long sleep knowing the difference between false and true.

James van Leiden played a part in last night's struggle. His feelings for Clarissa are evident whereas hers are not. This troubles Giovanni. He knows he is second in her eyes and probably always will be. The knowledge is painful – it burns - but if it means having her by his side he will bear it. What he could not bear is her coming to him blindfolded. She has choices to make. They need to be made clear to her and today before he leaves for Italy.

Realising he is no nearer Clarissa's love, Giovanni sighed, whereupon a hand took his. A worn hand, lined and wrinkled, it belonged to Phoebe Sarson: a lady so lost in grief she didn't mind whose hand she held.

* * *

They did not stay. There was little anyone could do. Clarissa hugged her aunt, trying to instil strength. 'Shall I come again tomorrow?'

'No, my dear! Not tomorrow! While I know he is relieved to see you he needs rest, and he will rest having seen you are happy. And you are happy aren't you, my dear, with this wonderful man to love you?'

'I am happy.' Clarissa smiled through her tears at her aunt who, even as they all stand together in the tiny sitting room, is unwilling to release Giovanni's hand. 'I am happier having seen you and knowing I can come again.'

'And you can but not yet! As you see, though our circumstances are humble, we are cared for. The Colonel and Mrs Phillips could not be kinder. And there is Dear Anneka, their daughter-in-law, and her husband, Thomas, who we've grown to care for these last months. We are not alone, and though you may not see it, dearest niece, we have sanctuary here.'

'I do see it and while I miss you I'm glad you've found comfort, though I admit to being puzzled as to how it all came about.'

'There is no need. We are here because of another kind man, Professor van Leiden, your uncle's staunch supporter this terrible year, who we see as a son to us, and to whom, if you've questions...' she dipped her head, denying further investigation, 'you must look to for further answers.'

They made their farewells: Uncle Sarson peering through a fog, Aunt Phoebe stretched and thin and yet strong within the love of her husband and the support of newfound friends.

* * *

Clarissa leant against the carriage's cushioned seat. She remembered Belgium and Alice van Leiden talking of her daughter's in-laws, Colonel and Mrs Phillips, who lived in Norfolk. They spoke of a woman helper called Phoebe who Anneka loved and who looked toward as a helper when the baby arrived. All this was happening under Clarissa's nose, and her aunt and uncle living but a few miles away supported by James van Leiden.

She recalled Great Aunt Sheba's ban against visiting and Aunt Phoebe's reluctance when further visits were mentioned, and how Uncle Sarson had recoiled from her embrace, his wasted body shrinking away.

Suddenly weary, she undid the fur bonnet and shook out her hair, unable to bear the weight of that *and* her thoughts. 'I think I must be the most short-sighted person.'

Giovanni frowned. 'Why do you say so?'

'Because of today and so many other things I thought I understood.'

'*Tale quale*? Such as?'

'Oh...such things as hothouse lilac, and letters, and people saying one thing and meaning another. Great Aunt said not to bother my uncle; he didn't want to see me. I didn't believe her. I thought it couldn't be that. It is exactly that! I saw it in their eyes today, especially Aunt Phoebe.'

'You are their niece. They want to see you as many times

as the sun rises in the sky. What they do not want to see is the mistake the professor made.'

'Mistake?'

'*Sì*! The debt! *Il livido*! The bruise.'

'I am a bruise to them?'

'Sadly yes. Your aunt clings to the hope her 'usband will survive. She closes the door on all hurtful things. There is nothing you can do about this. You can only wait until the bruise heals and they seeing you as you are.'

'My uncle is dying. He will never see me as I am.' A tear fell. She could not stop it. 'I shall always be a bruise to him.'

'Ah, do not weep, *amore mio*!' Giovanni pulled her into his arms. 'It will be better one day, this I promise!'

Tears falling, she clung to him. He let her weep, and then, tears subsiding, pulled away so he might see her eyes. 'Listen to me. I need to ask a question important to me and my life and I need you to answer true.'

Eyes questioning, she gazed at him.

'My question is this...today you learned James van Leiden brought your people to safety, and that he did this for love of you. My question is, why not choose happiness with him rather than difficulties with me?'

Still she looked at him, and he, catching the words, shook his head.

'Do not think I do not love for I do love as never before.' He took her hand. '*Io bisogno che tu facci quello ceh vuoi. Non quello che vorrie che facessi!* I need you to be sure of what *you* want not what I want. My life is not easy. It demands much and would demand the same of my wife. Not Italian born, nor of my chosen faith, it will be difficult for you. I do not want you to be unhappy. I would sooner lose you to a good man than see you suffer. James van Leiden is a good man. To be with him would not be so difficult.'

She was silent. He thought he had gambled and lost. 'I am a fool.' He gritted his teeth. '*Io dico così male.* I should be quiet and let what is be so.'

'It is all right. I understand what you are saying, truly I do. There has been little time to think beyond the moment. I know there are challenges, not least, as you say, in respect of faith. However, my immediate concern is with my family, as in Margret Hankin and Freya-Jasmine, and Jacob. What happens to these precious people? How will they live if I am with you?'

'They will live as they want to live, in comfort and safety. Once we are wed whatever is yours will be mine and mine always yours. As you say, you need time to think. I will give you and your precious people as much time as you, and they, need. It is as I said to Jacob: *Io sono Il Marchese di Lombardi. Mi prenderò cura di tutti voi!* '

'I know we would be safe in your care, Giovanni. But I need my life to be more than about caring and being cared for. I understand the expectations of the world regarding a wife; that is for her to love her husband, to bear his children, and be content within that role. If I were with the man I love I would be happy in all things. Yet within the role of wife and mother I would want to learn and grow. Not even so much in the world of art, though as you know, until lately I was partway through my Masters. Art is important to me but it's not everything. There is a world out there of learning. I need to be free to explore that world ...better yet, to explore with the one I love.'

Giovanni spread his hands. 'I know what you want. 'I have

always known, and say to you now, on my life, it would be my duty and my pleasure as your partner to assist in that need. For it is a good need and I welcome it.'

'You do understand?'

'*Certo*! So what do you say, Clarissa Morgan? Is it yes or no? I cannot leave Cambridge with this unknown. I am the strong man but not that strong.'

She pondered, and then: 'I say that if you give me time to work things out with those that need to know of this, and perhaps a little time for me to accept what this means, then my answer may well be yes.'

'Yes? You will marry me? Is that what you are saying?'

'*Si. Prometto di essere tua moglie.*'

'Hah!' He laughed. 'You learn this piece for me.'

'*Si*, last night, after you left.'

Eyes glowing, he captured her hands. 'You will come with me to Florence, beautiful girl, and anywhere else I go. We shall be together. None shall keep us apart! And we shall live and we shall learn, and while I know you do not love me on this day, I have all of the tomorrows to make the change.'

* * *

By the time they got to Croft House snow was falling thick and fast.

The carriage pulled up as James van Leiden was opening the door.

Charles Anouilh hovered. 'Shall I come with you, my lord?'

'No need. I am expected.' He climbed the steps. 'Forgive the late hour, Professor. I would've come at a more sociable time but leave for London and Italy this night.'

They entered the sitting room where Kasper van Leiden was waiting.

'Good to see you, Gianni.' They shook hands.

'And you.'

'You are on your way home?'

'*Sì*! The Milan Express Saturday.'

'I too am returning home. It is the holiday season and should be spent with those we love. I will leave you to talk. *Viaggio sicuro, amico mio*!'

'*Anche a te,* Kasper.'

They left alone, James van Leiden gestured. 'Please take a seat.'

'Thank you, I prefer to stand.'

'Very well. How can I help?'

'I am here on a small matter of business and also an issue of great importance.' Giovanni placed an envelope on the table. 'This is information regarding the Lorenzo Monaco. It suggests that, when restored, the painting is shared between major art galleries. Other issues with regard to restoration can be settled at a later date, however, in consideration of your help, the Fitzwilliam will be offered first showing.'

'That is generous offer. The Board will be delighted.'

'I hope so.' Giovanni went to the heart of his visit. 'You spoke on Wednesday of a debt. It is my belief you are the one who came to the aid of the Morgan household with regard to that. I am here tonight to thank you, and to beg you to allow me, as Miss Morgan's intended, to relieve you of the matter.'

James was silent.

'I understand you do not seek repayment as I understand

it was an act of kindness meant for the woman we both love. It was the good deed of a good man.' Hand on heart, Giovanni bowed. '*Un atto onorevole*, for which I am eternally grateful, and for which I swear by my life that from this day until my last I am of service to you.'

'Please say no more!' James held up his hand. 'I was happy to help.'

'This I know! Still it cannot remain, for no matter the heart behind the deed it leaves me in your debt. Please James, let me do this.' He laid a banker's draft on the table. 'Take from this what you need. Let me love this woman with a clean heart. I know she cares for you as you care for her. Set me free! Do not ask me to stand further under your shadow for it is a dark place to be. If we are to succeed and be happy, then Clarissa and *I* need to stand in the sun.'

Late Callers

Fitzwilliam Boardroom, Cambridge
Friday 13th December 1901

'You choose a strangely propitious time to leave us, Professor.'

James smiled. 'If by that you mean Friday the 13th, Vice-Chancellor, I must say I never would've supposed you a superstitious man.'

'You do like your little joke.' The responding smile was thin. 'I'm sure both students *and* faculty will miss your good nature as well as all else you brought. By propitious, I meant that, with the roof proving a longer issue, and the season upon us, we're allowed leeway in terms of finding another conservator. Will you be staying in Cambridge over Christmas or moving on?'

'I shall be at home with my mother for a while. As for the future, as yet I have no particular long-term plan.'

'And the painting? Might one ask if you have a plan regarding that?'

'It brought me here today. I have spoken with the Marchese with regard to that. He will be contacting you shortly. In the mean time I am to say that, once returned to good health, the Fitzwilliam will have first option of showing and promoting the same.'

'Oh I say, Professor van Leiden!' The Vice-Chancellor beamed and for once got the name right. 'You have done us great service.'

'I am pleased you think so.' James set the envelope on the desk. 'In this you'll find information regarding the sharing. As you know, the work needs careful handling. It can't take any more problems, which is why – your conservation area closed down - the Marchese wants further restoration to take place in Italy, and I to be in Florence in the new year, and the painting with me.'

'I see.'

'Do not be concerned, Vice-Chancellor. The move is merely a matter of convenience, or as it was put to me, the right locale for the right man. As for your fears of a change of heart, His Highness is an honourable man. If he says the Fitzwilliam is to be first at the table, you will be first. '

'I'm sure of it and again thank you for your help in this. The showing of such a find will be of enormous value to the City as well as to the Museum.' The Vice-Chancellor sighed. 'We have only known you for a short time. Judging the recent display of partiality on behalf of the students you will be missed. Speaking for myself, though we haven't always seen eye-to-eye, I am sorry you are not staying. I had great hopes of you, James.'

James gritted his teeth. 'As I had great hopes of my own.'

* * *

The museum is closed for the season. James didn't need to come today but in view of last night's visitor, and Kasper lamenting his fate into the early hours, he needed to get out. It appears Serena is pregnant and she and Kasper to wed in the new year.

'Marriage was never an aim,' this was Kasper. 'Lately I did have thoughts in that direction, but not to wed Serena; the thought makes me shudder.'

'Then why do it?'

'Because she is bearing my child.'

'Is she?'

'She says it is mine.'

'With respect, Kes, the woman is not known for the truth.'

'Maybe not, but this time I believe her. I dare do nothing else.'

It came to James then to tell of Serena's involvement in the bank loan, to let the whole thing out and be done with it, for once and all, but he couldn't do it; his brother was so unhappy he couldn't add to his misery.

'Where is Serena?'

'I don't know and I don't care. I'm guessing she's in Paris or on her way. She stayed at the hotel last night. I offered her a bed here. I knew you wouldn't mind. Considering her situation it seemed the right thing to do. She didn't want it. She said she'd sooner sleep on a bed of nails than with me.'

James was appalled: 'And this is the woman you are to wed!'

'It would seem so.'

'In God's name why? It's clear there's no love between you. Must you add to the poison? You said she offered a way out. Why didn't you take it?'

'Because of the child!' Kasper crunched his fist. 'I kept seeing Jacob's face when she walked into King's Chapel. I thought if she could make him look like that, plain terrified, how might she be with her own child.'

'It needn't be like that. Jacob is brother in name only. A piece of paper joins them together. Maybe with her own child she'd be different.'

'I can't take the chance. If this is my boy, come of my flesh and blood, I can't risk it. I have to get between him and whatever made Serena the way she is.' Eyes red-rimmed, he'd stared into the fire. 'It's not only her. It's the pair of them. Isabella is just as greedy and just as cold.'

He'd looked up. 'You never saw their place in San Nicolo, did you?'

'I never got that far.'

'I did. It was stacked from ceiling to floor with the spoils of war and they with minimum space to live. I didn't stay too long or look too hard, but what I did see turned my gut. It was the inside of a magpie's nest.' He threw back his head. 'I wish to God I'd realised what I was seeing. I might've picked up my heels and run. But this was early in our affaire, and, as usual, I was led by my cock rather then my brain. I'd like to run now, Gyr, but can't. I have to make myself worthy.'

'What do you mean worthy?'

'I have to do what King Belshazzar didn't do. I must stop striving for earthly things and find a better way of being, and that means looking after my boy. I must not be weighed in the balance and found wanting – not this time.'

He was gone before light this morning. Anneka having had her baby, a boy, Thomas Charles, Kasper went by way of Norfolk. Once upon a time they would've gone together, but while still brothers, they are not good company anymore. A woman stands between them, and this time it is not Serena, but a woman with silver hair and the pale eyes of a Mermaid.

* * *

Croft House, Cambridge
Saturday 14ᵗʰ December 1901

It was an evening of late callers. Joe Sissons was the first. He came with news of Archie, who'd been home these last two days, his mother dying, and he preparing for the funeral. 'He's been running about like a madman trying to set his mother to rest,' said Joe. 'Poor bloke! He said he used to work part-time in a mortuary and knows this time of year she could be on a slab for days. Anyway, a bit of luck, if that's what you can call it, the vicar at St Barts has a spot next Saturday. I've told him I'll be there. He was in tears. Apart from an aunty in Norfolk, and she on her way out, he has no one.'

'He has me, Joe,' said James. 'I'll be there too.'

'I knew you would, Guvnor. You're true blue. It's why I'm here. I was wondering about your choices for next year, in particular Italy.'

'You've heard that I might be going there?'

'Everybody's heard. It's the talk of the campus, you and that Museum.'

'The Uffizi?'

'That's the one. They're betting on you staying in Florence.'

'That might be the case. At this point I really don't know anything.'

'I don't suppose you do. I'm sorry about that.' A heavy hand patted James's shoulder. 'I know you'd set your heart on Doctor Morgan's girl.'

'Does everybody know about that too?'

'More or less and what they don't know they make up. It is said the Italian Marquis has offered his heart.'

'...and his soul too.'

'Anyway, Guvnor, I don't mean to keep you. I wanted to say that if you do decide to stay, could you find a place for me with you? I've heard bad tales about that country. While it is a wonderful place it can be dangerous, hot-blooded people and all. I don't like the thought of you being alone. I ain't much but I'm a tough old boy and I would make sure nothing ever got to you.'

'Why Joe?' Tears sprang into James's eyes. 'Would you do that for me?'

'Drop of a hat, sir. And I ain't alone. We talked about it, him and me, and both said the same. If you would 'ave us, it's me and Archie Johnson serving you til the end of the world.'

* * *

Joe left. Five minutes later there was a scratching at the back door. Once again gossip had been at work: Jacob was there with Amy, the dog, and Muffin, the cat, and all three covered with snow.

'I want to know if you'll take us with you when you go.'

James fetched them in, boy, cat, and dog, drying them with a towel.

'Does Miss Clarissa know you're here?'

'We told no one.'

'Right. Stay by the fire. I'll call the house. They will be worried.'

He dialled. Such an opportunity! Maybe the last he'll ever get.

'Hello.' She was anxious, the call immediately picked up.

'It's James. He's here with me.'

'Thank you for ringing. I was about to put on my coat and start looking, though I did think he'd be with you. He's anxious about the future, you know, as are we all. I tried settling his mind but I wouldn't do – it had to be you.'

'Do you want me to keep them overnight? They are cold and tired, and what with the heavy snow, there's no easy way back.'

'You're right, James.' The phone was silent for a while, and then her voice in his ear, so known and so loved. 'There is no easy way back.'

* * *

All three are settled in a back bedroom. The animals slept. Jacob fought to stay awake. 'You will not leave us?'

'I won't go anywhere without telling you what is happening, you can be sure of that. But isn't your home at Beeches with Miss Clarissa?'

'Not now. Beeches is to be sold. I heard Miss Clareessa talk with a lawyer. She says she must sell. It is the only way she can 'old up her head.'

'Hold up her head?'

'*Si*! She says she is obligated.'

'Obligated to whom?'

'I do not know only that the house will be sold.'

'And Miss Hankin? Does she speak of staying with Clarissa?'

'She will not go to Italy. She say *Il Marchese* has servants. Miss Clareessa will be waited on hand and foot and Miss Hanky will have to stand and watch. She say she can't live her life watching. She must have a purpose.'

Had this been another time, and another life, James might've smiled at the way the boy aped Margret Hankin's manner of speaking. But this is here and now, and people's lives are falling apart.

'Would you come with me if I did decide to stay in Italy?'

'Si!'

'You have bad memories of the place, Jacob.'

'Papa Samuel loved me. I have good memories too.'

'What about Cambridge and King's College and your music? You do know you are likely to be offered a scholarship there.'

'What good is that if my family is not here? I can make music anywhere. I do not have to go to school to do it.'

'What does Miss Clarissa say?'

'She said she would stay in Cambridge rather than leave me behind. But she cannot. She is unhappy here. People say bad things about her. *Il Marchese* will not let anyone speak badly of her. This I know.'

'He is a fine man.'

'So are you. You are my special father, my guardian as with an angel. Miss Clareessa trusts you. She would let me go with you.'

Other than to say any decision would include Jacob, there was nothing more to be said. James bade him sleep; they would talk in the morning.

He was closing the door when a sleepy voice whispered: 'I was glad to leave Italy and the Refugio. If you were with me, Mister James, I will be glad to go back. For then I shall have two families instead of one.'

* * *

James sat before the fire writing notes for next year's students while thinking of Friday's late caller. The problem was resolved, Giovanni's plea impossible to ignore. It was a strange meeting. On the surface it was about settling a point of honour: who should redeem the debt and who not; beneath the surface, where the past sits and the future grows, other words were said and other possibilities offered, inarticulate, and yet resounding in the ear.

It is those words and the visions they create he ponders. What did Giovanni mean by 'standing in shadow,' and why does it connect with today and Clarissa's echoing words: 'you are right. There is no easy way back.'

Since so many questions remain unanswered an interim stay in Italy is the answer. Giovanni did say it would be more convenient if restoration of the Lorenzo Monaco was continued in Florence, and that the Uffizi would be at James's disposal. The Villa del Rosa was offered by way of accommodation but then, the idea repugnant to both, Giovanni had shrugged. 'You must do what is best for the good of your soul. It is as I said when first meeting Clarissa: 'Go where your heart takes you. There you will find new paths and new ideas.'

* * *

The last of the callers arrived just before midnight. James was preparing for bed. He heard horses and looking out saw a woman in rich furs stepping down from a cab, and knew straightway who had come to trouble the night.

'Forgive me, James.' She stood in the hall, smiling sure of a welcome. 'Could you waken Kasper? I missed my train and am somewhat stranded.'

369

'Kasper left yesterday. He seemed to think you were already in Paris.'

'It is a mistake in communication. I was due to leave on Thursday but stayed over with friends. But *non importante*!' She turned back to the door. 'I must stop the cab before he leaves and return to those friends.'

'No, not at all. You must stay here.' He took her bag. 'Is there any more luggage to come?'

'Only this. The rest is gone ahead.'

He brought her inside. She shed her coat, and was magnificent in a black velvet evening gown and pearls, her perfume filling the air.

'Can I get you anything before I show you to a room, a drink perhaps or something to eat? There is a guest suite on the first landing. It is a comfortable room with a bathroom and other necessities.'

'Thank you, I am in need of nothing but sleep.' She glanced about. 'I do not see the bullfrog lurking. What happened? Did you step on him?'

'Excuse me?'

'Your Mr Johnson. He is not here.'

'His mother died. He has things to arrange.'

'Ah, for shame, Serena! The bullfrog's mother died.' Amused by her comment she smiled as she followed up the stairs. 'Will they have a funeral do you suppose, and a choir to sing the fair maiden to sleep? Bullfrogs do sing. There was a pretty little sewer not far from where I was born. They would sing every night. My father hated them. He would set traps and drop them into scalding hot water. It was not a good thing to do. I told him so.'

'This is your suite.' He pushed the door wide. 'You'll find

everything you need there. If not then let me know.'

Determined to have as little contact as possible he left her to it, closed all downstairs, and went to check on Jacob. The boy was asleep, long black lashes on his cheek; Amy, the dog, was awake and smiling, her tail wagging.

As he was closing the door the cat slid through, and knowing the way, skipped down the back stairs across the landing to James's room. There she jumped onto the bed and began licking her paws as if never having left.

Lights were on across the way and judging the noise the geyser was making, a bath was being taken. The key to the suite was in the outer lock. Musing on vampires, and other blood-sucking creatures, he was tempted to lock her in, but then, too weary to care, got into bed, turned down the gas, and slept.

* * *

Half a bottle of Beaujolais and an aching heart, he slept heavy and dreamt of Portia, the kindly whore from *Rue d'Aerschot,* a gift on his eighteenth birthday.

She sat in a chair at the bottom of his bed examining coloured patterns on her hands. It came to him that Portia had died, and the intricate designs on her hands, arms and feet, were symbolic of her death. He seemed to know that the tattooing was a gift from girls in the Parisian brothel who Portia had known and helped throughout the years, and who, when she died, sat with pots of henna, praying safe passage of the gods before wrapping their beloved sister in a shroud.

In the dream she sat with her head down, and single candle alight. She was quiet, and seemingly untroubled. He wanted to ask of Father, was he also at peace, or was he still chasing the rainbows he'd chased when alive.

With that thought Portia came and sat beside him on the bed. 'It is you, my elegant lover of long ago.' She kissed his cheek. 'You are grown now and so very handsome. I am so pleased to see you again.'

So was he! His body was on fire and he with a notable erection.

'Ah!' She slid her hand under the sheet. 'I see that you also are pleased.'

Smiling, she shed her robe, and was naked, the henna configurations on her body blazing like so many moons and stars dropped from the night skies.

She mounted him and leaning down, her hair a perfumed curtain, cupped her breasts offering herself. There was no hesitation. He was thick and strong inside her. Whatever bothered the eighteen-year-old didn't bother the man.

She began to move her hips, rocking back and forth. He wanted to speak, to say he hadn't forgotten that night, that she was always a loving memory. But she put her hand over his mouth, denying words.

'Don't.' He didn't like it. As a child he'd never liked anything across his mouth. It felt wrong, cruel and demanding. He shook his head trying to free his mouth but she, a sudden stranger, pressed down even harder.

'Don't!' He managed to speak. 'Don't do this!'

She smiled. 'Why not?'

'Because it feels wrong.'

She swapped her hands for her mouth, her lips hard and her breath hot. 'How can it be wrong when it feels so right?'

'No! I don't want this!' He put his hand out, and encountering warm flesh rather than a dream woke to Serena straddling his body.

* * *

He rolled away and was out of the bed gazing at her. This is not Portia. To have imagined a likeness is to insult the dead. 'You shouldn't be here.'

She sat back on her heels. 'Why not?'

'I don't want you here.'

'You don't want me? That's not the impression I was getting.'

'I don't care what impression you were getting. I want you dressed and out of my house by first light. '

'Why?' She leaned on her elbow, a body carved from silken alabaster and an empty soul. 'You seemed to be enjoying my company.'

'That was before I knew what poison was invading my bed.'

'There is no poison. There is you and me and an opportunity that might never come again. As for poison, if there is such,' she tossed her hair, her gaze languorous, 'who would not want to die sucking on the same.'

Furious, and with a double sense of being cheated *and* of cheating, he reached for a robe. 'Ah no, *mio caro*.' She slid across the bed, and ripping the robe away, wrapped her arms about his waist. 'I think I shall stay this night and the next, and we two making love until you never want me to leave.'

'I want you to leave now.' He did want her to leave but at the same time could not ignore her face against his groin and her warm breath.

'My dear, James!' She was smiling. 'You are in a puzzle, your mouth saying one thing and your body another.'

'That's because I am human and not above admitting it. For God's sake, Serena, can't you see the wrong in this.' He tugged on her arms. 'You are carrying my brother's child.'

'*Cos*i?' She shrugged. 'I am a generous creature with a generous body. I can accommodate the seed of both van Leiden brothers as I can waste that that I do not want.' She hung about his neck. 'Give me yours, dearest James, you who I love, and who I foolishly threw away in Assisi seeing glitter where had been true gold. You are the one I want and who I will continue to love no matter how many times you turn me away. Give me your children and I will treasure them as never before. As for the other one - the brother I tolerate – I do not care nor ever will.'

It was enough. He threw her off and taking his robe left the bedroom without looking back.

CHAPTER THIRTY-FOUR

Wanderers

Beeches, Lark Lane, Comberton
Saturday December 21ˢᵗ 1901

The day started well with a letter from Italy. It was not from Giovanni, but from his aunt, Senora Eufemia di Vallagra. Brief, little more then three or four lines, and yet a delight, the Senora wrote of her pleasure when meeting in Florence, and of her joy at the prospect of another meeting.

The letter remained in Clarissa's pocket. She would pull it out, read it, and put it back. A good thing, a sparkling thing, it offered a possible doorway into the future where before was a blank wall. Giovanni is behind this, talking with his aunt, promoting the idea, knowing what pleasure it would bring. It says much about the man and the kindness always waiting behind his eyes.

The day continued to shine with a gift of flowers. Admittedly, as the cart carried on back down the drive, she did experience a moment of regret, but that was only because she had grown accustomed to receiving hothouse lilac from that particular florist - and lilac is lovely whomsoever it's for.

Today the cart brought white roses. The card bore the Lombardi crest and the message: *'Con amore e devozionee.* With love and devotion.'

One rose was set aside for a visit to the cemetery this afternoon, the rest are now in a vase in the sitting-room, a delicate perfume sweetening the air.

The card went into Papa's cufflink box along with other souvenirs. Clarissa once owned a Chinese lacquer cabinet, a gift from Uncle Sarson when she was a child. Though more ornamental than useful, it was a lovely thing. Hand-painted dragons of red and gold guarded a hidden compartment in which one might've kept precious memorabilia, as in a lock of Mama's hair, and Papa's tie-pin, and now, perhaps, a gold-mounted card telling of adoration.

There was another card but that went adrift on the way back from Italy. She wonders about that and the message it carried. Giovanni never speaks of it as James van Leiden never mentions the note dropped in his pocket at Calais, the one carrying a small yet sincere declaration of her love; perhaps that too went adrift and he never to know how she felt.

This morning she woke from a dream where she floated down a river in a flat-bottomed boat. It was a heavy dream, hypnotic, from which she had trouble waking. Even now she could hear water lapping, and feel the motion of the current drawing the boat onwards. She would rise to the surface of waking only to fall back down again, limbs leaden, and she seeing through closed eyes patches of blue sky and banks of spear-like reeds either side of the river.

The Senora's letter helped reduce the drama of the dream as Giovanni's roses refined the heady mix from floral wreaths that lined the boat.

Closed eyes, hands clasped as in prayer and mourning wreaths, suggest a funeral scene as with Tennyson's soulful *Lady of Shallot,* and yet there was no sense of loss, only of motion and of all things moving toward a given end.

Clarissa feels the dream reflects her life, she irresistibly drawn toward a point in the future where, while knowing rivers have secrets, and that danger may be waiting round the bend, a safe harbour does seem possible.

A priest from the Catholic Church called on Wednesday. Before leaving for Italy, Giovanni asked support of the church for Clarissa with regard to rites of initiation. Her visitor, Father O'Connor by name, said she need have no fear of the future; God had reached down to bring her to safety. He talked for a good hour, until Tillie, the Jack Russell terrier, leapt on to his lap, as if to say, 'thank you, that'll do for today.' Things got easier then, the priest taking coffee and brandy in the kitchen while reminiscing of his dogs back home in Derry.

After he left Clarissa wondered how she'd arrived at this point, and how when Giovanni is here there is a sense of calm, but when returned to Italy, all seems complicated. She wishes Senora Eufemia was here. She'd have a friend to talk to. She used to have Margret and her sister. Now Sally walks a new path and beyond that has little to say. Margret doesn't talk at all.

'As I said, that is not how I want to live the last years of my life. I need to have things to do. I need purpose. I need to be wanted.'

'You are wanted!' Clarissa tried convincing her. 'You've been with me forever. I don't want to be without you.'

'Nor I without you but I can't live in a fairy castle. I'd be a spare cog in a wheel meaning nothing to no one. I know my limits. It doesn't matter how good his people are, I wouldn't fit it. How could I when I don't know their customs or speak their language.'

'We could learn together.' Still Clarissa tried. 'I might know a little Italian but nowhere near as much as I should. As for people's ways of thinking and being, surely that will come with time and patience.'

'I don't have that kind of patience. I am too old and set in my ways to start again in a foreign land. But you can take Freya-Jasmine! She will love it there, especially with that Mrs Pennington so eager to pamper her. I'll go to Norfolk with my Sally and be a spare part there.'

That was Sunday. Since then she hasn't mentioned the move and won't. Over the years Clarissa has seen enough of her old friend to know when a subject is done. Margret spends any spare time with Sally talking weddings and looking at the latest batch of photographs sent by the Reverend Charles.

Clarissa is happy for Sally. Gentle and kind, and with a love of people and gossip, she'll make a perfect vicar's wife. The congregation of St John the Divine in Diss will adore her and her pretty bonnets. Freya-Jasmine knows change is in the offing and that she would be welcome in Florence as she would be welcome in Diss. So far, a respectful child loving her aunt and grandmother, she makes no comment, though a latest visit to the library resulted in Stories of the Opera and an Italian phrase book.

One person did offer advice but was so certain of his opinion it felt more like being on the end of a lecture rather than the offering of helpful hints.

'I'm not sure you know what you're doing by going to Italy.'

This was Paul Brooke yesterday bringing medicine for Margret's cough and a roasting for Clarissa. 'It is a fair country with much to offer. I have travelled there myself and found the people warmly hospitable. I'd like to think you'll be happy there.

If not, I doubt it will be the fault of your intended.'

It was a dubious comment, and as always with this man, there is an undercurrent of reproof that she cannot allow to go unchallenged.

'So whose fault will it be if it doesn't work, mine for chancing it?'

He'd shrugged. 'Whose fault can it be but yours. You're chancing every misfortune in the world by going, not least a broken heart.'

'I don't see the need of that. I understand it's a gamble but in terms of marriage what isn't. We can't know a person until we live together.'

'Well, by God, you've certainly got some living to do to catch up on that! You've only known the man a matter of days never mind weeks. How can you hope to know anything about anyone in that amount of time?'

'Since when did time have anything to do with love?'

'It doesn't. Not a day or a second, but then we would have to be talking of love and not veiled hints and promises.'

'Giovanni di Lombardi does love me. He has sworn to protect me. Why would he break my heart?'

'I am sure he does love you. He would probably die for you, as would I, given the chance. That's not what I'm saying.'

'Then what are you saying?'

'I'm saying it is his heart that is at risk not yours.'

* * *

Clarissa should've left it there. It would've been the wisest thing to do, but she has spent most of her life defending her corner from masculine ideas as to what is right or wrong, and this is more than an idea – this is her life.

'Are you suggesting I won't make him happy? That I'm going into this marriage in a half-hearted manner determined not to do my best for him and his country - because if you are, that's a horrible thing to say!'

'I am not saying that as I am not trying to change your mind. It is your life and your decision. I am doing what you wanted me to do, offering an opinion. I know you'd do your best to make it work. You'd probably run yourself into the ground doing it and come home a nervous wreck. I've watched you over the years and know that once you set your mind to a purpose, the possibility of failure never enters your head. It is win or nothing.'

She'd gazed at him. 'If that is how you see me then you've been watching a stranger. I am afraid of failing. I might put on a good show but it is only a show, underneath I see myself a complete fraud.'

'I understand that. It's what we all do. But that's not what I am trying to say.' Paul saw himself deliberately misunderstood. He was angry, and being angry came closer to the truth than she would've liked. 'I doubt your reasons for going to Italy. Indeed, I doubt the reality of any of it.'

'Why do you?' She was more than a little taken aback by his manner, he usually so amenable. 'What am I doing that is *so* wrong? Every woman takes a risk leaving the nest. It's called following the heart.'

'Leaving the nest? What utter rot!' He was scathing. 'You're not leaving anything. You are running away. And don't look so miffed! You asked my opinion and for love of you I am giving it. You can tell yourself all the lies you like about why you are doing this but don't expect me to join in. If you really are following your heart then all I can say is you're going in the wrong direction, since any heart you had to give is already with James van Leiden. Italy is not a matter of doing your best or putting on a brave show, it is a matter of cheating yourself and the man you plan to marry.'

* * *

Last year Margret and Sally came with Clarissa to lay the Christmas wreath on the Morgan grave. Today the Hankins are with the dressmaker, Sally with a fitting for her wedding gown. It is bitterly cold in the cemetery and beyond a bedraggled crow pecking ivy on a nearby tomb not a soul in sight.

The day started so well. Now she is alone and lonely. Last week she wrote to the Fitzwilliam tendering her resignation and saying she would call in the new year regarding her Masters. While she thought she might get a note recognizing the same she didn't expect a letter from the Vice-Chancellor.

He said they were sorry to lose her, and looked forward to a 'chat after Christmas viz-a-viz the Masters, and what they can do to help in that direction, and to offer good wishes toward her new life in *La bella Italia*.'

Margret was clearing the breakfast table when the letter arrived, and looking over Clarissa's shoulder, momentarily stepped down from high dudgeon to offer a comment: 'That'll be about the Marquis and his money and the museum thinking to keep a warm hand on his purse.'

Though the comment was sour Clarissa chose not to be offended; that Margret was talking at all was some kind of relief. These days the house is so very quiet. Thank God for the animals, but for their comings and goings one would be living with shadows. Hazlett seems to have recovered from what ailed him and is back on form, kicking up a rumpus and generally misbehaving. While Amy is returned to the fold, the cat, Muffin, chose to stay with her former master. Rumour has it James is in Florence in the new year working on the Lorenzo Monaco. While she misses everything about the man - his face, his voice, the way he moves and talks, his every way of thinking and being - she prays he will have completed restoration before she arrives.

Clarissa is brave as she is stubborn. She has fought her way through more than one battle, and while not always emerging triumphant, at least she maintains her point of view. The hardest battle of the coming year will be parting with Beeches. She would have liked to keep the house but debts must be paid, and not just those caused by the bank loan.

For almost twenty years Margret and Sally Hankin have contributed toward the upkeep of the house; perhaps not in actual cash, yet in every other way.

Sally's wedding gown is already promised. She'd protested, saying she had a little money saved. Still, it won't do. Mama loved Margret. She would've wanted both sisters to go into the world armoured with some kind of settlement, therefore the house will be sold and loyalty repaid.

* * *

Clarissa knelt down placing a holly wreath on the snow-covered ground. She then took the rose and closing her eyes talked with her best friend.

'Dearest Papa, I miss you so much. I wake every morning thinking you are up and pottering then I remember you are gone and I am grieving again. I know you are aware of what is happening in Comberton and the world at large. I hope you agree with the idea of Italy and Giovanni. While not yet affianced, in my heart I am pledged to this man. He is honest and everything brave, and while his life is different to mine, I know he will help me find my way.'

She brushed snow from the headstone – their beloved names once again visible to the world. 'I am sorry about the house. But as you always said, a debt must not be left unpaid. I send love to you and Mama and ask you to be with me in the coming year. I think I can be happy in Italy as long as the way ahead remains clear and no hidden surprises - as in a sudden familiar footfall. If that were to happen, I think it would break my heart. God bless you, dearest Papa.'

For time she stayed on her knees hoping for a sign that would say her prayer had been heard, particularly in reference to the 'familiar footfall.' There was nothing, not even a ray of sunlight piercing the heavy skies. There was silence and the same bedraggled crow grubbing for dead bugs.

* * *

Back home she found Jacob in the kitchen and the-table laid for two.

'I make *la zuppa* with yesterday's left-overs. We eat and then we talk.'

Clarissa was cold from the cemetery, the soup was very welcome. She sat and ate, steam rising, and her thoughts with

Paul Brooke. One-by-one her supporters are dropping away. Now there's Jacob. Once upon a time he was open with his thoughts and feelings. Now he is silent. As a scholar he has choices: he can come to Florence as a beloved member of the Lombardi household and, as Giovanni suggested, take up music at the Institute of Rome. If preferred he can stay a boarding scholar at King's, returning to Florence during the Long Vac and other holidays.

Another way is to live with his guardian in Croft House. But with rumours of James leaving that idea is now uncertain, and once again, God the Fisherman, swooping to gather all in His net until we mortals decide what to do next.

It was the fear of his 'special father' leaving that saw Jacob steal out of the house last week throwing all into panic. He was returned the following day, James doffing his hat. 'I think a visit from Doctor Brooke would be in order.' The next day Jacob stayed in bed, a blanketed hillock, the dogs keeping guard. Clarissa asked what happened to make him ill but he wouldn't say. Perhaps now with the bowl of soup she will learn.

He pushed the bowl away. 'We are not a happy home.'

'No, we are not.'

'The time has come to choose where to go.'

'You don't have to choose anything. There is no need for a discussion never mind choices. You are to be with me now and always.'

He got up from the chair, took the bowls, washed and put them away. In his walking back and forth she noticed his foot dragging, the metal studs on his boot striking the stone floor, a sure sign he is unhappy.

'What is it, Jacob?'

He turned. 'I am glad to have lived in Beeches. It was my first real home as you are my first real family. I loved Papa Samuel and he loved me but we never had a home. We had places to stay, rooms where other homeless people lived and slept. Any food we had, we shared. Sometimes there were no rooms as there was no food. It was all right because Papa was there. He got sick and died then there was only a room with bars at the window. I never want to be in that room again and I don't want you or Mister James to be there either.'

'Jacob?' Clarissa was anxious. 'What is it you are trying to say?'

'I don't know.' He shrugged. 'I do not know what is coming, only that you and Mister James must be saved.'

'Saved from what?'

'Again I do not know.'

'I think we are safe and always will be. We are in the process of moving towards new worlds, that's all.'

'*Si*! New worlds. Miss Sally is to wed Mister Charles. Miss Hanky will go with them. You will be with *Il Signore Marchese*. All will be safe.'

'And where will you be?'

He looked up. 'With Mister James.'

'Oh I see. You have decided then.'

'*Si*! I have chosen my new world. It will be wherever he is.'

Clarissa thought then, that something untoward happened the night at Croft House, and that it had left him afraid for himself *and* for James van Leiden.

'*Signor Marchese* is a powerful man. He is brave and strong. If you go with him to *Firenzi* you will be safe from all things.' Jacob stared out of the window, his gaze fixed on unimagined views. 'The same is true for Freya-Jasmine, for Miss Hanky, and *me*, if I were to be with you. All will be safe. This I know.'

Clarissa was on her feet. 'Then come with us and be safe!'

But the Jacob she knew wasn't listening; another Jacob, the child, was remembering Spoleto and a room with bars at the window.

'When I played for the *turista* I met people from all over the world. Some would pay us to sing, others would steal the little money we had. Those that stole lived in a world of their own with rules of their own. Papa Samuel had a name for them. He called them the *Vagabondi* - the Wanderers.'

'What about them?'

'Papa said they were dangerous people who lived by their wits. They never settle. They are always on the move leaving darkness and destruction behind them, for the only home they care about is inside their head.'

Eyes heavy with tears, Jacob turned from the window. 'I would stay with you forever, Miss Clareessa, but I can't. You have the *Signore*. Mister James has no one. I must be with him if only to hold his hand when it gets dark.'

* * *

That night Clarissa dreamed the same dream of floating down the river. The boat she lay in was filled with flowers: Briar Roses, Kingcups and Queen Anne Lace strewn upon a carpet of lilac. She was dressed in a white shroud with lace at the throat and sleeves. Her hands were placed in an attitude of prayer, the wrists bound together by a jewelled rosary, sunbeams turning blood-red rubies to liquid fire. A letter was wedged between her palms.

The writing was of a woman's hand, but smudged and blurred where river water was seeping in through chinks in the boat.

She tried to read what was there: it seemed important to do so. But, even as she watched the ink dissolved, and she was left with a fragment:

'....beloved boy, we both knew how this would end. There could be no other way. And though my heart is broken in a million pieces, I promise the day we meet in Paradise, I shall be the first to kiss you and to forgive you.'

The boat was rapidly filling with water. Clarissa wasn't afraid. She knew it was but a dream. She would wake and life would begin again.

At that, a hand reached up out of the river - a woman's hand, a ring carved of emeralds on her finger as darkly green as the river itself. The hand caught hold of the rim of the boat and pushed down.

Water rushed in, and Clarissa woke remembering a warning.

'The Villa del Rosa is not a house. It is a shrine, testimony to the man's love of his wife. Carina di Vallagra was said to be the most beautiful woman in Italy, moonlight in her hair and eyes of topaz. You will never be happy there, for you share your life with a ghost that has haunted the villa these seven long years.'

CHAPTER THIRTY-FIVE

Noah

Croft House, Cambridge,
Saturday December 21ˢᵗ 1901

The last two days have been a whirlwind. Yesterday was taken up with college business, James meeting with students, awarding grades and certificates of merit, et cetera, so that none need come to grief.

They shared coffee and biscuits in the Library, where to his surprise he found some students in tears, and they begging an address where they might write of their progress. Truth to tell he had a hard time saying goodbye, every person, every stick and stone of the place once integral to his hopes of the future; now they are just another marker along the way.

Four o'clock he left the museum to join Joe Sissons at St Barts Cemetery supporting Archie Johnson. Three mourners and a boss-eyed curate in a shabby suit, it was a sad little ceremony, and being the last committal of the day – and the curate looking half-starved - James shunted them across the road to the *George and Dragon*.

He knows the ale house. A decent place serving wholesome food, one might say it was an introduction to Cambridge, he supping there the day he came at Kasper's request to escort the Parisi women to London. If he'd known the kind of people they were, and how they would influence his life to a point of ruin, he would've told his brother to find another fool to run his errands. But then he wouldn't have met Clarissa, nor would he have a beloved son in an orphan boy from Assisi. It seems whatever path you choose to take there are gains and losses to be understood.

In point of that - changes along the way - he takes the *Boston Herald* to catch up on home news. The sport's page of the latest edition carried a photograph of the baseball short-stop, Hans Wagner, aka The Flying Dutchman, with a telling quote: '*Play like the devil to win or don't play at all.*'

In the *George and Dragon* patrons celebrate the season with a fir tree covered in silver bells and a sprig of mistletoe hanging in a doorway hoping to steal a kiss from the unwary. The evening stretched out: Joe and Archie talking, their greying heads together like lovers, while the curate, stuffed to the gills with stewed beef and dumplings, slept in a corner of the settle.

Thinking on that quote and the idea of playing the game, James concluded he wasn't devil enough. He might have fallen in love with Clarissa Morgan but as Miss Hanky said, he never really tried to win her. He was too nice about everything. Instead of fighting in the old-fashioned way of declaring his feelings, he'd hovered, which left the way open for a more determined lover in Giovanni di Lombardi who, from the beginning, knew what he wanted.

James recalls the night of the Masked Ball and how, suffering a back injury, *il Marchese* stood on the edge of the ballroom observing all. A tall figure, silent and still, immaculate in swallow-tail coat and white waistcoat - the glittering Savoy Double Order of Chivalry about his neck - he embodied all that is honourable. The night progressed, dancers continued to whirl, and she, the exquisite beauty, wooed by all. Still the man watched and still he waited. It was as if, knowing his invited guest was mad for the girl, he gave the night and the opportunity to James. '*Eccoti qui, Signor Conservatore*! This is your moment to declare your position. Choose your weapons!'

James chose to act like a fool. Seeing Kasper as yet another contender for Clarissa's hand, he threw a tantrum, and cowardly, walked away. From that moment Giovanni put what armaments he had to good use. The following day saw his campaign in action, and while still *La Grande Signore* he was at war, reassuming youth with a smoothly shaved chin and trimmed locks, his battle colours flying by way of a yellow silk waistcoat.

* * *

Kasper had it right: as hunting birds go, the Gyrfalcon is singularly slow to strike. With that thought he decided to look toward a new phase of life by unshackling former chains, starting with the latest scrapbook. He burnt the lot, dropping once precious souvenirs of time and place into the flames: letters, theatre programmes, photographs, it didn't matter, they all went, for any value they might have had is lost to him and they merely ink and celluloid.

It came down to four items he now sees as rightly illustrating a chronic unwillingness to shoot from the hip: the photograph taken at the May Ball, Giovanni's address card, Father's suicide note and Clarissa's note.

The card was the first to burn followed by the suicide note and then the photograph of them dancing together. The image took an age to disappear, melting sooner than burning - Sweaty Steeds' fingerprints the last to go.

The note dropped into his pocket at Calais scorched his fingers even before going to the flames. For a moment he was tempted to read what she'd said, but then he let it go. He didn't want to know what she said anymore than why his father gave up on life; whatever the reality it is too little too late.

Sensing misery, the cat jumped on to his lap. He sat holding her thinking how easy paper burns as opposed to memories. A recent memory has heat of its own: Serena Parisi in her underwear hanging over the stairwell threatening to jump. 'I shall jump,' she says, 'and you left 'aving to explain to your college professors why I did it.'

She didn't jump, the theatre had entered her mind, and she having too much fun. 'You are cruel, James van Leiden and I am a fool to love you.'

She said other things, some meant to hurt and all to threaten, but nothing of real venom until Jacob appeared, when she rushed at the boy, throwing her arms about him, calling him, 'her adored brother! And happy she was knowing they were to be together again.'

Terrified, Jacob was on all fours covering his head with his arms, shutting her and the idea out. Sickened by it all, James's put him to bed and locked the door. Things said then don't bear repeating other than the theatrical mask was ripped away, and a Serena arriving who couldn't dent a man's armour but could pierce his heart through love of a boy.

There was no hysteria then. Hard facts were delivered through concrete lips; she'd contacted lawyers in Milan who said, irrespective of decisions made in England, she is Jacob's lawful sister as Isabella is his lawful step-mother, and his life and continuance is in their hands and theirs alone.

She retired then to change, leaving later with not a hair out of place.

'*Buon Natale caro, James*!' Hide of a rhinoceros she'd reached up to kiss his cheek. 'You'll be hearing from my lawyers and of course from me.'

Jacob was ill all night and afraid. It was pointless James saying it was going to be all right, because he didn't know that would be. He only knew that, Milan lawyers or not, he will fight to keep him.

* * *

Margret Hankin came to call as he was about leave for Norfolk, the house locked up, and cat and keys waiting on Archie Johnson, who, after dealing with his mother's affairs, will move into Croft House.

James wasn't surprised to see her. The woman needed an answer to her problem and until she had it wouldn't rest. While pleased to see her, he wondered at applying a temporary bandage to an age-old wound. Still, he drew her inside, another lost lamb to the fold, or in this case - the Ark.

With her brown hair plaited tight to her head, and clad head to toe in a snowy white Holland apron, she'd maintained a tidy appearance, and yet was adrift. 'I've come to ask a favour.'

'Okay then. Why don't you come in and take a seat.'

'I'm not sure I should. It don't seem right bothering you, but you're my last hope. Even then,' she sat down, 'I don't whether it's right to ask.'

'Ask and we'll find out.'

'It's a bit complicated,' she leaned forward in the chair, her face worn. 'I know what I want to do, but I'm fearful at the same time, seeing if it doesn't work for me, then it doesn't work for anyone.'

'Ask, Margret. You won't know until you do.'

'Very well then.' Head down, hands clasped together – she never seen so meek before – Margret made her plea. 'I want to know if when you go to Italy you'll take me as your cook and housekeeper.'

When he didn't speak she continued: 'I am a good cook. And though it's me that says so when I shouldn't, for years I managed a house of five people, food in the pantry, dust off the floor, and coal in the cellar for less time and money than any woman I know. My old employer, Doctor Morgan, used to say I saved pounds on housekeeping. You see, I didn't just look to the day, I looked to the morrow with apples off the tree and goosegogs and raspberries in jellies and jams. I don't know what fruit they grow in Italy or what veg. Even so, with a bit of practice, I could make something of it.'

A tear escaping, she shook her head. 'I don't expect an answer today or even one at all. I know I've a cheek asking and wouldn't except that yesterday a little birdie told me our lad has turned down the offer of being with Miss Clary in favour of you. I also heard as Archie Johnson, whose mother died the other day, God rest her soul, is coming with you as man-servant full-time.'

He nodded. 'There is some truth to that.'

'And Jacob? Is he really going to live with you?'

'While the situation is still very much up in the air, in view of certain legal niceties, I think that might well be the case.'

'Well there you are then! Italy or not, you're going to have people living with you who'll need care. They will want their shirts washed, and their beds made, and a nice salmon and broccoli pie put in front of them.'

He smiled. 'There is that.'

James didn't ask why she wouldn't go with Clarissa, he knew why. Proud and prickly, she couldn't bear the idea of taking a minor role. She knows that if she were to go as a member of the Lombardy household, while she would be treated well, she'd have no real position. Her role as housekeeper was here in England and the keys she once carried on her belt left behind.

Miss Hanky would be *La Senora Marchesa's* former servant, with no purpose to her life other than to see out her days while being paid to do so.

As if she caught his train of thought, she nodded. 'I wouldn't know a soul and I couldn't keep going to Miss Clary for help, or even for a gossip. As a Lady Marquis she will be streets above me, and while she wouldn't bother about that, the other servants would.'

'What about Freya-Jasmine? You are her grandmother. Surely she will want you close by her side.'

'No, she won't. She's eleven coming up one hundred and eleven. She knows what she wants and while she will miss me there are fancy Italian private schools to attend, and dancing lessons, and she with a book balanced on her head practising being a lady. Of course, if I was just down the lane, so to speak, she'd sleep a lot easier nights.'

'Does the Marchese plan to place Freya-Jasmine under his wing?'

'I believe he's only waiting for the nod and she signed up for a whole new world. Then, of course, as with Miss Clary, she'll receive religious instruction from a priest like the one who came to Beeches the other day.'

James blinked. 'Is it that much arranged?'

'I'll say! The Signore, as I'm to address him, is taking no chances. White roses for Miss Clary the other day and this morning a pony at the back door.'

'For Freya-Jasmine.'

'Yes. He knows where one goes the other will follow.'

'Well played, sir!' James was stunned. 'A battle plan indeed.'

'And a good one. You have to see it from his point of view. He's head over heels and anything that brings his beloved closer he will do.'

She sighed. 'I could go with Sally but she's settled with her vicar. Nothing but good will happen to them two, whereas, I don't know what's going to happen to my granddaughter and Miss Clary. They could be as happy as larks, I pray they will. Then again they might come up against all manner of problems. Freya-Jasmine is young. She can bounce back. It's Miss Clary I worry about. She'll be in a land of strangers. Some will love her and some will hate her just for being his wife. There's nothing like jealousy for ripping a house apart.'

'She has his love.'

'Let's hope it is enough.' She took his hand. 'I'm sorry to put this on you but I had to try, and not just for me, for you, because chances missed or not, you have to keep moving forward.'

He nodded. 'Thank you for coming Miss Hanky.

'Yeah all right,' she grimaced. 'I am a pain in the backside.'

'Not at all. You've given me food for thought.' He leaned down kissing her cheek. 'Now go home and do the best you can for your family while you have them. I don't know what's ahead but I can say this, I am due to go to Florence to work on a painting. If while I'm there I see any reason to prolong my stay, then you'll get a cable saying: 'pack your apron, Margret Hankin, and be ready to leave, and don't forget to bring some broccoli with you.'

* * *

Greys Farm, Norfolk

'How are you, Professor?' James leant over the bed. Beyond a squeeze of the hand there was no answer, which is as well for it was a foolish question: if his eyes didn't know the man's struggle then the torturous breathing would.

'It's good to see you, James.' Phoebe sat on the other side of the bed, hands in her lap and resignation on her face. 'As you can see, while it is not easy for him to speak, he knows you are here, and is glad.'

'I wanted to come. I felt I needed to enquire whether you have instructions for me with regard to the future.'

'I thought you might come with that intent.' She knew what he meant by future; that he referred to funeral rites, where and how, and if he could be of service. 'I think we might speak of that downstairs while you take bite to eat. I know we're not far from Cambridge, even so you travelled to be with us and I'm sure you'd appreciate a little refreshment.'

'Thank you.'

'Did you manage see the baby before you came up?' Conversation was shifted to smoother ground. 'Thomas Charles is growing fast. I am with him and Anneka most days and see the change. Mrs Phillips senior, who is not well, is unable visit

I am able to note the changes in the baby and relate back.'

'I'm sure she is glad of that.'

'As am I. That little man is our greatest joy. When I wake in the morning I have something good and pure to look toward.' She got to her feet. 'I'll leave you for a moment with my husband. I know you are pressed for time. It was good of you to think of us. Perhaps while I am making a pot of tea you might bring him up to date with news of Cambridge.'

'I will try.'

'Don't worry.' She smiled. 'Talking is difficult but he'll want to hear your news, as will I later, particularly I might say with reference to the Italian Marquis who called the other day with our niece. Delightful man! I can't tell you the comfort it gave knowing she is to be under his protection. '

James looked up. 'When was this, Miss Phoebe?'

'They came one day last week, or was it the week before. I think it was the Thursday. Yes, because the following day we received a letter, or rather John did. I didn't see it but whatever it was he took great relief from it.'

She leaned down. 'Didn't you, my love? The letter from His Highness - special delivery, you know - it gave comfort.'

Eyes fixed on James the old man nodded.

'All right then I'll leave you to chat.' Phoebe pressed James's hand. 'I know you two have secrets. I'm sure you'll find it easier with me away.'

They were here. James was left ruminating on the news. This is why Giovanni came that night to Croft House. He knew James had paid the debt and wanted to be free of obligation - what's more, he wanted Clarissa free.

'*Bravo Signore*! *Si Vince*!'

A whisper floated up: 'You can't beat him, you know.'

'You think not?'

'I know it. There are those born to fight and those to pick up the pieces. It is a question of deciding early who you are and sticking to it.'

'Don't worry about it.' James patted his arm. 'It will work itself out in the end.' Then knowing he'd a train to catch, he took the letters from his pocket.

The old man's eyes widened. 'You brought them back.'

'I thought it important. Things having settled down, and any foolish rumour well and truly scotched, I wondered if you might feel as I, that now is a good time to review the idea of delivering the same.'

James smiled. 'Don't misunderstand. If you want them delivered, one the Fitzwilliam and the other to the university, I will follow your instruction, as I would with that addressed to your niece. But now, things being the way they are, I can't help thinking there is no need of letters and no need of explanation. Help was needed and help arrived in the person of His Highness.

'You were hurt, John, and badly, and I am sorry for that. However any damage inflicted upon the Morgan family is healed and you and your niece reconciled. With that in mind...' He held out the envelopes. 'Don't you think it would be better left like that?'

John Sarson stared and then he nodded. 'Burn them. Burn them all!'

Lacquered Box

Greys Farm, Bressingham, Norfolk
Sunday December 29th 1901

John Matthew Sarson, Dsc, Dphil, Professor of Science Emeritus, died in his sleep sometime in the night of Friday December the 27th. He'd had a good day, drank a little soup, and slept a great deal. The doctor called - a brief visit, he on his way to dinner - he said he was glad to see the professor so cheerful, and while there was a long way to go, things might be taking a better turn.

That evening Anneka brought the baby to see John. They stood at the bedroom door, she in a beautiful gown of silver tissue and Mr Tom handsome in tails. They didn't come into the room, they thinking prevention was better than cure.

This was understood. The baby is tiny and open to all manner of germs. To see him was enough with his dear little face and silken tuft of red-gold hair on top of his head. John waved and smiled and the baby smiled back.

So they retired to bed that night, Phoebe and John, with a sense of gratitude. They said their prayers and, as always, asked a blessing on their niece and her companion, Signor di Lombardi. They finished by asking the Lord to bless James van Leiden, who is so bitterly disappointed in his hopes.

'I told him it wouldn't do.' John said he'd talked with him. 'He'd never beat the Marquis. I said he was a fighter and James is a negotiator.'

399

Phoebe thought that extremely unfair. If ever there was a case of still waters running deep, it is was James van Leiden. No one should ever think they know that man for one day he will yet surprise them all.

Those were her thoughts, and so much more, but finding her husband well enough to offer an opinion, she let him keep it. It was as well she did, for she woke just after three knowing he was gone. She seemed to think she heard him say farewell: 'Goodbye my dear and God bless you.'

She wept, of course, and wept again, until the Colonel came, and said she must go sit with Gladys in the Morning Room, and that he and his man, Carbury, would look to the arranging of things.

Fortunately, Anneka and Mr Tom were visiting friends that morning, and therefore saved the unhappy sight of the undertaker's cart, and of poor John being carried away in a coffin awaiting burial in the local mortuary.

The vicar from St John the Divine in Diss called earlier today. He'd heard of Phoebe's loss, and knowing the local vicar was down with a cold, came to offer comfort. Before John was taken poorly they had visited that parish. Such a pretty church there with a charming view of the Fens! They would've loved it to be *their* church, but sadly, it was a too far to go for Sunday worship, which is a pity, because she learned today this is the vicar due to wed Sally Hankin, sister to Margret Hankin, Clarissa's long-time housekeeper.

Such a shame! Hearing of this, Phoebe's first thought was to run upstairs to tell John. He always had a soft spot for Sally. When Flossie, their Cocker Spaniel, was alive, Sally asked if she might paint her. She was trying to set up a small business painting portraits of family pets, so people might have the remembrance of their beloved animals even after they were gone.

The portrait of Flossie hangs over the dresser in the sitting room downstairs. One can see it is her, one ear up and one inside out, but overall it doesn't quite work; one is never sure if one is looking at a dog or an amiable blob.

Flossie's been dead a good ten years. Phoebe and John were always going to get another dog but never did. Dependent as they were 'grace and favour' upon the university, they had to think about every penny spent.

Life was never certain. Now, with John dead, and minus a pension, Phoebe must make the best of what is left. She lunched with the family today as is her habit of late. The Colonel accompanied her back to the cottage. He asked if he might have a few words before leaving 'her to her meditation.'

He was nervous, the dear man, and walked up and down a lot, where really there isn't space to walk. He said he was concerned for the future. 'Under your instruction I called upon your niece yesterday imparting the sad news of your husband's demise. She said then, as she said before leaving the other day with the Marquis, that you have a home with her as long as you want it.'

He paused, and then continued. 'I am sure you would be happy with her. I must tell you I thought your niece a fine young woman, with a clear eye and a good heart. Equally, I was impressed by her companion. Though young, he is a gentleman of the old guard and true to his word. I don't wish to presume on your plans. It's likely you don't have a plan at the moment so much as a sense of numbness. Even so, before you commit yourself to anything, I very much want to assure you of your place and lifelong security here at Greys Farm.'

Phoebe seems to think she said something then but, over-thrown by his kindness, can't recall what. The Colonel left soon after with a gentle hand shake: 'Gladys hopes you will stay, as do my son and his wife, and indeed Baby Thomas. For my own part I would not want you to leave. The fact is I have grown used to you being here, Miss Phoebe. I see your sweet smile and loving presence as a gift to us all, particularly me.'

While desperately sad - a place within her body that be-longed to John now utterly incapable of feeling - the Colonel's visit did relieve her mind, in that, knowing she doesn't have to move, gives her time to think.

One thing is sure - she won't be going with Clarissa. She could no more live with her than fly. Alas, though knowing it unfair, and incredibly unjust, Phoebe blames Clarissa for John's death. He worried so much about the effect of the debts on her it dragged him down to a place where he couldn't get up.

If she doesn't blame Clarissa, then Phoebe blames Charles Morgan, her father, for bringing those wretched Italian women into their lives.

Phoebe knows she is wrong about Clarissa and twisted in her notions but she can't seem to stop feeling this way. Even now, the thought of her coming through that door brings such rage, she wants to pick up the poker and throw it, scarring that lovely face, wanting her to grieve as she grieves, and to answer the only question that matters – why are you alive when John is dead.

'I am sorry Patricia but I can't seem to stop feeling this way.'

Hearing her thoughts, and knowing her sister, Clarissa's mother, would be appalled to know she felt this way, Phoebe hung her head. 'One day I'll ask your forgiveness for such thoughts, but for now please ignore what seems like cruelty. See it as the madness of grief - for that is really what it is.'

Last night, time on her hands, she decided to carry out John's wishes regarding the letters. John did say he'd asked James to destroy them but had changed his mind. 'I said he should leave them with me. I need to be the one watching them burn and getting the greatest pleasure from doing it.'

Poor John! He didn't get to see anything burn unless it was his last sunset here on earth. He died, God rest his soul, smiling and relieved, his hand under his cheek the way he used to sleep when he was young and handsome.

Those letters were a source of grief. John talked of them, wringing his hands, wishing he'd never written them, saying, they would make a bad situation worse. His relief when James brought them back was beyond measure.

* * *

There are, in fact, four letters to be destroyed where there were supposed to be three: one to the University, another to the Museum, and a third to Clarissa. The fourth letter is from James and meant for Clarissa.

That it is here along with the others suggests a pact between the two men. It's possible that, since they were both stung by the same hornet in Serena Parisi, the letters are meant to burn together as a sacrificial job-lot.

It has a kind of grim humour to it: burn one – burn all.

Phoebe fed the first letter to the flames with a sense of *déjà vu, of* having done this before, kneeling before a fire wanting to be rid of a mistake.

One-by-one, they burned to a dull ash. Then there was James's letter to Clarissa. In it he tells of redeeming the debt. He mentions Serena:

'*I did care for Serena. I have no excuse for that nor do I believe I need one. For three days in Assisi I was blinded by what I took to be the sun, but was soon to learn of another kind of glare and none of it kind.*'

He writes of the debt: '*I paid the debt to ease the Professor's burden but also for love of you, for I do love you, Clarissa, and deeply, as I loved you the first time I saw you that day in the April snows, you with your arms filled with lilac, and I with my eyes, and my heart, filled with you.*'

Phoebe had to stop reading. It felt wrong to peer into a man's heart, for it was a beautiful letter, declaring a strong and a mighty love. She was so moved by his declaration, that her feelings for her niece were challenged. She was made to see the unfairness of bitterness, and how wrong she and John were to deny their niece, hiding away in Norfolk like guilty children.

Overcome with shame she sat down. She could hear John: 'If there is a finger to point, my dear,' he was saying, 'aim in the right direction; first to Serena for dishonesty, and then to me, your foolish husband, for a moment of weakness.'

John Sarson died leaving nothing but his love. While it would seem Phoebe has a life and purpose at Greys Farm, she too is likely to die equally poor. Everything they own is in this cottage, and all of little earthly value. Even so, knowing she was wrong, Phoebe will offer her niece a memento of her uncle, and one to cherish in remembrance of happier times.

On the dresser in the sitting-room sits a pretty lacquered box. John brought it back from China years ago. Initially there were two cabinets, a matching pair, both with red-gold dragons, Phoebe had one and Clarissa the other, which, sadly, was to go the way of Italy never to be seen again.

Clarissa loved that box. As a child she would play with it for hours, hiding precious bibelots in the secret compartment, which really is secret, one having to know which dragon's eye to press to unfold the mystery.

Today the drawer is empty; any treasure Phoebe might've had is now waiting to be buried in Bressingham cemetery, and another reason to stay in Greys Farm - the loving duty of tending a grave.

She read James's letter one last time, and this time allowing tears to fall, for it is a tender letter, and a declaration of love Clarissa will never get to hear.

It was with that sad thought in mind - the howl of love unspoken – that Phoebe folded the letter to fit inside the drawer: such a small space to hold such feeling. She then added another memento, a china broach in the shape of lilac blossom, a gift from Patricia, her sister, Clarissa's mother.

The drawer slid shut: love locked away for another time and another day.

Air and Angels

Silent Noon

Prologue
The Night Watch

The Bardia Fiorentina, Florence
Sunday March 9th 1902

The Benedictine monks see the hour before dawn as a time when the soul is conflicted, and therefore prey to Satan's wiles. Charles Anouilh and sleep are strange bedfellows thus any time of the night he is prey to Satan.

It was just before dawn when he knelt at the Bardia Fiorentina altar rail. He would've preferred a time of day less acid to the gut, but His Highness, the Marchese di Lombardi, returns to Fiesole today; the Palazzo at Como to be shut down, and this, his servant, come ahead to ensure all is well at the Villa.

In terms of Charles and the Benedictine Order, the adage 'old habits die hard,' has a sense of literal truth, since as a youth, until swapped for a sword, a monk's habit was his daily wear. In the monastery he served the Lord God with a willing heart and bruised spirit - memories of his childhood like bleeding sores. Many years have passed. Now he serves a lord of human flesh and temporal power, Giovanni di Lombardi: a man with a pure and loving heart, and so, while the childhood sores remain, they no longer bleed.

In the world of Fine Art, the Marchese is known as *Il Maestro*, a collector of priceless antiquities willing to wrangle for the rarest of treasure, and then, having won the same, willing to give it away. In France he is regarded as *un homme calme:* one who knows the business and secure within the knowledge. *Il Maestro, un Homme Calme,* or as in Britain, somewhat bitterly, *the Assassin*, Charles has heard it all. At such times he doesn't disagree, for in the cut and thrust trading of such rarefied commodities, as with a Titian painting or a Donatella sculpture, these epithets apply. Of the other man, the flesh and blood creature, people remain silent, for only the few get to meet him.

When first brought to Charles, the lordling was a babe in arms. He was a tiny creature, fiercely brave. When in pain or aggrieved, he would ball his little fists and shout. Water might gather in his eyes, but then, as now with the man, he was rarely seen to weep.

The old Marchese, his father was the same, as was *il Divino*, Leonora, the Marchesa, Giovanni's mother. An inbuilt disinclination to complain or explain is a family trait. It masks a passionate soul. The young Marchese is in love, the mask wearing thin, and passion breaking through.

Giovanni's one desire is to bring the beloved to Italy and the safety of his arms. The need devours him, working its way into his brain to the exclusion of all else. He loved like this once before – it nearly killed him.

The villa in Fiesole is undergoing change, although it might be more correct to say adjustment. An existing energy within the house needs to be restrained, so that another, more gentle element, might find space to grow.

The Villa del Rosa is a fine old building of gracious proportions. Every room is furnished with priceless antiques and decorated with a particular artistic time-scale in mind. The house and the grounds – particularly the rose gardens - are celebrated throughout Italy. People come to stare. All leave declaring the beauty of the place and yet if asked, none would want to live there.

As in the castle in the children's nursery tale, *La Belle au Bois Dormant,* a curse was once laid upon the House of Lombardy, where two lives were lost and a third given away. It was just before dawn, seven years ago, when a last breath was taken, a soul fled away, and a house became a prison.

Time stood still, the hands on every clock fixed on a particular hour. Vines sprang up about the walls. Thickly entwined, and with raking thorns, they stole the light, blocking the outside world from view. Such infestation may not be apparent to the eye, yet it is there, stifling, so that all life within the castle, even to that of a mouse, stumble their way through a perpetual night.

The rearranging is meant to bring light to gloom. All alterations are at the behest of the Marchese, and brought into being with one thought in mind, and that - *si Dieu le veut*! - of winning Clarissa Morgan's love. Consequently, he ever willing to advance his beloved charge, Charles is getting to know *Les Anglais*, following their history and polishing his knowledge of their tongue.

This association sits uncomfortably on his shoulders, as it would with any true Frenchman, and yet, to be of service, Charles will prosper.

He has met the young lady. He thought her beautiful and kind, but more than a little blind to the machinations of the wider world, thus easily bruised. That His Highness sees the same resulted in the rearranging of the villa.

Cela n'a pas d'importance! Good or bad, any changes will be met with resistance from those who would prefer time to stand still. With those ancient animosities in mind, Charles Anouilh is soon to travel to Cambridgeshire, his charge that of emissary, bearing gifts, while supporting his master's lady.

'*Prenditi cura del mio amore, Lucciole!* ' was the message. ' *Vedi che nessuno è tra di noi.*' Take care of my love. See that none comes between us.'

* * *

The bell rings: the Vigil is done. Today's penitents are mostly old men with rheumy eyes and housemaids with shawls about their heads. A tourist, Baedeker in hand, stumbles out into the sunlight, followed by a lady and her female companion - she in furs and her companion in galoshes.

Such people are always here, even this early in the day. Usually they travel in groups, a guide at their head with poor Italian and a passion for Giotto.

The Badia Fiorentina is a building of great beauty. A man is nothing here, not so much as an echo. Charles has come to regard the abbey as a life-line to God. He brings his pain here and his fury at those who robbed him of sight, and as always, prays for the Marchese, for if all is well with him, then all is well with the world.

Today, between begging forgiveness for his sins, Charles Anouilh recalls the pyre of ash and fire that has been his life. As a child he learned of sin, every lesson accompanied by a birch

410

twig lashing the heart as well as the skin.

Pride, lust, *et cetera*, seven sins are thought to be worthy of Eternal Damnation. Charles's mother, Sophie Anouilh, once a lady of the cloister, learned, to her cost, there were many more, and hung a list upon a door.

Every night before sleeping Charles was required to understand a particular sin. All sin being incomprehensible to a child, he struggled with his lessons, and the birch twigs resolutely applied so that on a bad day the scars on his back are clearly visible. His mother would weep and strike her breast: 'What did I do wrong, Lord, to give life to such a son?' It was a question he couldn't answer, any more than he understood words like wrath and lust. What do such words mean? Is a sloth a three-toed creature crawling along the ground, or is it a man seen earlier asleep in the gutter an empty wineskin clasped to his breast?

The lessons, and the punishments, continued until his seventh birthday when *maman* sought her own salvation through a sharp blade at her wrist.

At seven, an underfed whelp, he was taken into the monastery in *La Haute-Loire*. The brothers cared for him the same way they cared for the three-legged dog that lay under the water-trough, a pat for a good day and a kick for bad.

At eighteen he left, swapping the Black Habit for the wine and women that was the *chambrée* of the *Regiment de Touraine*. Still an underfed whelp, yet gaining strength with every killing, he fought in various wars, moving through the ranks, until 1866 when, at twenty-one, he was deployed West of the River Mincio to Lombardy - Italy having declared war against Austria.

At twenty-four, a Captain, handsome and brave, he was elected for the Pontifical Guard, a post he never gained, for in Rome he came under the gaze of his master, His Highness, Carlo Arello di Lombardi. More significantly, he came to serve Her Highness, the Marchesa Leonora Maria, a woman of great beauty and kindness for whom Charles would've gladly died.

Time passes; the sun rises and the sun sets. Now a man of fifty-three, half priest and wholly butcher, the wall behind his cot is bare, no crucifix hangs there. Over the years the list has grown and every variation known.

Anger, murder and hate, he comes to the abbey asking the Lord God to forgive those sins already known while allowing for those still to come.

* * *

The bell tolls another day. Thirsty for his morning *cafe* the sacristan rattles his keys. Charles continues on his knees, for what, he no longer knows.

Outside the weather changes: lightning flashes and rain fills the sky.

People seek shelter, their shadows passing back and forth before Charles's wounded eyes, images forming of well-fed people with scant souls.

While there is space at the rail one chooses to kneel beside Charles.

A familiar shadow, gaudily clothed, it belongs to the worker of stone, Vincenza di Vallagra, brother of the late-lamented, Carina di Vallagra.

'*Bonne journée M'sieur Anouilh. Comment ca va?*'
'*Je vais bien, merci, Chevalier di Vallagra.*'

The shadow moves closer, his whiskers hinting of costly

cologne and his soul stinking of the latrine. *'Dites-moi: qui est cette fille, Clareessa Morgan?'*

When there is no reply the shadow leaned close, displaying linguistic skills.

'I hear she is beautiful with snow white flesh and lips like honeyed cherries. And that my saintly brother is alive again. Is this true, *Lucciole?* Has he at last confessed his guilt, or does he still stumble behind my sister's bier? I am curious to know, old man, what will befall this union – if it happens at all.'

Charles sighed. There is nothing he can say, no answer he can give while under the suffering gaze of the Lord Jesus Christ. Instead, he will take today's prayer to the other fellow, Satan, who understands there is pleasure to be found in the contemplation of sin, and in the hope of one day throttling a particular snake with one's bare hands, thus putting an end to seven years of lies, and of torment, and of a beloved son's pain:

'*In nomine patris et filii sancti, amen.*'

Printed in Great Britain
by Amazon

66482241R00246